# 新聞英語

## NEWS 必備指南
### —— 關鍵字

金利 主編

學習新聞英語，既能讓你的英文突飛猛進，
也能使你跟上國際趨勢！

這是一個全球化的時代，掌握世界動向、
了解全球形勢，已經成為人生致勝法則！

崧燁文化

# 目錄

# 前言

在語言學習過程中，詞彙的重要地位眾所周知。詞彙的學習和掌握是英語學習的關鍵。沒有扎實的詞彙作基礎，一切語言應用都無從談起。在日常交流和國際事務中，離開單字我們會寸步難行。

對於廣大英語學習者而言，學習單字也成為了最令人苦惱的一件事情。許多人在背單字的路上屢戰屢敗，因為無法突破單字，英語學習受挫。因此，我們希望這本書可以幫助讀者消除這個困擾。

本書具有以下特色：

## 1. 單字來源原汁原味，主要突破聽力能力

為了幫助廣大英語學習者突破單字關，保證讀者學到的都是最實用的單字，本書利用精心製作的詞頻篩選軟體，從原汁原味的材料中收錄出現頻率最高的單字。即：在 VOA、BBC 和 CNN 等新聞中精選出 1100 個高頻單字，以保證單字的實用性。同時，從 VOA、BBC 和 CNN 等新聞中收錄的主要是聽力單字，側重解決聽力問題。

## 2. 按照詞頻進行分級，結合難度科學排列

本書打破了從 A 到 Z 的常規單字排列方式，從最實用的角度出發，將所有單字按照出現頻率，分成 20 個 Level，每個 Level 涵蓋 55 個關鍵字。同時，根據單字的難度，使書中的難易單字交錯排列，避免因為難詞集中而產生較強的挫敗感。這樣，保證讀者最先學到的單字是出現頻率最高、最實用的，而且學起來會比較輕鬆。

## 3. 經典例句重現場景，用法講解即學即用

本書中的每個單字都配以精心挑選的例句，保證讀者所學到的都是原汁原味的道地表達。即：從 VOA、BBC 和 CNN 等新聞中精心選擇經典聽力例句。同時，結合材料的特點，著重從聽力角度來講解，包括常用搭配、常用句型、同類詞拓展等，力求讓讀者在生活中即學即用，起到事半功倍的效果。

　　我們希望本書不僅能夠幫助讀者攻克聽力單字大關，學到最實用的單字，還能提高讀者的英文聽力水準，實現輕鬆聽英語的夢想。

# Level 1

## president ['prezidənt] n. 總統；(大學) 校長；董事長

【例】President Obama said the figures were positive but not good enough. 歐巴馬總統表示，這些資料比較樂觀，但仍不夠理想。(BBC)

【用】 president 在新聞中經常出現，president+ 人名，就表示「某某總統」，如：President Bush 即「布希總統」。

## news [njuːz] n. 新聞，消息

【例】But first, we got something about Syria that United Nations representative called the first hopeful news in the very long time. 但是首先，我們帶來了敘利亞方面的消息，聯合國代表稱這是長期以來第一個令人振奮的消息。(CNN)

【用】 新聞報導相關詞：report 報導；bulletin 新聞簡報；column 專欄；title 標題。

## government ['g8v4nm4nt] n. 政府

【例】To tackle property price hikes, the government has issued a series of policies year after year. 為抑制房價上漲，政府每年都會發表一系列政策。(CRI)

【用】 「中央政府」即 central government，「地方政府」則是 local government。

## country ['kʌntri] n. 國家

【例】But a recent decision by Mexican officials to curb U.S. anti-drug agents access in the country will likely dominate discussions. 但墨西哥官員最近決定限制美國的掃毒專員進入該國，這項決策或將引發大量爭議。(NPR)

【用】 developed country 表示「先進國家」；developing country 表示「發展中國家」。

## state [steit] n. 國家；州；狀態 v. 說明

【例】Barak said Israel would not make any compromises when it comes to the security of the state. 巴瑞克稱，一旦涉及國家安全問題，以色列將絕不妥協。(VOA)

【用】 「美國」除了用 America 表示外，也被稱為 the United States，簡稱 US。

## report [rɪˈpɔːt] v./n. 報導；報告

【例】A report for the US Labor Department shows that 67,000 new private sector jobs were created last month. 美國勞工部的報告顯示，上個月新增 6.7 萬個私營企業就業職位。(BBC)

【用】 It is reported that... 是新聞英語聽力材料中的常見句型，表示「據報導……」。

## united [juːˈnaitid] a. 統一的；團結的

【例】The United States promised to track down who ever is behind the killings. 美國承諾追查殺戮背後的真凶。(CNN)

【用】 the United Nations 表示「聯合國」，簡稱 UN；UN Security Council 表示「聯合國安理會」。

## economy [iˈk3n4mi] n. 經濟；節約

【例】Americans are feeling more confident about& the economy and their incomes. 美國民眾現在對經濟和收入越來越有信心。(NPR)

【用】 與經濟相關的內容在新聞中經常出現，常用片語包括：market economy 市場經濟；national economy 國民經濟；global economy 全球經濟；knowledge economy 知識經濟。

## grain [grein] n. 穀物；顆粒；少量

【例】The agency also sent out warnings to grai storage companies nationwide. 該機構也向全國的糧食倉儲公司發出了警告。(NPR)

【用】 農業相關詞：barn 穀倉；hay 乾草；irrigate 灌溉；graze 放牧；orchard 果園；pest 害蟲

## minister [ˈministə] n. 部長，大臣

【例】Defense Minister Ehud Barak took a softer approach. 國防部長埃胡德 · 巴瑞克採取了更為溫和的方法。(VOA)

【用】 新聞中常用片語包括：Prime Minister 首相；總理；foreign minister 外交部長；finance minister 財政部長。

## official [əˈfiʃəl] n. 官員 a. 官方的；正式的

【例】Officials in the Philippines say at least a hundred people have died in floods and landslides in the north triggered by a week of heavy rain. 菲律賓官員稱，北部持續一週的暴雨引發了洪水和山崩，導致當地至少 100 人死亡。(BBC)

【用】 official 不僅可以作為名詞使用，還可以用作形容詞。其形容詞常用片語包括：official document 官方文件；official visit 正式訪問；official statement 正式聲明。

## international [ˌintəˈnæʃənəl] a. 國際的

【例】We continue to work very closely with our European allies on the threat from international terrorism. 我們將繼續與歐洲盟友密切合作，共同對抗來自國際恐怖主義的威脅。(CNN)

【用】 常用片語包括：international cooperation 國際合作；international market 國際市場；international community 國際社會；international situation 國際形勢。

## court [kɔːt] n. 法院 v. 獻殷勤；追求

【例】The 26 reforms include putting the military under the control of civilian courts. 26 項改革措施包括將軍事案件置於民事法院的管轄之下。(VOA)

【用】 與 court 相關的法律英語常用片語包括：Supreme Court 最高法院；federal court 聯邦法院；higher court 上級法院。

## right [raɪt] n. 權利 a./ ad. 正確的（地）v. 糾正

【例】We know that much remains to be done on human rights, on democracy, fighting poverty and achieving lasting peace. 在保障人權、實行民主、消除貧困和實現持久和平等方面，我們還有很多工作要做。(BBC)

【用】 right 在新聞中常作名詞，表示「權利」，常用片語包括：human rights 人權；have the right to do sth. 有權做某事；rights and interests 權益。

## percent [pəˈsent] n. 百分之...... a./ad. 百分之......的（地）

【例】If people can work until age 70, their monthly benefit will be 75 percent higher than it is at 62. 如果人們能夠工作到 70 歲，他們的月福利將比 62 歲時高 75%。(CNN)

【用】 基本用法是「數詞 +percent」，「百分之十」就是 10 percent。

## found [faund] v. 創建

【例】To me, that is the essential core principle behind our founding documents—the idea tha we are all created equal. 對我來說，這是建國文獻基本的核心原則——每個人都生而平等。(VOA)

【用】 注意該詞與 find（v. 發現）的區別，find 的過去式、過去分詞是 found，而 found 的過去式、過去分詞是 founded。

## law [lɔ:] n. 法律，法規

【例】A law banning the sale of large-sized containers of sugary drinks in New York City has been overturned a day before it was due to come into effect. 禁止在紐約市銷售大容量含糖飲料的法規在原定生效日前一天被推翻。(BBC)

【用】 法律相關詞：amendment 修正案；constitution 憲法；bill 法案；pass 通過；lawyer 律師。

## federal [ˈfedərəl] a. 聯邦（制）的；聯邦政府的

【例】The president's plan is just one proposal in just one part of the federal budget process. 總統的計畫僅僅是聯邦預算過程中的一項提議。(CNN)

【用】 採用聯邦制的國家主要有美國、澳洲、俄羅斯。「聯邦政府」即 federal government；「聯邦法律」即 federal law；「聯邦法院」即 federal court。

## health [helθ] n. 健康；衛生

【例】Health officials say that region seems to be the starting point for a dangerous new virus. 衛生官員表示，該地區似乎成為一種新型危險病毒的發源地。(CNN)

【用】 World Health Organization 表示「世界衛生組織」。

## million [ˈmiljən]num. 百萬 n. 百萬，無數

【例】For a giant abstract painting that's sold for more than 13 million. 一幅巨型抽象畫賣出了高於 130 萬美元的價格。(NPR)

【用】 數字相關詞：hundred 百 ；thousand 千；billion 十億；number 數字。

## pope [pəup]n.（天主教）教皇，羅馬主教

【例】He had to send a messenger to Rome to ask the Pope to help him. 他不得不派信使去羅馬向羅馬教皇求援。(CNN)

【用】 Pope 的首字母常大寫，且常與定冠詞 the 連用。

## item [ˈaitəm] n. 條款；（新聞等的）一條，一則

【例】The BBC has apologized for any offence the item may have caused. 英國廣播公司已經為這則新聞可能引起的任何冒犯而道歉。(BBC)

【用】 item 作名詞時是可數名詞，如：a news item 一則新聞。該詞也可用於商務談判或法律條文中。

## political [pəˈlitikəl] a. 政治上的;政黨的,黨派的

【例】It was two decades later that she decided to return to the public spotlight and enlarge her own political career. 直到 20 年後,她才決定重返公眾視線並繼續自己的政治生涯。(CNN)

【用】 政治相關詞:party 政黨;guideline 方針;policy 政策;politician 政客。

## prime [praim] a. 首要的 n. 全盛時期

【例】British Prime Minister David Cameron welcomed the agreement. 英國首相大衛·卡麥隆欣然接受了這項協議。(VOA)

【用】 prime 作形容詞表示「首要的」,含有「最」的意味,所以沒有比較級和最高級形式。

## power [ˈpauə] n. 權力,勢力;能力

【例】As a permanent member of the United Nations Security Council, Russia has the power to veto resolutions. 作為聯合國安理會的常任理事國,俄羅斯對決議享有否認權。(BBC)

【用】 表示「能力」時,power 常用複數,powers of mind 表示「思維能力」。但是 power 作「權力,勢力」解釋時是不可數名詞。

## corn [kɔːn] n. 穀物;玉米

【例】Monsanto expects to be ready in a few years to market its first corn seeds genetically engineered to resist drought. 孟山都公司預期在幾年內推廣上市第一批利用基因工程培育的抗乾旱玉米種子。(VOA)

【用】 在英式英語中,corn 常指「穀物;穀粒」,尤指「小麥」。在美式英語中,corn 常指「玉米」。

## major ['meidʒə] a. 主要的 v. 主修 n. 少校

【例】One of the major challenges as a president would be dealing with other coun-tries. 總統面對的一個重要挑戰就是如何處理與其他國家的關係問題。(CNN)

【用】 major 作不及物動詞時常與介詞 in 連用，表示「主修」。如：He majored in biology. 他主修生物學。

## former ['fɔ:mə] a. 以前的 n. 前者

【例】Annette Pacas, a former teacher and now a single mother of six, later learned about her son's final moments. 安妮特・帕卡斯以前是一名教師，現在是六個孩子的單身母親，她後來得知了兒子臨終時的情況。(NPR)

【用】 the former 表示「前者」，the latter 表示「後者」，兩者相對，只可用於兩個人或物之間。former 常用在美語中，英式英語常用 ex- 表示「前任的」。

## company ['kʌmpəni] n. 公司；陪伴；同伴（們）

【例】The company racked up more than $20 billion in debt and its share price has dropped to a record low of about three cents. 該公司積累的債務超過了兩百億美元，股票價格也跌至有史以來最低的三美分左右。(VOA)

【用】 常用表達：parent company 母公司；listed company 上市公司；trading company 貿易公司。

## include [in'klu:d] v. 包括

【例】 The government admits that it's tough but insists that the alternative, which could include default and the collapse of the banking system, would be catastroph-ic. 政府承認這很艱難，但也堅稱替代方案涉及欠債以及銀行系統癱瘓，可能導致災難性的後果。(BBC)

【用】 including 常作介詞，與其後的名詞或代詞構成介賓片語。如：The astronauts spent their workdays conducting experiments, including biomedical research. 太空人在工作日會進行各種實驗，包括生物醫學研究。

## system [ˈsɪstəm] n. 系統；制度

【例】In the past, these events were used to help scientists understand the size of the solar system and the distance between planets. 過去，這些事件被用來幫助科學家理解太陽系的大小以及行星間的距離。(CNN)

【用】 常用搭配：judicial system 司法系統；digestive system 消化系統；security system 安保系統；transportation system 運輸系統。

## tax [tæks] n. 稅（款）；負擔 v. 對......徵稅

【例】It's incredibly important that companies and individuals pay the tax that is due. 企業和個人按時繳納應付稅款非常重要。(NPR)

【用】 常用搭配：income tax 所得稅；tax revenue 稅收；tax evasion 漏稅。

## job [dʒɔb] n. 工作；職業；職責

【例】Yesterday he was approved by the senate for that job. 昨天，參議院批准他從事那個工作。(Scientific American)

【用】 job 常用的片語有：job hunting 找工作；out of job 失業；inside job 監守自盜，內部人員作案。

## space [speɪs] n. 太空；距離

【例】The repairs carried out in May by the crew of the Space Shuttle Atlantis are expected to be the last. 五月，亞特蘭提斯號太空梭上的工作人員維修了太空梭，這或將是最後一次。(VOA)

【用】 space 作「太空」或「距離」講時，前面一般不加冠詞。表示「太空」時強調空間的概念，因此只用單數形式。另外，在科技新聞中，常出現「美國國家航空暨太空總署」的縮寫 NASA，其完整形式是：National Aeronautics and Space Administration。

## department [diˈpɑːtmənt] n. 部，部門

【例】The bill approved by the Republican-controlled House is designed to ease deep cuts across the Defense Department that came into effect last week. 共和黨控制的眾議院通過此法案的目的是減弱國防部上週實施的大幅削減開支力度。(BBC)

【用】　在英國，人們習慣用 ministry 來表示「部」，用 department 來表示「司」；而美語中習慣用 department 來表示「部」，「司」則是用 bureau 表示。

## foreign [ˈfɔrən] a. 外國的；對外的

【例】The Secretary of State is the president's top advisor on foreign policy. 國務卿是總統在外交政策方面的首席顧問。(CNN)

【用】　foreign 的常見搭配有：foreign affairs 外交事務；foreign policy 外交政策；foreign trade 對外貿易；foreign investment 外來投資。

## home [həum] n. 家，家鄉；本國；原產地 a. 國內的

【例】It is now logical for the U.S. to want to bring manufacturing back to its home soil since manufacturing is the largest source for employment. 因為製造行業能創造最多的就業機會，所以現在，美國希望將其從海外轉回國內的想法是合理的。(CRI)

【用】　home 的基本意思是「家，故鄉」，此外可指植物或動物的「產地，生長地，發源地」，這個含義在新聞中更常出現。

## place [pleis] n. 場所；場合 v. 放置；安排

【例】It says the state gains federal dollars for every native child it places into its foster care system. 據稱，美國為本國每個納入寄養體系的兒童都籌備了聯邦資金。(NPR)

【用】　place 的常用片語有：in place of 代替；take the place of 也可指「代替」；但是 take place 表示「發生」。

## party [ˈpɑːti] n. 社交聚會；政黨；當事人

【例】Party officials have called for African solutions to African problems. 政黨官員要求用非洲的方法來解決非洲的問題。(VOA)

【用】 美國總統大選是熱點新聞，兩大政黨在新聞中經常出現，分別為：Democratic Party 民主黨；Republican Party 共和黨。

## oil [ɔil] n. 石油，燃料油

【例】The money will fund new developments aimed at turning Brazil into a major oil exporter. 籌集到的資金將用於新的發展，使巴西成為主要石油出口國。(BBC)

【用】 經濟新聞中常會提到石油，與其有關的搭配有：crude oil 原油；oil price 油價；off-shore oil 近海石油；deep-sea oil 深海石油。

## expect [ikˈspekt] v. 預料，盼望；要求

【例】 The speech includes some of the big issues that Parliament expects to face during its new session. 演講的內容涉及議會在下一任期可能面臨的重大問題。(CNN)

【用】 expect 多用作及物動詞，可接名詞、代詞、動詞不定式或 that 從句。

## case [keis] n. 事例；案件

【例】Among the reported bird flu cases, children and elderly people seem to be the most vulnerable groups. 在已報導的禽流感病例中，孩子和老人似乎是最易感染的人群。(CRI)

【用】 in case of 是一個比較常用的片語，指「假如……發生，以防……發生」。in case 表示「萬一；假使」，也可接從句。

## care [keə] v. 關心；介意 n. 照顧

【例】More specifically, Native American children are provided health care by a federal program directly through the Indian Health Service. 確切地說，印第安衛生局直接通過聯邦專案為印弟安兒童提供衛生保健服務。(NPR)

【用】 care 作動詞時常用的片語搭配有 care about 和 care for，都表示「在乎，關心」。

## university [ˌjuːniˈvəːsiti] n. 大學

【例】To save costs, the university plans to cut its one teaching position. 為了節省開支，這所大學計畫削減一個教學的職位。(VOA)

【用】 學校教育相關詞：alumni 校友；campus 校園；school 學院；professor 教授。

## kill [kil] v. 殺死；打發（時間）

【例】British and Canadian scientists say they have identified a potential treatment for sleeping sickness which kills about 50,000 people a year in Africa. 英國和加拿大科學家稱他們發現了一種有望治療昏睡症的方法，該疾病在非洲每年會奪走大約 5 萬人的生命。(BBC)

【用】 kill 表示「殺死」，引申義為「消磨（時間）；緩解（疼痛）」等含義。

## public [ˈpʌblik] a. 公眾的；公共的 n. 公眾

【例】Public opinion can influence political leaders. 公眾輿論會對政治領袖產生影響。(CNN)

【用】 public 作名詞時，表示「公眾」，是集合名詞，前面要加定冠詞 the。in public 表示「公開地」。

## according [əˈkɔːdiŋ] ad. 依照

【例】According to a statement issued by the provincial health department, another infection case was confirmed in neighboring Zhejiang Province on Monday. 根據省衛生部門的聲明，週一在浙江省又確認了另一例感染病例。

【用】according to 根據表示「根據，依據」。

## secretary [ˈsekrətəri] n. 祕書；書記；部長

【例】At the White House, Press Secretary Jay Carney urged the public to withhold judgment until all the facts were clear. 白宮新聞發言人傑伊‧卡尼竭力主張公眾應在明瞭所有事實之後再作判斷。(NPR)

【用】　新聞中常見與 Secretary 有關的各種職務：Secretary of State 國務卿；Secretary of Defense 國防部長。

## budget [ˈbʌdʒit] n. 預算 v. 編預算

【例】Oil and gas exports account for almost 70 percent of Russia's export earnings and cover half of the federal budget. 石油和天然氣占俄羅斯出口利潤的近 70%，這足夠擔付一半的聯邦預算。(VOA)

【用】　經濟新聞中常見與 budget 有關的搭配：fiscal budget 財政預算；military budget 軍費預算；budget deficit 預算赤字。

## support [səˈpɔːt] v. 支持；供養；維持

【例】Voters are widely expected to support retaining their current status. 普遍預期選民們會支持保持現狀。(BBC)

【用】　常用片語：economic support 經濟支援；emotional support 精神支持；social support 社會支持；support for 支持。

## military [ˈmilitəri] a. 軍事的 n. 軍隊

【例】He seized the power when the military took control of the government in 1961. 1961 年，軍隊控制了政府，於是他奪取了政權。(CNN)

【用】　與 military 有關的片語：military ase 軍事基地；military spending 軍費開支；military service 兵役；military coup 軍事政變。

## general [ˈdʒenərəl] a. 普遍的；一般的；大體的

【例】The general rules of the patent system have been established in statutes and Supreme Court case law for over 150 years. 專利制度的通用規則在法令和最高法院判例法得以確定，已有 150 多年了。 (NPR)

【用】 in general 表示「大體上，一般來說」。另外，general 也可作名詞，表示「將軍；一般」。


## global [ˈgləubəl] a. 全球的

【例】Commercial jets pump out some 700 million tons of CO2 a year—about two percent of global emissions. 商【用】飛機每年排放約 7 億噸的二氧化碳，約占全球排放量的百分之二。 (Scientific American)

【用】 與 global 有關的片語：global market 全球市場；global phenomenon 全球性現象；global problem 全球性問題；global warming 全球化變暖。


## future [ˈfjuːtʃə] a. 將來的 n. 將來；前途

【例】Experts are predicting that the United States could become more active in settling disputes in the future. 專家預測未來美國將會更加積極主動地解決爭端。(VOA)

【用】 in future 和 in the future 都是正確的表達方式，in future 常指「從現在開始到今後」，in the future 則是「將來」的意思，但 in the near future，in the distant future 等片語中的 the 不可省略。另外，future 作為名詞，還可以表示「期貨」，在商務英語中比較常見。


## bank [bæŋk] n. 銀行；( 河等的 ) 岸

【例】Among bills passed already by the assembly are the creation of a solidarity fund and a law giving the government powers to impose capital controls on banks. 議會通過的法案內容包括：創立團結基金以及授權政府對銀行進行資金管制。(BBC)

【用】 該詞常用於經濟類新聞中，常見用法有：central bank 中央銀行；world bank 世界銀行；investment bank 投資銀行；bank loan 銀行貸款。

# Level 2

## set [set] n. 裝置 v. 安置 a. 固定的

【例】Her dream of being a professor was set aside. 她想當教授的夢想被擱置了。(CNN)

【用】 set 的常用搭配有：set aside 留出，撥出；set up 設置；set sb. to do sth. 使某人開始做某事。

## center [ˈsentə] n. 中心；a. 中心的；中央的

【例】But labor costs in the U.S, despite signs of a decrease, are still much higher than that of traditional manufacturing centers like China or India. 美國的勞動力成本有下降跡象，但與中國或印度這樣傳統的製造業中心相比，仍高出很多。(CRI)

【用】 常用片語：center on 以……為中心；business center 商業中心；trade center 貿易中心；financial center 金融中心。

## billion [ˈbiljən] n./a. 十億（的）

【例】But the rockets currently under development just aren't powerful enough, and the agency's $17.7 billion budget is being squeezed. 但正在研發的火箭功率不夠強大，而且機構原有的 177 億美元預算也被壓縮了。(NPR)

【用】 billions of 表示「數以億計的」。

## deal [diːl] v. 處理 n. 交易；政策，協議

【例】 The deal, which will have to be approved by the state legislature, includes plans for billions of dollars in budget cuts, but no tax rises. 該協定需要經過州議會批准，協定涉及數十億美元的預算削減計畫，稅收增長不在其中。(BBC)

【用】 deal 的常用搭配有：deal with 處理；deal in 從事。在商務領域中，常表示「交易」，比如：make a deal 成交；fair deal 公平交易；package deal 一籃子交易。另外，這個詞在新聞中也常表示「協議」。

## cut [kʌt] v. 切；削減；中斷

【例】Greek lawmakers agreed to cut 15,000 jobs by the end of 2014. 希臘立法者同意在 2014 年年底之前削減 1.5 萬個職位。(CNN)

【用】　常用片語：cut down 削減；cut in 插入；cut off 切斷；cut across 抄近路。

## clear [klɪə] a. 明白的；暢通的 v. 清空

【例】Secretary of State John Kerry made it clear this week that American foreign policy decisions affect the lives of Americans. 國務卿約翰‧克里在本週明確表示，美國的外交政策決定影響著美國人的生活。(VOA)

【用】　常用句型：sb. make it clear that... 表示「某人表明......」。

## nation [ˈneiʃən] n. 國家，民族

【例】The northern Philippines have been pounded by heavy rain following the second typhoon in just over a week to hit the nation. 菲律賓北部遭受了暴雨的襲擊，一周後，第二場颱風再次侵襲該國。(BBC)

【用】　與 nation 有關的片語，如：United Nations 聯合國；the Chinese nation 中華民族；most favored nation clause 最惠國條款。

## safety [ˈseifti] n. 安全；保險裝置；安全場所

【例】None of the boys was trained in proper safety procedures and none was warned about the dangers of breaking up the corn, says Piper. 這些男孩中沒有一個人接受過正規的安全規程方面的訓練，也沒有人警告過他們，將穀物弄碎很危險，派珀說道。(NPR)

【用】　相關片語：safety of person 人身安全；safety belt 安全帶；safety regulation 安全規則。另外，需要注意與 security 的區別：safety 強調自身無傷害；security 強調防範外界或敵人所造成的傷害。

## scientist [ˈsaɪəntɪst] n. 科學家

【例】Using a sediment core as a detailed history of climate change, scientists can see how the forested Arctic gradually became covered in ice and snow. 科學家們利用沉積岩的岩心研究氣候變化的詳細歷史，從中可以看到樹木叢生的北極是如何逐漸被冰雪覆蓋的。(VOA)

【用】 科技新聞中常見的單字還有：research 研究；analysis 分析；report 報告；result 結果。

## senate [ˈsenɪt] n. 參議院

【例】A push to overhaul U.S. immigration laws has been gaining momentum in the Senate, where a bipartisan reform bill was unveiled last month. 推進美國移民法改革的勢頭在參議院中非常強勁，就在上月，參議院公開了一個兩黨共同起草的移民改革法案。(VOA)

【用】 通常與 House 相對而言，Senate 是「上議院」，House，即 House of Representative 則稱為「下議院」，兩者共同構成美國的國會。

## own [əun]] a. 自己的 v. 擁有

【例】Even so, the disturbing tumor photos did lead many to question their own standards about what exactly we're all eating. 即便如此，腫瘤照片令人不安，許多人開始質疑日常飲食的標準。(CNN)

【用】 常用片語：on one's own 獨立地；主動地；hold one's own 堅持自己的立場；own up (to) 坦白地承認。

## research [rɪˈsəːtʃ] n./v. 研究，調查

【例】NASA's budget provides $78 million to start researching the mission, but ultimately Congress must approve the funding. 美國航空航太管理局提供了 7800 萬美元，用作研究專案的啟動資金，但這筆錢最終必須經由國會批准。(NPR)

【用】 作名詞時，research 的常用片語有：do a research 做個調查；research result 調查結

果；research group 研究小組；market research 市場調查。作動詞時，常用搭配為：sb. have/has researched on... (field) 某人在某一領域進行研究。

## bin [bin] n. 箱櫃；倉

【例】The work went well at first, with the boys shoveling corn toward a cone-shaped hole at the center of the bin. 工作起初進行得很順利，男孩們將穀物鏟進穀倉中央的錐形洞中。(NPR)

【用】 其他「容器」的說法：cabinet 儲藏櫥；dustbin 垃圾桶；cupboard 櫃櫥；bookcase 書櫃；locker 寄物櫃。

## congress [ˈkɔŋgres] n. 代表大會；議會，國會

【例】With the U.S. unemployment rate at 9.7 percent, the president said he hopes Congress will soon approve incentives for small businesses to add workers. 隨著美國失業率跌至 9.7%，總統表示他希望國會能盡快批准激勵措施，以鼓勵小型企業增加雇員數量。(VOA)

【用】 congress 一般是國家的立法機關，如：congress party 國大黨（印度）；Congress 國會（美國）。

## information [ˌinfəˈmeiʃən] n. 訊息；通知

【例】 For a one-month period, next January, FIFA will reward players, officials and administrators who come forward with useful information. 明年一月，國際足聯將獎勵提供有用資訊的球員、官員和管理人員，時間將持續一個月。(BBC)

【用】 每則新聞消息都要具備以下特點：accuraey 準確性；timevalidity 時效性；readability 可讀性。

## republican [riˈpʌblikən] a. 共和政體的；[R-] 共和黨的 n. [R-] 共和黨人

【例】He also said Democrats and Republicans need to work together on the problems facing the country. 他也表示，民主黨和共和黨需要共同協作，解決美國面臨的問題。(CNN)

【用】 美國兩黨分別是 Republican Party「共和黨」和 Democrat Party「民主黨」。由於兩黨的黨徽分別是大象和驢子，因此，有時口語中也用 elephants 代表「共和黨人」，用 donkeys 代表「民主黨人」。

## policy [ˈpɔləsi] n. 政策，方針

【例】 Often officials and policy makers don't have the most up-to-date information. 通常，官員和政策制定者都沒有掌握最新的資訊。(VOA)

【用】 該詞通常表示「政策」，常用片語：foreign policy 外交政策；fiscal policy 財政政策；monetary policy 貨幣政策。常用句型：It is sb.'s policy to do sth.。但在經濟領域 policy 可以表示「保險單」，表達這個含義時為可數名詞。

## die [dai] v. 死亡；停止運行；消逝

【例】One man died after he was injured in clashes outside the parliament. 在議會大廈外面，一名男子在衝突中受傷，隨後死亡。(BBC)

【用】 常用片語辨析：die of 一般指由於疾病、情感等原因引起的死亡；die from 一般常用於由外傷、衰老引起的死亡；die out 表示「滅絕，滅亡」。注意：die 不能用於被動語態，強調動作，是瞬間動詞，不能與表示一段時間的狀語連用。

## death [deθ] n. 死亡；破滅；毀滅

【例】 It causes blurred vision, rapid breathing, heavy sweating, confusion, headaches, nausea and at the very worst cases, convulsions, paralysis and death. 這種疾病會導致視力模糊、呼吸急促、大量出汗、意識混亂、頭痛和噁心，最糟糕時還會導致抽搐、癱瘓，甚至死亡。(CNN)

【用】 常用片語辨析：to death 表示「十分，很；到極點」；而 to the death 表示「直到死；到最後」。death 表示一個人的「死亡」時不可數；但表示「某種類型的死亡」或「死亡人數」時是可數名詞。

## researcher [riˈsəːtʃə] n. 研究員

【例】That would be a so-called biosafety level 3 lab, where researchers can keep this demonstrably dangerous virus under tight control. 那將成為一個三級生物安全實驗室，在這個實驗室裡研究者們能夠嚴格控制住這種病毒，這種病毒經證實非常危險。(NPR)

【用】 researcher 是 research 的派生詞，前面可以加形容詞作定語，一般為課題方向，如：a political researcher 一個政治研究員。

## start [stɑːt] v. 開始；創辦；著手

【例】Researchers started by feeding 120 volunteers a daily, 18-ounce serving of low-fat yogurt. 研究員在實驗的開始階段每天給 120 名志願者提供 18 盎司的低脂優酪乳作為食物。(Scientific American)

【用】 start 作為動詞的常見搭配有 start to do sth. 開始做某事。同時，start 也可用作名詞，常用片語：the start of... 的開頭。

## least [liːst]（little 的最高級）a. 最少的；最不重要的 ad. 最少

【例】At least 77 of the Catholic Church's 115 cardinals chose the new Pope during a vote in the Vatican in Rome. 在 115 位天主教堂的紅衣主教中，至少 77 位主教在羅馬教廷的投票中選擇了新任教皇。(VOA)

【用】 常用片語：at least 至少，其反義詞為：at most 最多。在演講中，尤其是在競選演講中，經常會聽到 last but not the least，表示「最後，但也非常重要的一點」，這是慣用法。但在書面語中，直接用 last but not least 即可。

## market [ˈmɑːkit] n. 市場；股市 v. 銷售

【例】The benchmark price is published by these agencies underpaying billions of dollars of transactions in the oil markets. 這些機構發布了基準價格，導致石油交易市場出現數十億美元的損失。(BBC)

【用】 market 在聽力中經常出現，on the market 待售，出售；at the market 照市價；in the market 在市場上。market 作為「市場」時是可數名詞，但作為「銷路」時不可數。

## issue ['i5ju:] n. 議題；(報刊的)一期 v. 頒布

【例】It's Thursday, and today the U.S. Senate could start debating the issue of guns. 今天是週四，美國參議院可能會就槍支問題展開辯論。(CNN)

【用】 issue 常用片語有：at issue 在討論中；make issue of 大做文章。

## growth [grəuθ] n. 增長；生長

【例】The price has also been hit by the lower-than-expected GDP growth here in China. 在中國，國民生產總值的增長低於預期，這在很大程度上對價格產生了影響。(CRI)

【用】 變化相關詞：increase 增長；decrease 減少；enlarge 擴大；reduce 縮小。

## given ['givən] prep. 鑑於 a. 規定的；假設的

【例】But given the force of the storm, the toll might have been even higher. 但鑒於這場風暴威力很大，傷亡人數可能還會增加。(NPR)

【用】 作形容詞時，一般用作定語，如 a given time 規定的時間；在作介詞時，放在句首，引導條件狀語從句。

## union ['juːnjən] n. 工會；聯盟；聯合

【例】European Union countries have struggled to find common ground as they worked out a budget agreement in Belgium this month. 本月在比利時，歐盟各國就有關預算協定的問題好不容易達成了共識。 (VOA)

【用】 團體相關詞：department 部門；team 團隊；Student Union 學生會；company 公司。

## nuclear [ˈnjuːkliə] a. 原子能的；核心的

【例】Turkey and Japan have signed a deal to build a large nuclear power plant on the Turkish Black Sea coast. 土耳其和日本簽訂了一份協議，他們將在土耳其黑海岸邊建造一座大型核電站。(BBC)

【用】 常見片語有 nuclear weapon 核武器，nuclear power 核能，nuclear bomb 核彈。nuclear family 這個詞與核輻射無關，它的意思是「核心家庭」。

## service [ˈsəːvis] n. 服務；行政部門

【例】Administration officials credit early warnings from the national weather service for giving residents precious additional minutes to take shelter. 政府官員讚揚了國家氣象局，他們及時預警，為居民們爭取了額外的寶貴時間來避難。(NPR)

【用】 常用片語：at sb.'s service 聽任某人差遣；the Civil Service 公務員；see service 服役；service charge 服務費。

## process [ˈprəuses] n. 過程 v. 處理

【例】Gamers also became quicker at processing information. 遊戲玩家們處理資訊的速度更快。(Scientific American)

【用】 process 作為名詞，表示「過程」，常用片語為 in the process （of）在（......的）過程中；在電腦專業英語中，也表示「進程」；而作為動詞，表示「加工，處理」，多用於被動語態，be processed。

## race [reis] n. 競爭；人種 v. 參加比賽

【例】Italian authorities say it is a race against time to stop a massive oil slick flowing down Italy's longest river. 義大利當局稱，要爭分奪秒地阻止浮油大規模地流入該國最長的河流中。(VOA)

【用】 在體育競技中，race 通常表示「比賽，競爭」，常用習語：a race against time 與時間賽跑；爭分奪秒。此外，還表示「人種，種族」，常見的搭配：the human race 人類；race relations 種族關係。

## business [ˈbiznis] n. 交易；商店；工作

【例】Swiss business leaders who campaigned hard against the measures are bitterly disappointed. 堅決反對該措施的瑞士商界領袖們徹底失望了。(BBC)

【用】 business 通常指商業上的「交易，生意，工作」等，但口語中也經常用到，如：It's not your business. 這不關你的事。Business is business. 公事公辦。Get down to business. 言歸正傳。

## war [wɔ:] n. 戰爭；競爭 v. 作戰

【例】The tradition goes back to nearly 150 years started out with a way to pay tribute to troops who died during the Civil War. 這個傳統可以追溯到將近 150 年前，用來悼念內戰期間犧牲的士兵。(CNN)

【用】 政治新聞常見片語：Civil War 內戰；Cold War 冷戰；the Second World War 第二次世界大戰；而在經濟話題中，商家之間的「價格戰」可以用 price war 表示。

## control [kənˈtrəul] n. 控制（能力），支配 v. 控制

【例】His major was aircraft control, so he was quite familiar with the feeling of flying without restrictions. 他的專業是飛行控制，所以他對不受限飛行的感覺十分熟悉。(CRI)

【用】 常用介詞片語：in control 在控制中；out of control 失控；under control 在控制範圍內。用名詞修飾 control 時，多用於政府職能方面，表示「管制，控制」如：price control 物價管制；traffic control 交通管制。

## agency [ˈeidʒənsi] n. 代理；（政府等的）專門行政部門

【例】As it did in 1993, the agency delivered a warning to the industry. 就像 1993 年一樣，機構向該產業發出了警告。(NPR)

【用】 news agency 或 press agency 專指「新聞社，通訊社」。全球主要知名通訊社有：Xinhua News Agency 新華社；AP (Associated Press) 美聯社；Reuters 路透社；AFP (Agence France Press) 法新社。

## chief [tʃiːf] a. 主要的 n. 首領

【例】The BBC's chief technology officer has been suspended pending a top-level investigation, and the team running the failed five-year project has been disbanded. 英國廣播公司首席技術官因一項最高級別的調查而被停職，其運營團隊也被解散，該團隊 5 年來都沒有成功運營專案。(BBC)

【用】 chief 作為名詞泛指「首領」，但在不同場合有不同稱謂，如：Chief Executive Officer 首席執行官；Air Chief 空軍上將；the chief of a tribe 酋長；the police chief 警察局長；chief editor 總編輯。

## continue [kənˈtinjuː] v. 繼續；延續

【例】If the trend continues, it's estimated one out of two new graduates in this class will not have a job lined up. 如果這種趨勢持續發展，這個班一半的應屆畢業生在畢業後都會找不到工作。(CNN)

【用】 continue 多用於不及物動詞，後面要加介詞才能與名詞連用，如：continue with 繼續做；continue 後面也可以加不定式和動名詞，如：continue to do 或 continue doing；在表示新聞、電視、電影等有後續報導或內容時，可以用 to be continued。

## capital [ˈkæpitəl] n. 資本；首都 a. 首要的

【例】In the hours that followed, two bombs, also targeting police, exploded in the capital. 在隨後的幾小時中，首都兩顆炸彈爆炸，目標鎖定在員警身上。(VOA)

【用】 在商業領域，capital 多用來表示「資本，資金」，如：human capital 人力資本；capital and interest 本金和利息；capital market 資本市場；venture capital 風險投資。在政治領域，capital 不僅可以指國家的「首都」，也可以指政治、經濟、文化、娛樂等的「中心，核心」。

## parliament [ˈpɑːləmənt] n. 國會，議會

【例】Parliament in Cyprus has narrowly ratified the country's bailout deal imposing tough conditions in exchange for a loan. 賽普勒斯議會勉強批准了該國的財政救援

協議，即為獲取貸款，接受更為苛刻的條件。(BBC)

【用】 parliament 常見片語：House of Parliament 國會大廈（英國）；Parliament Building 國會大廈（加拿大）；Member of Parliament 議會成員。另外，要注意的是，parliament 常指英國或加拿大等國的議會，通常用大寫形式；congress 指美國等國的國會，也可指「代表大會」。

## program [ˈprəugræm] n. 程式；專案

【例】It's all part of a program to revitalize Detroit schools. 這是振興底特律學校專案的環節之一。(CNN)

【用】 在科技領域，computer program 表示「電腦程式」；在經濟、教育建設範疇內，development program 表示「發展計畫」；在媒體領域，TV program 表示「電視節目」。

## member [ˈmembə] n. 成員，會員

【例】After member states failed to agree on the issue, the European Union's executive body said it would impose a moratorium on the chemicals. 成員國未在就該議題達成一致，歐盟執行機構表示他們將暫停使用這些化學物質。(BBC)

【用】 由 member 衍生出來的詞 membership 表示「會員資格；全體會員」。

## announce [əˈnauns] v. 宣布；預告

【例】You might remember that a group of U.S. Senators announced an immigration reform plan earlier this week. 你們可能還記得，一些美國參議員在本週早些時候宣布了一項移民改革計畫。(CNN)

【用】 新聞常用句型：It is/was announced that... 「據宣告稱......」announce 的名詞形式為 announcement，表示「宣告」，也可用 sb. makes/made an announcement that... 「某人發表宣言稱......」。

## attack [ə'tæk] v./n. 攻擊，抨擊

【例】The April 15th Boston attack left three people dead and 176 injured. 4 月 15 日發生的波士頓襲擊事件導致 3 人死亡、176 人受傷。(CRI)

【用】 attack 作動詞可以表示「襲擊某人；進攻某地」，也可以用作被動語態；作為名詞，make an attack 的含義相當於動詞本身，常用片語 air attack 表示「空襲」。

## act [ækt] v. 表現 n. 行為；法令

【例】That's what happened when Congress moved to undo large parts of a popular law known as the Stock Act last week. 上週，國會廢除了熱門法——證券法的大部分條文。(NPR)

【用】 act 通常表示「表演；表現；行為」，派生詞有：actor 男演員；actress 女演員；action 動作；activity 行動。但在新聞或政治領域，act 表示「法案，法令」，如：Act of Parliament 議會法案。

## hold [həuld] v. 掌握（權力）；容納；舉行

【例】 People seem to be holding an unannounced parade on the sidewalks and around the trees. 在人行道上，在大樹周圍人們似乎正在遊行，事先其他人對此一無所知。(NPR)

【用】 常用片語：hold a meeting 舉行會議；hold on 堅持，稍等；get hold of 控制 ( 常用反身代詞 )。hold 表示「拿著，握住」，引申為「掌握，控制」，過去式為 held，過去分詞為 held 或 holden。

## industry ['indəstri] n. 工業，產業

【例】The regulation had been challenged by drinks manufacturers and other industry groups. 這項規定受到了飲料製造商和其他行業組織的質疑。(BBC)

【用】 表示「產業」時，是可數名詞，複數為 industries，如：automobile industry 汽車產業。另外，industry 還可以表示「勤奮」，其形容詞為：industrious 勤勉的。

## medical [ˈmedikəl] a. 醫學的，醫療的

【例】Consuming too much sugar will eventually lead to diseases and cause immense medical expenses. 攝入過量的糖分會最終導致疾病，讓你花費巨額的醫療費。(CNN)

【用】 就醫相關詞：medicine 藥，內科；hospital 醫院；operation 手術；recovery 痊癒；complication 併發症。

## hit [hit] v. 擊中；碰撞 n. 擊中

【例】Authorities say there are still six adults who have not been accounted for since Monday's monstrous twister hit. 有關部門表示，週一可怕的龍捲風來襲後，仍有六名成年人不知去向。(NPR)

【用】 作為動詞，過去式與過去分詞都是 hit；作為名詞，表示「擊中」，通常用於擊打類體育運動；引申為「成功」，如：The singer became a hit. 這位歌手紅了。

## history [ˈhistəri] n. 歷史（學）；（某物的）來歷

【例】So your listening history helps determine whether you'll like a new song—or tell it to hit the road. 所以，過去聽過的音樂會對自己今後的音樂喜好有重大影響。(Scientific American)

【用】 在表示「……的歷史」時，既可以用名詞加上 history，也可以用「the history of+ 名詞」來表示。history 的派生詞有：historical 歷史的，史學的；historic 有歷史意義的；historian 歷史學家。

## fire [ˈfaiə] n. 火災 v. 射出（子彈等）；解雇

【例】They will fire darts from small air rifles to collect blubber and skin for genetic testing, and to attach satellite-tracking tags to monitor the whales. 他們會用小型來複氣槍發射飛鏢來收集鯨脂和外皮以供基因實驗使用，他們還會給鯨魚貼上衛星追蹤標籤來監測它們。(VOA)

【用】 常用片語：on fire 著火；on the fire 在審議中；under fire 遭到攻擊。fire 可單獨成句，在軍事行動中，表示「開槍射擊」。

## justice ['dʒʌstis] n. 公平；司法；法律制裁

【例】And we will do everything we can to bring them to justice. 我們會盡我們所能將他們繩之以法。(CRI)

【用】 justice 表示「公平，公正」，如：a sense of justice 公平意識；在法律範疇，常用片語有：justice department 司法部門；court of justice 法院。

## region ['riːdʒən] n. 地帶；範圍

【例】 More than 6,000 soldiers and doctors have been deployed to the region, as part of the rescue operation. 救援行動包括，在該地區部署 6000 多名士兵和醫生。(NPR)

【用】 與 region 相似，area、zone、district 都可以表示「地區，範圍」，但在使用時各有側重。area 最常用，使用範圍最廣；zone 強調按溫度劃分的 5 個地帶；district 側重行政區域的劃分；而 region 既可指按行政區域劃分的地帶，也可以指按溫度、大氣劃分的地帶。

## pay [pei] v. 支付，交納 n. 工資

【例】It is a yearly effort that is paying off, with a river that is once again starting to look like a river. 一年以來的努力沒白費，這條河又恢復了原樣。(VOA)

【用】 pay 的過去式和過去分詞為 paid，常用片語有：pay back 還錢，償還；pay up 付清全部欠款；pay off 成功，行得通。作名詞時，同義詞有：payment、salary、wage。

## vote [v4ut] n. 選舉，投票 v. 投票

【例】Italy's new coalition government has easily won a vote of confidence in the lower house of parliament. 義大利新的聯合政府輕鬆贏得了下議院的信任票。(BBC)

【用】 vote 在總統大選、制定法律的程式中很常見，通常是 one man one vote（一人一票制），get the vote at 18（18 歲有投票權）。作為動詞，常見片語有：vote for 投票贊成；vote on 就……表決；right to vote 投票權。

## plan [plæn] n. 計畫；示意圖 v. 計畫

【例】So Detroit today is announcing a big plan, shutting down more than 40 of its schools. 所以底特律今天宣布了一個重大的計畫，準備關閉市內的 40 多所學校。(CNN)

【用】 plan 作名詞時是可數名詞，大到城市的發展計畫 (development plan)，小到個人的工作計畫 (work plan) 都可以用 plan 表示。

# Level 3

## record [riːˈkɔːd] n. 記錄；最高紀錄 v. 登記

【例】And records of background checks have to be destroyed within 24 hours after a gun buyer is approved—which hampers investigations. 槍支買家通過審核後 24 小時內背景審查記錄必須銷毀，這妨礙了調查。(NPR)

【用】　常用片語：keep the record 保持紀錄；break one's record 打破某人的記錄。record 作名詞和動詞時發音不同，注意分辨。

## force [fɔːs] n. [pl.] 軍隊；力 v. 強迫

【例】And not just force equals mass times acceleration. 不只是簡單的「力等於品質乘以加速度」。(Scientific American)

【用】　表示「力量」時，force 相當於 strength、might；表示「軍事力量」時，可以指 army。美國總統專機就被稱為 Air Force One（空軍一號）。

## project [ˈprɔdʒekt] n. 專案，工程 v. 設計

【例】Now, the U.N. Food and Agriculture Organization, the FAO, hopes to change that with a new project called Voices of the Hungry. 如今，聯合國糧食及農業組織 (FAO) 希望通過一個名為「飢餓的聲音」的新專案來改變這種現況。(VOA)

【用】　常見片語：Project Hope 希望工程；science project 科研專案。

## data [ˈdeitə] n. 資料，資料

【例】But even though pictures of both brothers were in public databases, the computers that searched that data missed them, and came up empty. 儘管兄弟兩人的照片都在公共資料庫中，用電腦還是搜尋不到，搜尋結果顯示為「無」。(CNN)

【用】　data 表示「資料」，是 datum 的複數形式。常見句型：The data shows... 資料顯示……

## crisis [ˈkraisis] n. ([pl.] crises) 危機；關鍵階段

【例】The financial hit to the government from bailouts during the financial crisis is shrinking. 金融危機期間，政府因對外緊急救助而受到金融衝擊，這種衝擊正在逐漸減弱。(NPR)

【用】 新聞常見片語：financial crisis 金融危機；political crisis 政治危機；economic crisis 經濟危機。

## opera [ˈkraisis] n. 歌劇

【例】The opera was composed using an ink containing traces of iron, but the last page was smudged out using a different substance containing no traces of metal. 這部歌劇是用一種含有微量鐵元素的墨水寫成的，但最後一頁被另一種不含金屬元素的不同墨水弄髒了。(BBC)

【用】 常用片語：opera house 歌劇院；Beijing Opera 京劇；soap opera 肥皂劇。藝術相關詞：symphony 交響樂；ballet 芭蕾舞；acrobatics 雜技；concert 音樂會；drama 戲劇。

## director [diˈrektə] n. 導演；主管；董事

【例】She is the director of the Center for Retirement Research at Boston College. 她是波士頓學院退休研究中心的主任。(CNN)

【用】 director 在藝術領域，表示「導演、指揮」，從 direct（指揮，命令）引申而來，同根詞有：direction 方向；indirect 間接的。

## organization [ˌɔːgəniˈzeiʃən] n. 團體，機構，組織

【例】Statistics from the World Health Organization show Indonesia has the biggest bird flu death toll in the world. 世界衛生組織的統計資料顯示，印尼的禽流感死亡人數居全球首位。(CRI)

【用】 注意組織機構名稱的首字母大寫，也可直接用大寫字母組合縮寫，如：WTO World Trade Organization 世界貿易組織。

## civil [ˈsɪvəl] a. 公民的；國內的；民事的

【例】President Obama's nominee to lead the Labor Department has been one of the most aggressive advocates for civil rights in decades. 歐巴馬總統提名的勞工部領導是數十年以來最激進的民權宣導者之一。(NPR)

【用】　與 civil 相關的常出現的有 civil right 民權；civil war 內戰等。civil 也可表示「有禮貌的」，civility 是其名詞形式，表示「禮貌；客氣」。

## bill [bɪl] n. 帳單；法案；鈔票

【例】Accordingly, he has sent a bill to parliament that would transfer responsibility for various tasks from the Interior Ministry to other agencies. 因此他向國會遞交了一份法案，要求內政部將部分職責移交給其他機構。(VOA)

【用】　常用片語：bill of lading 提貨單；bill for 送交罰單；pay the bill 付帳。

## head [hed] n. 首腦 v. 主管；使朝......行進

【例】Passengers will feel weightless for up to five minutes before heading down through the atmosphere and gliding back to earth. 乘客在前 5 分鐘會有失重感，然後，穿過大氣層，滑翔返回地球。(BBC)

【用】　head 通常表示「頭」，指身體部位。但在新聞英語中，head 通常表示各國首腦或是會議的牽頭人。作動詞時，常用片語有：head for 向......挺進；head off 阻攔，攔截。

## energy [ˈenədʒi] n. 精力；能量；能源

【例】China is very interested in energy supplies of the Middle East. 針對中東地區的能源供應問題，中國非常感興趣。(NPR)

【用】　常見片語有：full of energy 充滿力量。如今，energy saving（節能）與 new energy（新能源）成為政府和新聞媒體的關注點。energy 的派生詞也常出現在新聞中，如：energetic 精力充沛的。

## condition [kənˈdiʃən] n. 狀況；[pl.] 形勢；前提

【例】To test this kind of body perception in anorexic patients, researchers recruited 39 women, 19 with anorexia and 20 without the condition. 為了測試厭食症患者的身體知覺，研究者招募了 39 位女性，其中 19 位患有厭食症，另外 20 位沒有。(Scientific American)

【用】 condition 與 situation，circumstance 一樣，都有「狀況」之意。condition 強調產生影響的原因或環境；situation 指明確的環境或處境；circumstance 多指周邊的情形與情況。

## peace [piːs] n. 和平；平靜

【例】U.S. Secretary of State John Kerry travels Monday to the Middle East for talks on holding a Syrian peace conference. 美國國務卿約翰‧克里星期一訪問中東發表了演講意在解決敘利亞危機。(VOA)

【用】 peace 首字母大寫時，表示「和約」，如：The Peace of Versailles 凡爾賽和約。常用片語：at one's peace 保持沉默；at peace 和睦；make peace 和解；peace negotiations 和談。

## point [pɔint] n. 點；觀點；目的；進展的階段，程度

【例】 The corporation's head of strategy, James Purnell, said it had reached the point where good money was being thrown after bad. 公司的策略主管詹姆士‧珀內爾稱該公司已經到了這樣一種境地：為彌補損失，不斷投入資金，但未見成效，資金有去無回。(BBC)

【用】 常用句型：There's no point in doing sth. 做……毫無意義。口語中，常用 That's my point. 我就是這意思。

## hope [həup]] n./v. 希望，期望

【例】I hope the court rules that a student's race and ethnicity should not be considered when applying to the University of Texas. 我希望法庭裁定：學生申請德克薩斯大學時，不應將其種族情況納入考核標準。(CNN)

【用】 hope 作為動詞，後面既可以加不定式 to do sth.，也可以加從句。與 hope 近似的詞為 wish，兩者相較，hope 表示可能實現的期望，而 wish 表示心裡美好的願望。

## church [tʃəːtʃ] n. 教堂；禮拜；教會

【例】Pope Francis is urging church leaders to go out into their communities and help the poor around rather than focus on the internal politics. 弗朗西斯教皇呼籲教會領袖們走出去，深入到社區去幫助身邊的窮人，而不是專注於內政。(NPR)

【用】 church 通常出現在與宗教相關的新聞中。相關片語：the Church 全體基督教徒；Church of England 英國國教會；go to the church（去教堂）做禮拜。

## huge [hjuːdʒ] a. 龐大的

【例】Our skins play host to a huge variety of microbes, but previous studies focused on bacteria. 我們的皮膚是多種微生物的宿主，但以前的研究重點在於細菌。(Scientific American)

【用】 huge，immense，giant，vast 都表示「大」。huge 強調體積、容量的「龐大」；immense 指體積、數量、程度上遠遠超過一般標準；giant 強調體積「龐大」；vast 的「龐大」，不涉及重量。

## criminal [ˈkriminəl] n. 罪犯 a. 犯罪的

【例】They say the attacks are purely criminal, and the country is safe for foreign students. 他們聲稱襲擊事件只是單純的刑事案件，而這個國家對於留學生來說依然是安全的。(VOA)

【用】 犯罪相關詞：sentence 判決；judge 審判；punishment 懲罰；death penalty 死刑；witness 證人；victim 受害人。

## risk [risk] n. 風險；冒險 v. 冒......的危險

【例】There's already evidence at eating a lot of red and processed meat can raise the risk of stomach cancer. 已經有證據表明，如果大量食用紅肉和加工過的肉類，

患胃癌的風險會增大。(BBC)

【用】 at risk 表示「處境危險」。

## local [ˈləukəl] a. 本地的；局部的 n. [ 常 pl.] 當地人

【例】A local archeologist called the pyramid's destruction an incredible display of ignorance. 一位當地的考古學家稱，對金字塔的破壞行為體現了人們是多麼無知。(CNN)

【用】 常用片語：local authority 地方政權；local government 當地政府；local news 當地新聞。需要注意的是，local 作為名詞時，相當於 local people，表示「本地人」，通常用作複數形式 locals。

## charge [tʃɑːdʒ] n. 費【用】；管理；控告

【例】Mubarak is still being held in connection with the corruption charges against him. 穆巴拉克因涉嫌貪汙罪，仍被關押。(CRI)

【用】 常用片語：in charge (of) 主管；take charge 掌管，接管；free of charge 免費。charge 表示「控告」時還有動詞詞性，與 accuse 可以互換，但 charge 側重罪行嚴重，比 accuse 更為正式。

## speech [spiːtʃ] n. 講話；言論

【例】The president used this speech to promote his health care law. 總統發表演講，來宣傳他的醫改法案。(NPR)

【用】 常見片語：freedom of speech 言論自由；speech contest 演講比賽；make a speech 發表演講。國外大學畢業時，通常邀請名人校友在畢業典禮上演講，因此，speech-day 也被稱為「畢業典禮日」。

## senior [ˈsiːnjə] a. 資格較老的；年長的 n. 較年長者

【例】Senior African finance officials say per capita income in Africa fell for the first time in a decade because of the global economic recession. 非洲的高級金融官員稱，由於全球經濟衰退，非洲的人均收入十年來首次下降。(VOA)

【用】 senior 不僅可以指年齡大，也可以指資格老，即「有經驗的」，與其相對的就是 junior。另外，國外也會有重名的時候，這時按照年齡，在名字後面加上 Senior 表示年長的一位，而 Junior 則表示年輕的一位。

## effort [ˈefət] n. 努力，嘗試；成就

【例】A new study says energy generation today is almost as dirty as it was 20 years ago despite efforts to introduce cleaner technologies. 一項新的研究表明：儘管我們做出了巨大的努力引進清潔技術，但是能源生產過程中的汙染很嚴重，不比 20 年前少。(BBC)

【用】 常用片語：make an effort to do sth. 努力嘗試做某事。

## means [miːnz] n. 手段；財產

【例】Until relatively recently, much of the medical profession disdained patents, except as a means to ensure quality. 直到最近，許多醫學界人士都很輕視專利權，僅用於保證品質。(NPR)

【用】 常用片語：by means of 依靠；by no means 一點也不；means of communication 通訊手段。需要注意的是，means 在這裡是獨立的可數名詞，要與 mean 作為動詞時的第三人稱單數形式區分開來。

## area [ˈeəriə] n. 面積；地區；範圍

【例】One method was to sell oil in one area of the country for much less than the oil was worth. 其中一個方法是在該國的一個地區以很低的價格出售石油。(VOA)

【用】 area 是表示「地區」指較大的、界限不明顯的區域；district 主要以行政區域劃分；belt 主要指廣闊的長條地帶；而 zone 則是指圓形或弧形地帶。

## role [rəul] n. 作【用】；角色

【例】Among them was American Jody Williams, who won the 1997 Nobel Peace Prize for her role in the campaign to ban landmines. 其中美國人裘蒂・威廉姆斯因在禁雷運動中扮演重要角色而獲得了 1997 年的諾貝爾和平獎。(VOA)

【用】 常用片語：play a role 發揮作用；role of ……的角色；role play 角色扮演。通常說「發揮重要作用」，用 play an important role。

## expert [ˈekspəːt] n. 專家 a. 熟練的

【例】Without the extra money, the experts say, NASA would have to work with private companies now trying to embark on commercial space flights. 專家稱：如果缺乏額外的資金支持，美國國家航空暨太空總署將不得不與私營公司合作，開啟商業化模式的太空航行。(BBC)

【用】 expert 表示「專家」，具有一定的 authority（權威性）；與之相對的就是 amateur（外行，生手）。常用片語有：expert in 熟於，在......是行家；expert at 擅長。

## free [friː] a. 自由的；免費的；不受（規章）控制的 v. 使自由

【例】You might be able to post what you want, but Facebook is free to take it down and cancel your account. 你可以隨心所欲地在臉書上發布內容，但臉書有權刪除它們並註銷你的帳號。(CNN)

【用】 Feel free. 表示「感到自在。」相當於 Enjoy yourself.「請自便。」作形容詞時，還可以表示「空閒的」，相當於 available；名詞形式為 freedom，表示「自由」。

## agreement [əˈɡriːmənt] n. 同意；協定；一致

【例】China and Iceland have signed a Free Trade Agreement. 中國和冰島簽訂了一項自由貿易協定。(CRI)

【用】 agreement 常見片語有：reach agreement 達成一致；sign an agreement 簽署協定；bilateral agreement 雙邊協議；in agreement with sb. 與某人意見一致。

## build [bɪld] v. 建造；建立 n. 體型

【例】So with the engineer, we are actually being able to build a very economic and very rational tower. 所以有了這位工程師，我們就能夠用合理的價格建造一座牢固的塔樓。(CNN)

【用】 build 的過去式和過去分詞為 built，可用於被動語態。新聞中會引用一句話：Rome was not built in a day. 引申為「冰凍三尺非一日之寒。」

## final [ˈfaɪnəl] a. 最後的；決定性的 n. [ 常 pl.] 決賽

【例】The final troops would return, he said, with the heads held high and with the backing of the American people. 他說，最後的部隊一定會在美國人民的支持下昂首挺胸地歸來。(BBC)

【用】 在體育競技中，the final 特指最後的「總決賽」，其派生詞有：finally 最後地；finality 最終。

## commission [kəˈmɪʃən] n. 委員會；傭金 v. 委託

【例】The Joint Commission points to federal findings that identify more than 560 alarmrelated deaths in hospitals. 聯合委員會表明聯邦調查結果發現醫院內有超過 560 起的死亡事件都與報警器失常有關。(NPR)

【用】 在表示「委員會」時，首字母通常大寫，即 Commission。常用片語有：in commission 可用；在服役期間；out of commission 不可使用；退役。

## win [wɪn] v. 贏得 n. 勝利

【例】No party is expected to win a majority in the election which will be closely monitored by the organization for security and cooperation in Europe. 選舉將在歐洲安全與合作組織的密切監測下進行，預計沒有黨派能在選舉中贏得大多數選票。(BBC)

【用】 win 的過去式和過去分詞為 won。通常說的「雙贏」即 win-win；「贏家」則是 winner。

## community [kəˈmjuːnəti] n. 社區；共同體

【例】We need co-operation on the part of the international community. 我們需要加強與國際社會的合作。(CNN)

【用】 the community 特指「社區」，常用片語：community centre 社區中心；sense of community 社區意識。

## key [kiː] n. 關鍵；答案 a. 主要的

【例】 Contending that genes can be patented are the biotech and pharmaceutical industries, which see patents as the keys to new scientific exploration. 生物技術行業和製藥行業主張基因可以申請專利，這對於科學探索新發現來說很關鍵。(NPR)

【用】 「......的答案；......的關鍵」用 the key to...，這裡使用的介詞是 to，而不是 of。

## team [tiːm] n. 隊，組

【例】The team was very energized going into this court. 這支隊伍精神抖擻地走進球場。(VOA)

【用】 team 經常在商務類、體育類新聞中出現，如：football team 足球隊；national team 國家隊；team work 協作；team spirit 團隊精神。

## technology [tekˈnɔlədʒi] n. 技術，工藝

【例】Without their research, modern communications technology including digital cameras and the Internet might not exist. 如果沒有他們做研究，數位相機和網際網路等現代通訊技術可能都不會存在。　(BBC)

【用】 經常說的 IT 產業，即 Information Technology 資訊技術產業。technology 派生詞有很多，也大都用於科技英語範疇，如：technological 技術的；technically 技術上；technique 技術；technician 技師。

## reform [ri'fɔːm] v. 改革 n. 改革

【例】Republicans have promised to make the health care reform law a major issue in midterm Congressional elections in November. 共和黨人承諾將醫療改革法列為 11 月份國會中期選舉的主要議題。(VOA)

【用】 reform 常常用在政治和經濟方面：政治上，institutional reform 體制改革；educational reform 教育改革；經濟上，reform and opening-up 改革開放；economic reform 經濟改革。

## visit ['vizit] v./n. 參觀，訪問

【例】On Sunday Mr. Kerry said during his visit to Istanbul that it would be better to wait for the right conditions. 星期日，克里先生訪問了伊斯坦布爾，期間他提出最好等待合適的時機。(BBC)

【用】 常用句型：It's one's first visit to... 這是某人首次拜訪......

## council ['kaunsəl] n. 委員會，理事會；議會

【例】Those actions led the United Nations Security Council to expand existing sanctions against that country. 那些行為使聯合國安理會加重了對該國現有的制裁。(VOA)

【用】 council 常出現在政治新聞中。State Council 國務院；the Council 議會。

## follow ['fɔləu] v. 跟隨；遵照；領會

【例】We intend to follow those rules. 我們打算遵守那些規則。(CNN)

【用】 在動詞時，可以用 follow sb. 跟隨某人；as follow 如下所述。

## evidence ['evidəns] n. 證據，根據

【例】Other studies suggest the evidence is contradictory, and that scientists don't know for sure what is happening to sharks across the Atlantic. 其他研究表明這個證據自相矛盾，科學家們不確定大西洋裡的鯊魚到底怎麼了。(NPR)

【用】 常用片語：in evidence 顯而易見地。常見句型為：There isn't enough evidence to prove... 沒有足夠的證據證明……

## provide [prəuˈvaid] v. 供給，提供

【例】 But overall, the study shows that Twitter can provide cheap and useful information. 但總的來說，研究表明推特網能夠以低廉的價格為大家提供有用的資訊。(Scientific American)

【用】 通常與 with，for 連用，表示「提供……」。

## current [ˈkʌrənt] a. 現行的；流通的 n. 潮流

【例】 Russia's known oil reserves only allow for production to continue at current levels for 20 years. 按照現在的生產水準，俄羅斯已探測到的石油儲備只夠維持 20 年。(VOA)

【用】 常用片語：current situation 現狀，目前形勢；current status 當前狀態。

## supreme [sjuˈpriːm] a. 最高的，至上的；極度的

【例】U.S. Supreme Court sessions start in October. 美國最高法院會議於 10 月開始。(CNN)

【用】 supreme court 最高法院；supreme commander 最高指揮官。

## decade [ˈdekeid] n. 十年

【例】 The mobile phone and computer giant Apple has reported its first quarterly drop in profits for almost a decade. 據報導近十年來手機和電腦巨頭蘋果公司的季度利潤首次下降。(BBC)

【用】 與 decade 相關的，在新聞調查報告中會出現的是：in the past decade 在過去的 10 年裡……；from decade to decade 每 10 年。

## station [ˈsteiʃən] n. 車站；駐地 v. 安置

【例】Two astronauts left the International Space Station today on a mission to find and end ammonia leak. 今天，兩名太空人離開國際空間站，任務是找到氨氣洩漏的源頭並將其堵住。(CRI)

【用】 station 最常見的含義是「車站;駐地」，如：police station 警察局；bus station 公交網站；railway station 火車站。

## release [riˈliːs] v./n. 釋放；發行

【例】They say the arrested miners must be released by Sunday or they will apply to the high court to order their release. 他們要求在週日前釋放被捕礦工，否則他們將申請高等法院釋放他們。(BBC)

【用】 常用片語：on release 在公映，發行。release 與 free 不同，它更強調放鬆限制、解除監禁或免除義務。

## professor [prəuˈfesə] n. 教授

【例】Professor MacGregor says lowering salt can do a lot to reduce hypertension, but increasing potassium in the diet also helps. 馬基高教授表示，減少食鹽攝入量有助於緩解高血壓的症狀，不過增加飲食中鉀的含量對降壓也有幫助。 (VOA)

【用】 professor 既可以指一個人的職業，也可以說明這個人的職位，通常用 Professor 加上人的姓氏，如：Professor Lee 李教授。教授也分很多種，如：Visiting Professor 客座教授；Honorary Professor 名譽教授。

## king [kiŋ] n. 國王

【例】Consumed by ambition and spurred to action by his wife, Macbeth murders

King Duncan and takes the throne for himself. 受妻子唆使，野心勃勃的馬克白謀殺了鄧肯國王，自己繼承了王位。(CRI)

【用】 王室相關詞：queen 王后；prince 王子；princess 公主；knight 騎士；royalty 皇室。

## committee [kəˈmiti] n. 委員會

【例】Officials say two committees will be set up in reaction to the protests. 官員稱將成立兩個委員會來應對示威活動。(VOA)

【用】 committee 與 comission 均含「委員會」的含義，前者指一般的委員會，後者指由於某種原因而成立的委員會。

## lead [liːd] v. 致使，引導 n. 榜樣

【例】Critics say it could lead to sharply higher inflation. 評論家稱這會導致更嚴重的通貨膨脹。(BBC)

【用】 需要注意的是，lead 的過去式與過去分詞為 led。常用句型：It leads to... 這導致……。

## form [fɔːm] n. 形式；表格 v. 形成

【例】Only by safeguarding nature's resilience can we hope to have a resilient form of food production and ensure food security in the long term. 只有依靠大自然的自我修復能力，我們才有望長期擁有一個彈性的糧食生產形式，並確保食品安全。(CNN)

【用】 form 在作為名詞時，可以用 a form of 表示「一種……的形式」；在作為動詞時，搭配 form up 表示「將某人編入隊伍」，在軍事新聞中需要注意該用法。

# Level 4

## mount [maunt] n. 山峰 v. 登上

【例】UNESCO said Mount Fuji had 「inspired artists and poets and been the object of pilgrimage for centuries」. 聯合國教科文組織稱富士山「激發了藝術家和詩人的靈感,幾個世紀以來都是人們的朝聖之地」。(BBC)

【用】 作為名詞,mount 常見用法是首字母大寫,加上山峰的名稱,如:Mount Everest 珠穆朗瑪峰;作為動詞,mount to 表示「登上,爬上」;mount up 表示「(量或強度的)增加,上升」;另外,注意「發起(攻擊、戰爭等)」,也可以用 mount。

## patient [ˈpeiʃənt] n. 病人 a. 忍耐的

【例】So far, only one H7N9 patient has been discharged from hospital after treatments. 目前,只有一位 H7N9 禽流感患者經過治療後出院了。(CRI)

【用】 patient 兩個詞性的用法都很常見。作為名詞,複數形式為 patients;作為形容詞,其反義詞為 impatient「沒有耐性的」,副詞為 patiently「有耐性地」。

## air [eə] n. 空氣;航空

【例】Instead, he wants to know how he will feel and deal with the extreme cold, thin air and low oxygen levels in the Himalayas. 相反,他想探索自己在極度寒冷、空氣稀薄、缺氧的喜馬拉雅山上感覺如何,又會如何應對。(VOA)

【用】 常用片語:fresh air 新鮮空氣;by air 乘飛機;air force 空軍。air 在表示「空氣」時,可引申為「氛圍,環境」。

## receive [riˈsiːv] v. 收到;遭到;接待

【例】I received over 2,200 letters on this topic. 我收到了 2200 多封關於這一話題的來信。(CNN)

【用】 在表示「收到」時,accept 強調主動或自願接受;receive 陳述「收到」的事實,不含採取主動或積極行動的意思。

## brain [breɪn] n. 腦;智慧

【例】Their mother underwent surgery for brain injuries. 他們的母親因腦損傷做了手術。(CRI)

【用】 brain 除了表示「腦」這一人體器官之外,可引申為「智慧,頭腦」,如:use your brain 發揮你的聰明才智;也可以引申為「人才」,如:brain drain 人才流失;brain gain 人才引進。

## gene [dʒiːn] n. 基因

【例】Some companies modify the genes of animals and plants that are part of our food chain. 有些公司修改了食物鏈上的動植物基因。(CNN)

【用】 該詞常用於科學、醫學、生物學等相關文章中。常見片語:gene mutation 基因突變;gene pool 基因庫;gene engineering 遺傳工程。

## measure [ˈmeʒə] n. 測量;措施;尺寸

【例】 The continued recession highlights the struggles brought down by austerity measures.經濟一直很蕭條,這更加突出地說明了:時政緊縮措施的影響很大。(NPR)

【用】 常用片語:effective measure 有效措施;beyond measure 無可估量,極度;in some measure 在一定程度上。

## special [ˈspeʃəl] a. 特殊的;專門的 n. 特價

【例】The FBI Special Agent in charge, Richard says all the evidence is now being analyzed. 負責本案的聯邦調查局特工理查稱,現在正在分析所有的證據。(CRI)

【用】 special 作形容詞時,通常作定語,修飾名詞,如:special delivery 專遞;special train 專列;作名詞時,有複數形式,可表示「特價菜」,也可表示「號外」。

## product [ˈprɔdʌkt] n. 產品,產物

【例】Thousands of genetic tests carried out across the European Union have found that almost 5% of processed beef products on sale have been contaminated with horsemeat. 歐盟國家進行了數千次基因測試，表明市場上高達 5% 的牛肉加工製品都摻雜了馬肉。(BBC)

【用】 產品相關詞：produce 製作；design 設計；marketing 行銷；advertisement 廣告。

## cost [kɔst] n. 價格；損失 v. 使付出（代價）

【例】For the past few decades, U.S. companies have been outsourcing its manufacturing business to places where labor costs are low and raw materials abundant. 在過去的幾十年中，美國公司紛紛將製造業外包、因為海外勞動力成本低、原材料豐富。(CRI)

【用】 作動詞時，注意與 spend，take，pay 的區別：spend 主語是人，常用 spend (time/money) in doing sth；take 一般用形式主語 it，句型為 it takes sb. (time/money) to do sth.；pay 表「支付」，與 for 連用；cost 主語是物，句型為 it costs sb. (time/money) to do sth.

## administration [ədˌminiˈstreiʃən] n. 管理；行政機關

【例】When the Federal Aviation Administration said it would have to close about 150 towers to cut costs, the airports protested, some even threatened to sue. 聯邦航空管理局表示必須關閉約 150 個塔台以削減成本，但機場紛紛表示抗議，一些機場甚至威脅要提起訴訟。(NPR)

【用】 當管理的物件是人時，通常用 management；管理的物件是事物、工作、系統時，則用 administration。常用片語：administration expenses 行政費用；administration department 行政部門。

## army [ˈɑːmi] n. 軍隊，陸軍

【例】The present constitution was written by the army in 1982 after it seized power in a coup in 1980. 現行的憲法是當地軍隊在 1980 年的政變中取得政權後，於 1982 年改革的。(VOA)

【用】 army 泛指「軍隊」，但是側重「陸軍」，「海軍」為 marine，「空軍」為 air force。常用片語：red army 紅軍；join the army 參軍。

## science [ˈsaiəns] n. 科學；學科

【例】Cathie Martin, professor of political science at Boston University, says she is shocked by the tragedy. 波士頓大學的政治系教授凱西 · 馬丁稱，她聽聞這個悲劇感到很震驚。(CRI)

【用】 常用固定搭配：science fiction 科幻小說；computer science 電腦科學；science and technology 科學與技術。

## fact [fækt] n. 事實，真相

【例】In fact, he says, figuring out what you owe and paying your debt is the foundation of the US tax system. 他表示，事實上，核算欠款、督促還債是美國稅務系統的基礎性工作。(NPR)

【用】 除了 in fact 可以表示「事實上」之外，也可以用 in actual fact，in point of fact，in view of the fact。

## victim [ˈviktim] n. 受害者

【例】The victim was a twenty-three-year-old medical student. 受害者是一名 23 歲的醫學學生。 (VOA)

【用】 常用片語：fall victim to 成為……的犧牲品；fashion victim 時髦追隨者。

## create [kriːˈeit] v. 創造；引起，產生

【例】Scientists in the United States say they've created a human embryo through cloning. 美國科學家稱，他們已經利用克隆技術創造了人類胚胎。(BBC)

【用】 常用派生詞：creation 創造；creative 有創造力的；creatively 有創造力地；creativity 創造力；creature 生物；人。

## film [film] n. 影片；膠片 v. 拍攝

【例】The film was edited by a highly skilled technician so that the joints are imperceptible. 這部影片是由一位技術高超的技術人員剪輯的，因此連接處令人難以察覺。(VOA)

【用】 常用片語：film star 電影明星；film test 試鏡；film industry 電影業。

## result [ri'zʌlt] n. 結果；成果 v. 導致

【例】The opposition though, alleges the results are fraudulent. 但是反對黨宣稱結果具有欺騙性。(CRI)

【用】 常用片語為 as a result of 由於，result in 導致，result from 起因於。

## focus ['fəukəs] n. 焦點；中心 v.（使）聚焦

【例】The political analyst believes Cairo would be better off to focus on issues close to home, whether successful or not. 政治分析家認為無論成功與否，開羅都應該關注那些更加切實的問題。(VOA)

【用】 常用片語：focus on 集中於；the focus of ......的焦點；in focus 清晰；focus in 專注於......。

## gun [gʌn] n. 槍，炮

【例】The two days of violence erupted after a group of local youths allegedly shot two immigrants with a pellet gun. 據傳一夥當地青少年用彈丸槍擊中了兩名移民，引發了為期兩天的暴亂。 (VOA)

【用】 gun 表示戰鬥中的武器，與 gun 相關的固定片語有：stick to one's guns 堅持自己的立場；jump the gun 搶先行動；with all guns blazing 全力以赴。

## legal [ˈliːgəl] a. 法定的；合法的

【例】Argentina became the first Latin American country to make same-sex marriage legal in 2010. 2010 年，阿根廷成為第一個將同性婚姻合法化的拉丁美洲國家。(VOA)

【用】 該詞與法律，政策等相關，常見用法有：legal system 法律制度；legal services 法律服務；legal protection 合法保護。常見派生詞：legally 法律上；illegal 不合法的。

## amount [əˈmaunt] n. 總額 v. 合計

【例】We actually know there's particular environment that water was there for significant amount of time, that it was neutral, wasn't too salty. 我們可以確定的是，在很長一段時間裡，那裡環境特別，有水存在，這種水是中性的，且鹽度不高。(BBC)

【用】 作名詞時，the amount of 表示「......的總數」，a large amount of 表示「大量的......」，但要注意後面加不可數名詞；作動詞時，常用片語為 amount to 表示「達到......」。

## rate [reit] n. 比率；價格 v. 對......估價

【例】An analyst says the program could help increase test scores, but it could also increase dropout rates. 一位分析師表示該計畫可能有助於提高學生的考試成績，但是也可能導致輟學率上升。(CNN)

【用】 employment rate「就業率」一直是每個國家的一個熱門話題，相對而言，unemployment rate「失業率」也逐漸被人們所關注。

## coast [kəust] n. 海岸

【例】They breed in the Maritime Provinces of eastern Canada and winter along the Atlantic coast. 它們在加拿大東部的沿海諸省繁殖，同時冬季遷徙到大西洋沿岸。(CNN)

【用】 海濱相關詞：beach 海灘；coastguard 海岸警衛隊；coastline 海岸線；bank 河岸。

## accuse [əˈkjuːz] v. 譴責，控告

【例】He accused Venezuela's enemies of attacking the president with cancer. 他譴責委內瑞拉的敵人用癌症迫害總統。(VOA)

【用】 最常用的片語就是 accuse sb. of sth. 控告某人某事，需要注意的是。of 後面加名詞或是動名詞。該詞有被動語態，便成為 be accused of，表示「由於……而被控告」。

## majority [məˈdʒɔrəti] n. 大多數，多半

【例】The government majority say this was necessary to make a clean break with the previous constitution. 政府中多數人表示有必要與之前的憲法劃清界限。(BBC)

【用】 與其相對的是 minority，表示「少數」。the majority 表示「大多數人；多數黨」，在政黨、選舉中經常出現。

## rescue [ˈreskjuː] v./n. 營救，拯救

【例】 That suggests that British troops were involved in the rescue although there has been no confirmation of that. 那就暗示了英國軍隊參與了營救行動，儘管這一點還沒有得到確認。(BBC)

【用】 rescue 常見於自然災害或人為造成的重大突發事件的新聞報導中，如：rescue mission 救援任務；rescue team 救援小組。

## pressure [ˈpreʃə] n. 壓強；壓（力）v. 迫使，使……增壓

【例】The World Health Organization says high blood pressure affects one billion people worldwide. 世界衛生組織稱全世界有 10 億人患高血壓病。(VOA)

【用】 常用片語：high blood pressure 高血壓；under pressure 壓力之下；relieve pressure 緩解壓力；atmospheric pressure 大氣壓力。pressure 還有動詞詞性，在句中相當於 push，如：Don't pressure me. 不要逼我。

## labor ['leibə] n. 勞動；勞工

【例】The labor department released its producer price index fell 0.70% in April, the steepest dropping more than three years. 勞工部四月公布的生產價格指數下跌了 0.70%，遭遇三年多來最大跌幅。 (NPR)

【用】 也作 labour，常見片語：Labor Day 勞動節；labor force 勞動力；labor market 勞動力市場。如今，發展中國家，多為勞動密集型（labor-intensive）產業；而先進國家，多為技術密集型（tech-intensive）產業。

## famous ['feiməs] a. 著名的，出名的

【例】The famous Maracana football stadium in Rio de Janeiro reopened shortly after nearly three years of renovations to prepare for Brazil's hosting of the 2014 World Cup. 經過近三年的整修，里約熱內盧著名的馬拉卡納足球館重新開館，迎接巴西主辦的 2014 年世界盃。(BBC)

【用】 最常見的片語是：be famous for 因……而著名。注意與 notorious 的區別在於，notorious 表達的是「聲名狼藉的，臭名昭著的」。

## conference ['kɔnfərəns] n. ( 正式 ) 會議；討論 ( 會 )，商談 ( 會 )

【例】In a press conference, the Minister of Interior named three men arrested for alleged involvement in the terror plot. 內政部長在新聞發布會上給出了三名因涉嫌恐怖陰謀而被捕的男子的姓名。 (NPR)

【用】 conference 表示比 meeting 更正式、規模更大的會議，而不是單純的會面，如：press conference 記者招待會；news conference 新聞發布會；international conference 國際會議；in conference 正在開會。當今，會議的方法也有很多，如：video conference 電視會議；teleconference 電話會議。

## gas [gæs] n. 氣體；煤氣；汽油

【例】In addition, the sediment comes from a window of time during the Pliocene Epoch, when greenhouse gas levels were only slightly higher than they are today. 此

外，沉積物形成於上新世時期的一段時間，那時的溫室氣體量比現在略高。(Scientific American)

【用】 gas 一詞在新聞中出現，可以表示日常使用的「天然氣」，還可以表示「天然氣資源」，同時也可表示車輛用的「汽油」，如：gas station 加油站。

## flu [fluː] n. 流行性感冒

【例】In fact, the urgency increased this weekend with the discovery that a 7-year-old girl in Beijing fell ill with this new bird flu last Thursday. 事實上，上週四在北京出現了一個新型禽流感疑似病例，患者為一名 7 歲女童，這週末情況變得愈發緊急。(NPR)

【用】 常見片語：bird flu 禽流感；seasonal flu 季節性感冒；flu shot 流感疫苗；have/catch a flu 患感冒。

## march [mɑːtʃ] v. 前進 n. 行軍；遊行示威

【例】Earlier, he had called for a march to peacefully protest against the results, and to demand the National Electoral Council to recount Sunday's votes. 此前，他號召了一次和平的示威遊行以抗議投票結果，並要求國家選舉委員會重新計算週日的投票。(CRI)

【用】 在軍事新聞中，march 通常表示「行軍，行進」，quick march 表示「齊步走」，也有可能表示「示威遊行」，如：the organizer of the march 遊行的組織者；另外需要注意，m 大寫後，變成專有名詞 March「三月」。

## unemployment [ˌʌnimˈplɔimənt] n. 失業；失業人數

【例】Critics argue that the steps Greece is taking to get the bailout money are increasing unemployment without really helping the country's economy. 評論家認為，希臘為獲得救助資金採取了一些措施，導致失業率上升，沒有對該國經濟起到真正的幫助。(CNN)

【用】 常見用法：unemployment rate 失業率；unemployment insurance 失業保險；unemployment benefit 失業救濟金；失業津貼；unemp-loyment compensation 失業補償金。

## describe [diˈskraib] v. 描寫；說明

【例】Mr. Obama described the program which he compared in scope to mapping the human genome as enormous mystery waiting to be unlocked. 歐巴馬先生描述了這一計畫，他將其比作繪製人類基因圖譜，巨大迷團有待被揭開。(BBC)

【用】 其名詞形式為 description，表示「描述，形容」。常用片語有：describe as 把……描述為；describe with 用……來描述。

## sale [seil] n. 出售；廉價出售；銷售額

【例】Whole sale prices are down sharply, driven lower by cheaper energy and food. 由於能源和食品價格下降，批發價大幅下跌。(NPR)

【用】 sale 相關的片語有很多，常見的有：on sale 廉價出售；for sale 出售，待售；direct sale 直銷。

## patent [ˈpeitənt] n. 專利權（證書）；a. 專利的

【例】On the other side are doctors, patients and many scientists, who see gene pat-ents as an attempt to monopolize and block future exploration in the new universe of genetics. 另一方面，醫生、患者和多位科學家認為基因專利權壟斷並阻礙了未來遺傳學的發展。(NPR)

【用】 常用片語：patent law 專利法。表示「申請專利」，用 apply for a patent 來表示。

## seafood [ˈsiːfuːd] n. 海鮮；海味

【例】It's too early to determine what impact April's deadly BP (British Petroleum) oil rig explosion will have on the nation's seafood and the restaurant industry. 英國石油公司鑽井平台在 4 月發生了一起嚴重的爆炸事件，這將給全國海產及餐飲業帶來怎樣的影響，現在還不得而知。 (CNN)

【用】 海產相關詞：shrimp 蝦；crab 螃蟹；lobster 龍蝦；salmon 鮭魚。

## order ['ɔ:də] n. 順序；訂單；命令

【例】Mr. Kerry told business leaders in Cairo that in order to get the economy back on its feet, it was vital to establish a sense of security. 克里先生在開羅告訴商界領袖，建立民眾安全感對於經濟復甦非常重要。(BBC)

【用】 order 作名詞的幾個意思都較為常見。表「順序」的常用表達：in order 按順序；表「命令」的常用表達：give orders 下令；表「訂單」的常用表達：delivery order 提貨單。常用片語還有：in order to 為了......；in order that ... 以便；out of order 出故障。

## ground [graund] n. 地面；場地；根據

【例】The state is seeking hundreds of millions of dollars to detect and remediate ground water contaminated with that chemical. 州政府正在籌集數億美元以檢測並淨化被化學物質汙染的地下水。(NPR)

【用】 常表示「地面」，on the ground 在地面上；to the ground 到地面上；也可指與天空相對的「地面」，通常用在軍事領域，如：ground operation 地面作戰。

## line [lain] n. 線；航線 v. 排齊

【例】Countries like Britain want their EU contributions to fall in line with national austerity cuts. 英國等國希望自己對歐盟的出資能削減到與本國的財務緊縮削減相符合水準。(BBC)

【用】 作名詞時，常見片語：bottom line 底線；dividing line 分界線；作動詞時，line up 表示「排成直線；準備好」。

## person ['pə:sən] n. 人

【例】The artists visit the students in person, mentor them, teach master classes and give encouragement. 藝術家們和學生見了面，給予學生指導和鼓勵並講授了專業課程。(NPR)

【用】 片語 in person 較為常見，表示「親自」。在法律領域，legal person 就指「法人」。注意：person 指「一個人」，是可數名詞，但在表示多個人時，用 people，persons 用於正式或法律語言中。

## course [kɔːs] n. 課程；路線

【例】This is a rigorous course, and the students are just dead tired. 這是一門要求嚴格的課程，學生們已經感到精疲力竭。(VOA)

【用】 常見片語：public course 公共課；specialized course 專業課；required course 必修課；course of study 學科；of course 當然。

## plant [plɑːnt] n. 植物；工廠 v. 種植

【例】Microbes, plants, insects, mammals—we all experience circadian rhythms, due to molecular clocks in our cells. 無論是微生物、植物、昆蟲還是哺乳動物——細胞中都有分子生理時鐘，即晝夜節律。 (Scientific American)

【用】 plant 作為可數名詞表示「工廠」的釋義在新聞中較為常見，如：a chemical plant 化工廠；作為動詞，plant sth. 可以表示「種植某物」，可進一步引申為「安置」的意思，如：plant sth. on sb. 將某事栽贓給某人。

## test [test] n./v. 試驗

【例】Initial tests on those two letters indicated they were tainted with a poison called ricin. 對這兩封信進行的初步檢測顯示，它們被一種名為蓖麻毒素的毒藥汙染了。(CNN)

【用】 常見片語：test on 在……身上做實驗；test for 探測；test tube 試管。test 既可以指「（單科的）實驗、檢測」；也可以整體指「測驗、考試」，如：take a test 參加考試。

## further[ˈfɜːðə]a. 更遠的； ad. 進一步地；此外

【例】Mr. Kerry added that further talks will focus very quickly on how to accomplish the goal. 克里補充道，會很快進行下一步對話，以實現這個目標。(BBC)

【用】 是 far 的比較級，其最高級為 furthest。可作定語，如：further education 繼續教育；也可修飾動詞，如：go further 走得更遠。

## shark [ʃɑːk] n. 鯊魚

【例】However, studies showing that blue sharks have sharply declined focus on a limited region. 然而研究表明藍鯊數量在一定區域內大幅減少。(NPR)

【用】 shark 除了可以用來描述一種動物，也可以用來描述一群人，即「坑蒙拐騙的人」，loan shark 就表示「放高利貸的人」。

## college [ˈkɔlidʒ] n. 大學，學院

【例】Having a college degree does increase job prospects, though, compared to a high school graduate. 與高中文憑相比，大學文憑意味著更好的就業前景。(CNN)

【用】 常見片語：in college 在大學；college student 大學學生。注意與 university 的區別：university 指綜合大學，一般由多個學院組成；college 多指大學內的學院或科目較少的高等學校，但泛指大學時，通常用 college。

## decide [diˈsaid] v. 決定

【例】Guo then decided that his career would take a different path. 郭後來決定要走一條與眾不同的職業道路。(CRI)

【用】 常用片語：decide to do sth. 決定做某事；decide on 決定。在口語中，You decide. 表示「由你決定。」

## hard [hɑːd] a. 堅固的；艱苦的；猛烈的

【例】They blow so hard that you can hear them as they toss the American flags that surround the monument. 風很大，你甚至可以聽到它們吹動紀念碑周圍的美國國旗的聲音。(VOA)

【用】 hard 釋義很多，相關片語：work hard 努力地工作；hard work 艱苦的工作；hard attack 猛烈的攻擊；hard disc 硬碟；hard cash 現金；hard boiled 煮老了的。

## access [ˈækses] n. 入口；接近（或進入，享用）的機會

【例】Originally, Google had said it would help bring its high-speed Internet to those who don't have access. 起初，谷歌表示會為那些無法高速上網的人們提供服務。(NPR)

【用】 常用片語為 have access to do sth. 表示「有機會做某事」，access 還可以表示「存取」，如：access time 存取時間。

## troop [truːp] n. 軍隊；隊 v. 成群結隊而行

【例】It was the first vote since the departure of U.S. troops more than a year ago. 這是在美軍撤離一年後進行的首次選舉。(BBC)

【用】 troop 雖然也表示「軍隊」，但與 army 不同，可以用 a troop of 表示「一大群……」；還可作動詞，troop in 成群結隊而行。

## launch [lɔːntʃ] v. 發動；推出（產品）；發射

【例】The video sharing site YouTube is launching its first pay channels which will allow content providers to sell its subscriptions through their videos. 影片分享網站 YouTube 正在推出首個付費頻道，該頻道將允許內容發布者透過其影片來銷售訂閱源。(BBC)

【用】 常用片語：launch into 開始，著手；launch out at sb. 攻擊或抨擊某人；表示「發射」時，通常用在航空航太領域。

# Level 5

## address [əˈdres] n. 地址；演說 v. 對......發表演說

【例】He began his final address with his voice ringing out in the air. 他開始發表最後的演說，聲音在空氣中迴盪。(VOA)

【用】 address 用作「演說」時，經常用在總統、政要的公開演講中，如：the President's inaugural address 總統的就職演講。

## environment [inˈvaiərənmənt] n. 環境；周圍狀況

【例】This kind of feeding environment creates a good condition for the virus to mutate. 這樣的飼養環境為病毒變異創造了有利條件。(CRI)

【用】 environment 可以表示大範圍的「環境」，是一個全球都關注的問題，如：natural environment 自然環境；ecological environment 生態環境；environmental protection 環境保護；與此同時，也可以表示小範圍的「氛圍，氣氛」，如：home environment 家庭環境，家庭氛圍。

## approve [əˈpruːv] v. 贊成；批准

【例】Neighboring Maryland also approved the first hike in its gas tax in more than two decades. 二十年來，鄰近的馬里蘭州首次批准上調汽油稅。(NPR)

【用】 通常與 of 連用。而 agree 是表示「贊成」中最普通的一個用法，通常與 with 連用。

## base [beis] n. 基礎；總部 v. 以......為根據

【例】There are still many questions surrounding the mass shooting at the America's largest military base, but one of them has now been answered. 發生在美國最大軍事基地的群眾槍擊事件還存有很多疑點，但其中一個現已得到了答覆。(BBC)

【用】 作為「基礎」，常用表達是 the base of ...... 的基礎；作為「總部，基地」，多用於軍事方面，有：naval base 海軍基地；air base 空軍基地；set up a base 建立根據地。

## remain [rɪˈmein] v. 保持；留下；剩餘

【例】Meanwhile, the four-year-old boy infected by the H7N9 virus remains in stable condition. 與此同時，目前感染 H7N9 病毒的四歲小男孩病情穩定。(CRI)

【用】 表示保持事物的原本狀態，如：remain silent 保持緘默；remain calm 保持冷靜；同時，remain 也有名詞詞性，表示「殘留物」，引申為「遺物、屍體」。

## online [ˈɒnˈlain] a. 線上的；連線的 ad. 線上地

【例】They bought tax-free things online or in another state—and they failed to pay tax on their purchase in their home state. 他們在網上或其他州購買免稅商品——這樣就不用為這些商品支付自己所在州的稅款了。(NPR)

【用】 現在很多事情都可以線上完成，如：online shopping 網上購物；online tutorial 線上輔導；online games 網路遊戲；online bookstore 網上書城。

## injure [ˈindʒə] v. 傷害

【例】At least sixty-five demonstrators were injured in protests earlier in the week. 在本週早些時候，至少 65 名示威者在抗議活動中受傷。(VOA)

【用】 常用派生詞：injured 受傷害的；injury 傷害，受傷處；injurious 有害的。

## species [ˈspiːʃiːz] n. 種類，物種

【例】It could mean a sharp decline in rainfall in some areas, flooding in others and extinction of about half of all the world's animal and plant species. 這可能意味著某些地區的降雨量大幅降低，而另一些地區則出現洪澇災害，世界上大約一半的動植物物種滅絕。(BBC)

【用】 達爾文著作《物種起源》即 The Origin of Species。值得注意的是，species 作為可數名詞，複數不變，仍是 species。

## cause [kɔːz] n. 原因；事業 v. 使發生

【例】It also guarantees that fishing companies do not cause serious harm to other life in the sea, from coral to dolphins. 這也確保了漁業公司對珊瑚礁海豚等其他海洋生物不會造成嚴重的危害。(NPR)

【用】 作名詞時，常用表達有：cause and effect 因果關係；for a good cause 為了公益事業；作動詞時，cause 表示「導致」，相當於 lead。

## development [diˈveləpmənt] n. 生長；發展

【例】These changes help us understand details about the development of Ice Ages. 這些變化幫助我們理解一些細節，有關冰河時代的歷史。(Scientific American)

【用】 該詞由動詞 develop「發展」衍生而來。其他衍生詞有：developing 發展中的，正在發展著的；developed 發達的，成熟的。

## Internet [ˈintənet] n. 網際網路

【例】 The Internet company Yahoo has bought an application created by a British teenager in a deal reported to be worth tens of millions of dollars. 網路公司雅虎購買了一款由一名英國少年製作的應用程式，據報導，這筆交易價值數千萬美元。(BBC)

【用】 該詞一般首字母大寫，surf the Internet 表示「上網」。由於網路的發達，各種相關服務也得以發展，如：Internet Banking 網上銀行。

## fine [fain] n. 罰金 a. 健康的；極好的

【例】The fine ended up at just $42,000. 最終罰款僅為 4.2 萬美元。(NPR)

【用】 fine 作名詞，表「罰金」，是可數名詞，在政府行政或法律法規中經常出現，相當於 penalty。

## statement ['steitmənt] n. 陳述；結算單

【例】The ruling military council issued a statement designed to calm the increasingly febrile atmosphere. 執政軍事委員會發布了一項聲明，目的是平息日益緊張的局勢。(BBC)

【用】 該詞由動詞 state「陳述」衍生而來，表示「聲明」。在國家、地區發生重大事件時，通常第一時間都由職能部門發表聲明，即 The government issued a statement that...。

## fund [fʌnd] n. 基金

【例】Women are more successful in getting funds for documentaries. 女性在為紀錄片爭取資助的方面更加成功。(VOA)

【用】 International Monetary Fund 為「國際貨幣基金組織」，這在經濟新聞中經常出現。

## board [bɔːd] n. 董事會 v. 登機；寄宿

【例】Authorities say more than 50 Lebanese passengers boarded the plane as well as more than 20 Ethiopians, in addition to the crew members. 當局稱，除了機組人員外，還有 50 多位黎巴嫩乘客和 20 多位衣索比亞乘客登機。(VOA)

【用】 常見片語：above board（協議或交易）合法誠信的，公開的；across the board 全面地；on board 在飛機（火車、輪船）上；sweep the board（在競賽、選舉中）大獲全勝。

## increase [inˈkriːs] v. 增加

【例】European Union Finance Ministers have agreed to increase the EU budget for this year by 7.3 billion Euros. 歐盟各國財政部長一致同意今年為歐盟增加 73 億歐元的預算。(BBC)

【用】 其反義詞為 decrease，表示「減少」。這兩個詞通常用來表示資料的增減。

## severe [si'viə] a. 嚴重的；嚴厲的；劇烈的

【例】Symptoms include fever and severe respiratory problems. 其症狀包括發燒及嚴重的呼吸道感染。(CNN)

【用】 severe 可以用來修飾天氣的惡劣，如：severe winter 嚴寒；severe summer 酷暑；severe storm 劇烈風暴。在醫藥學領域，severe 表示「重症」，如：severe pneumonia 重症肺炎。

## content [kən'tent] n. 內容；目錄；a. 滿足的

【例】Starting Monday, Facebook will no longer allow ads on pages that contain sexual or violent content. 從週一開始，禁止在臉書頁面上出現含有色情或暴力內容的廣告。(CNN)

【用】 作形容詞時，反義詞為 discontent，表示「不滿的」。常用片語為 to one's heart's content 心滿意足的。

## site [sait] n. 位置；場所 v. 使坐落在

【例】Investigators with a National Transportation Safety Board are being dispatched to the site of collapsed bridge in Washington state. 國家運輸安全委員會的調查人員正被派往華盛頓州橋梁倒塌的事故現場。 (NPR)

【用】 相關片語：on site 現場；in site 原位；web site 網址；construction site 施工場地。

## due [dju:] a. 應得的；適當的；到期的

【例】Toyota has been inundated with lawsuits due to safety concerns that have led to the recall of more than eight-and-a-half million vehicles worldwide. 出於安全考慮，豐田公司在全世界範圍內召回了超過 850 萬輛汽車，公司現在已無力招架相關訴訟。(VOA)

【用】 常用片語：due to 由於；in due course 在適當的時候；due for 應該得到。

## virus [ˈvaiərəs] n. 病毒

【例】The best way to avoid catching the virus is simple: wash your hands and avoid coughing and sneezing in public. 避免感染這種病毒的最好方法很簡單：洗手，以及避免在公共場合咳嗽、打噴嚏。(BBC)

【用】 常用於醫學領域，如：flu virus 禽流感病毒；也可用在網路領域，如：computer virus 電腦病毒。

## allow [əˈlau] v. 允許；同意給

【例】Facebook says it's tried to find a balance between cracking down on hateful content and allowing for freedom of expression. 臉書稱他們試圖在嚴格把控惡意內容的發布和允許言論自由之間尋求平衡。(CNN)

【用】 常用搭配為 allow sb. to do sth. 允許某人做某事。注意：allow 可以放在被動語態的句子中，但一般為否定句，表示「不允許……」，「禁止……」。

## price [prais] n. 價格；代價

【例】On monetary policy, Roosevelt and the Congress decided that the dollar should no longer be tied to the price of gold. 在貨幣政策方面，羅斯福及國會決定放棄美元與金價掛鉤。(VOA)

【用】 相關片語：at any price 不惜任何代價；cheap at the price 物有所值；of great price 極其寶貴的。問價格時，除了用 How much? 還可以用 What's the price of ...?

## climate [ˈklaimit] n. 氣候；風氣

【例】At recent climate change conferences, advocates for water management tried to put the issue high on the agenda but were not always successful. 在最近的氣候變化會議上，一些人倡議將水資源管理提上日程，但並不總是奏效。(VOA)

【用】 常用搭配：climate change 氣候變化；global climate 全球氣候。在表示「風氣」時，相當於 environment，可譯成「環境；氣氛」。

## pass [pɑːs] v. 傳遞；通過（考試等）n. 通行證

【例】The Senate pass the food-safty bill. It will give the FDA(Food and Drug Administration more power to order product recalls. 參議院通過了食品安全法案，這將給食品及藥物管理局更多授權；命令召回產品。(CNN)

【用】 pass 既可以用於法律上，如：pass a bill 通過法案；也可以用於教育中，如：pass an exam 通過考試。

## education [ˌedjuːˈkeiʃ ən] n. 教育

【例】Local governments and businesses are still trying to figure out how the technology could transform sectors like education, health care and the arts. 當地政府和企業在試圖弄清這項技術對教育、衛生保健和藝術的改革做出了哪些貢獻。(CRI)

【用】 現在 early education「早教」非常流行，不僅僅要學習文化知識，更要重視 intellectual education（智育）、moral education（德育）、physical education（體育）。

## rule [ruːl] n. 規則；統治 v. 統治

【例】Burma's financial industry has suffered from years of mismanagement under military rule. 在軍隊的管理模式下，緬甸的金融業經歷了多年的管理不善。(VOA)

【用】 rule 作為名詞，有複數形式 rules。rules and regulations 指「規章制度」；as a rule 表示「通常情況下」；break a rule 表示「破壞規則」。

## cell [sel] n. 細胞；小牢房

【例】However, other experts say there are easier, cheaper and less controversial sources of stem cells. 然而，其他專家表示獲取幹細胞，還有更廉價、更簡便的方法，且爭議性更少。(BBC)

【用】 該詞常見於醫學、遺傳學等相關領域的文章中，如：cancer cell 癌細胞；red blood cell 血紅細胞；cell division 細胞分裂。

## population [ˌpɑpjuˈleiʃən] n. 人口；人口密度

【例】So if we could get the population as a whole to retire at 70, most people will be able to support themselves in retirement. 所以，總的來說，如果我們能夠讓人們在 70 歲退休，大多數人將能夠在退休時養活自己。(CNN)

【用】 人口相關詞：a population drift 人口流失；talent introduction 人才引進；urbanization 城市化；rural migrant worker 農民工；emigration wave 移民潮。

## sustainable [səˈsteinəbl] a. 可以忍受的；足可支撐的；養得起的

【例】The survey finds the provision of energy to be among the core elements of the sustainable development agenda, along with food and nutrition security. 調查發現：能源供給、食品安全和營養保障都是可持續發展議程中的核心要素。(VOA)

【用】 常用片語為 sustainable development 可持續發展。

## private [ˈpraivit] a. 私人的；祕密的；私立的

【例】Saudi Arabia has, for the first time, officially sanctioned sports activities for girls in private schools. 沙烏地阿拉伯首次正式批准私立學校女生進行體育活動。(BBC)

【用】 其名詞為 privacy，表示「隱私」；副詞為 privately，表示「私人地」。西方人重視個人權力，尤其是隱私，如：private property 私有財產；private income 個人所得；private house 私人住宅。值得注意的是，private 作為名詞可以表示「士兵」。

## lower [ˈləuə]] a. 較低的；下麵的 v. 放下

【例】One goal will be to help lower performing students to do better. 其中的一個目標是説明表現欠佳的同學做得更好。(CNN)

【用】 該詞原為 low 的比較級，但經過形容詞動詞化，也可表示「降低，放下」，如：The price is lower than before. 價格比原來要低。 lower the price 降低價格。

## journal [ˈdʒəːnəl] n. 定期刊物；日誌

【例】The study appeared in the Journal of the International Neuropsychological Society. 這項研究被發表在《國際神經心理學協會雜誌》上。 (NPR)

【用】 journal 通常出現在科研、新聞等領域，如：core journal 核心期刊；a medical journal 醫學期刊。

## authority [ɔːˈθɒrəti] n. 官方；專家

【例】The Prime Minister says responsibility for meeting that electoral deadline does not rest entirely with the interim authority. 總理稱趕上選舉最後期限的責任並非完全在於臨時政府。 (VOA)

【用】 該詞常作複數 authorities，表示「官方，當局」，具有一定的權威性。常見片語：local authority 地方當局。常用句型：sb. have it on good authority that... 某人有可靠的資訊來源……。

## serious [ˈsiəriəs]] a. 嚴重的；重大的；嚴肅的

【例】It could have included tests to establish if the symptoms she's been suffering from have been caused by an infection or a potentially more serious underlying problem. 檢查可能包括一系列測試，以確認症狀是由感染引起還是存在潛在的更嚴重問題。 (BBC)

【用】 口語中，常見句子：I'm serious. 相當於 I mean it. 表示「我是認真的。」而 serious 在表示「嚴重的」時，用來修飾名詞的程度，如：a serious mistake 一個嚴重的錯誤；a serious illness 一個嚴重的疾病。

## coalition [ˌkəuəˈliʃən] n. 同盟；聯合；聯合政府

【例】He also co-chairs the coalition that wrote the report. 他同時也是編寫這個報告的聯盟聯合主席。 (NPR)

【用】 coalition 常用於政治、軍事領域的文章中。常見片語：coalition force 聯軍；international coalition 國際聯盟；coalition government 聯合政府。

## post [pəust] n. 職位 v. 郵寄；貼出

【例】About six million people worldwide post to Twitter, producing some 650,000 new tweets daily. 每天世界上有大概 600 萬人在推特網上發布資訊，產生約 65 萬條新微博。(Scientific American)

【用】 固定搭配：post office 郵局；post up 公布。相關拓展詞有 postcard 明信片；postman 郵遞員；postmark 郵戳；postcode 郵遞區號。

## responsible [riˈspɔnsəbl] a. 有責任的；負責的；可信賴的

【例】It seems that when the FED is responsible for monetary policy and bank supervision, its performance in both suffers. 聯邦儲備局負責制定貨幣政策，對銀行進行監管，表現似乎不盡如人意。(VOA)

【用】 常見句型：be responsible for sb./doing sth. 對......承擔責任。反義詞為 irresponsible 不負責任的；名詞為 responsibility 責任，義務，相當於 duty。

## status [ˈsteitəs] n. 地位；身份；情形

【例】Iceland recognized China's status as a complete market economy. 冰島承認中國是完整的市場經濟體。

【用】常見符號：狀態符號社會代表的象徵；平等與......同樣的地的狀態位； social status 社會等級。

## correspondent [ˌkɔriˈspɔndənt] a. 符合的 n. 記者

【例】This method enabled the oiler ant the correspondent to get respite together. 這個辦法使加油工和記者可以一起稍事休息。(VOA)

【用】 在作「記者」講時，與 reporter，journalist，newsman 含義類似，但 correspondent 側重表示「通訊記者」。常用片語有：special correspondent 特約記者；war correspondent 戰地記者。在作「符合的」講時，常用 be correspondent with 與......相符合。

## defense [diˈfens] n. 防禦；答辯

【例】Turkey has increased security forces in the area and its NATO allies have installed missile defense systems there. 土耳其已在該地區增加了安保部隊，其北約同盟國也在那部署了導彈防禦系統。(CNN)

【用】 美語中，常用 defence。首字母大寫時，即 the Defense 表示「國防部」。相關常用片語：defense attorney 辯護律師。

## drug [drʌg] n. 藥物；毒品

【例】The Justice Department has reached the biggest drug safety settlement today with a generic drug maker. 今天，（美國）司法部與一家仿製藥生產商就是最大的藥品安全案達成和解協定。(NPR)

【用】 需要注意的是，drug 雖然有「毒品」的意思，如：on drugs 吸毒；但 drug store 意為「藥店」，在這裡 drug 表示一般的「藥物」，如：antiviral drug 抗病毒藥物；drug therapy 藥物治療。

## protect [prəuˈtekt] v. 保護，保衛

【例】 Conservation biologists study biodiversity to protect species and habitat. 生物保護學家們負責研究生物的多樣性，保護物種和它們的棲息地。(Scientific American)

【用】 同義詞：defend，guard。protect 指用某種手段作為防禦工具以防危險或傷害；defend 強調用武力保持不受侵害；guard 強調長期保持警惕以防可能的攻擊或傷害。

## check [tʃek] v. 檢查 n. 檢查；支票

【例】The panel is expected to approve three other bills which include a ban on the assault weapons and tougher background checks on people buying guns. 專家組將批准其他三項法案，包括攻擊性武器的禁令以及對購買槍支的人員進行更嚴格的背景調查。(BBC)

【用】 需注意：check 不能用於被動語態中。生活、商務領域常用：check in 辦理登機或入住手續；keep/hold sth. in check 控制。

## sign [saɪn] n. 標記；跡象 v. 簽署

【例】Experts see this as a sign that the U.S. economy is improving. 專家將這視為美國經濟正在復甦的跡象。(CNN)

【用】 常用片語：sign language 手語；sign in 簽到；註冊。在醫學領域，sign 表示「病症；症狀」。

## side [saɪd] n. 旁邊；方面；一方

【例】Mark advised us to gather the people to our side. 馬克建議我們把人聚集到我們這一邊。(VOA)

【用】 通常人們喜歡用 A coin has two sides. 形容事物具有兩面性。常用片語：side by side 肩並肩；be on one's side 站在某人的一邊；支持某人。

## step [step] n. ( 腳 ) 步；步驟 v. 踩

【例】Having a seed strain is the first step in making a vaccine. 得到種子毒株是研製疫苗的第一步。 (NPR)

【用】 常用片語：step by step 逐步地；take steps 採取措施；step in 介入，插手。

## land [lænd] n. 陸地；土地 v. ( 使 ) 登陸

【例】He said the mission wouldn't land but rather fly within 100 miles of Mars and then use its gravitational pull to return to earth. 他表示這次的任務不是在火星著陸，而是在距火星 100 英里內的地方飛行，再利用引力返回地球。(BBC)

【用】 相關合成詞：landmark 路標；landowner 土地所有者。

## traffic [ˈtræfik] n. 交通

【例】Air traffic controllers are being spared further furloughs after government felt the rough of a traveling public affected by hundreds of flight delays. 政府察覺到上百架航班延誤給民眾的出行帶來了負面影響，於是空中交通管制員未來的休假計畫被取消了。(NPR)

【用】 與 traffic 有關的常見問題有：traffic accident 交通事故；traffic jam 交通堵塞；rush hour 上下班高峰期；drunk driving 酒後駕駛；speeding driving 超速駕駛；fatigue driving 疲勞駕駛。

## average [ˈævəridʒ] n. 平均；a. 平均的；普通的

【例】About a million passengers pass through the airport each month, on average. 機場平均每月的人流量大約為 100 萬。(CRI)

【用】 on average 是最常用的一個片語，表示「平均；一般」。該詞也可以專門用於數學領域，表示「平均數」。

## catholic [ˈkæθəlik] a. 天主教的；普遍的

【例】The University of San Diego is a private Catholic college. 聖地牙哥大學是一所私立的天主教學校。(CNN)

【用】 首字母大寫時，Catholic 特指「天主教的」，常見片語：Roman Catholic 天主教的。

## lawmaker [ˈlɔːˌmeikə] n. 立法者；立法機關成員

【例】Still Obama says the plan should appeal to centrist lawmakers with its balance of deficit reduction and new investment. 歐巴馬仍然表示該計畫將在削減赤字和增加投資之間取得了平衡，對中立派議員來說很有吸引力。(NPR)

【用】 lawmaker 是合成詞，由 law「法律」和 maker「製作者」合成。像這樣的單字還有，如：bookkeeper 記帳員；takeaway 外賣。

## extra [ˈɛkstrə] a. 額外的 ad. 特別地 n. 額外的事物

【例】Several member states including Britain are opposed to the extra funding which's been seen as a political compromise. 包括英國在內的幾個成員國對帶有政治妥協意味的額外資助持反對意見。(BBC)

【用】 通常用來作形容詞，如：extra time 額外的時間；extra work 加班；extra charge 附加費。注意：extra money 可特指「超速罰款單」。

## matter [ˈmætə] n. 事情；物質 v. 有關係

【例】The fact of the matter is you will not see him walking on this earth again. 事實就是你不會再看到他出現在這個世界上。(CNN)

【用】 在口語中較為常見，如：It doesn't matter. 沒關係。It matters to me. 對我來說很重要。常見片語：as a matter of fact. 事實上。

## property [ˈprɔpəti] n. 財產；性質；房產

【例】According to the central bank's survey, 14.8 percent of respondents say they will buy property in the next three months. 中央銀行的調查顯示，14.8% 的受訪者稱他們會在未來三個月購買房產。(CRI)

【用】 該詞常見於金融、經濟、財政等領域的新聞中，如：personal property 私有財產；public property 公共財產；property right 產權。

# Level 6

## internal [in'tə:nəl] a. 內部的；國內的

【例】The French authorities point out however that most of the Easyjet staff lived and paid their taxes in France and many were working solely on internal flights between Paris and Nice. 然而法國當局指出，大部分易捷航空員工住在法國，並在法國繳稅，而且許多人只在巴黎和尼斯之間的國內航班上工作。 (BBC)

【用】 按地域範圍，新聞可分為：internal news 國內新聞和 international news 國際新聞。

## worth [wə:θ] n. 價值，財產 a. 值得......的

【例】In the last quarter alone, Monsanto sold seed, much of it modified, worth more than $4 billion. 僅在最後一個季度，孟山都公司就出售了價值超過 40 億美元的種子，而這些種子大部分都是轉基因的。(CNN)

【用】 常見片語：net worth 淨資本；present worth 現市值；well worth 很值得。常見派生詞：worthless 沒用的；worthwhile 值得做的；worthy 有價值的。

## believe [bi'li:v] v. 相信；認為

【例】Originating from the Huizhou area of east China's Anhui Province, Hui Opera is believed to be the predecessor of Peking Opera, China's national opera. 徽劇起源於中國東部的安徽省徽州地區，它也被認為是中國國劇——京劇的前身。(CRI)

【用】 Believe it or not. 表示「信不信由你」。常用片語為 believe in 信仰。有句諺語叫作 Seeing is believing. 表示「眼見為實。」

## sort [sɔ:t] n. 種類 v. 分類，整理

【例】I had never done that sort of work, and it was not the right job for me. 我之前從來沒做過這類工作，而且這個工作不適合我。(VOA)

【用】 sort 與 kind 都表示「種類」，用法也相似，例如：a sort of 一種；of sorts 各種各樣；sort of 後面加形容詞，表示「有幾分，有點」。sort 作為動詞，可與 out 連用，表示「分類，整理」。

## raise [reiz] v. 舉起，提高；飼養

【例】Men, women and even young children raise their cellphones and cameras and take pictures. 無論是男人還是女人，甚至連小孩子都舉起了他們的手機和相機來拍照。(VOA)

【用】 常見片語：raise money 籌款；raise up 舉起。

## train [trein] n. 火車 v. 訓練

【例】This train conveys over five thousand passengers every day. 這列火車每天運送 5000 位旅客。(VOA)

【用】 作名詞時，train 是可數名詞，「上、下火車」可以用 get on/get off 或 on board，注意固定搭配 in train 表示「準備妥當」。

## event [iˈvent] n. 事件；專案

【例】One of the most memorable musical events took place here in 1938. 最令人難忘的音樂活動之一就是 1938 年在這個地方舉辦的。(VOA)

【用】 常用片語：in any event 無論如何；in the event 如果；in the event of 萬一。注意區分近義詞：accident 更側重「不幸事件」；incident 可指「政治事變」；event 尤指「歷史重大事件」。

## period [ˈpiəriəd] n. 時期，( 一段 ) 時間；句號

【例】The girl's bones date to a period known to historians as The Starving Time. 這個女孩的骨骼可以追溯到歷史學家所熟知的「大飢荒時期」。(BBC)

【用】 通常用來表示一段時間，如：a period of ......的時期；long period 長期的；transition period 過渡時期。

## threat [θret] n. 威脅，恐嚇

【例】The World Health Organization is calling it a threat to the world. 世界衛生組織

稱其對世界構成威脅。(CNN)

【用】 常用片語：pose a threat 構成威脅；a threat to sth. ......的威脅。

## media [ˈmiːdiə] n. 大眾傳播媒介，新聞媒體

【例】International media can contact the page to confirm details or talk to eyewitnesses. 國際媒體可以透過訪問頁面或者與目擊者溝通來確認細節。(BBC)

【用】注意：該詞的複數形式為 medium。常見搭配：mass media 大眾傳媒；advertising media 廣告媒體；print media 平面媒體；digital media 數位媒體；new media 新媒體，這些都是新聞的載體。

## situation [ˌsitjuˈeiʃən] n. 形勢，局面，處境

【例】Speaking after his election, Mr. Napolitano said Italy faced difficult situation and he called on all political parties to act responsibly. 納波利塔諾先生於當選後發表演講，稱義大利面臨艱難處境，並且呼籲各政黨肩負起責任。(BBC)

【用】 situation 在大背景下譯為「形勢，局勢」，如：overall situation 大局；win-win situation 雙贏局面；competitive situation 競爭態勢。此外，也可以表示事情的「狀況，情況」，如：actual situation 實際情況；current situation 現狀。

## staff [stɑːf] n. 全體職工，工作人員

【例】There are reports of at least two-hour flight delays due to staff shortages. 有報導稱由於人員短缺，航班延誤了至少兩個小時。(NPR)

【用】 該詞是一個集合名詞，是對一部分人的總稱，如：medical staff 醫務人員；office staff 辦公室職員。

## significant [sigˈnifikənt] a. 重要的，意義重大的

【例】The birth of the new British royal could also make a significant contribution to the British economy. 英國王室新成員的誕生也可能對英國經濟的發展作出巨大的貢獻。(VOA)

【用】 常見片語：significant development 重大進展；significant event 有意義事件。同時，該詞可引申為「顯著的」，如：significant change 顯著變化；significant difference 顯著性差異。其名詞形式為 significance「重要性」。

## improve [imˈpruːv] v. 改進，改善

【例】A third area is building data systems that not only measure student success, but also inform teachers how to improve. 第三部分是致力於打造一個資料系統，該系統不僅能衡量學生的成就，還能通知老師在哪些方面改進。(VOA)

【用】 我們常說 improve the environment 改善環境。表示「在某方面改進」可用 improve in。常用派生詞：improved 改良的；improvement 改進。

## similar [ˈsimilə] a. 相似的

【例】As of yesterday afternoon, officials hadn't said whether ricin was found on the letter addressed to the White House, although they did say the letters were similar. 截至昨天下午，官員也沒有透露是否在寄到白宮的信件中發現了蓖麻毒素，雖然他們表示相關信件很相似。(CNN)

【用】 similar 可以用作表語或定語，修飾名詞。常用片語：be similar to 像......；similar test 相似實驗；similar taste 相似的口味。

## memorial [miˈmɔːriəl] n. 紀念物，紀念碑 a. 紀念的

【例】His statue stands inside a stone memorial. 他的雕像矗立在一座石碑內。(VOA)

【用】 作為名詞，常用於 a memorial to sb./sth. 的結構中，表示「對......的紀念」；memorial hall 表示「紀念館」。另外，Memorial Day 特指（美國）陣亡將士紀念日。

## language [ˈlæŋgwidʒ] n. 語言；措辭；說法

【例】Even a little knowledge of the language can make a difference in attitude when you meet people from other countries. 和外國友人會面時，即使只會講一點當地的語言也會讓別人對你刮目相看。(BBC)

【用】 常用搭配有：Chinese language 中文；foreign language 外語。在語言研究方面，常用表達有：language learning 語言學習。

## bailout [ˈbeilaut] n. 緊急（財政）援助；緊急融資；跳傘

【例】As Mr. Obama admitted in last week's State of the Union address, the federal bailout of big financial institutions has been unpopular. 在上週的國情咨文演講中歐巴馬總統承認，聯邦政府為大型金融機構提供金融救助的做法已不得人心。(VOA)

【用】 常見金融專業詞彙：bailout period 投資返還期；government bailout 政府緊急援助；bailout loans 緊急援助貸款。同時，bailout 可用於航空緊急情況中，如：bailout door（跳傘）安全門；bailout area 應急跳傘出口。

## consider [kənˈsidə] v. 考慮；認為

【例】Russia is considering building a Moon colony in what satellite images suggest are lunar caves. 俄羅斯正考慮建立一個月球殖民地，在衛星圖像上可以看出他們選定的地方顯示為月球洞穴。(BBC)

【用】 注意：表示「考慮做某事」時，consider 後面要加動名詞形式。

## astronaut [ˈæstrənɔːt] n. 太空人

【例】 Other video shows astronauts fl ying through their large, open workspace or performing graceful somersaults outside the bounds of gravity. 在其他影片裡太空人或者飄浮著穿梭在他們的大型開放式工作區，或者優雅地表演不受重力限制的翻筋斗動作。(VOA)

【用】 astronaut 的同義詞：spaceman。但與 pilot 的區別在於：astronaut 指在外太空（outer space）的太空人；pilot 指不進入外太空的飛機駕駛員。

## attorney [əˈtəːni] n. 律師

【例】The ruling said he was not made aware of his constitutional right to remain silent and consult an attorney before police questioning. 這項裁決表示，他在警方審訊前，不知道按照憲法規定，可以有權保持沉默和諮詢律師。(VOA)

【用】 在美國更常用 attorney，與 lawyer 近義。常用搭配：defense attorney 辯護律師；civil/criminal attorney 民事／刑事律師；power of attorney 代理權。

## concern [kənˈsəːn] v. 關心 n. 擔心

【例】They won't take part because of concerns about fraud and security. 他們因為擔心存在欺詐和安全隱患，所以不會參與其中。(BBC)

【用】 常用片語：concern oneself with 對……關心。常用派生詞：concerned 關心的；concerning 關於。

## sense [sens] n. 感覺；意識 v. 意識到

【例】 The concept that we're talking about today is a fairly common sense and non-radical idea. 我們今天要討論的概念還算是一個常識，並不激進。(CNN)

【用】 跟 sense 相關的有視覺（sight）、聽覺（hearing）、嗅覺（smell）、味覺（taste）、觸覺（touch）五種感官。sense 的常用片語有：common sense 常識；sense of humor 幽默感；make sense 講得通。

## chairman [ˈtʃeəmən] n. 主席，會長，董事長

【例】 Ji Guoping, vice chairman of China's Dramatists Association, says "Psycho" interprets the famous Shakespeare work very well using Hui Opera's unique style. 中國戲劇家協會副會長季國平表示，《驚魂記》運用徽劇的獨特風格出色地演繹了莎士比亞的作品。(CRI)

【用】 注意：chairman 下一級就是 vice chairman 副主席；the chairman of ……的主席；chairman of the board 董事長。

## mark [mɑːk] n. 記號；分數 v. 作記號於

【例】Confession is one mark of repentance. 坦白是悔悟的一個標誌。(BBC)

【用】 mark 作為動詞，有 mark up 一片語，表示「提高……的價格」，可出現於市場競爭話題。

## potential [pəuˈtenʃəl] a. 潛在的 n. 潛力

【例】China, as the world's second largest economy can offer huge market potential and investment opportunities for Iceland. 中國作為世界第二大經濟體，能夠為冰島提供潛在而巨大的市場和投資機會。(CRI)

【用】 經濟類常見片語：potential customer 潛在客戶；potential risk 潛在風險；potential benefit 潛在優勢。

## experience [ikˈspiəriəns] n. 經歷；體驗 v. 經歷

【例】Bernie Sucher is an American entrepreneur with 20 years experience in Russia. 伯尼・蘇赫爾是一位美國企業家，在俄羅斯有 20 年的行業經驗。(VOA)

【用】 其形容詞為 experienced，表示「有經驗的」，可作定語和表語。常見搭配：related work experience 相關工作經驗；lack of experience 缺乏經驗。

## blood [blʌd] n. 血液；血統

【例】The hospital's director said a nine-month pregnant woman from the Philippines was brought in suffering from extremely high blood pressure. 醫院院長說，一位來自菲律賓、有 9 個月身孕的婦女因身患嚴重高血壓而被送進醫院。(BBC)

【用】 有句諺語說：Blood is thicker than water. 即「血濃於水。」而 new blood 直譯為「新鮮血液」，可以引申為「新人」。

## fuel [fjuəl] n. 燃料 v. 給……加燃料

【例】US automakers continue taking steps towards increasing fuel economy. 美國

汽車製造商繼續採取措施提高燃油經濟性。(NPR)

【用】 常用片語有：fossil fuel 礦物燃料；fuel consumption 燃料消耗

## class [klɑːs] n. 課；種類；等級

【例】In one class, kids are learning to play music on new keyboards donated by Yamaha. 在一堂課上，孩子們正在用雅馬哈公司捐贈的新鍵盤學習演奏音樂。(NPR)

【用】 class 表示「等級」時，相關片語有：the working class 工人階級；upper class 上層階級。

## nature ['neitʃə] n. 自然界；本性

【例】The experiment is seen as a major breakthrough in efforts to understand the fundamental nature of the universe. 這項實驗被認為是瞭解宇宙本質的一個重大突破。(BBC)

【用】 表「自然」時，常用 against nature 表示「違反自然的」；表「本性」時，常用 It's nature for sb. to do sth. 表示「對某人來說，做某事是很自然的。」

## detail ['diːteil] n. 細節

【例】The FBI has refused to disclose any more details, but is vowing to hunt worldwide for those responsible. 聯邦調查局拒絕透露更多的細節，但誓稱將在全球範圍內追捕相關責任人。(CRI)

【用】 該詞多用於調查研究，如：go into details 詳細描述；in some detail 相當詳細地。

## challenge ['tʃælindʒ] n. 挑戰 v. 向......挑戰；對......質疑

【例】The road ahead for Libya and its people will be difficult and full of challenges. 利比亞及其人民的未來之路將很艱難，並且充滿挑戰。(BBC)

【用】 作名詞時，「接受挑戰」用 accept a challenge；作動詞時，「對某人產生質疑」用 challenge sb. 即可。

## effect [iˈfekt] v. 生效 n. 效應

【例】Analysts say the economy's effect on the auto industry is far-reaching. 分析師稱，經濟對汽車行業的影響很深遠。(VOA)

【用】 常見用法：come into effect 表示「實行，實施」；take effect 表示「生效」。

## facility [fəˈsiləti] n. 設施，設備

【例】Meanwhile the US sent about 50 marines to Libya to help secure American facilities there. 與此同時，美國向利比亞派遣了約 50 名海軍陸戰隊員，以保障當地的美國設施的安全。(CNN)

【用】 該詞複數形式為 facilities，如：medical facilities 醫療設備。

## previous [ˈpriːviəs] a.（時間或順序上）先的，前的

【例】But when the cod population plunged to a fraction of previous levels, the Canadian government banned cod fishing—putting thousands of people out of work. 但是當鱈魚數量驟降到以前數額的幾分之一後，加拿大政府開始禁止捕撈鱈魚，這導致了成千上萬的人失業。(NPR)

【用】 作定語，修飾後面的名詞，如：previous year 前年。在網路領域，previous page 表示「返回上一級菜單」。

## investment [inˈvestmənt] n. 投資；投入

【例】The changes will allow more foreign investment and include the creation of a new regulatory agency. 此舉將會吸引更多外資，成立新的監管機構。(BBC)

【用】 表示「投資」時，常用於財經新聞等方面，如：international investment 國際投資；capital investment 資本投資。

## warn [wɔːn] v. 警告

【例】But experts also warn that traditional Chinese opera must never abandon its roots and core elements. 但專家也發出警告，中華傳統戲曲絕不能丟了根，失了魂。(CRI)

【用】　常見片語：warn against 警告……不要。其名詞形式為 warning 表示「警告」，為可數名詞。

## incident ['insidənt] n. 事件，事變

【例】Maroni said the immediate reaction on the part of security officials from the start of the disorder ensured the violence did not degenerate into more serious incidents. 馬羅尼表示，騷亂一開始安保官員的反應就很迅速，確保了這次暴力行為沒有演變成更嚴重的事。(VOA)

【用】　注意：incident 指的「事件」，是在政治上有所影響的事件；accident 指的是「事故」，強調其偶然性。

## recession [ri'seʃən] n. 後退；（經濟的）衰退

【例】The Euro currency zone recession is now in a sixth quarter. 歐元區經濟衰退，已經連續六個季度。(NPR)

【用】　該詞通常用於經濟新聞中，如：in recession 處於（經濟）衰退期。

## standard ['stændəd] n. 標準，規則 a. 標準的

【例】The quality standards of our customers are very high. 我們客戶對品質標準要求非常高。(VOA)

【用】「生活標準」既可以用 living standard，也可以用 standard of living。

## independent [ˌindiˈpendənt] a. 獨立的；單獨的

【例】An independent report was handed to the government in Nicosia this week after months of investigation. 經過幾個月的調查，本周有一份獨立報告遞交到尼古西亞政府手中。(BBC)

【用】 在新聞中，除了 independent 外，其名詞 independence 也很常用，如：United States Declaration of Independence《美國獨立宣言》。

## conservative [kənˈsəːvətiv] a. 保守的；傳統的 n. 保守派

【例】He is known for his conservative beliefs. 他是出了名的保守派。(VOA)

【用】 首字母大寫時，尤指英國主要政黨之一「保守黨」，與 Labor「工黨」構成英國主要政黨。

## attempt [əˈtempt] n./v. 嘗試，企圖；努力

【例】He subsequently attempted to set off a bomb on a Northwest Airlines fl ight traveling to Detroit. 隨後他試圖在一架前往底特律的西北航空公司的航班上引爆炸彈。(VOA)

【用】 表示「嘗試做某事」可以用 attempt to do sth. 或 attempt at doing sth.。

## finding [ˈfaindiŋ] n. 調查（或研究）的結果；（陪審團的）裁決

【例】The authors say more research is needed to back up their findings and to try to explain these differences. 作者們稱他們需要做更多研究來證實調查結果，嘗試解釋這些差異。(BBC)

【用】 作為名詞，常用其複數形式 findings，相當於 research results。

## fail [feil] v. 失敗；不及格

【例】The Australian leader says his government is committed to international legal action if discussions fail to convince Japan to stop killing whales in the Antarctic. 澳洲領導人表示，如果討論結束後日本仍然在南極捕殺鯨魚，他們將準備訴諸國際法庭。(VOA)

【用】 常用片語：fail in 失敗；never fail to 一定會......。其名詞形式為 failure「失敗，不足」。

## figure ['fɪɡə] n. 數字 v. 想；計算

【例】Figures from the National Bureau of Statistics indicate that housing costs rose 0.5 percent month on month in March, with rent up 1.2 percent. 國家統計局的資料顯示，3 月份，住房成本同比上漲了 0.5 個百分點，同時租金上漲了 1.2 個百分點。(CRI)

【用】 figure out 解決；算出。

## conflict ['kɔnflɪkt] v./n. 衝突，爭論

【例】 Journalists can't work freely in the conflict areas of north-eastern Nigeria because they are so dangerous. 記者無法自由地在尼日利亞東北部的衝突地區工作，因為那兒非常危險。(BBC)

【用】 該詞多用於解決國際爭端。常見片語：in conflict with 和......衝突；in conflict 不一致；conflict of interest 利益衝突；class conflict 階級矛盾。

## dozen ['dʌzən] n. ( 一 ) 打，十二個

【例】 Over the weekend protests like this one happened at dozens of countries around the world. 整個週末，在世界範圍內的數十個國家都爆發了類似的抗議活動。(CNN)

【用】 計數相關詞：quarter 四分之一；score 二十；million 百萬；billion 十億。

## emergency [iˈməːdʒənsi] n. 緊急情況，緊急事件

【例】Boston hospitals always staff up their emergency rooms on Marathon Day to care for runners with cramps, dehydration and the occasional heart attack. 波士頓醫院通常在馬拉松日為急診室增加員工，以照顧痙攣、脫水和突發心臟病的運動員們。(NPR)

【用】 該詞用於緊急突發事件中，生活中也較為常見。常見搭配：emergency button 應急按鈕；emergency room 急診室；emergency exit 緊急出口。

## fight [faɪt] v./n. 打架，打仗

【例】Alipay began fighting the problem of fishing sites at the end of 2007. 在 2007年底，支付寶開始致力於解決釣魚網站的問題。(CRI)

【用】 fight 一詞不僅可以用於軍事領域，也可以用於網路科技、體育賽事等領域，常用片語：make a fight of it 奮力抵抗；fight back 反擊；fight or flight 或進或退。

## add [æd] v. 增加；把......加起來

【例】He says that means adding one million new jobs every month for the next two decades. 他說，這意味著在未來 20 年，每個月會增加一百萬個就業機會。(VOA)

【用】 最常用的搭配：add up 合計。在商業領域，產品所具有的附加值，可以用 add value 來表示。常用拓展詞：addition 附加；additional 另外的。

## victory [ˈvɪktəri] n. 勝利

【例】Both sides have claimed victory and warned of the dire consequences if the other candidate wins. 雙方都宣稱自己是勝利方，並警告對方如果獲勝，將會有嚴重的後果。(BBC)

【用】「勝利」也有很多種，如：landslide victory 以絕對優勢取得勝利；narrow victory（以微弱優勢）險勝。

## produce [prəuˈdjuːs] n. 產品；農產品 v. 生產

【例】Scientists have cloned for the first time human embryos that can produce some cells opening the door for treatments of various diseases. 科學家們首次克隆了人類胚胎用於製造胚胎細胞，供治療多種疾病之用。這些細胞開啟了治療多種疾病的大門。(NPR)

【用】 作名詞時，produce 是不可數名詞，如：farm produce 農產品；dairy produce 乳製品；native produce 土特產品。作動詞時，produce「生產」，是與 consume「消費」相對的。

## exchange [iksˈtʃeindʒ] n. 交換；兌換 v. 交換

【例】It is illegal for public officials to solicit money in exchange for favors. 公務員以提供便利來索取金錢作為交換是非法的。(CNN)

【用】 常用於國際金融、貨幣領域，如：foreign exchange 外匯；indirect exchange 間接套匯；exchange rate 匯率；stock exchange 證券交易所。也可用在教育領域，如：exchange student 交換生。

# Level 7

## list [list] n. 目錄，名單 v. 列出

【例】The list of Oscar winners is usually dominated by American films and actors but 2009 has seen a more international flavour to the ceremony. 奧斯卡得主名單上通常大多數是美國電影和美國演員，但 2009 年的奧斯卡頒獎禮上出現了很多來自其他國家的演員和作品。(BBC)

【用】 on the list「在名單之列」，尤其用在軍事、刑事犯罪領域，on the list 引申為「在抓捕名單之上」。 list 也可用於商業領域，如：price list 價目表；shopping list 購物清單；packing list 裝箱單。

## campaign [kæmˈpein] n. 戰役；( 政治或商業性 ) 活動

【例】The campaign targeted Facebook pages that celebrated or joked about violence against women. 這一活動針對那些鼓勵女性使用暴力或藉此開玩笑的臉書頁面。(CNN)

【用】 該詞多用於政治性的活動，尤其是選舉活動，如：election campaign 選舉活動。也可用於維護權利的大型社會活動，如：campaign against racial discrimination 反對種族歧視的活動。

## spokesman [ˈspəuksmən] n. 發言人，代言人

【例】A Chrysler spokesman says the company has received reports of 26 accidents and two injuries. 一位克萊斯勒公司的發言人表示，該公司已經收到 26 起事故的報告，其中 2 人受傷。(NPR)

【用】 注意：與之相對的是 spokeswoman 女發言人；複數形式為 spokesmen。常見片語：brand spokesman 品牌代言人；press spokesman 新聞發言人。

## cancer [ˈkænsə] n. 癌

【例】There's more evidence that vegetarians are less likely than meat-eaters to develop cancer. 有更多證據表明素食者相較於肉食者患癌症的可能性更小。(BBC)

【用】 在醫學相關報導中，常見的癌症有：lung cancer 肺癌；skin cancer 皮膚癌；breast cancer 乳腺癌。表示「死於」某種癌症，可以用片語 die of。

## militant [ˈmilitənt] a. 好戰的；好暴力的 n. 激進分子

【例】The militants have progressively moved South. 激進分子已逐步南移。(VOA)

【用】片語：militant Islamists 激進伊斯蘭主義者；militant groups 激進組織。

## constitution [ˌkɔnstiˈtjuːʃən] n. 憲法；組成

【例】The legislative branch, Congress, makes the laws, but it's the judicial branch's job to interpret those laws and decide if they violate the Constitution. 國會是立法部門，負責立法，但如何解釋法律並判決它們是否違憲則是司法部門的職責。(CNN)

【用】 the Constitution 特指《美國憲法》；amendments to the constitution 憲法修正案；unwritten constitution 不成文憲法；written constitution 成文憲法。

## memory [ˈmeməri] n. 記憶（力）；回憶

【例】But here's the good news: Brain researchers say there are ways to boost brain power and stave off problems in memory and thinking. 但好消息是：大腦研究者稱，有辦法增強腦力並緩解大腦在記憶和思維方面可能出現的問題。(NPR)

【用】 常用片語：in memory of sb. 紀念某人。memory 在科技領域，還表示「記憶體」，如：memory card 記憶體卡，記憶卡。

## marathon [ˈmærəθən] n. 馬拉松長跑

【例】US Law enforcement officials say the explosive devices used in the deadly bombings at the Boston Marathon were placed in dark colored bags. 美國執法官員稱，波士頓馬拉松致命爆炸案中所使用的爆炸裝置被放於深顏色的背包中。(CRI)

【用】 該詞還可引申為「漫長而艱苦的過程」。

## critic [ˈkritik] n. 評論家，批評家

【例】Critics say it could be used to increase the president's power to use deadly force against suspected terrorists. 評論家說，這可能被用來增加總統對恐怖分子嫌疑人使用致命武力的權力。(VOA)

【用】 一般用在文體領域，如：theater critic 劇評家；film critic 影評人；literary critic 文學批評家；sports critic 體育評論員。同時，也可以對時政、軍事、財經等領域進行評論。

## available [əˈveiləbl] a. 可利用的；可取得聯繫的；可得到的

【例】But a new analysis of all the available research has backed the view that it was a giant asteroid that wiped out the dinosaurs. 但針對現有研究進行的一項新的分析認為：一顆巨大的小行星撞擊了地球，造成了恐龍滅絕。(BBC)

【用】 在口語中，available 指「有空的」，如：Are you available this afternoon? 今天下午你有空嗎？而 Are you available? 也可表「你有男／女朋友嗎？」

## aid [eid] n. 幫助 v. 援助

【例】However, aid agencies say it will be more difficult to fight the disease in poorer countries. 然而援助機構稱，在那些相對貧窮的國家，與疾病作鬥爭時會面臨更多困難。(VOA)

【用】 新聞中常見片語：first aid 急救；legal aid 法律援助；humani-tarian aid 人道主義援助。

## reduce [riˈdjuːs] v. 減少，縮小

【例】The researchers say that dogs fed high fat diets are less fatigued after exercise, which reduces panting and sensitizes sniffing. 研究人員稱，食用高脂肪狗糧的偵緝犬在運動後不會那麼疲勞，喘氣不那麼厲害，嗅覺也會更加靈敏。(Scientific American)

【用】 常用於環保話題，如：reduce waste 減少浪費；reduce expenditure 節流。

## autism [ˈɔːtizəm] n. 自閉症，孤獨症

【例】U.S. health authorities announced in March that autism is more common than previously thought. 美國衛生部門在 3 月宣稱，自閉症比人們先前認為的更為常見。(CNN)

【用】 注意區分形近詞：amnesia 表示「健忘症」。

## freedom [ˈfriːdəm] n. 自由

【例】If you have an aim you must sacrifice something of freedom to attain it. 如果你有目標，你就要犧牲一定的自由以達到它。(CNN)

【用】 常見於公民權利的社會新聞中。常用片語有：freedom of speech 言論自由；personal freedom 人身自由；political freedom 政治自由。

## claim [kleim v. 聲稱 n. 要求；聲稱

【例】No individual or group has, so far claimed responsibility for the fatal attack. 至今為止，還沒有任何個人或團體聲稱對此次致命襲擊事件負責。(CRI)

【用】 作動詞時，claim 常與 for 連用，表示「要求；索取」。

## treatment [ˈtriːtmənt] n. 治療；對待

【例】Mr. Mandela who is 94 spent 18 days in hospital in December to receive treatment for a lung infection and gallstones. 94 歲高齡的曼德拉先生於 12 月入院，接受了 18 天的肺部感染和膽結石治療。(BBC)

【用】 treatment 表「治療」時，一般是醫學或科學實驗領域；表「對待」時，不可數名詞，一般是人權、社會領域，如：wastewater treatment 汙水處理。

## disease [diˈziːz] n. 疾病

【例】Officials have found some clusters of cases where the disease has been transmitted between family members or in a health care setting. 官方已經發現一些病例，在這些病例中，疾病在家庭成員間相互傳染或透過衛生保健設施得以傳播。(CNN)

【用】 常見片語：heart disease 心臟病；occupational disease 職業病；infectious disease 傳染病；Parkinson's disease 帕金森症。

## rest [rest] n. 剩餘部分；休息 v. 休息

【例】We must persuade the rest of the committee to our point of view. 我們必須說服委員會的其他會員支持我們的觀點。(CNN)

【用】 在聽力中，在舉【例】說明後，以 and the rest 結尾，表示「等等」，省略不說。

## progress ['prəugres] n./v. 前進；進展

【例】 I think it's fair to say that the American people are frustrated with the lack of progress on some key issues. 公平地說，美國人民對某些關鍵問題缺乏進展感到失望。(VOA)

【用】 該詞用途廣泛，可指任何領域的進步或發展。常見片語：social progress 社會進步；economic progress 經濟發展；in progress 在發展中。

## express [ik'spres] v. 表示 a. 特快的 n. 快車；快遞

【例】「I hope the show expressed well that money doesn't buy you happiness,」 says Evans. 「我希望這場表演生動地詮釋了金錢買不來幸福的理念。」埃文斯說道。(NPR)

【用】 作名詞時，常表示「快車；快遞」，如：常見的 EMS 全稱為 Express Mail Service 郵政特快專遞。

## vice [vais] n. 缺點，弱點 a. 副的

【例】Former Vice President Dick Cheney spoke recently on ABC's This Week program. 前副總統迪克·切尼最近在 ABC 電視台的《本週》欄目中發表了演講。(VOA)

【用】 常首字母大寫，用於職位、職稱之前，表示「副......」，如：Vice Chairman 副主席；
Vice Premier 副總理。另外，固定用法 vice versa 表示「反之亦然」。

## trade [treid] n. 貿易，商業 v. 貿易

【例】The European Union has initialed an agreement to end one of the world's lon-
gestrunning trade disputes over bananas. 歐盟起草了一份協定以終止世界上持續時
間最長的香蕉貿易爭端。(BBC)

【用】 常用於商貿領域的新聞中，如：foreign trade 對外貿易；international trade 國際貿易；
trade sth. for sth. 以物易物。

## manufacture [ˌmænjuˈfæktʃə] v. 製造 n. 製造，製造業

【例】He and his family manufacture toys for buyers from as far away as the united
states. 他和家人為遠在美國的買家們生產玩具。(VOA)

【用】 表示「製造」，最普遍的詞為 make，指製造的具體事物；produce 側重大量生產；
manufacture 則更為正式，側重機器大規模生產。

## league [liːg] n. 聯盟，同盟，聯賽；聯合會

【例】In doing so, the League becomes the first leading domestic competition to approve a goal-line technology system. 這樣做的話，該聯賽將成為國內認可門線技術
系統的領頭羊。(CRI)

【用】 該詞多用於體育領域，尤指足球項目，如：the football league 足球聯賽；American
league 美國棒球聯賽。另外，Ivy League 指「常春藤聯盟」。

## admit [ədˈmit] v. 承認；准許......進入

【例】He also admitted to falsely stating that he'd obtained a prestigious qualification
from the Sorbonne University in Paris. 他也承認自己謊稱取得了巴黎索邦大學的榮
譽證書。(BBC)

【用】 admit 後面可加賓語，也可加從句。常見片語：admit of 允許。

## deny [dɪˈnaɪ] v. 否認；拒絕......的要求

【例】It is a charge that Australian officials have strongly denied. 澳洲官員極力否認這項指控。(VOA)

【用】 在新聞報導中，常用於權威部門對事件的回應，如：The government denied the rumor at the first time. 政府第一時間對流言予以否認。

## summit [ˈsʌmɪt] n. 頂點，極點；峰會

【例】Mr. Obama said the summit had made a real contribution to a safer world. 歐巴馬先生表示，此次峰會為建設一個更安全的世界作出了實實在在的貢獻。(BBC)

【用】 表「峰會」時，常用於經濟、政治、軍事等領域。summit 常指世界範圍內的，且會議結果對全球有重大影響的大型會議，如：Global Summit 全球峰會。

## view [vjuː] v. 看 n. 觀點；視野

【例】 Overseas real estate developers have shifted their focus onto the Chinese market in view of China's fast-growing economy and the continuing economic crisis in western countries. 由於中國經濟增長迅猛，西方國家經濟危機仍在持續，海外房地產開發商將他們的重點轉向中國市場。

【用】 常見片語：in view of 鑑於；point of view 立場；with a view to 著眼於。

## demand [dɪˈmɑːnd] n./v. 要求，需求；需要

【例】 Additionally, changes in health care laws give millions more Americans access to health insurance and care, which means demand for nurses will grow even more. 此外，醫療法的改革使數百萬美國人能夠享有醫療保險和醫療保健，這意味著對護士的需求會增加。(VOA)

【用】 在經濟領域，與 demand「需求」相對應的就是 supply「供給」，supply and demand

即「供求」。注意，demand 在作動詞時，主語可以是人，也可以是物。

## consumer [kən'sjuːmə] n. 消費者

【例】This is good bid for folk consumers because they get more choices. 這個報價對消費者有利，這使他們有了更多的選擇。(NPR)

【用】 商業鏈條中，有 consumer「消費者」，就有 producer「生產者」。consumer price index 就是常說的「消費者物價指數」。

## arrest [ə'rest] v./n. 逮捕

【例】We're learning more as well about one of the two key suspects who were shot and arrested at the crime scene. 我們也正在進一步追蹤瞭解兩名重要嫌疑人的其中一人，該嫌疑人在犯罪現場被擊中並逮捕。(CNN)

【用】 用於刑事、法律領域。arrest 表示「逮捕」時，有被動語態，也可引申為「吸引……的注意」，如：arrest one's attention 吸引某人的注意。

## term [təːm] n. 學期；期限；條款

【例】Under the terms of its bailout, Greece must sell state assets worth more than $12 billion. 根據援助條款，希臘必須出售超過 120 億美元的國有資產。(BBC)

【用】 表示「條款」，一般使用複數形式 terms。而在金融領域，term 表示「一段時間，期限」，如 term investment 長期投資；term loan 長期貸款。

## debate [di'beit] n./v. 辯論，討論

【例】The debate centers around a legal principle known as the Miranda Warning. 這場辯論圍繞著「米蘭達警告」的法律原則展開。(VOA)

【用】 debate 表示「辯論」，如：debate on 關於……進行辯論；還可在正式場合表示「探討；磋商」。

## series [ˈsiəriːz] n. 一系列，連續；( 電視 ) 連續劇

【例】I recommend that you start by reading the first article in this series. 我建議您從閱讀這個系列的第一篇文章開始。(BBC)

【用】　常用片語：series of 一系列。在新聞英語中，常見主題為政治、經濟，如：series of sanction measures 一系列制裁措施。

## suffer [ˈsʌfə] v. 遭受；受痛苦

【例】But he suffered enormous mental anguish. 但他遭受了巨大的精神折磨和痛苦。(CRI)

【用】　常用片語為 suffer from，可譯為「遭受；患……病」，如：suffer from flood 遭受水災；suffer from cancer 患癌症。

## struggle [ˈstrʌgl] v./n. 奮鬥，努力；鬥爭

【例】His struggle for civil rights changed the lives of millions of Americans. 他為爭取公民權利而努力奮鬥，這改變了數百萬美國人的生活。(VOA)

【用】　表示「與……鬥爭」，用介詞 against，如：struggle against terrorism 與恐怖主義作鬥爭。還可以說：class struggle 階級鬥爭；power struggle 權力鬥爭。

## target [ˈtɑːgit] n. 目標；靶子

【例】But the weapons missed their target by 300 meters, killing the civilians in Marjah. 但武器偏離目標 300 公尺，導致瑪律亞多名平民死亡。(BBC)

【用】　該詞可用於軍事、商務、經濟、政治等多個領域，如：target group 目標群體；target market 目標市場。同時，target 也可以表示「( 批評、辱罵、嘲笑的 ) 物件」。

## tough [tʌf] a. 強硬的；艱苦的；嚴格的

【例】It's a tough challenge, but if you can overcome the challenge, you will be a strong man. 這很有挑戰性，但如果你能夠直面它，你將變得堅強。(CRI)

【用】 tough policy 表示「強硬政策」，用於政府對內對外政策的態度。tough 也可指人意志品質，相當於 strong。

## network [ˈnetwəːk] n. 網路

【例】It's a costly business that involves using a network of 500 instrument towers worldwide. 這個業務成本高昂，需要用到全球 500 個裝置塔構成的網路。(Scientific American)

【用】 network 常見於公共設施建設、網路發展等相關領域。常見片語：railway network 鐵路網；transportation network 交通網路；network system 網路系統。

## collapse [kəˈlæps] v./n. 崩潰，倒塌；虛脫

【例】More than 80% of the residential houses built with mud and brick have collapsed. 80% 以上用泥磚建造的居民住宅都已倒塌。(BBC)

【用】 該詞可用於表示實物、抽象物質，也可以用來表述人的精神狀態，如：the building's collapse 大樓的倒塌。

## response [riˈspɔns] n. 回答，回應；反應

【例】We also may disclose such information in response to a law enforcement agency's request. 我們也可能會按照執法部門的要求，公開相關資訊。(CNN)

【用】 常見搭配：in response 作為回應；in response to 回答；回應。通常在國際新聞，涉及兩國及以上之間產生對話或交易時。

## design [diˈzain] n. 設計；圖樣 v. 設計

【例】Synthetic biologists design and make biological devices and systems for useful purposes. 合成生物學家以實用性為宗旨設計製造了生物設備和系統。(Scientific American)

【用】 design 一方面用於新事物的設計、創造，如：design a plan 設計一個計畫；另一方面

用於貶義，表示「圖謀，策劃」。

## giant [ˈdʒaiənt] n. 巨人 a. 巨大的

【例】The surveys will be done annually in collaboration with survey giant Gallup. 我們每年都將與調研巨頭蓋洛普合作完成調研。(VOA)

【用】 該詞可引申表示在某一領域占絕對優勢的人或公司，如：giant of enterprise 商業巨頭，商業巨鱷。

## monetary [ˈmʌnitəri] a. 貨幣的

【例】The International Monetary Fund has told governments across the world that further action is needed to help return the global financial system to stability. 國際貨幣基金組織要求各國採取進一步行動，使全球金融系統恢復穩定。(BBC)

【用】 常見於金融、財經新聞中。常見片語：monetary policy 貨幣政策；international monetary system 國際貨幣制度。

## movement [ˈmuːvmənt] n. 運動；進展

【例】Mrs. Parks who died in 2005 is widely regarded as the mother of the civil rights movement in the U.S. 帕克斯女士於 2005 年去世，人們普遍認為她是美國民權運動之母。(BBC)

【用】 該詞用途廣泛，各個領域的「運動」都可以利用 movement，常用其複數形式，如：troop movements 調兵；labour movement 工人運動；population movement 人口遷移。

## avoid [əˈvɔid] v. 避免；逃避

【例】Residents have been told to avoid drinking tap water. 居民們被告知不要飲用自來水。(VOA)

【用】 表示「避免做某事」，後面加動名詞形式，即 avoid doing sth.。商業中，可以依法規避風險（avoid risks）；法律上，avoid a contract 表示「撤銷合約」。

## trial [ˈtraɪəl] n. 試驗；審訊；試用

【例】It's the longest state trial in New Hampshire history. 這是新漢普郡歷史上為期最長的州立審判。(NPR)

【用】 表「試驗」時，可見於醫學領域，如：on trial 在試驗中；trial and error 反覆試驗；clinical trial 臨床試驗；而 on trial 也可以表示「在受審」，用於法律領域。

## cabinet [ˈkæbinit] n. 內閣；貯藏櫥

【例】President Tandja was meeting with cabinet ministers at the presidential palace when the coup took place. 政變發生時，總統坦賈正在總統府會見內閣大臣。(VOA)

【用】 該詞可以表示「儲藏櫃」，但是更多出現在政治領域，首字母須大寫，表示「內閣」，如：the Cabinet meeting 內閣會議。

## revenue [ˈrevənjuː] n.（尤指大宗的）收入；（政府的）稅收

【例】That's turned into a big source of revenue for local affiliates, totaling $2.3 billion last year. 這變成了當地分公司的一大收入來源，去年的收入總額達到了 23 億美元。(NPR)

【用】 該詞比 income 的收入來源更廣、數量更大，多用於政府、大型企業的「收入」和「稅收」。常見經濟片語：tax revenue 稅收；fiscal revenue 財政收入；source of revenue 收入來源；net revenue 淨收入。

## trauma [ˈtrɔːmə] n. 精神創傷；外傷

【例】Hospitals in many states are seeing fewer gunshot injuries according to doctors at one California Trauma Center. 據加州創傷中心的醫生表示，醫院發現該州在槍擊中的受傷人數在減少。(VOA)

【用】 常見於與醫學、心理學相關的新聞中，如：psychological trauma 心理創傷；primary trauma 原始創傷；internal trauma 內傷。

## urge [əːdʒ] v. 催促 n. 迫切的要求

【例】President Obama has urged Congress to pass a bill to avert billions of dollars of automatic spending cuts which are due to start taking effect on Friday. 歐巴馬總統敦促國會通過一項法案，有關削減開支，阻止預計在週五生效的方案。(BBC)

【用】 作動詞時，urge 褒義的一面，側重「鼓勵，激勵」，如：urge consumption 鼓勵消費；貶義的一面，側重「慫恿，煽動」。

## affect [əˈfekt] v. 影響

【例】Passengers are already feeling the impact of furloughs that affected the Federal Aviation Administration. 乘客們已經感受到了此次休假給美國聯邦航空管理局帶來的影響。(NPR)

【用】 常用派生詞：affected 受到影響的；affective 表達情感的；affection 愛情；affecting 感人的。

## destroy [diˈstrɔi] v. 破壞，毀滅

【例】It says bridges have been knocked out, hospitals and care facilities have been damaged or destroyed. 據稱橋梁已被擊垮，醫院和衛生保健設施也遭到了破壞甚至摧毀。(VOA)

【用】 其同義詞是 undermine，表示「破壞；漸漸破壞」。

## zone [zəun] n. 地區，區域

【例】The Euro Zone is offering a ten-billion euro loan while insisting on extra cash from Cyprus itself. 歐元區提供了 100 億歐元的貸款，並要求賽普勒斯提供更多的現金。(BBC)

【用】 該詞可用於軍事領域，如：war zone 戰區；danger zone 危險地帶；militarized zone 軍事區；也可指地理位置，如：time zone 時區；tropic zone 熱帶地區。

## survey [səˈvei] n. 調查

【例】To do the analysis, researchers turned to a survey that's been given to about 15,000 highschool seniors every year since 1976. 研究者透過調研來做分析，自 1976 年起，每年都有 1 萬 5 千名高中生參與該調研。(NPR)

【用】 新聞中，常見句式：The survey shows ... 調查表明......。「關於......的調查」可用 survey of ... 表示，也可以用 survey about ... 表示。

# Level 8

## sanction [ˈsæŋkʃən] v. 批准 n. 批准；制裁

【例】The sanctions actually did stop production because foreign operators pulled out. 由於國外運營商撤資，制裁措施確實導致了停產。(VOA)

【用】 經濟、政治新聞中的常見片語：sanction against ... 對......的制裁；sanction of ... 對...... 的批准；officially sanction 正式批准。另外，the sanction of tradition 表示「約定俗成」。

## block [blɔk] v. 阻礙 n. 大塊；街區

【例】His victory gives the Democrats 60 votes in the senate and the potential to overturn Republican efforts to block legislation. 他的勝利給民主黨在參議院爭取了 60 個席位，並且有可能使共和黨人阻撓立法通過的幻想破滅。(VOA)

【用】 block 作名詞時，可指「大型建築」或「街區」，如：office block 辦公大樓；noisy blocks 喧鬧的街區。作動詞時，有「阻塞」之意，如：block the traffic 阻礙交通。

## weapon [ˈwepən] n. 武器

【例】The resolution aims to impede the growth of ballistic weapons programs. 該項 決議旨在阻止彈道武器專案的進展。(BBC)

【用】 大規模殺傷性武器（weapons of mass destruction）和核武器（nuclear weapon）一直 是全球政治、軍事的重要因素，在新聞中也常出現。

## mission [ˈmiʃən] n. 任務

【例】The U.N. Security Council has lifted its arms embargo on Liberia for one year, primarily to allow its peacekeeping mission there to receive military equipment. 聯 合國安理會解除了對賴比瑞亞的武器禁運，解禁期為一年，目的是讓在當地執行維 和任務的軍隊接受軍事裝備。(VOA)

【用】 常見於國際軍事新聞中，固定搭配：strategic mission 策略任務；rescue mission 營救任務。

## press [pres] n. 壓力；新聞界 v. 壓

【例】Most of what was said at the press conference can't be independently verified. 新聞發布會上的大多數消息無法被獨立證實。(BBC)

【用】 the Press 特指「新聞界；報界」，常見片語：press conference 新聞發布會；press comment 報刊評論；press freedom 出版自由；press cutting 剪報。

## involve [inˈvɔlv] v. 包含；牽涉；使捲入

【例】The harsh journey involved sleep deprivation, debilitating cold, and unrelenting heat as the sailors passed through severe oceanic and climactic extremes. 在艱苦的旅程中，水手們被剝奪睡眠，時而寒風凜冽，時而酷暑難耐，經歷了惡劣的海洋極端氣候。(CRI)

【用】 通常用於被動語態，如：sb. is involved. 某人被牽涉進來了。be involved in the trouble 陷入麻煩。

## native [ˈneitiv] a. 當地（人）的 n. 本國人

【例】The 22-page report from the tribes also charges that the state has a financial incentive to remove Native American children from their tribes. 這份來自部落的長達 22 頁的報告也控訴道，州政府將原住民兒童從部落中趕出存在其經濟動機。(NPR)

【用】 Native Americans 作為固定用法，表示「美洲原住民」，go native 表示「入鄉隨俗」，native speaker 表示「說母語者」。

## argument [ˈɑːgjumənt] n. 爭論，辯論；論點

【例】The argument comes ahead of Sunday's election and on the anniversary of his return to power. 這次辯論發生在週日的競選之前，當天也是他重掌政權的周年紀念日。(BBC)

【用】 常用句型為：have an argument with sb. about sth. 與某人關於某事展開爭論。對於論點的立場，同意或支持用 for，反對或抵抗用 against。

## impact [ˈɪmpækt] n. 影響（力），作用；衝擊

【例】We have been working very hard to use high technology to create a strong visual aesthetic impact on stage. 我們一直在努力運用高科技打造舞台效果，給人以強烈的視覺衝擊，充滿美感。(CRI)

【用】 impact 表「衝擊」，引申為「影響」，如：environmental impact 環境影響；impact of 影響。

## reject [rɪˈdʒekt] v. 拒絕，抵制

【例】The justices unanimously rejected an Indiana farmer's argument that cheap soybeans purchased from a grain elevator are not covered by the Monsanto patents. 法官一致駁回了一名印第安那農民的起訴，這名農民認為從穀倉購買的廉價大豆不包括在孟山都公司的專利範圍之內。(NPR)

【用】 法律領域，reject 表示「駁回」，其名詞為 rejection，可獨立成句，通常用於庭審過程中，律師對對方說法的不贊同，可以說：Rejection! 反對！

## suspend [səˈspend] v. 吊，懸；暫停

【例】The BBC says it's suspending its FM radio broadcasts to the country because of continued interruption and interference in the program. 英國廣播公司稱，由於節目一直遭到阻止和干擾，該公司準備暫時停播在該國的調頻廣播節目。(BBC)

【用】 表「吊，懸」時，常用於被動語態。但在新聞中，常以「中止，暫停」出現，如：suspend production 停產。

## link [lɪŋk] v. 連接 n. 聯繫

【例】Climate change and food security are tightly linked. 氣候變化和食品安全是緊密相連的。 (VOA)

【用】 常見片語：link up 連接；link with 與……有關。作為名詞，在新聞中，表示國家或地區之間的聯繫，如：commercial link 商業往來。

## governor [ˈgʌvənə] n. 省長，州長，主管

【例】That program was defunded last year by Florida's current governor, Rick Scott. 去年，佛羅里達州現任州長里克‧斯科特從這個專案撤資。(NPR)

【用】 政府相關詞：secretary 書記；minister 部長；monarch 君主；president 總統。

## ensure [inˈʃuə] v. 確保，保證，擔保

【例】President's spokesman said the date was shifted from April 27th to April 22nd to ensure that everyone in Egypt can vote. 總統的發言人稱，選舉日期由 4 月 27 日改為 4 月 22 日，以確保每個埃及人都可以投票。(BBC)

【用】 ensure 相當於片語 make sure「確保」，如：ensure supplies 保證供應；ensure safety 確保安全。

## activity [ækˈtivəti] n. 活動；活躍

【例】The activity in the states comes in contrast to the gridlock in Washington. 這幾個州非常活躍程度，而華盛頓卻陷入了僵局，兩者形成了鮮明對比。(NPR)

【用】 activity 既可用在生活領域，如：cultural activity 文化活動；也可用在政治、外交領域，表示較大型的活動，如：political activity 政治活動。

## favor [ˈfeivə] n. 贊成；支持；偏愛

【例】A great number of states are in favor of country or region labeling for process food. 許多州都支援國家或地區為加工食品貼上相應標籤。(BBC)

【用】 常見片語：in favor of 有利於；支持；贊同；in favor with 受......寵愛。口語中常有：Do me a favor. 幫我個忙。

## flight [flait] n. 飛行；航班

【例】Because climate change may stir up more turbulence over the North Atlantic, causing bumpier fl ights there. 由於氣候變化，可能引起北大西洋上空出現更多渦流，導致航班更加顛簸。(Scientific American)

【用】 航空交通常見片語：in flight 在飛行中；flight number 航班號；flight crew 機組人員；direct flight 直航。

## exempt [igˈzempt] v. 使......免除或豁免 a. 被免除的

【例】The outrage over the IRS's conduct in targeting certain tax-exempt groups is based on a misunderstanding. 美國國稅局指定了特定免稅群體，人們對此感到憤慨，但這可能是因為存在誤解。(CNN)

【用】 該詞主要用於法律領域。稅收方向，如：tax exempt 免稅；權利方向，如：exempt from military service 免服兵役。

## resident [ˈrezidənt] n. 居民，定居者 a. 居住的

【例】Authority evacuated more than 60 people while allowing residents to return to their homes Thursday. 週四，當局在幫助居民返鄉的同時疏散了 60 多名群眾。(NPR)

【用】 在社會方面，resident 主要用於城市、人口等相關主題，如：local resident 當地居民；resident population 常住人口；city resident 城市居民。

## document [ˈdɔkjumənt] n. 文件，文檔

【例】This document embodies the concern of the government for the deformity. 這個檔案體現了政府對殘疾人的關懷。(VOA)

【用】 該詞可用於法律、商業、金融等領域，如：secret government document 政府祕密檔；document management 文件管理；transport document 運輸單據。

## ministry [ˈministri] n.（政府的）部門；牧師

【例】The country's Ministry of Health, Welfare and Family Affairs will be turning off all the lights at 7 pm. in a bid to force staff to go home to their families and, well, make bigger ones. 該國保健福祉家庭部力求在晚上七點的時候，讓公司全線熄燈，來強迫員工回到家人身邊中，當然，任務是增加家庭成員。(BBC)

【用】　常用片語：the Ministry of Defence 國防部；Foreign Ministry 外交部；Justice Ministry 司法部；Finance Ministry 財政部。

## crime [kraim] n. 罪行，犯罪

【例】They said they'd been abducted from various parts of Mexico and forced to work for organized crime. 他們稱自己是從墨西哥各處被綁架到這裡，被迫參與集團犯罪工作。(BBC)

【用】　主要用於法律、安全領域，常見搭配：crime rate 犯罪率；economic crime 經濟犯罪；minor crime 未成年人犯罪。

## debt [det] n. 債務

【例】A recently downgraded debt rating could make Greece's attempt to get the money more difficult. 最近債務評定等級下調，這可能使希臘向外借款更加困難。(VOA)

【用】　debt 通常用於經濟領域，如：in debt 負債；national debt 國債；bank debt 銀行借款。但值得注意的是，debt 也可用於宗教領域，指「罪孽」。

## degree [diˈgriː] n. 度，程度；學位

【例】A new study on climate change says catastrophic 4 degree rise in global temperature is increasingly likely to occur within many people's lifetimes. 一項關於氣候變化的新研究表明，在許多人的有生之年，可能會親眼目睹全球溫度升高 4 度，這個災難性事件發生的可能性越來越大。(BBC)

【用】　在教育領域，表示「學位」，如：bachelor degree 學士學位；而「在某種程度上」，可以用 in some degree，也可以用 to some degree。

## earthquake [ˈə:θkweik] n. 地震

【例】Sichuan province is no stranger to earthquake. 四川是地震頻發地。(NPR)

【用】 地震誘發災害擴展詞：debris flow 泥石流；landslide 山體滑坡；tsunami 海嘯；flood 山洪。

## protest [prəuˈtest]] v./n. 抗議，反對

【例】At least 7 people have been killed across the country during violent clashes at opposition protests. 全國至少 7 人在抗議示威活動的暴力衝突中喪生。(CRI)

【用】 常用片語：protest against 反對；without protest 心甘情願地；protest about 對……提出抗議。

## individual [ˌindiˈvidjuəl] n. 個人，個體 a. 單獨的

【例】It will use surveys of individuals to gather information on the extent and severity of hunger. 透過對個體調查可以收集到關於飢餓的程度和嚴重性的資訊。(VOA)

【用】 individual effort 表示「個人努力」。常用擴展詞有：individually 個別地；individualism 個人主義。

## natural [ˈnætʃərəl] a. 自然的，天然的

【例】Snow from the snow generators mixes with natural snow that falls and then the snow ploughs rake it over. 造雪機的人造雪和天然降雪混合在一起，然後被雪犁耙平了。(CRI)

【用】 常用於環境、資源領域，如：natural disaster 自然災難；natural resource 自然資源；natural gas 天然氣；pure natural 純天然的。

## addition [əˈdiʃən] n. 加法；增加的人（或物）

【例】France was a notable addition to the list. 「法國」出現在新名單上，這值得注意。(NPR)

【用】 常用片語：in addition to 除......外。其形容詞為 additional，表示「附加的」，如：additional charge 附加費用。

## crew [kru:] n. 全體船員，一隊工作人員

【例】The Discovery crew is set to launch early Tuesday to deliver nearly 8,000 kilograms of equipment to the International Space Station. 「發現號」機組人員將在週二一早出發，為國際空間站運送近 8000 公斤的設備。(VOA)

【用】 與 staff、family 一樣，crew 也是集合名詞，crew 更側重「船上工作人員」。

## guilty [ˈgilti] a. 有罪的；內疚的

【例】If charged and found guilty, he could be jailed for three years. 如果他被指控並判有罪，那麼他可能被監禁三年。(BBC)

【用】 與 criminal 都表示「犯罪的」，但 guilty 有兩層含義。可指在法律上的「犯罪」，也可指在道德上的「愧疚」。在法律領域，常用句型：sb. is found guilty of sth. 某人被判......罪名。

## relation [riˈleiʃən] n. 關係，關聯；親戚

【例】The new FTA(Free Trade Agreement) will set an example as how China and European countries can work to boost trade relations through eliminating trade barriers as much as possible. 中國與歐洲國家努力通過消除貿易壁壘來促進貿易關係，新自由貿易協定將此作為大家學習的榜樣。(CRI)

【用】 「與......有關」用詞組 in relation to。新聞中常見搭配有：diplomatic relation 外交關係；public relation 公共關係。

## income [ˈiŋkʌm] n. 收入，所得，收益

【例】In April, Americans' confidence about their incomes and the short term state of the economy increased moderately, surprising many economists. 4 月，美國人對

於他們的收入和短期內的經濟狀況充滿信心，這令許多經濟學家感到驚喜。(NPR)

【用】 常與經濟、法律、社會領域內容聯繫在一起，如：income tax 所得稅；family income 家庭收入；annual income 年收入。修飾「收入」的多少，用 high 或 low。

## elect [iˈlekt] v. 選舉，推舉

【例】The settlers helped elect right-wing Prime Minister Benjamin Netanyahu, but now they accuse him of abandoning his nationalist ideals. 在居民們的幫助下，右翼者班傑明‧納坦雅胡當選總理，但現在他們指責班傑明放棄了他的民族主義理想。(VOA)

【用】 該詞用於政治領域，如：elect a new leader 選舉一位新領導人。但作形容詞時，用於名詞後，表示「當選尚未就職的」，如：monitor elect 候任班長。

## scandal [ˈskændəl] n. 醜聞

【例】Her predecessor as head of the IMF, Dominique Strauss Kahn, who was also French, had to resign in the midst of a sex scandal. 她的前任多明尼克‧史特勞斯‧卡恩是國際貨幣基金組織的負責人，同樣也是法國人，不得不因捲入性醜聞而辭職。(BBC)

【用】 新聞中常見片語：sex scandal 性醜聞；political scandal 政治醜聞；corruption scandal 貪汙醜聞。一般用於政治、經濟、娛樂領域。

## influence [ˈinfluəns] n. 影響，影響力

【例】He talked of teenagers at the start of their careers coming under the influence of criminal gangs. 他談到，青少年在他們職業生涯的開端會受到犯罪團夥的影響。(BBC)

【用】「對......有影響」，用片語 influence on，後面可以加人、事、物。under the influence of sb./sth. 表示「在某人／某事的影響下」，而 under the influence 也特指「醉酒」。

## institute ['institju:t] n. 學院，協會

【例】The Blue Ocean Institute has a similar system. 藍色海洋協會擁有一個類似的系統。(NPR)

【用】 通常以公共組織的縮寫形式出現，其中 I 表示 institute，如：Massachusetts Institute of Technology (MIT) 麻省理工學院；the Institute for Space Studies 空間研究所；the National Cancer Institute 國家癌症研究所。

## appeal [ə'pi:l] n./v. 吸引力；上訴；呼籲

【例】The city authorities said they would appeal. 市政府表示他們將會上訴。(BBC)

【用】 國際新聞中，sb. has appealed... 某人呼籲……，常用於環保領域。appeal to sb. 可以表示「對某人有吸引力」；appeal to sth. 則可表示「向……上訴」。

## approach [ə'prəutʃ] v. 接近 n. 方法

【例】They are trying a different demolition approach. 他們正在嘗試一種不同的拆遷方式。(CNN)

【用】 慣用 easy of approach 表示「平易近人」。其形容詞為 approachable，表「親切的，可接近的」。

## immigrant ['imigrənt] n. 移民，僑民

【例】The British Prime Minister David Cameron has announced plans to tighten the rules on state welfare to immigrants. 英國首相大衛‧卡麥隆宣布了限制移民享受國家福利的計畫。(BBC)

【用】 注意與 emigrant 的區別：immigrant 表「（入境）移民」，emigrant 表「（出境）移民」。而 migrant 總指「移民」，沒有方向性。常用搭配：illegal immigrant 非法移民；immigrant wave 移民潮。

## relate [rɪˈleɪt] v. 有關聯；講述

【例】There's underlying issues that relate to demographic growth—there's ever more people to feed. 人口增長帶來了潛在問題，更多的人需要養活。(VOA)

【用】「與......有關」常用 relate to 表示。其形容詞 related 也很常見，如：close related 密切相關的。

## annual [ˈænjuəl] a. 每年的 n. 年報

【例】China's three major state-owned airlines including China Southern posted sharp drops in annual profi t for 2012 last month. 包括中國南方航空公司在內的中國三大國有航空公司均於上月公佈了 2012 年度利潤，利潤急劇下滑。(CRI)

【用】常見用法有：annual conference 年會；annual profit 年利潤；annual sales 年銷量；annual rainfall 年降雨量。

## faith [feɪθ] n. 信任，信仰

【例】There has been a decrease in the Catholic faith within Europe. 在歐洲，信奉天主教的人有所減少。(VOA)

【用】常用於宗教、商務、人際交往領域，如：break faith with sb. 失信於人；loyal to one's faith 忠於自己的信仰；in faith 真正地。

## democracy [dɪˈmɔkrəsi] n. 民主制度，民主國家

【例】They are trying to establish that dictatorship or democracy is a frame of mind. 他們試圖證實獨裁或者民主是一種思維狀態。(BBC)

【用】與 democracy「民主」相對的是 despotism「專制」。用於國家政體、政治領域。

## abuse [əˈbjuːz] v./n. 濫【用】；虐待

【例】It's well known that adults abused as children frequently exhibit violent behavior. 眾所周知，那些在童年時受過虐待的人成年後會經常表現出暴力行為。(VOA)

【用】 常見片語：woman and child abuse 虐待婦女兒童；abuse of power 濫用職權；personal abuse 人身攻擊。

## active [ˈæktɪv] a. 積極的；主動的

【例】I made an active decision to do it for income and pension planning. 我是為了我的收入和養老金計畫，主動決定做這個的。(The Guardian)

【用】 與 active 相對的為 passive「被動的;消極的」。在化學領域，表示「活性的，活躍的」，如：active material 活性材料；active volcano 活火山。

## austerity [ɔˈsterəti] n. 樸素；艱苦；(經濟的)緊縮

【例】The Greek parliament has given its initial approval to a new austerity bill designed to tackle the country's deepening debt crisis. 希臘議會初步批准了新的財政緊縮法案，旨在應對該國日益嚴重的債務危機。(BBC)

【用】 用於經濟領域，常見片語：austerity budget 緊縮財政預算；austerity measures 財政緊縮措施；austerity program 財政緊縮方案。

## crash [kræʃ] n./v. 碰撞；墜毀

【例】Three people were remaining critical condition from yesterday's commute train crash in Connecticut. 在昨天的康乃狄克州通勤火車相撞事故中，有 3 人仍處於危險狀況。

【用】 通常指公共交通的事故，也可特指經濟領域的破產，如：crash landing 緊急迫降；air crash 空難；car crash 車禍；stock market crash 股市崩盤。

## lack [læk] v./n. 缺乏，不足；沒有

【例】The former pope resigned the position because, at age 85, he said he lacked the strength to continue his work. 前教皇表示，由於自己已有 85 歲的高齡，沒有精

力再繼續工作，因此退位。(VOA)

【用】 注意：該詞不能用於被動語態。常用片語：lack of 缺乏；lack in 在……缺少；lack of power 乏力。

## offer [ˈɔfə] v. 提供 n. 提議；報價

【例】The company is retaining the right to expand further the offer of new shares if there is sufficient demand. 如果有足夠的需求，公司還獲得進一步擴大新股發行的權利。(BBC)

【用】 表「報價」時，主要用於商務往來領域，如：offer price 要價；on offer 出售中；public offer 公開報價；special offer 特別優惠。表「提供」時，有 offer sb. a job 或 job offer 工作機會。

## arrive [əˈraiv] v. 到達，到來；達成

【例】A team of experts from the World Health Organization are also set to arrive in China later this week to assess the H7N9 influenza in the country. 來自世界衛生組織的專家小組也定於這週晚些時候到達中國，他們將評估 H7N9 流感對中國的影響。(CRI)

【用】 表「到達某地」，arrive 不能單獨使用，後面必須加介詞 in 或 at，如：arrive in Paris 到達巴黎。其名詞形式為 arrival，與其相對的是 departure「出發；離開」。

## industrial [inˈdʌstriəl] a. 工業的，產業的

【例】Campaigners say there is huge interest from industrial corporations in developing so-called killer robots. 活動家表示，工業企業對開發所謂的殺手機器人抱有極大興趣。(VOA)

【用】 該詞源於 industry「工業」，有許多派生詞，如：industrialism 工業主義；industrialist 企業家；industrialization 工業化；industrialized 工業化的。

## particular [pəˈtikjulə] a. 特定的；特別的 n. 詳情

【例】「I don't think we have any particular plan to single out any class or caste of taxpayers,」 he said. 他說，「我想我們沒有特殊的方法可以篩選出特定階級或社會團體的納稅人。」 (NPR)

【用】 常見片語：in particular 尤其，特別。particular case 表示「特殊情況」。注意：be particular about/ over sth. 對……挑剔的。

## trap [træp] n. 陷阱 v. 使中圈套，使陷入困境

【例】If you're trapped in grain up to the waist, it takes over 600 pounds of force plus your body weight to free you from the grain. 如果你從腰部以下被困在糧食堆中，加上你的體重，總共需要超過 600 磅的力量才能使你從中掙脫出來。(NPR)

【用】 表示「陷入……的圈套」，可用 trap into 這一動詞片語。be trapped 表示「被陷害；陷入困境」。

## workforce [ˈwəːkfɔːs] n. 勞動力

【例】A growing number of mothers in the United States are joining the workforce, from fewer than 50 percent in the 1970s to close to 75 percent today. 在美國，越來越多的母親外出工作，其比例從 1970 年代的不到 50% 增長到現在的接近 75%。(VOA)

【用】 與 staff 同義，表示「員工，勞動力」，不表個人，而表示一個群體。

# Level 9

## discuss [dis'kʌs] v. 談論，討論

【例】NATO (North Atlantic Treaty Organization) defense ministers are likely to discuss troop levels on a meeting formally in Bratislava next week. 下週於布拉提斯拉瓦舉辦的會議上北約各國防部長可能會正式討論部隊兵力的問題。(BBC)

【用】 常用 discuss sth. with sb. 表示「與某人談論某事」。其名詞形式為 discussion，under discussion 表示「正在討論中」。

## exactly [ig'zæktli] ad. 確切地，恰好

【例】Exactly what happened to the child is not clear. 在這個孩子身上究竟發生了什麼還尚不清楚。(NPR)

【用】 對事情細節回答 Not exactly. 表示「不完全是這樣。」通常用於口語中，可單獨成句。

## seize [si:z] v. 抓住；奪取

【例】She was seized of vast estates. 她依法占有大片地產。(VOA)

【用】 seize hurriedly 匆忙抓住；seize today 把握今天。

## personal ['pə:sənəl] a. 個人的，私人的

【例】A book containing George Washington's personal copy of the American Constitution has been sold in New York for $10m. 一本含有喬治·華盛頓的親筆書寫的《美國憲法》的書以 1000 萬美元的價格在紐約出售。(BBC)

【用】 一般作定語，常見片語：personal affair 私事；personal account 個人帳戶；personal property 個人財產。

## delay [di'lei] v./n. 耽擱，推遲

【例】The researchers say extra-virgin olive oil contains aromatic compounds that block the absorption of glucose from the blood, delaying the recurrence of hunger.

研究人員說特級純橄欖油含有芳香族化合物，該物質會阻止血液中葡萄糖的吸收，從而延緩飢餓感的再次出現。(Scientific American)

【用】 多用於交通、通訊領域。火車、飛機的晚點，也可用 delay 表示。常用片語：without delay 立即；time delay 延時；short delay 短暫停留。

## attention [ə'tenʃən] n. 注意，注意力

【例】The crime has also brought attention to the issue of women's rights in India. 這起犯罪行為也引發了對印度女性權利問題的關注。(VOA)

【用】 常用片語：pay attention to (sth.) 關注（某事）。另外，attention 在軍事領域，特定表示「立正」的命令，可單獨成祈使句。

## opportunity [ˌɔpə'tjuːnəti] n. 機會

【例】He said there was no need to be sad and that the night was an opportunity to celebrate the singer's achievements. 他說，不必悲傷，今晚正是慶祝這位歌手取得成就的大好機會。(BBC)

【用】 常見片語：job opportunity 工作機會；equal opportunity 機會均等；opportunity cost 機會成本；employment opportunity 就業機會。

## miss [mis] v. 錯過；惦念

【例】We're going to miss him until the last day of our lives but we carry on his legacy here and we will carry it on with strength. 我們會終生懷念他，我們將不遺餘力地繼承他的遺志。(VOA)

【用】 miss 作動詞時，常見用法有：miss the mark 沒打中目標；miss out 錯過；miss the point 沒有抓住要領。在體育領域，miss 表「未擊中（球）」。

## poverty ['pɔvəti] n. 貧窮

【例】Poverty is not first thing that comes to mind when you think of Japan. 一提到日

本時，你首先想到的不會是貧窮。(VOA)

【用】 新聞常用片語：reduce poverty 消除貧困；Poverty Project 扶貧工程；in poverty 貧困；poverty gap 貧富差距。

## channel [ˈtʃænəl] n. 頻道；海峽

【例】The Iraqi government says the channels promoted violence and sectarianism. 伊拉克政府稱這些管道宣揚了暴力和宗派主義。(BBC)

【用】 在特指「海峽」時，首字母要大寫，如：English Channel 英吉利海峽。也可引申為「管道」，如：marketing channel 銷售管道。

## infrastructure [ˈinfrəˌstrʌktʃə] n. 基礎設施

【例】 Obama says his budget will curb spending and cut corporate tax breaks — while boosting funding for infrastructure and education. 歐巴馬表示他的預算將削減開支和削減企業稅收優惠，同時增加基礎設施和教育基金的投入。(VOA)

【用】 用於政府宏觀規劃領域，如：economic infrastructure 經濟基礎建設；transport infra-structure 交通基本建設；infrastructure project 基礎設施工程。

## finance [faiˈnæns] n. 財政，金融

【例】Speculation continues that it may ask for a bailout for its public finances. 不斷有人猜測：政府可能會為公共財政尋求救援。(BBC)

【用】 新聞英語常用詞彙：public finance 公共財政；Finance Ministry 財政部；international finance 國際金融；national finance 國家財政。

## govern [ˈgʌvən] v. 控制；統治

【例】Given that this government needs to govern Italy, I hope that it is done by Italians. 考慮到該政府需管理義大利，我希望此事能由義大利人完成。(CNN)

【用】 其名詞形式為 government「政府」。govern 表「控制」，小到個人情緒，如：govern

your temper，大到地區、國家、政府，如：govern an area。

## gather [ˈgæðɔ] v. 聚集；採集

【例】Supporters of Mubarak have gathered outside the Police Academy in Cairo on hearing the country's ruling. 在聽到國家的裁決後，穆巴拉克的支持者聚集在開羅員警學院外。(CRI)

【用】 與 gather 相關片語：gather together 集合在一起；gather in 收集。其名詞形式為 gathering，表示「聚會」。

## identify [aiˈdentifai] v. 認出，識別，鑑定

【例】Current tests for human flu viruses don't identify this one. 現有的人類流感病毒測試無法識別這種病毒。(CRI)

【用】 常見用法是 identify with，表示「認同；理解」。

## worldwide [ˈwɔːdwaid] a. 全世界的 ad. 在全世界

【例】The United Nations top health official has said the worldwide spread of swine flu is now unstoppable. 聯合國高級衛生官員表示，現在已經無法阻擋豬流感在全球蔓延。(BBC)

【用】 與該詞相關搭配：worldwide sales 全球銷售額；worldwide organization 全球性組織。

## willful [ˈwilful] a. 任性的，故意的

【例】 Let's strike hard at the people responsible for this, and their willful support structures. 讓我們嚴厲打擊對此負有責任的人，以及背後有意支援他們的組織。(CNN)

【用】 也作 wilful。相關片語：willful murder 故意殺人；willful act 故意行為。在指人的性格時，表示「任性的，固執的」，可作定語或表語。

## sector ['sektə] n. 部分，部門；扇形

【例】This pattern worked fine when the economy was robust and there were ample job opportunities in other sectors. 當經濟發展勢頭強勁，且其他部門有充足的就業機會時，這種模式的優越性才能體現出來。(CRI)

【用】 表「部門」時，常用於國家職能領域，如：government sector 政府部門。在軍事方面，sector 表「防禦區」，如：the British sector 英國防區。

## emission [i'miʃən] n.（光、熱等的）散發

【例】Its aim was to cut greenhouse emissions by 5% over the next ten years. 目標是在未來的十年內將溫室氣體排放量減少 5%。(BBC)

【用】 在環境領域，emission 表示「（廢棄物的）排放」，如：emission control 廢物排放控制。

## infect [in'fekt] v. 傳染，感染

【例】Currently, there are eight kinds of bird flu viruses which can infect human. 現在，有八種禽流感病毒能傳染給人類。(CRI)

【用】 一般指「病菌」的傳染，用 infect ... with ... 表示「把……傳染給……」。在醫學方面，infect agent 病原體。其名詞形式為 infection。

## revolution [ˌrevə'ljuːʃən] n. 革命

【例】The man expected to be Japan's next Prime Minister has held his party's election victory as a revolution. 作為下一屆首相的準候選人，他將其所代表的黨派的成功競選視為一次革命。(BBC)

【用】 前面可以加定語，如：industrial revolution 工業革命。但在天文領域，表示「公轉」。

## violent ['vaiələnt] a. 暴力的；強烈的

【例】 But the situation was much more violent at the American consulate in Benghazi, Libya. 但在位於班加西的美國駐利比亞領事館，局勢更為暴力。

【用】 常用片語：violent crime 暴力犯罪；violent earthquake 強震；violent debate 激烈的辯論。其名詞形式為 violence「暴力，暴行」。

## fishery [ˈfiʃəri] n. 漁場；漁業

【例】Researchers point to the collapse of the herring fishery in the Irish sea as helping to increase the numbers of jellies there. 研究人員指出，愛爾蘭海域的鯡魚漁業的崩潰使得當地水母的數量有所增加。(BBC)

【用】 該詞可用於環境、生產生活領域，如：fishery resource 漁業資源。在法律上，fishery 表「捕魚權」。

## massive [ˈmæsiv] a. 巨大的，大規模的

【例】A massive earthquake followed by the threat of tsunamis, for people in Indonesia, that combination could bring up tragic memories. 一場大地震再加上隨之而來的海嘯威脅，可能會使印尼人留下悲慘的回憶。(CNN)

【用】 用來修飾事物的程度，如：massive investment 大規模投資；massive increase 巨大增長。但在地質領域，表示「塊狀的」，massive structure 表示「土壤的塊狀構造」。

## allege [əˈledʒ] v. 斷言，宣稱，指稱

【例】India auditors allege corruption in farm loan waivers. 印度審計員指稱在農業貸款減免方面存在腐敗行為。(BBC)

【用】 常用同義詞有：declare，state。

## passenger [ˈpæsindʒə] n. 乘客，旅客

【例】Its passengers included people with developmental disabilities. 其乘客中存在發育障礙者。(NPR)

【用】 多用於交通領域，如：passenger safety 乘客安全；passenger train 客運列車。

## citizen [ˈsitizən] n. 市民，公民

【例】It would include a path for undocumented immigrants, people who are in the country illegally to become citizens. 這為非法移民提供了一個成為合法公民的途徑。(Scientific American)

【用】 在法律範疇，citizen 是具有權利與義務的。範圍最廣的就是 citizen of the world 世界公民；科技領域的有 net citizen 線民。

## seek [siːk] v. 尋找，追求

【例】Several leaders and foreign ministers from the European Union, which Turkey is seeking to join, welcomed the result. 幾位歐盟領導人和外交部長對該結果表示滿意，而土耳其正在設法加入歐盟。(VOA)

【用】 常見片語：seek for 尋找；seek out 搜出；seek after 追求。「尋求幫助」可以用 seek help，而「徵求建議」可以用 seek advice。

## diversity [daiˈvəːsəti] n. 多樣，千變萬化

【例】 The school says race is one of many factors it uses to achieve diversity on campus. 學校表示種族是實現校園多樣性的眾多因素之一。(CNN)

【用】 常用搭配：species diversity 物種多樣性；biological diversity 生物多樣性。這也是國際討論的熱門話題。

## generation [ˌdʒenəˈreiʃən] n. 一代人；產生

【例】She says fewer people live in three-generation households, where the parents and grandparents work. 她說，與沒有退休的父母和祖父母共同生活的三代同堂的家庭越來越少了。(VOA)

【用】 常見片語：generation gap 代溝。另外，asexual generation 可以表示植物領域的「無性生殖」。

## publish [ˈpʌblɪʃ] v. 出版；公布，發表

【例】More than 15,000 children under 18 months took part in the study, which has been published in the New England Journal of Medicine. 該研究有 15000 多名一歲半以下的兒童參與，其研究結果發表在《新英格蘭醫學雜誌》上。(BBC)

【用】 常用句式：sb. has published (his/her) book/novel/thesis...。publish 也可【用】於被動語態，如：It will be published in July. 它將在 7 月出版。

## deficit [ˈdefɪsɪt] n. 赤字

【例】Obama says the plan should appeal to centrist lawmakers with its balance of deficit reduction and new investment. 歐巴馬表示這個方案能夠吸引中立派立法議員，因為它在削減赤字與增加投資之間達到了平衡。(NPR)

【用】 常用於政府財政、貿易經營方面，如：budget deficit 預算赤字；trade deficit 貿易逆差。

## scale [skeil] n. 刻度，規模 v. 攀登

【例】Policy Research warn that future growth depends on large-scale job creation to employ the next generation of workers. 政策研究室警告說，未來的經濟增長取決於為新一代的勞動力創造大量的就業機會。(VOA)

【用】 與 large-scale「大規模」相對的就是 small-scale「小規模」；表示「比例」時，常用片語有 on the scale of 按……的比例，常用於計算、數學領域。

## muscle [ˈmʌsl] n. 肌肉

【例】He said muscle atrophy was a major concern. 他說，肌肉萎縮是一個主要的顧慮。(VOA)

【用】 主要用於醫學領域，也可用於體育領域。「肌肉拉傷」為 muscle strain；「肌肉收縮」為 muscle contraction；「肌肉組織」為 muscle tissue。

## choose [tʃuːz] v. 選擇；決定

【例】Voting is underway in Venezuela to choose a successor to the late President Hugo Chavez. 委內瑞拉正在進行投票，以選出已故總統烏戈‧查維茲的接班人。(BBC)

【用】 其名詞形式為 choice，表示「選擇；精品」。口語中，經常用 as you choose 表示「隨你的便」。

## agriculture [ˈægrikʌltʃə] n. 農業，農學

【例】 It collects, preserves and maintains the raw genetic material used in agriculture. 它收集、保存並維護用於農業的原始基因。(VOA)

【用】 產業相關詞：forestry industry 林業；animal husbandry 畜牧業；fishery 漁業；tourism 旅遊業。

## prevent [priˈvent] v. 阻止，妨礙

【例】A key goal is to prevent multi-national firms exploiting legal loopholes to minimize their tax payments. 一個主要目標就是防止跨國公司利用法律漏洞來偷稅漏稅。(BBC)

【用】 常與 from 連用，表示「妨礙……做某事」，from 後要加動名詞形式。

## domestic [dəuˈmestik] a. 國內的；家（庭）的

【例】 Domestic manufacturers of auto parts are looking outside India for business, and steel companies are also feeling the pinch. 國內的汽車零件製造商正在印度以外的國家尋找業務機會，鋼鐵企業也感受到了壓力。(VOA)

【用】 domestic 可指小到「家庭」，domestic water 家庭用水；大到「國家」，domestic flight 國內航班。新聞中常見的「國內生產總值」即為 gross domestic product (GDP)。

## square [skweə] n. 平方；廣場；正方形

【例】The plan also includes restaurants, a new town square, pedestrian areas and 383 car parking spaces. 該計畫還包括多家餐廳、一個新型城市廣場，步行區和 383 個停車位。(BBC)

【用】 在表示計量單位時，square metre 表示「平方公尺」；square kilometer 表示「平方公里」。注意：fair and square 表示「光明正大地」；all square 表示「勢均力敵」。

## widely [ˈwaidli] ad. 廣泛地

【例】It was widely used as a building material from the 1950s to the mid-80s. 從 1950 年代到 80 年代中期，它被廣泛地用作建築材料。(BBC)

【用】 由形容詞 wide「廣的」派生而來，常用來修飾動詞的過去分詞或用在被動語態當中。片語有：widely read 廣泛閱讀。

## range [reindʒ] n. 範圍；射程 v.（在某範圍內）變動

【例】The symptoms can range from mild to severe. 這些症狀輕重程度不一。(CNN)

【用】 常用片語：in the range of ... 在......的範圍內。

## quality [ˈkwɔləti] n. 品質；品質 a. 優質的

【例】To improve the water quality of the springs, Florida regulators have set targets for reducing the amount of nitrates. 為提高泉水的水質，佛羅里達州的監管機構設定了減少硝酸鹽含量的目標。(NPR)

【用】 與 quality「品質」相對的是 quantity「數量」。在生活各領域，都可遇見該詞，如：service quality 服務品質；environmental quality 環境品質；quality of life 生活品質。

## fear [fiə] n./v. 害怕，恐懼；擔心

【例】But security fears did not stop runners from turning out on Sunday. 但是對安全

問題的擔憂並沒有阻止走私者們在週日聚首。

【用】 固定搭配：for fear 以免；in fear 害怕。而 no fear 要注意，表示「當然不」。

## brotherhood [ˈbrʌðəhud] n. 手足情誼，兄弟關係；兄弟會

【例】We live and work together in complete equality and brotherhood. 我們完全平等，如兄弟般地在一起生活和工作。(BBC)

【用】 與 brotherhood 相對的就是 sisterhood，表示「姐妹會」。

## grand [grænd] a. 宏偉的，壯麗的

【例】In many towns, however, the grand ambitions inspired by the Olympics do not seem to have been realised. 然而在許多城鎮，受到奧運會感染而激發的遠大目標似乎並沒有實現。(BBC)

【用】 固定用法：a grand old man 表示「元老，前輩」。

## source [sɔːs] n. 來源；發源地

【例】Poultry and wild birds are currently the only known source of infection. 家禽和野生鳥類是目前唯一的已知感染源。(NPR)

【用】 片語有：at source 在源頭。常用 the source of，可表示「……的產地」，如 the source of wine 紅酒產地，也可表示「……的來源」，如：the source of the news 新聞來源。

## executive [igˈzekjutiv] n. 行政主管，決策者 a. 行政的

【例】 They have also opened a criminal investigation into two of the bank's former senior executives. 他們還對該銀行的兩名前任高級主管啟動了犯罪調查。(BBC)

【用】 一般出現在商務、政治、經濟新聞中，如：executive management 行政管理；executive ability 執行力；executive position 行政職務。

## grant [grɑːnt] v. 授予；同意 n. 授予物

【例】A Russian multimillionaire who is wanted on charges of fraud by the authorities in Moscow has been granted asylum in Britain. 被莫斯科當局以詐騙罪通緝的俄羅斯富豪已經在英國獲得政治避難權。 (BBC)

【用】常用片語：take for granted 認為……理所當然。在政治方面，grant 還可指「（政府）撥款」，如：student grant 學生助學金。

## overall [ˈəuvərɔːl] a. 全面的，綜合的 ad. 總共

【例】It's one thing experts look at to get an idea of how the overall economy is doing. 專家觀察這件事是為瞭解整體經濟是如何運作的。(CNN)

【用】相關搭配：overall consideration 全盤考慮；overall situation 大局；overall planning 整體規劃。

## material [məˈtiəriəl] n. 材料，原料 a. 物質的

【例】Police also found more than 20 pounds of explosive material and a computer that had instructions on how to make bombs. 警方還發現了 20 多磅的爆炸性原料和一台裝有炸彈製造步驟說明的電腦。(NPR)

【用】常用片語：raw material 原材料；reference material 參考資料。注意，material 還有形容詞性，表示「物質的」，與其相對的是 mental「精神的」。

## resource [riˈsɔːs] n. 資源

【例】It says there will be a higher demand on resources as the world's population expands from seven-point-one billion today to eight billion people. 它說當世界人口從現有的 71 億增長到 80 億人時，更多的資源需求將會出現。(VOA)

【用】常以複數形式出現。在商務領域的常見片語有 human resource，即常說的 HR，人力資源。在資源有效利用方面，會涉及 resource allocation 資源配置；resource management 資源管理；resource protection 資源保護。

## deadly ['dɛdlɪ] a. 致命的；死一般的 ad. 極度地

【例】The race was cancelled in 2011 when the government crashed pro-democracy rallies with deadly force. 由於政府動用致命武力與民主集會人員產生衝突，2011 年的比賽被取消了。(BBC)

【用】 通常作定語，如：deadly enemy 死敵；deadly seriousness 極其嚴肅。

## type [taip] n. 類型 v. 打字

【例】But there are many unknowns about a vaccine against this type of virus. 但對於這種類型病毒的疫苗，還有許多未知的情況有待被瞭解。(NPR)

【用】 作動詞時，有 type in，表「輸入」；作名詞時，有複數形式，常用 type of 表示「......型」。

## edge [edʒ] n. 邊

【例】Scientists say the earthquake in Japan in March 2011 was so big that its effects were felt at the edge of space. 科學家稱，2011 年 3 月在日本發生的地震非常強烈，連太空邊緣都感受到了地震效應。 (BBC)

【用】 需要注意的是，edge 雖然表示「邊緣」，但 on edge 的意思是「緊張不安」。

# Level 10

## responsibility [rɪˌspɑnsəˈbɪləti] n. 責任，職責，責任心

【例】We say that you have a responsibility, too,not just the student. 我們要說的是不僅是學生有責任，你也有責任。(CNN)

【用】 常用於社會新聞中，如：sense of responsibility 責任感；social responsibility 社會責任。其同義詞為 duty，與「責任」相對的就是 obligation「義務」。

## resolution [ˌrezəˈluːʃən] n. 決心；決議；解析度

【例】U.S. officials say they hope to bring a resolution to the U.N. Security Council this month, while France holds the rotating presidency. 美國官員表示他們希望在本月，給聯合國安理會提交一項決議，法國這個月擔任輪值主席國。(VOA)

【用】 New Year's resolutions「新年決心」是西方國家的傳統。在科技領域，image resolution 表示「圖像解析度」；high resolution 表示「高解析度」。

## journalist [ˈdʒɜːnəlist] n. 記者，新聞工作者

【例】The Pulitzer Prize-winning journalist and best selling author, Haynes Johnson died today after suffering a heart attack. 普立茲獎獲獎記者、暢銷書作家海恩斯·詹森因心臟病發作在今天去世。(NPR)

【用】 該詞源於 journal「日記，雜誌」。常用拓展詞有：journalism 新聞業；journalistic 新聞業的。

## contain [kənˈtein] v. 包含

【例】Researchers are interested in the dust clouds because they may contain material that could form planets. 研究人員們對塵埃雲感興趣，是因為它們可能包含可以形成行星的物質。 (CNN)

【用】 involve，include 都有「包含」之意，區別在於：involve 的客體一般是無形的；include 側重整體對其中獨立個體的包含；contain 客體可以有形，也可無形，並且強調包容關係。

## judge [dʒʌdʒ] n. 法官 v. 判斷;審判

【例】The White House is announcing confirmation of the first South Asian American in US history to serve as a circuit court judge. 白宮方面宣布確認美國歷史上首位南亞裔美國人成為巡迴法庭法官。(NPR)

【用】 作動詞時,無被動語態。作名詞時,High Court judge 表示「高等法院的法官」。另外,judge 也可表示「裁判」,用於體育領域。

## wild [waild] a. 野生的;狂熱的;野蠻的

【例】Consistent with the pre-dawn noises observed in wild fowl, the roosters began to crow about two hours before their rooms lit up. 經觀察,野禽會在黎明前鳴叫,同樣,房間亮燈前兩小時左右公雞就開始鳴叫。(Scientific American)

【用】 常見片語:wild animal 野生動物;in the wild 野生的。wild 也可指性格中的「狂野」,引申為「難駕馭」,如:run wild 失去控制。

## relationship [riˈleiʃənʃip] n. 關係,聯繫

【例】The countries have been allies for decades, and as part of that relationship, the two countries run joined military exercises every year. 這兩個國家結盟已經幾十年了,作為彼此的盟國,兩國每年都舉行聯合軍事演習。(CNN)

【用】 用途廣泛,有 interpersonal relationship 人際關係;cooperative relationship 合作關係;direct relationship 直系親屬關係。還可暗指「男女之間的曖昧關係」。

## refugee [ˌrefjuˈdʒiː] n. 難民

【例】The attacks occurred in a town that shelters Syrian refugees. 襲擊事件發生在一個供敘利亞難民避難的小鎮。(NPR)

【用】 常見片語:refugee camp 難民營。為免於迫害而對別國申請境內停留的公民,稱為 political refugee 政治難民。

## ability [əˈbiləti] n. 能力

【例】The Turkish government appears to have strong faith in Japan's ability to get it right. 土耳其政府似乎堅信日本有能力使其恢復正常。 (BBC)

【用】 指先天或學習來的各種能力，如；learning ability 學習能力；cognitive ability 認知能力；physical ability 體能。

## episode [ˈepisəud] n. 一段情節；一集

【例】The series has since aired 33 seasons and nearly 800 episodes with 11 actors portraying the Doctor over time. 這部電視劇至今已經播出了 33 季，近 800 集，期間共有 11 名演員扮演過博士這一角色。(CNN)

【用】 主要用於電影、電視、小說、詩歌等作品中，表示「插曲」，可以引申為「一段經歷」。

## corruption [kəˈrʌpʃən] n. 腐化；貪汙；墮落

【例】He was accused of corruption. 他被指控犯有貪汙罪。(VOA)

【用】 該詞是國內新聞的熱點話題，如：combat corruption 反腐；crime of corruption 貪汙罪；fighting corruption 打擊貪汙腐敗。

## rare [reə] a. 罕見的；( 肉類 ) 半熟的

【例】Rare bipartisanship has emerged on both issues, boosting prospects for legislative action. 此次兩黨合作實為罕見，提出了兩個議題，推進實施立法行動。 (VOA)

【用】 在飲食上，rare 表示「半熟的」，如：rare steak 五分熟牛排；在自然資源領域，rare 表示「稀有的」，如：rare metal 稀有金屬。

## territory [ˈteritəri] n. 領土，領域，範圍

【例】 Though a recent referendum showed overwhelming support for remaining a

British territory. 然而，最近進行了一次公投，大家普遍支持維護英國領土完整。
(NPR)

【用】 一般用於地理、國家主權領域，如：dependent territory 附屬地；但在商業領域，表示
「勢力範圍」，sales territory 銷售範圍。

## desert [ˈdezət] n. 沙漠 v. 離棄

【例】In southwestern Africa's Namib Desert, the lack of rainfall keeps grass sparse.
在非洲西南部的納米比沙漠，降水過少，草地稀疏。(Scientific American)

【用】 在新聞中，要注意該詞在拼寫和讀音上與 dessert「飯後甜點」的區別。

## review [riˈvjuː] n./v. 複習，回顧；評論

【例】The oil company had warned that it may be irreparably harmed by the high levels of the compensation and it's appealing to have the process reviewed. 石油公司
警告稱，過高的賠償標準可能給公司造成無法挽回的損失，並呼籲重新評審該程式。
(BBC)

【用】 學術領域，有 Literature Review 文獻綜述；大部分情況下都表示「回顧」，如：general review 總複習。review 表「評論」時，有 film review 影評。

## interview [ˈint4vjuː] n./v. 面試；會見，採訪

【例】Camalier interviewed Mick Jagger and Keith Richards for the film. 卡馬利爾就
此部電影採訪了米克‧賈格爾和基斯‧理查茲。(VOA)

【用】 在新聞中，interview 常表示「採訪」，如：telephone interview 電話採訪；在職場中，
interview 常表示「面試」，如：job interview 求職面試。

## priority [[praiˈɔrəti] n. 優先權，優先考慮的事

【例】The top priority is diagnosis—the capability to be able to pick up this virus,
should it emerge outside of USA. 當務之急是進行診斷——如果這種病毒在美國以外

的地方出現，我們要能夠將其分辨出來。(NPR)

【用】 常見片語：give priority to 優先考慮；order of priority 優先秩序；according to priority 依次。

## asset [ˈæset] n. 資產

【例】Spain is setting up what has been called a bad bank to take over the toxic assets held by country's banks following the property crash. 西班牙正建立一個被稱為壞帳托收銀行的機構，以接管繼房地產崩盤後國家銀行持有的不良資產。(BBC)

【用】 常見用法有：fixed asset 固定資產，real estate 不動產；intangible asset 無形資產。

## anniversary [ˌæniˈvəːsəri] n. 週年紀念

【例】And in order to commemorate that anniversary, nearly 200 buglers and trumpeters gathered at Arlington National Cemetery over the weekend. 為慶祝週年紀念日，整個週末近 200 名軍號手和小號手聚集在阿靈頓國家公墓。(CNN)

【用】 表示「（幾）週年」時，用 the + 序數詞 + anniversary，如：the 10th anniversary 10 週年紀念。

## estimate [ˈestimeit] v./n. 估計，估量

【例】A Pentagon report released this month estimated as many as 36 thousand service members may have been sexually assaulted last year. 美國國防部這個月發布報告，稱去年軍中可能有多達 36000 人遭到了性侵犯。(NPR)

【用】 用於商業領域，cost estimate 成本估算；rough estimate 粗算。較為常用的搭配是 estimate for 對……進行估價。

## modern [ˈmɔdən] a. 現代的

【例】They were able to sequence the genomes of 11 different strains of blight, and then to compare these older specimens to 15 modern ones. 他們能對十一個不同

種類的枯萎菌株基因進行排序，然後將這些早期的樣本與 15 個現代的樣本作比較。
(Scientific American)

【用】 常被人們音譯為「摩登」，表示「現代的」，也可引申為「時髦的」。但在文化領域，
modern 表示一個時間段，如：modern Chinese 現代漢語。

## officer [ˈɔfisə] n. 軍官；官員

【例】 The United States army has formally charged the military officer accused of
carrying out last week's mass shooting at the Fort Hood military base in Texas. 上
週在德克薩斯州胡德堡軍事基地發生了大規模槍擊案，美國軍隊已正式地對該軍官
提出指控。(BBC)

【用】 常見用法：police officer 警官；military officer 軍官；customs officer 海關官員。在新
聞中，officer 常指有一定權力的人。

## airline [ˈeəlain] n. 航空公司；航線

【例】The airline has been the most aggressive of the Chinese carriers in its Australian expansion. 該航空公司是中國航空公司中向澳大利亞擴張業務的最積極的一家。
(CRI)

【用】 在國際交通運輸領域，有 airline industry 航空公司；international airline 國際航線；
major airline 主要航線。

## scene [siːn] n. 景色；場，景

【例】Federal investigators are on scene trying to discover the cause. 聯邦調查員正
在案發現場試圖找到起因。(NPR)

【用】 在影視、戲劇、小說中，指「場景、布景」，如：behind the scene 幕後；new scene
新建場景。注意，scene 還可表示「現場」，Crime Scene Investigation 犯罪現場調查。

## necessary [ˈnesəsəri] a. 必要的;必然的

【例】But he says it was necessary to prevent the U.S. financial system from collapsing. 但他表示有必要防止美國金融體系崩潰。(VOA)

【用】 if necessary 如果必要的話;necessary for 所必需;necessary condition 必要條件;when necessary 在必要的時候。

## successor [səkˈsesə] n. 接班人,繼任者

【例】Sir Alex has played a central part in the selection of his successor. 亞歷克斯爵士在為自己選擇繼任者上起著至關重要的作用。(BBC)

【用】 常用片語:legal successor 法定繼承人。

## illegal [iˈliːgəl] a. 違法的

【例】 New York's mayor wants to make it illegal for restaurants to serve sugary drinks that are larger than 16 ounces. 紐約市長希望將那些供應超過 16 盎司的含糖飲料的餐廳行為定為非法。(CNN)

【用】 常見搭配有:illegal activity 違法行為;be illegal 違法的。其反義詞為 legal 合法的。

## total [ˈtəutəl] a. 總的;完全的 n. 總數

【例】 Estimates of the total cost of bringing the asteroid to the astronauts are currently around $2.6 billion. 將太空人帶到小行星上的總成本目前估計約為 26 億美元。(NPR)

【用】 常用片語為 in total,表示「總計」。其副詞形式為 totally,常用於句首,表示「總的來說」。

## digital [ˈdidʒitəl] a. 數字的;數位的

【例】 Armed with digital cameras, they record the most spectacular displays of fall foliage. 他們配備了數位相機，把最美麗的秋葉景色記錄了下來。(Scientific American)

【用】 在科技領域，數字時代也是新聞的熱門話題之一，如：digital technology 數位技術；digital library 數字圖書館；digital media 數字媒體。

## message [ˈmesidʒ] n. 訊息

【例】In a final message on his official Twitter account, he thanked his followers for their 「love and support.」 他在其 Twitter 官方帳戶的最後一條消息中感謝了關注者們的「關愛和支持」。(VOA)

【用】 生活中常用 leave a message 表示「留口信」，用於電話通話情境。而表示「收、發簡訊」時，則用 receive 和 send。

## strike [straik] v. 打，撞 n. 罷工

【例】 We are going to be talking about teachers'strike and a new case of disease that's usually associated with middle ages. 我們將討論教師罷工事件和一個與中年人息息相關的全新病例。(CNN)

【用】 作名詞，用於社會、權力等話題，如：on strike 在罷工中；air strike 空襲；general strike 大罷工。

## murder [ˈməːdə] n./v. 謀殺

【例】Meanwhile, Macbeth, which is full of tension, conspiracy, murder and remorse, provides a perfect grounding for Hui Opera performers to act upon. 同時，《馬克白》的表演充滿張力，融入了陰謀和謀殺的元素，夾雜著深深的懊悔之情，用徽劇的形式呈現得唯妙唯肖。(CRI)

【用】 用於法律、軍事、犯罪領域，如：commit murder 謀殺；mass murder 大屠殺。

## fatal [ˈfeitəl] a. 致命的；災難性的

【例】The number of teenage drivers in fatal car crashes has dropped dramatically in the past decade. 在過去十年裡，因車禍死亡的青少年司機人數急遽下降。(NPR)

【用】　該詞要注意的是，比較級和最高級，在詞前加 more 和 most。可以用來表示事件的程度，如：fatal illness 絕症。

## accept [əkˈsept] v. 接受

【例】But the chairman of the Liverpool Supporters'Club, Richard Pedder, says everyone should accept the ban and move on. 但利物浦球迷俱樂部主席理查‧裴達德表示，每個人都應該接受該禁令，繼續向前看。(BBC)

【用】　其反義詞為 decline「拒絕」，賓語可以是人，也可以是物。

## heritage [ˈheritidʒ] n. 遺產，繼承物；傳統

【例】Many of the children were later adopted, losing their connection to their families and heritage. 許多孩子後來被收養，和曾經的家人和傳統不再緊密相聯。(NPR)

【用】　新聞中常見片語：cultural heritage 文化遺產；natural heritage 自然遺產。其同義詞有：tradition，legacy。

## various [ˈveəriəs] a. 各種各樣的

【例】Firstly, we hope consumers do not use the same pass code for various accounts online. 首先，我們希望用戶不要對網上不同的帳戶設置相同的密碼。(CRI)

【用】　相當於 all kinds of，通常放在名詞前面，如：various meetings 各種會議。

## regular [ˈregjulə] a. 規則的，有規律的；經常的

【例】Venice gets regular flooding at this time of year but this was the fourth deepest on record. 威尼斯在每年這個時候都會發生洪災，但這次是有記錄以來的第四次。(BBC)

【用】 其反義詞為 irregular，表示「不規則的」。

## suppose [sə'pəuz] v. 推測，猜想；假設

【例】Government agencies that were supposed to monitor and regulate fishing were often doing a lousy job. 政府機構應該對漁業進行監督和管理，但他們往往做得不盡人意。(NPR)

【用】 可用於句首，引導祈使句，表「讓......」。其常用派生詞有：supposed 假定的；supposition 假定；猜測。

## decline [di'klain] v./n. 下降，減少；拒絕

【例】Because a study finds that elderly people who played a video game for at least 10 hours gained three years of protection from cognitive decline. 因為研究發現，那些玩電子遊戲長達 10 小時的老人，其認知能力下降的時間被推遲了 3 年。(Scientific American)

【用】 decline 表「拒絕」是較為委婉的，而 refuse 則更為直接。在表「下降」時，有 on the decline 在衰退中；economic decline 經濟衰退。

## allegation [ˌæli'geiʃən] n. 指控；宣稱，聲稱

【例】Police here in Britain have arrested the editor of a national newspaper, his deputy and two other former editors over phone hacking allegations. 英國警方已經逮捕了一家全國性報紙的主編、副主編及其他兩名前任編輯，他們被指控進行電話竊聽。(BBC)

【用】 常用於法律領域，如：bribery allegation 賄賂指控；allegation of defendant 被告的申訴。

## strategy ['strætidʒi] n. 策略，策略

【例】Among other things, the president denounced changing strategy including less reliance on unmanned drone to target enemies. 除其他事項外，總統還對策略的改

變予以譴責，比如減少使用無人機定位敵人。(NPR)

【用】 該詞可用於經濟、政治、軍事等多個領域，如：marketing strategy 行銷策略；branding strategy 品牌化策略；dominant strategy 優勢策略。

## career [kəˈriə] n. 職業，事業，生涯

【例】 He joined the Washington Post where he did work the rest of his newspaper career and became one of most influential political journalists in the country. 他加入了《華盛頓郵報》並將餘生的報業生涯全部貢獻在這裡，成為了全國最有影響力的政治記者之一。(NPR)

【用】 常見片語：career objective 職業目標；career development 職業規劃。

## vulnerable [ˈvʌlnərəbl] a. 易受攻擊的

【例】Analysts say the oil boom will give the U.S. economy a competitive advantage with cheap energy supplies no longer vulnerable to global geopolitics. 分析師說，油價暴漲將對美國經濟帶來競爭優勢，因為廉價的能源供應將不再輕易受到全球地緣政治的影響。(VOA)

【用】 多用於生態環境、經濟政治競爭等領域。vulnerable groups 就表示「弱勢群體」。常見用法為 be vulnerable to 表示「易受……攻擊的」。

## require [riˈkwaiə] v. 需要；要求，命令

【例】He also announced plans to cut another 30,000 public-sector jobs and added that civil servants would be required to work an extra hour a day. 他還宣布了削減另外 3 萬個公共部門職位的計畫，並要求公務員每天額外工作一小時。(BBC)

【用】 常用派生詞有：required 必需的；requirement 必需品。

## understand [ˌʌndəˈstænd] v. 理解，懂，明白

【例】 Just like the many meditators we have often seen, we can't understand why they can still maintain a healthy condition despite no eating and drinking. 我們經常看到許多冥想者，很難理解在沒有進食、喝水的條件下，他們為什麼仍然可以保持健康的身體狀態。(CRI)

【用】 常見派生詞：understandable 可以理解的；understanding 諒解。

## intend [in'tend] v. 打算

【例】They are intended to alert caregivers of potential problems. 他們打算讓看護者意識到潛在的問題。(NPR)

【用】「打算做某事」用 intend to do sth.；與 for 連用時，則表示「為......做準備」。

## variety [vəˈraiəti] n. 種類；多樣化

【例】The environment is changing to the point where farmers can no longer maintain the seeds of the varieties that they always used. 環境變化很大，使農民再也不能繼續使用他們曾經用過的種子品種。(VOA)

【用】 是 various 的名詞形式。常見搭配為：variety of 各種各樣的。

## minority [maiˈnɔrəti] n. 少數；少數民族

【例】The deal will see Hansen take the Maloof family's 53% share of the team as well as minority owner Bob Hernreich's 12% stake. 這項交易見證了漢森接替馬魯夫家族在國王隊53%的股份以及僅占12%股份的小股東鮑勃·赫恩賴奇的股份。(CNN)

【用】 與其相對的為 majority「多數」。常用 ethnic minority 表示「少數民族」。多用於宗教、民族、種族等領域。

## discover [disˈkʌvə] v. 發現，發覺

【例】If they discover it, they say it could be a nifty way to treat infestations without pesticides. 他們表示如果成功發現的話，那可能成為一個不用農藥對付蟲害的好辦

法。　(Scientific American)

【用】其名詞形式為 discovery，首字母大寫，也是著名電視節目名稱。


## devastate [ˈdevəsteit] v. 毀壞

【例】President Obama says he wants to avoid a repeat of last year's failure of several banks and other financial firms, which devastated the U.S. economy. 歐巴馬總統表示，他希望避免去年多家銀行及其他金融公司再次失敗的情況，因為那曾經摧毀了美國經濟。(VOA)

【用】同義詞：destroy，damage 都表示「毀壞」。


## manager [ˈmænidʒə] n. 經理，管理人

【例】The people of Switzerland have voted overwhelmingly to adopt measures restricting the salaries of top managers. 瑞士人民以壓倒性票數通過了限制高管薪水的措施。(BBC)

【用】源自 manage「管理」，其派生詞常用的還有 management「管理」。常用於經濟、商貿領域。

newspaper [ˈnjuːsWpeip4] n. 報紙

【例】It's expensive to tie up reporters on intensive projects, and newspaper budgets are tight. 讓記者為密集型專案工作的成本是昂貴的，而報紙的預算很緊張。(NPR)

【用】新聞中常用片語：newspaper reporter 新聞記者；newspaper report 新聞報導。注意：「看」報用 read，在報紙「上」用 in。


## proper [ˈprɔpə] a. 合適的，正當的

【例】With the proper use of technology, we will be able to say we have a degree of border security that will enable people to move toward a path to citizenship. 隨著技術的恰當利用，我們就能在一定程度上保障邊境安全，進而使人們能夠享受合法公民身分的權利。(VOA)

【用】 常作定語，修飾名詞，如：proper time 適當的時間；proper chance 適合的機會；proper operation 正確操作。

## positive [ˈpɔzətiv] a. 積極的；正的；明確的

【例】The key point I'm making right now is that the economy is moving in a positive direction. 我現在要說的關鍵問題是經濟正朝著積極的方向發展。(BBC)

【用】 其反義詞為 negative「消極的」。片語 positive response 表示「積極的回應」。

# Level 11

## refuse [riˈfjuːz] v. 拒絕

【例】The group has refused discussions with the United States and Israel. 該團體拒絕與美國和以色列開展討論。(VOA)

【用】 作動詞時，其名詞形式為 refusal「拒絕」。通常用 refuse to do sth. 拒絕做某事。

## commerce [ˈkɔməːs] n. 貿易，商業

【例】The Commerce Department says sales rose at 0.1% in April as more people purchased clothes and cars. 商務部稱，四月份的銷售額增長了 0.1%，因為更多的人購買了衣服和汽車。(NPR)

【用】 固定用法：Commerce Department 商務部。常見拓展詞：commercial 商業的；commercialize 使商業化。

## spread [spred] v. 展開；散布 n. 傳播

【例】Health officials don't know much about how the virus spreads, but at this point, travel warnings have not been issued. 衛生部官員對於病毒的傳播方式尚不清楚，但目前還沒有發布有關旅行的警告。(CNN)

【用】 spread 一般用於修飾消息、疾病、味道等的「蔓延，擴散」，可用於被動語態。片語有：spread out 展開；spread over 遍布於。

## daily [ˈdeili] a. 每日的 ad. 每日 n. 日報

【例】For the first time in human history, daily measures of CO2, which is an important factor in global warming, have topped 400 parts per million. 二氧化碳的排放是全球變暖的一個重要因素，其每日測量值在人類歷史上首次超過百萬分之四百。(BBC)

【用】 與 monthly，yearly 一樣，表示事物的週期性。

## explain [ikˈsplein] v. 解釋，說明

【例】The White House cited the independent report in explaining why the president signed the bill. 白宮引用了一份獨立報告來解釋總統為何簽署了這項法案。(BBC)

【用】 常見片語：explain oneself 為自己辯解；explain clearly 闡明。其名詞形式為 explanation 表示「解釋；說明」。

## fraud [frɔːd] n. 詐騙，欺騙；騙子

【例】Football's world governing body FIFA (Federation International Football Association) has provisionally suspended an executive committee member accused of fraud. 世界足球管理機構——國際足聯，暫時對一名被控有欺詐罪的執行委員會委員實施停職處分。(BBC)

【用】 常用於經濟犯罪話題中，如：accounting fraud 做假帳；credit fraud 信用欺詐；charity fraud 詐捐門。也會在體育競技中出現，如：soccer fraud 黑哨。

## audience [ˈɔːdiəns] n. 聽眾，觀眾

【例】The performances have been widely acclaimed by audiences and critics alike. 表演受到了觀眾和評論家的廣泛好評。(CRI)

【用】 target audience 指「目標觀眾」，經濟領域，也指「目標消費者」。廣播、電視尤其注重的「收視率」則為 audience rating。

## certain [ˈsɜːtən] a. 某種；肯定的，確信的

【例】He says there no definite answer on why people on certain age group are more vulnerable. 他說，關於特定年齡段的人更易感染原因，現在還沒有確切的答案。(CRI)

【用】 常見片語：a certain extent 一定程度上；for certain 肯定地；certain of 確信；under certain circumstance 在某種情況下。

## maintain [menˈtein] v. 維持;維修,保養

【例】Foreign policy analysts say Mr. Obama's trip is mainly about maintaining the alliance—or dropping in on friends. 外交政策分析人士說,歐巴馬先生此行主要是為了維護聯盟關係,也可以說是拜訪朋友。(VOA)

【用】 表「維護」時,有 maintain world peace 維護世界和平,常見於國際會議中;表「保養」時,可用被動語態。

## ambitious [æmˈbiʃəs] a. 有抱負的,雄心勃勃的;宏大的

【例】The Australian parliament has rejected government plans to introduce ambitious carbon trading scheme to tackle global warming. 澳洲議會否決了政府利用宏偉的碳交易計畫來應對全球變暖的方案。(BBC)

【用】 該詞源於 ambition「野心;抱負」,其副詞詞性為 ambitiously。一般用於商業、政治等競爭領域,如:ambitious plan 雄心勃勃的目標。

## legislation [ˌledʒisˈleiʃən] n. 立法;法律,法規

【例】The bill passed the Senate late yesterday and President Obama is expected to sign the legislation today. 昨天晚些時候參議院通過了該法案,預計歐巴馬總統今天將簽署該立法。(NPR)

【用】 主要用於法律、政府領域,如:labour legislation 勞工法。常用派生詞有:legislative 立法權;legislature 立法機關;legislator 立法者。

## coup [kuː] n. 政變

【例】A coup attempt appears to be under way in Niger. 一場政變正在尼日爾進行。(BBC)

【用】 通常用於政治、軍事領域,如:military coup 軍事政變;armed coup 武裝政變。

## present [ˈprezənt] a. 出席的 n. 現在 v. 提出

【例】It is to be presented to African leaders at their upcoming summit in Ethiopia. 在衣索比亞即將舉行的峰會上，它將被提交給非洲國家領導人。(VOA)

【用】 常用片語：at present 現在；present situation 現狀。作動詞時，present oneself 表示「出席」，而作名詞，表「禮物」時，與 gift 同義。

## advance [ədˈvæns] v./n. 前進 a. 預先的

【例】Reservations have to be made months in advance for menus that cost in excess of $260. 超過 260 美元的菜品必須提前幾個月預訂。(BBC)

【用】 常用片語：in advance 提前。advance 作動詞時，有 advance on 或 advance toward 的表達，指「向……前進」，可用於軍事領域。

## capacity [kəˈpæsəti] n. 能力，容量

【例】It's hoped the plant's capacity will reach 500 megawatts by 2020. 工廠的生產能力有望在 2020 年達到 500 兆瓦。(BBC)

【用】 可用來形容工廠的生產能力，即「production capacity」；也可以描述環境的承載力，即「environmental capacity」。

## behavior [biˈheivjə] n. 行為；舉止

【例】These disorders generally affect social interaction, behavior and language. 這些疾病通常影響一個人的社交生活、行為舉止和語言表達。(CNN)

【用】 可用多種形容詞修飾 behavior，如：good，aggressive，criminal 等。該詞源於動詞 behave「表現」，常用 behave oneself 表示「讓某人好好表現」。

## certify [ˈsə:tifai] v. 證明，保證；證實

【例】The constitutional court has two weeks to certify the provisional results. 憲法法院有兩週的時間來證實暫定的結果。(VOA)

【用】 與 prove，demonstrate 意思相近。prove 最常用，demonstrate 常用於理論、學說、定律的證明，而 certify 側重具有法律效益。

## credit [ˈkredit] n. 信用；貸款 v. 把......歸於

【例】Already pressure is mounting on Portugal which has also seen its credit rating downgraded today, although it remains above junk status. 葡萄牙已經倍感壓力，因為今天其信貸評級也被降級，雖然還沒有被調至垃圾級別。(BBC)

【用】 主要用於金融、銀行領域。常見片語：credit account 信用帳戶；credit card 信用卡；credit rating 信用等級。

## calm [kɑːm] a. 平靜的 v.（使）平靜；（使）鎮靜

【例】He says they tell him to calm down, get married, smoke a water pipe and not think about anything. 他說，他們告訴他要冷靜下來，把婚結了，抽一管水煙，不要亂想。(NPR)

【用】 常見搭配：calm down 冷靜下來；keep calm 保持冷靜。另外，Calm down. 可以獨立成句，表示「冷靜冷靜。」

## culture [ˈkʌltʃə] n. 文化

【例】The long history of Chinese opera has given rise to numerous regional branches, each of which is imprinted with the distinctive local culture of the region. 歷史悠久的中華戲劇在眾多地區都有衍生的分支，每一個分支都烙有獨特的當地文化印記。(CRI)

【用】 culture 前可以用形容詞來限定，如：traditional culture 傳統文化；western culture 西方文化；enterprise culture 企業文化。

## foster [ˈfɔstə] v. 培養；領養 a. 收養的

【例】But they have told NPR in the past that they strongly reject the notion that the state has a financial incentive to place children in foster care. 但之前他們已經告訴過美國國家公共電台，他們堅決反對該州為寄養兒童提供財政獎勵的想法。(NPR)

【用】 與 foster 類似，nurture 也可表示「培養」。但 nurture 的客體側重是人，而 foster 可以是人，也可是物。

## construction [kənˈstrʌkʃən] n. 建設；結構；建造

【例】Growth in the UK construction sector slowed in April, according to a closely-watched survey. 一份備受觀注的調查顯示：4 月份英國的建築業增長開始減緩。(BBC)

【用】 常用於城市建設 (urban construction) 領域：in construction 建設中；economic construction 經濟建設。

## criticism [ˈkritisizəm] n. 評判，批評

【例】Turkey's Prime Minister has rejected criticism of police violence against protesters. 土耳其總理反對警方使用武力鎮壓抗議者。(VOA)

【用】 常見片語：literary criticism 文藝評論；objective criticism 客觀批評。在修飾「批評」的程度時，可用 heavy 和 light。

## threaten [ˈθretən] v. 威脅，恐嚇

【例】Many of the world's coral reefs are threatened by ocean acidification and pollution, among other things. 除其他方面外，世界上很多珊瑚礁還受到海洋酸化和海洋汙染的威脅。(VOA)

【用】 常用 threaten sb. with sth. 表示「以......來威脅某人」。

## formal [ˈfɔːməl] a. 正式的，正規的

【例】Business manners are renowned for being very formal. 商務禮儀以其正規而著稱。(BBC)

【用】 用於嚴肅的大型場合，如：formal contract 正式合約；formal organization 正規組織；formal training 正規訓練。

## comment ['kɔment] n./v. 評論

【例】Instead, he struggled to explain his comment that he's「not concerned about the very poor.」相反，他試圖解釋他那條「不關心窮人」的評論。(NPR)

【用】 作名詞時，有 fair comment 公正評論。作動詞時，常用 comment on... 表「對……的評論」。口語中，No comment. 表示「無可奉告。」

## boost [buːst] v. 提高，增加 n. 增加

【例】It has 35 weekly return fl ights to four cities, and plans to boost it to 55 services within two years. 該航空公司每週有 35 趟飛往 4 座城市的往返航班，並計畫在 2 年內增加到 55 個。(CRI)

【用】 表資料、進度、過程的「迅猛增長」，也可表示「促進」，如：boost local business 促進地方商業。

## tragedy ['trædʒidi] n. 悲劇；災難

【例】It may be hard to comprehend the twisted logic that led to this tragedy. 造成這場悲劇的扭曲邏輯可能很難被世人理解。(BBC)

【用】 用於表演、文藝領域，但也可用來形容事件，如：tragedy life 悲劇的一生。反義詞為 comedy「喜劇」。

## determine [diˈtəːmin] v. 確定；決定

【例】They are these little pieces of code that determine the characteristics of living things, and all living things have them. 正是這些小小的密碼決定著生物的特徵，並且所有的生物都擁有這樣的密碼。(CNN)

【用】 常用搭配：determine to do sth. 決定做某事。decide 表「決定」，側重經過思考、討論；

determine 表「決定」，強調深思熟慮過並付諸行動。

## amid [əˈmid] prep. 在......中間，被......圍繞

【例】The Russian city of Sochi is saving this year's snow amid fears there won't be enough for next year's Winter Olympics. 因為擔心明年冬奧會時沒有足夠的雪，俄羅斯城市索契正在儲藏今年的雪。(CRI)

【用】 同義詞辨析：between「在（兩者）之間」，among「在（三者或以上）之間」，amid 指在某個地方的中間或被某個東西包圍著。

## reserve [riˈzəːv] v. 保留；預訂 n. 儲備（物）

【例】Over $40 billion worth of the new shares will go to the government to pay for the right to exploit Brazil's offshore reserves. 價值超過 400 億美元的新股票將流向政府，用於購買巴西近海石油儲存的開採權。(BBC)

【用】 reserve，preserve，conserve 均有「保留」之意。reserve 為正式用詞；preserve 側重為防止損害、變質等而保存；conserve 一般指保存自然資源，保全人的精力、力量等。

## crowd [kraud] n. 人群，群眾 v. 擠

【例】Crowds of people have listened to speeches, demonstrated and protested here. 成群的人就是在這裡聆聽了演講，並舉行了示威抗議。(VOA)

【用】 the crowd 表示「人群」。

## promote [prəuˈməut] v. 促進；提升

【例】So that is the reason why we are here to promote peace. 所以這就是我們為什麼在這裡促進和平。(BBC)

【用】 多數用在工作晉升的場合。promote sb. to sth. 提升某人至某職位。其名詞形式為 promotion，gain promotion 獲得晉升。

## insurance [inˈʃuərəns] n. 保險，保險費

【例】This fall people can begin signing up for insurance exchanges to get health coverage. 今年秋天，民眾就可以開始到保險交易所註冊以獲得健康保險。(NPR)

【用】 通常用於金融行業，如：insurance company 保險公司；personal insurance 人身保險。注意：保險費用 insurance premium，而不用 fee。

## analysis [əˈnæləsis] n. 分析

【例】The bill would require the ICC(International Chamber of Commerce) to do a cost benefit analysis when writing new regulations. 該法案規定國際商會在擬定新規時要進行成本效益分析。(NPR)

【用】 常見於資料統計、科學計算、學術交流等領域，如：statistical analysis 統計分析；case analysis 個案分析。其動詞形式為 analyze。

## export [ikˈspɔːt] v./n. 出口（物），輸出（品）

【例】Its garment industry makes up nearly 80 percent of the country's exports. 該國的服裝業占出口總額的近 80%。(CNN)

【用】 export licence 出口許可；export trade 出口貿易。反義詞為 import「進口」，都用於經濟、商貿領域。

## allegedly [əˈledʒidli] ad. 依其申述；據稱

【例】The man, Bryce Reed, is being held for allegedly possessing a destructive device. 該男子名為布萊斯·里德，據說他因持有破壞性的危險裝置而被拘留。(BBC)

【用】 該詞後面一般加動詞分詞形式。其動詞形式為 allege，表示「宣稱」，常用於司法、犯罪領域。

## distribution [ˌdistriˈbjuːʃən] n. 分發，分配；分布

【例】English is the dominant language of the Internet, which skews the language distribution in bilingual cities like Montreal. 英語作為網路的主要語言，讓蒙特利爾這樣的雙語城市的語言分布情況發生了改變。(Scientific American)

【用】　常見搭配有：distribution of population 人口分布；distribution of wealth 財產分配。其動詞形式為 distribute，表「分配」。

## awareness [əˈweənis] n. 意識；察覺

【例】It says awareness and open discussion of the problem is key to prevention. 它表示，能夠意識到問題並對其進行公開討論是預防的關鍵。(VOA)

【用】　表示人各方面的意識，如：environmental awareness 環境意識；political awareness 政治覺悟；general awareness 普遍意識。

## investigate [inˈvestigeit] v. 調查

【例】Ian Lipkin is leading a team of scientists at Columbia University to investigate the virus, which is in the same family as SARS and the common cold. 伊恩‧利普金正帶領著哥倫比亞大學的一個科學家團隊研究這種類型的病毒，這種病毒與非典型肺炎及普通感冒病毒同屬一個族群。(CNN)

【用】　表示「對......進行調查」，用 investigate into。investigate 的物件可以是科學課題，也可以是犯罪案件。其名詞形式為 investigation。

## politics [ˈpɔlitiks] n. 政治

【例】 Democrats charge that Republicans are playing politics at a time when lawmakers should be focused on the economy. 民主黨指責共和黨，在立法者應當專注於經濟發展時卻在玩政治把戲。(NPR)

【用】　在黨派鬥爭、政治動盪主題的新聞中，常有 play politics「玩弄政治權術」。politics 在句中多為貶義。

## broadcast [ˈbrɔːdkæst] n. 廣播 v. 廣播，播放

【例】This reunion of our former president and South-African president was broadcast on TV. 在電視上播放了前總統與南非總統的這次聚會。(VOA)

【用】 作為媒體的一種形式，通常用 on air 表示正在直播過程中。常見搭配有：broadcast station 廣播電臺；broadcast news 廣播新聞。

## multiple [ˈmʌltɪpl] a. 多樣的；多重的 n. 倍數

【例】She suffered for more than decades with multiple sclerosis. 她患多發性硬化症已經幾十年了。(NPR)

【用】 該詞用途較廣，如：a multiple crash 連環撞車事故；multiple shop 連鎖商店；multiple choice 多項選擇；multiple sclerosis 多發性硬化症。

## diet [ˈdaɪət] n. 日常飲食；規定飲食 v. 節食

【例】But now researchers have discovered a way to enhance a detection dog's schnoz: change its diet. 但現在研究人員已發現一種使探測犬嗅覺更靈敏的方法：改變其飲食。(Scientific American)

【用】 on a diet 固定搭配，既可指「指定的飲食」，也可指「在節食中」。常出現在與健康相關的主題新聞中。

## serve [səːv] v. 為......服務；擔任；服役

【例】A teenager who admitted murdering 58-yearold Seamus Fox in west Belfast last year is told he must serve at least 13 years in prison. 這名少年承認自己去年在西貝爾法斯特謀殺了 58 歲的謝默斯‧福克斯，他被告知必須要在監獄服刑至少 13 年。(BBC)

【用】 通常用 serve as 或 serve in 表示「在......供職；在......服役」。

## effective [iˈfektiv] a. 有效的，生效的

【例】It's a nice try and points to an effective way of reviving and promoting Chinese opera to a wider audience. 這是一次很好的嘗試，它為復興和推廣中國戲曲提供了有效方法。(CRI)

【用】 該詞用途廣泛，如：effective measure 有效措施；effective method 有效方法，均可用於經濟、政治、文化、生活等多個領域。

## resign [riˈzain] v. 辭職

【例】Some observers said the comment was a reply to his surprising decision to resign. 一些觀察者表示該評論是對他突然決定辭職行為的一個答覆。(VOA)

【用】 用於企業、政府對職務的卸任，其名詞形式為 resignation。另外，resign oneself to sth./doing sth. 表示「聽任，順從」。

## surface [ˈsəːfis] n. 表面，面

【例】After about 10 months, the tube pops off the shark and floats to the surface, beaming all the information via satellite to Campana. 大約 10 個月後，管子從鯊魚身上脫落漂浮到水面上，並透過衛星將所有資訊傳送給坎帕納。(NPR)

【用】 on the surface 表示「在表面上，從外表上」。還可引申為「地面」，用於軍事領域，如：surface-to-air 地對空的（導彈）。

## strength [streŋθ] n. 力量；強度

【例】The former state-owned carrier once symbolized the strength of the country's postwar economic boom. 之前的國有航空公司曾一度是國家戰後經濟復甦的象徵符號。(VOA)

【用】 與 strength 相似，power、force、vigor 都可表示「力量」。但 strength 和 power 都可指物體或人體的內在力量，而 force 和 vigor 則強調能量的應用。

## cite [saɪt] v. 引用 n. 引文

【例】Mr Green says he can cite 57 laws that have corrupted Britain in that time. 格林先生表示他可以引用 57 條在當時曾導致英國腐敗的法律。

【用】 主要用於公開講話、正式文章中的引用，其名詞形式為 citation「引文，語錄」。cite 還可用於法律領域，表示「傳喚」。

## ban [bæn] v. 禁止 n. 禁止，禁令

【例】Some opponents of these GMOs(Genetically Modified Organisms) want them banned. 一部分轉基因生物的反對者希望禁止它們。(CNN)

【用】 作動詞時，「禁止某人做某事」用 ban sb. from doing sth.。作名詞時，表示「對某方面的禁令」，用介詞 on，如：a ban on smoking 吸菸禁令。

## isolate [ˈaɪsəleɪt] v. 孤立；隔絕

【例】The restaurant says it's working with agency staff to try to isolate the source of the infection. 餐廳表示他們正與政府機構的人員合作，試圖隔離感染源。(BBC)

【用】 常用搭配：isolate from 從……脫離出來。其形容詞形式為 isolated，表示「隔離的，孤立的」。

## appear [əˈpɪə] v. 出現；好像

【例】Senator Derban also appeared on Fox news Sunday. 參議員德爾班也出現在周日的福克斯新聞中。(NPR)

【用】 常用句式：It appears as if，後面加從句，表示「看來……」。常用片語：appear to「似乎」。

## dominate [ˈdɒmɪneɪt] v. 支配，控制；在……中占首要地位

【例】Congress is not in session this week so investigations into recent scandals continue to dominate the Washington political agenda. 本周國會沒有舉行會議，所

以近期華盛頓的政治議程仍以對醜聞的調查為主。(VOA)

【用】 通常用來形容龐大機構、組織或團體。同義詞：possess 持有，占有。

## advisor [əd'vaizə] n. 顧問

【例】In Washington President Obama's top security advisor said things appeared to be moving in the right direction. 在華盛頓，歐巴馬總統的高級安全顧問表示事情似乎正朝著正確的方向發展。(BBC)

【用】 源於動詞 advice「建議」。常見片語：financial advisor 財務顧問；investment advisor 投資顧問。

# Level 12

## session [ˈseʃən] n. 會議,會期;一段時間

【例】The session was not included on Obama's daily public schedule for Thursday. 此次會議沒有納入歐巴馬週四的每日公開日程之中。(VOA)

【用】 常用片語:in session 在開庭;在開會;special session 特別會議;regular session 例會。session 比 meeting 更為正式。

## rally [ˈræli] n. 集會 v. 集合;重新振作

【例】Massed rallies have been taken place across Portugal to demonstrate against the government's austerity measures. 葡萄牙各地舉行了大規模集會,人們示威抗議政府的財政緊縮政策。(BBC)

【用】 作名詞時,除了表示「集會」,還可用於體育競賽領域,表示「拉力賽」,如:Rally Championship 冠軍拉力賽。

## accountable [əˈkauntəbl] a. 應負責的;(對自己的行為)應作解釋的

【例】The FDA(Food and Drug Administration) says the rules will hold importers accountable for observing the same safety standards as domestic producers. 美國食品和藥物管理局表示,這些規則將使進口商負責遵守與國內生產者同樣的安全標準。(VOA)

【用】 常用句式:accountable to sb. for sth. ......負責。其名詞形式為 accountability 有責任。

## represent [ˌrepriˈzent] v. 代表;表示;描繪

【例】They may represent a new way to monitor climate change. 它們可能代表著一種監測氣候變化的新方式。(Scientific American)

【用】 常用搭配:represent for 代表;象徵。其名詞形式為 representation「代表;表述」,在企業、商務領域常用 make a representation「做報告」。

## graduate ['grædʒueit] v. 畢業 n. 畢業生 a. 研究生的

【例】NPR's Jim Howard reports college graduates hoping to enter the job market still face a daunting economy. 美國國家公共電台的吉姆‧霍華德報導，那些期待進入就業市場的大學畢業生們仍面臨著嚴峻的經濟形勢。(NPR)

【用】 graduate student 通常指「研究生」，而「本科生」為 undergraduate。「從......畢業」可以用 graduate from，也可以用 graduate at。

## perform [pə'fɔːm] v. 做；表演；執行

【例】All 39 women walked through portals of varying sizes while performing a distracting memorization task. 所有的 39 名婦女走過大小不等的門並同時執行一個分散記憶力的任務。(Scientific American)

【用】 在醫學領域，perform an operation 表示「做手術」。perform 其名詞形式 performance 為「表演」的意思。

## indeed [in'diːd] ad. 真正地；確實

【例】One of the first things that they learned was yes, indeed, humans were capable of reacting to situations unanticipated. 確實，他們首先學到事情就是人類確實能夠應付意料之外的狀況。(VOA)

【用】 口語中，indeed 一般用於對事物的再次肯定語氣，用於句首或句尾。諺語有：A friend in need is a friend indeed. 患難見真情。

## ancient ['einʃənt] a. 古代的，古老的

【例】Archaeologists in Mexico say they've uncovered three ancient playing fields at a pre-Hispanic site in the eastern state of Veracruz. 墨西哥考古學家稱，在維拉克魯斯州東部的前西班牙時期遺址中發掘了 3 處古競技場。(BBC)

【用】 常用片語：ancient history 古代歷史；ancient Greece 古希臘；ancient times 古代。一般用於文化、歷史、科研領域。

## round [raund] a. 圓的 ad. 在附近 n. (一)場

【例】He was eliminated in the very second round. 他在第二輪比賽中就被淘汰了。(VOA)

【用】 形狀相關詞：square 正方形；rectangle 長方形；ellipse 橢圓；triangle 三角形；diamond 菱形；sector 扇形。

## position [pə'ziʃən] n. 位置；職位；立場

【例】They say the body position may be linked to development in the brain. 他們稱體位可能與大腦的發育有關。(VOA)

【用】 常用片語：in one's position 以某人的立場；position on 看法，觀點；in position 在位。

## opponent [ə'pəunənt] n. 對手；反對者 a. 對立的

【例】 Opponents of the practice has staged large rallies, for occasionally it turned violent. 該做法的反對者舉行了大型集會，因為該做法有時會引發暴力衝突。(NPR)

【用】 在政治新聞中，常見片語：political opponent 政敵。同義詞有：rival、enemy。

## contact ['kɔntækt] n./v. 接觸；互通資訊

【例】Three people who have had close contact with him have not exhibited any abnormal symptoms. 與他有過密切接觸的三個人都沒有任何異常症狀。(CRI)

【用】 常用片語：make contact 保持聯繫；contact with sb. 與某人保持聯繫。另外，contact lens 專指「隱形眼鏡」。

## volunteer [ˌvɔlən'tiə] n. 志願者 v. 自願(做)

【例】The volunteers came into Rogalski's memory lab and were given a barrage of tests. 志願者們來到洛加爾斯基的記憶實驗室接受一連串的測試。(NPR)

【用】 通常用作名詞，如：volunteer services 志願者服務；volunteer work 義工。另外，

volunteer 用於軍事領域，專指「志願軍」。

## remove [ri'mu:v] v. 移開；消除；免除

【例】Thousands of volunteers turned out on a recent weekend to remove the trash that has been deposited by winter rain storms. 近期數千名志願者在週末出動，清除下冬季暴雨時堆積的垃圾。(VOA)

【用】 常用 remove from 表示「移開」，引申為「遠離」；remove oneself 引申理解為「走開」。

## commitment [kə'mitmənt] n. 承諾，許諾；獻身

【例】Its commitment to that policy is now being severely tested. 它對於該政策方針的堅守正在經受嚴峻的考驗。(BBC)

【用】 表示「做出承諾」時，用動詞 make，make a commitment。

## reveal [ri'vi:l] v. 揭示；揭露；顯示

【例】While Big Data can uncover correlations between data points, it doesn't reveal causation. 雖然大資料能夠揭示資料點之間的相關性，但它無法揭示其因果關係。(NPR)

【用】 其同義詞有：uncover，expose。uncover 指「移去遮蓋物」，可指陰謀、祕密等；expose 指「暴露在外」，可指醜聞、壞人或陰謀；reveal 指顯示一直隱藏或隱祕的東西。

## interior [in'tiəriə] n. 內部 a. 內部的；國內的

【例】More detailed knowledge of the solar interior has actually deepened some other scientific mysteries. 隨著對太陽內部構造瞭解增多，其他一些科學奧祕顯得更有神祕感。(Scientific American)

【用】 反義詞為 exterior「外部的；國外的」。在政治方面，the interior 可特指「內政」。

## synthetic [sɪnˈθɛtɪk] a. 合成的，人造的

【例】A voice—even a synthetic one—is packed with information our brains are programmed to decode, like gender or age. 任何一個聲音，甚至是合成音都飽含人類大腦需要解碼的資訊，性別和年齡也是如此。(NPR)

【用】 可用於科技、醫學、生物等多個領域，如：synthetic diamond 人造鑽石；synthetic rubber 合成橡膠。其相對詞為 natural「天然的」。

## salt [sɔːlt] n. 鹽

【例】 Many studies have shown that reducing salt or sodium in the diet can lower the risk of stroke and other health problems. 許多研究表明，降低飲食中鹽分或鈉的攝取能夠降低患中風和引起其他健康問題的風險。(VOA)

【用】 salt 指「鹽」，但也可引申為動詞「用鹽醃制」。相關片語有：worth (one's) salt 有能力的；the salt of the earth 社會中堅。

## reporter [rɪˈpɔːtə] n. 記者

【例】 Reuters and Bloomberg News have beefed up their enterprise reporting and hired many experienced newspaper reporters. 路透社和彭博新聞社已加強了各自的報導強度，並聘請了很多有經驗的新聞記者。(NPR)

【用】 該詞用於媒體領域，TV reporter 電視記者；news reporter 新聞記者。注意：在法律領域，reporter 表示「法庭筆錄員」。

## suspect [səˈspɛkt] v. 懷疑 n. 嫌疑犯

【例】It was named after a Supreme Court decision in 1966 that found that a robbery suspect named Ernesto Miranda had been wrongfully convicted. 它根據最高法院在 1966 年的一項判決而命名，在該判決中一個名叫埃內斯托·米蘭達的搶劫嫌疑犯受到了誤判。

【用】 作動詞時，suspect of「懷疑......」；作名詞時，crime suspect 犯罪嫌疑人。其形容詞

形式為 suspicious「可疑的」。

## tourist [ˈtuərist] n. 旅遊者，觀光者

【例】Chinese tourists have overtaken Germans and Americans as the world's biggest spending travelers. 中國遊客已經超過德國和美國的遊客，成為全世界消費高的。(BBC)

【用】 用於旅遊業的新聞中，常見搭配有：tourist resources 旅游資源；tourist attraction 觀光勝地；outbound tourist 出境游客。

## vehicle [ˈviːikl] n. 交通工具，車輛；媒介

【例】People who trade in their animals will receive money, a new vehicle or help with a business plan. 用動物做交易的人們將會得到金錢和新車一輛，獲得一份商業計畫的協助。(BBC)

【用】 vehicle 是車輛的總稱。motor vehicle 機動車輛；passenger vehicle 客運車輛；electric vehicle 電動車。

## mass [mæs] n. 塊；品質 a. 大量的

【例】The Potato Famine in Ireland killed a million people and led to mass emigration. 愛爾蘭大飢荒造成了 100 萬人的死亡，並導致大規模移民。(Scientific American)

【用】 常用搭配：a mass of 大量……；in the mass 總體上說；mass media 大眾傳播媒介。

## definitely [ˈdefinitli] ad. 明確地，確切地

【例】Guo says the physical difficulties onboard were definitely not the toughest he has endured. 郭表示身體病痛絕對不是他在船上所經歷過的最艱難的事。(CRI)

【用】 對一般疑問句的肯定回答，可單獨成句，譯為「當然。」而 Definitely not. 表示「絕對不會。」常用於動詞之前。

## acknowledge [əkˈnɔlidʒ] v. 承認；對......表示感謝

【例】The current Socialist leader Martine Aubry acknowledged defeat after today's second round of voting in a primary election. 現任社會黨領導人馬蒂娜·歐布里在今天初選的第二輪投票後認輸。(BBC)

【用】 表「承認」時，有 be glad to acknowledge 很樂意承認和 refuse to acknowledge 拒絕承認；表「感謝」時，其名詞形式 acknowledgment「致謝」，常出現在論文最後。

## associate [əˈsəuʃieit] v. 把......聯繫在一起；聯合 n. 夥伴

【例】Most of the cases and illnesses have been associated with the elderly and those with preexisting or severe underlying medical conditions. 大多數的病例與疾病都發生在老年人及那些有病史或有嚴重潛在病情的人們身上。(CNN)

【用】 表「聯繫」時，有 associate with 將......聯繫起來；而 associate oneself with sth. 表示「某人贊同某事」。

## underway [ˈʌndəˈwei] a. 正在進行中的

【例】With mopping up still underway, the authorities say they don't yet know the final cost of repairs. 清理工作仍在持續進行，當局表示他們還不清楚最終的修繕費用是多少。(BBC)

【用】 常用 get underway 表示「開始；啟程」。作名詞時，可表示「海底隧道」。

## agenda [əˈdʒendə] n. 議程；日常工作事項

【例】President Obama's trying to a shift focus back to his second term agenda. 歐巴馬總統試圖將焦點轉回到他第二任期的議程中。(NPR)

【用】 通常用於大型機構、企業、團體及政府等。常用搭配為 the item on the agenda 議程專案。

## direction [diˈrekʃən] n. 方向;指示;指導

【例】Testing a similar crystal, the team of scientists from Rennes University in France shows that by rotating it you can find the point where the two beams converge and that indicates the direction of the sun. 法國雷恩大學的科學家也測試了相似的水晶,他們表示透過將其旋轉,你可以找到兩個光束的聚點,這個聚點就指示著太陽的方向。(BBC)

【用】 常見片語:in the direction (of) ......的方向。其形容詞形式為 directional,表示「定向的」。

## collect [kəˈlekt] v. 收集

【例】The agents have also collected pieces of nylon black bag or backpack they suspect that has been used to carry the explosives. 特工們也收集了被懷疑用來攜帶炸藥的黑色尼龍包或背包的碎條。(CRI)

【用】 collect up 或 collect together 表示「收集」,可表示一種愛好,如:stamp collecting 集郵。

## propose [pr4uˈp4uz] v. 打算;求婚;提

【例】The president spoke at a meeting of a White House advisory panel set up to study the problems facing the middle class and to propose solutions. 總統在白宮顧問小組的一次會議上發表演講,該小組是為研究中產階級面臨的問題及提出相關解決方案而成立的。(VOA)

【用】 常見句型:sb. propose that... 某人提議......。該詞還可表示「求婚」,其名詞形式為 proposal「求婚(行動)」。另外,propose a toast 祝酒,通常用於聚會場合。

## benefit [ˈbenifit] n. 益處;津貼 v. 得益

【例】Officials said a deeper recession had resulted in more government spending on benefits and further recapitalization of troubled banks. 官方稱更嚴重的經濟衰退

使政府增加了在福利方面和進一步重組受困銀行的開支。(BBC)

【用】 作動詞時，常用 benefit from sb./sth. 從……受益；作名詞時，有 unemployment benefit 失業救濟；ecological benefit 生態效益。

## sink [siŋk] v. 下沉，沉沒 n. 水槽

【例】Many deep sinkholes have been sinking for over 10 years. 許多深層的汙水坑已經下沉了 10 餘年。(CNN)

【用】 片語 sink into 表示「沉入；落水」，注意其過去式為 sank，過去分詞為 sunk。

## extend [ik'stend] v. 延展，延長

【例】 In recent weeks the European Union and the United States voted to extend sanctions against South Africa's neighbor. 在最近幾週，歐盟和美國就延長對南非鄰國的制裁活動進行投票。(VOA)

【用】 同義詞為 enlarge、spread。其名詞形式為 extension「延長；範圍」。

## representative [ˌrepriˈzentətiv] n. 代表 a. 有代表性的，典型的

【例】Each user must agree to a two-year test period for the system, the representative said. 代表稱，每個用戶都必須接受為期兩年的系統測試期。(CNN)

【用】在國事訪問的新聞報導中，常有 a representative of... 表示「……的代表」。

## gross [grəus] n. 總額 a. 總的；粗野的

【例】And as a result the EU's seven-year budget will cost less than one percent of Europe's gross national income. 而且歐盟的 7 年預算將消耗不到百分之一的歐洲國民總收入。(VOA)

【用】 在經濟新聞中，出現的 GDP，GNP 分別表示 gross domestic product「國內生產總值」和 gross national product「國民生產總值」。

## album [ˈælbəm] n. 相冊；唱片，唱片集

【例】The Scottish singer Emeli Sande has beaten a record set by the Beatles of the album with the most consecutive weeks in the British top 10. 蘇格蘭歌手艾米麗‧桑迪的專輯在英國前十榜上連續停留的時間最長，打破了披頭四樂隊創下的紀錄。(BBC)

【用】 常見片語：photo album 相冊；record album 唱片。

## obtain [əbˈtein] v. 獲得，得到

【例】While urine may be a plentiful and less invasive way to obtain stem cells, some experts are skeptical about its value as a source of stem cells. 雖然可以從尿液中獲取充足的幹細胞且尿液對幹細胞的創傷程度較低，但一些專家懷疑尿液作為幹細胞來源的價值。(VOA)

【用】 obtain 用法比較正式，強調透過努力得到盼望已久的東西；gain 側重有意識的行動，取得某種成就或獲得某種利益或好處。

## clash [klæʃ] n. 衝突；撞擊聲 v. 發生衝突

【例】He's being impeached over his role in the death of 17 people last week in clashes between the police and landless farmers. 上週員警和失去土地的農民之間發生衝突，導致十七人死亡，他因在衝突中扮演的角色而被彈劾。(BBC)

【用】 常用片語：clash with sb./ sth. 與……發生衝突；culture clash 文化衝突。

## unique [juːˈniːk] a. 唯一的，獨一無二的

【例】It's what makes each species, each person unique from others. 它讓每個物種、每個人都與其他物種和其他人有所不同。(CNN)

【用】 同義詞有 individual，distinct，都指「獨特的，獨一無二的」。注意：在數學領域，unique 指「唯一性」，如 unique solution 唯一解。

## compare [kəmˈpeə] v./n. 比較，比喻

【例】Those with busy social lives were half as likely to develop dementia, compared with those with minimal social activities. 與那些很少有社交活動的人相比，那些忙於社交生活的人患痴呆症的可能性要減少一半。(NPR)

【用】 常見片語：compare with 與......相較；compare to 把......比作；compare notes 交換意見。

## overhaul [ˌəuvəˈhɔːl] v./n. 翻修；仔細檢查；革新

【例】Polls show majorities of Americans favor stricter gun laws and an immigration overhaul. 民意調查顯示，大多數美國人贊成實施更嚴格的槍支法以及對移民法案全面修訂。(VOA)

【用】 通常可指機器的大型整體檢修，如：major overhaul 全面檢修；complete overhaul 大修。

## complete [kəmˈpliːt] a. 十足的；完成的 v. 完成

【例】When he was away, renovation work was completed on the monastery. 在他離開的這段時間，修道院的修繕已徹底完工。(NPR)

【用】 作形容詞時，可作定語、表語，同義詞有 entire、whole；作動詞時，同義詞為 finish、end。

## attend [əˈtend] v. 出席，參加；照料

【例】President Obama has attended a dedication ceremony in Washington for a new memorial to the assassinated Martin Luther King. 歐巴馬總統在華盛頓出席了一個新的紀念館的落成典禮，該紀念館為了被暗殺的馬丁·路德·金恩建造。(BBC)

【用】 一般「出席」的場合，較為正式的會議、聚會、儀式、典禮，如：attend the meeting, attend the ceremony。

## track [træk] v. 跟蹤 n. 軌道

【例】Since a deadly bombing attack on hotels in Jakarta last year, Indonesian security forces have tracked down the militants responsible and prevented other attacks. 自去年雅加達的酒店發生致命爆炸襲擊以來，印尼安全部隊已追蹤到對此負有責任的激進分子，並阻止了其他的襲擊的發生。(VOA)

【用】 該詞可用於軍事、國際形勢、犯罪等領域，如：track down 追捕；作名詞時，on the track 在軌道上，未離題，可用於會議、談話、演講中。

## handle [ˈhændl] v. 處理 n. 柄，把手

【例】A Bangladeshi minister said his government has turned down offers of international help because it was confident it could handle the rescue operation. 孟加拉的一位部長表示，政府已經拒絕了國際援助，因為他們有信心處理好救援行動。(BBC)

【用】 handle with「處理」相當於 deal with，而日常生活中，handle with care 表「小心輕放」。

## supply [səˈplai] n. 供給 v. 供應

【例】They had more new neurons, stronger connections between neurons, and increased blood supply to a number of regions in the brain. 他們的新神經元更多，神經元之間的聯繫更加緊密，並且對多個腦部區域的供血更充足。(NPR)

【用】 常見片語：supply chain 供應鏈；supply and demand 供應與需求；in short supply 供應不足。

## tradition [trəˈdiʃən] n. 傳統

【例】It means that for the first time under Greece's constitution, the tradition of civil service jobs for life will end. 這意味著希臘憲法首次規定公務員工作終身制的傳統時代結束了。(BBC)

【用】 常用於文化、歷史等方面，有 cultural tradition 文化傳統；oral tradition 口頭傳統。

## aim [eim] n. 目的 v. 把......對準；旨在

【例】Its aim is to guide the country's environmenta policies and future laws to protect natural resource and ensure safe economic development. 其目標是指導該國制定環境相關的政策和未來的法律，以保護自然資源並保證經濟安全發展。(VOA)

【用】 aim to 表示「目的是......」。作名詞時，相當於 goal、target。

## witness ['witnis] n. 目擊者，證人 v. 目擊；證明

【例】Witnesses report seeing the plane on fire before it crashed. 目擊者報告說看到飛機在墜毀前起火了。(VOA)

【用】 主要用於有關法律的場合。 witness 表示「在法庭上作證」，具有權威性。

## newly ['nju:li] ad. 新近地；重新地

【例】This newly designed car is the only zero emission car on the market. 這款新設計出來的汽車是市場上絕無僅有的「零排放」車型。(CNN)

【用】 new 的副詞形式。意義相近的詞有 recently、last。

## tour [tuə] n./v. 旅行

【例】Hotels, tour guides and eating places all benefit from the guests. 酒店、導遊和飲食場所都能從客人身上獲益。(VOA)

【用】 相當於 traveling 或 visit。通常用於生活、旅遊、娛樂範疇。

## substantial [səb'stænʃəl] a. 大量的；可觀的；實質的

【例】 And then the crowding out of other sectors by energy would diminish and at that time we will see a substantial revival of Russian manufacturing. 隨後能源產業對其他經濟領域的排擠會有所減少，到那個時候，我們將看到俄羅斯製造業的大幅復甦。(VOA)

【用】 可用於社會、經濟、政治等多領域，如：substantial shareholder 大股東；substantial order 大宗訂單。

## cast [kæst] v. 投，扔 n. 全體演員

【例】The cast and crew of British movies will no longer be hailed as the underdogs at awards ceremonies. 英國電影的演員和工作人員在頒獎典禮上將一雪前恥，揚眉吐氣。(BBC)

【用】 cast 作動詞時，相當於 throw，有：cast off 拋棄；釋放；作名詞時，有集體概念，跟 crew、family、staff 類似。

# Level 13

## marine [məˈriːn] a. 海的；海事的

【例】Biologist Susanna Fuller, co-director of marine programs at Canada's Ecology Action Centre, agrees. 生物學家及加拿大生態行動中心海洋專案的聯合主任蘇珊娜．富勒同意這一點。(NPR)

【用】 與「海」相關，常用於軍事、航海、交通等領域。marine life 海洋生物；Marine Corps 海軍陸戰隊。

## nationwide [ˈneiʃ ənwaid] ad./a. 全國性（的）；遍及全國（的）

【例】China has 77 H7N9 cases reported nationwide, including 16 deaths. 中國全國有 77 例 H7N9 報導，包括 16 例死亡病例。(CRI)

【用】 作形容詞時，多用作定語，指在一定範圍內。 nationwide campaign 全國性活動；nationwide research 全國性的調查研究。

## discrimination [disˌkrimiˈneiʃ ən] n. 歧視；區別；辨別力

【例】The real danger for most of us is discrimination by statistical inference. 對我們大多數人來說，真正的危險是因為不能對統計資料作出精準識別與判斷。(BBC)

【用】 就業領域，「歧視」主要體現在：sex discrimination 或 gender discrimination 性別歧視；政治領域，主要體現為 racial discrimination 種族歧視。

## tourism [ˈtuərizəm] n. 旅遊業

【例】So tourism seems to be booming right now. 因此，旅遊業現在似乎正在蓬勃發展。(VOA)

【用】「旅遊產業」為 tourism industry，其中包括 tourism resource 旅遊資源；tourism company 旅遊公司；tourist 旅遊者；tourism activities 旅遊活動。

## profit [ˈprɔfit] n. 利潤．收益

【例】They could not sell their oil for that low a price and still make a profit. 他們不可

能在以這樣的低價售油的同時還能盈利。(VOA)

【用】 用於經濟領域，常見片語：profit margin 利潤率；net profit 淨利潤；profit and loss 盈虧帳目；gross profit 毛利。「獲得利潤」，可用動詞 make 或 gain。

## disorder [disˈɔːdə] n. 混亂；騷亂 v. 擾亂

【例】Autism is the general term used for a group of developmental disorders. 自閉症是對一組發育障礙疾病的統稱。(CNN)

【用】 在醫學領域，表示「障礙；疾病」，如：mental disorder 精神病；在社會領域，表示「騷亂」，如：in disorder 混亂。

## possibility [ˌpɔsəˈbiləti] n. 可能，可能性

【例】The researchers did a study of adult beliefs about the possibility of health risks to children from third-hand smoke. 研究人員調查了成年人對於兒童吸入三手煙的健康隱患的看法。(VOA)

【用】 production possibility 生產可能性；success possibility 成功可能性。其反義詞為 im-possibility「不可能」，兩詞均源於 possible「可能的」。

## account [əˈkaunt] n. 帳戶；解釋 v. (在數量、比例方面) 占

【例】In humans, when we're awake, our brain accounts for 20% of the energy we use when just sitting around. 對人類來說，當我們保持清醒僅僅是坐著的時候，大腦消耗的能量也要占總消耗能量的 20%。(BBC)

【用】 作名詞時，bank account 銀行帳戶；take into account 考慮；作動詞時，account for 對......負有責任。

## slash [slæʃ] v. 砍；大幅度削減 n. 砍

【例】More than $9 million in initial fines were slashed nearly 60 percent. 最初超過 900 萬美元的罰款被削減了近 60%。(NPR)

【用】 一般用於經濟等跟金錢相關領域，都表示「大幅削減」，相當於 cut。 slash costs 削減成本； slash taxes 削減稅收； slash prices 削減價格。

# historic [hiˈstɔrik] a. 有歷史意義的；歷史的

【例】 The streets surrounding Mexico City's historic center have been closed for hours in anticipation of President Obama's arrival. 墨西哥城歷史中心周圍的街道已戒嚴數小時，以迎接歐巴馬總統的到來。(NPR)

【用】 該詞一般與歷史、文化、旅遊等領域連接， historic site 歷史遺址； historic interest 歷史遺跡。該詞還用於語言學， historical linguistics 歷史語言學。

# respond [riˈspɔnd] v. 回答；做出反應

【例】Mr. Niebel was responding to a continuing scandal in Europe with tests in one country after another detecting horsemeat in products labeled as beef. 一個又一個的歐洲國家在標注為牛肉的食品中發現了摻雜的馬肉，尼貝爾先生目前仍在對這一醜聞做出回應。(BBC)

【用】 常見句型：sb. respond to sth. with sth. 某人對某事做出反應／做出回應。其同義詞有 reply，react。

# praise [preiz] v. 讚揚 n. 稱讚，讚美

【例】German Chancellor Angela Merkel praised the long-term spending plan. 德國總理安格拉‧默克爾稱讚了這一長期支出計畫。(VOA)

【用】 常見片語：full of praise 讚不絕口； praise for 因為......讚美； in praise of 歌頌。

# shock [ʃɔk] n. 衝擊；震驚 v.（使）震驚

【例】 I think everybody is pretty shocked and we tend to think this sort of thing doesn't really happen in Boston. 我想大家都非常震驚，而且我們傾向於認為這樣的事情並不會真的在波士頓發生。(CRI)

【用】 shock 既可以是物質上的衝擊，也可以是精神上的震驚，如：earthquake shock 地震衝擊；culture shock 文化衝擊。在醫學領域，shock 表示「休克」。

## conversation [ˌkɔnvəˈseiʃən] n. 交談，談話

【例】Jones choked back tears as she recalled the conversation. 當鐘斯回憶對話內容時，她強忍著眼淚。(NPR)

【用】「與……交談」用介詞 with；「正在交談過程中」用介詞 in；表示「談話」這一動作時，通常用 have a conversation 或 make a conversation。

## oversea [ˈəuvəˈsiː] a. 海外的 ad. 在海外

【例】The regulatory authority in UAE has said that it is because RIM is the only firm that automatically sends users' data to oversea servers. 阿聯酋的監管機構表示，這是由於 RIM 是唯一一家會自動將使用者資料發送到海外伺服器的公司。(BBC)

【用】 常見片語：oversea study 留學；oversea student 留學生；oversea Chinese 華僑。

## toll [təul] n. 過路（橋）費；傷亡人數

【例】On April 15, another death from H7N9 bird fl u was reported in China bringing the nationwide death toll to 14. 4 月 15 日，中國再次報導了一例 H7N9 禽流感死亡病例，全國死亡總人數上升至 14 人。(CRI)

【用】 該詞可用於災害後的傷亡人數統計，也可用於公共交通領域，如：death toll 死亡人數；road toll 養路費；toll free 免費通行。

## blame [bleim] v. 責備 n. 過錯；責備

【例】 Education is under threat, but the Internet and the growth of Massive Open Online Courses are not to blame. 教育正面臨著巨大威脅，但是網路的使用以及大量公開網路課程的增加都不是罪魁禍首。(CNN)

【用】 常用搭配：blame sth. on sb. 在……上責怪某人。

## terminal [ˈtə:minəl] a. 末端的，終點的 n. 終點（站），航站樓

【例】The terminal here is packed with people wherever you can find space. 在這個航站樓，到處都是人。(CNN)

【用】 terminal 可指「終點站」，也可特指「機場的航站樓」。

## locate [ləuˈkeit] v. 找出；（使）坐落於

【例】Both universities are located near rivers, and rowing is a popular and prestigious sport. 兩所大學都坐落在河流附近，而且賽艇是一種流行且久負盛名的運動。(CRI)

【用】 locate in/at 表「坐落在……」，可用被動語態。

## tackle [ˈtækl] v. 處理；對付

【例】There is an urgent need for the US to tackle the deficit in the government's finances, according to IMF. 據國際貨幣基金組織稱，美國迫切需要解決政府財政赤字。(BBC)

【用】 注意：tackle 在橄欖球、曲棍球中表示「攔截動作」，在體育新聞中比較常見。

## shoal [ʃəul] n. 魚群；淺水處 a. 水淺的

【例】The shoal was created from dune rock around 30, 000 years ago. 魚群來自於三萬年前的沙丘岩。(BBC)

【用】 與 shoal 有關片語：shoal area 淺水區；shallow shoal 淺灘；a shoal of 一大群。

## complicated [ˈkɔmplikeitid] a. 複雜的

【例】Measuring the scope of world hunger is a long and complicated process. 衡量世界飢餓程度是一個漫長而複雜的過程。(VOA)

【用】 同義詞：sophisticated 複雜的，精妙的；intricate 複雜的。

## connect [kəˈnekt] v. 連接；聯繫；給......接通電話

【例】After all is said and done, Google is expected to spend about $94 million for the Kansas City project to connect roughly 149,000 homes to the high-speed network. 說到底，人們希望谷歌投資大約 9400 萬美元在坎薩斯城專案上，讓大約 149,000 個家庭接入高速網路。(NPR)

【用】 通常與介詞 with 或 to 連用，表示「與......相連」，也可用 connect up 表示「連上」。

## convict [kənˈvikt] v. 定罪 n. 罪犯

【例】If convicted, he could face the death penalty, although no one has actually been executed under the US military justice system for almost 50 years. 如果罪名成立，他可能被判死刑，雖然近 50 年來在美國軍事司法系統中沒有人真正被執行過死刑。(BBC)

【用】 convict 是法律用詞，指審判後判定有罪，但未作最後判決。

## emerge [iˈməːdʒ] v. 浮現

【例】But elements of the strategy have begun to emerge in comments by officials involved in, or familiar with, the process. 但評論裡已經開始顯現出策略要素，這些評論來自於親身參與這一過程或是對此過程十分熟悉的官員。(VOA)

【用】 常見片語：emerge from 從......浮現；clear emerge 清晰浮現；suddenly emerge 突然出現。

## manage [ˈmænidʒ] v. 管理；經營

【例】The Wall Street Journal reports on an initiative in New Jersey to manage traffic. 《華爾街日報》報導了紐澤西的一則交通管理法案。(NPR)

【用】 常用 manage to do sth. 表示「設法做成某事」，含有成功之義。對比 try to do sth. 指「嘗試做某事」，不知道結果如何。

## ceremony [ˈserimǝuni] n. 儀式；典禮

【例】He was unable to attend swearingin ceremonies for another term in office in January. 他無法出席將於 1 月舉行的下一任期的就職儀式。(VOA)

【用】 新聞中與 ceremony 相關的片語：opening ceremony 開幕典禮；inauguration ceremony 就職典禮；award ceremony 頒獎儀式。

## immediate [iˈmiːdiǝt] a. 立即的；直接的

【例】And he met with the first responder who helped in the storm immediate aftermath. 他會見了暴風雨後第一個立即提供幫助的人。(NPR)

【用】 常見片語：immediate cause 直接原因；immediate action 立即行動。

## firm [fǝːm] n. 公司 a. 堅實的

【例】They were looking for evidence that the firms had submitted distorted data to price reporting agencies. 他們試圖收集這些公司向報價機構提供虛假資料的證據。(BBC)

【用】 作形容詞時，可用於經濟類新聞中，如：firm price 穩定的物價。

## easily [ˈiːzili] ad. 容易地

【例】So it 's unclear that people with close contact to poultry may be more easily infected. 所以尚不清楚密切接觸家禽的人是否更容易被感染。(CRI)

【用】 其形容詞形式為 easy。口語中，Take it easy. 表示「別著急（慢慢來）。」

## value ['v1lju:] n. 價值 v. 重視；評價

【例】Higher number equals higher value for those stocks. 對於那些股票來說，數值越高就等於價值越高。(CNN)

【用】 常見用法：economic value 經濟價值；social value 社會價值。

## temporary [ˈtempərəri] a. 短暫的;臨時的

【例】The deal is believed to include a temporary ceasefire and a framework agreement for future talks. 人們普遍認為此次交易包括一個臨時停火協定和一個未來談判的框架協議。(BBC)

【用】 新聞中常見的與 temporary 有關的片語有:temporary construction 臨時工程;temporary connection 暫時聯繫;temporary job 臨時工作。

## establish [iˈstæbliʃ] v. 建立;確定

【例】Officials in the town have suspended rescue efforts until they can establish that the ground is safe. 該鎮官員在確定地面安全後才開展了援助行動。(BBC)

【用】 establish,屬於短暫性動作,不用於完成時態中。常用片語有:establish in 使立足於;establish as 確立為。

## sharp [ʃɑːp] a. 鋒利的;明顯的 ad. 準時地

【例】Officials are predicting a sharp rise in heart disease and related problems. 官員們預測患上心臟病及相關疾病的人數會急遽上升。(VOA)

【用】 可指人說話風格「犀利」,也可指言辭「激烈」,表程度。注意:首字母大寫,可指日本電商「夏普」公司。

## trick [trik] n. 詭計;竅門;技巧 v. 欺騙

【例】Mr.Hoff says the trick is that nature does not dig a hole like we humans do to plant seeds. 霍夫表示大自然的神奇之處就是它不會像人類一樣,需要挖坑來種下種子。(VOA)

【用】 trick sb. into doing sth. 誘騙......做......;trick out 打扮,裝飾。另外,Treat or trick. 也是西方萬聖節的一個標誌語言。

## endangered [inˈdeindʒəd] a. 有危險的；有滅絕危險的

【例】In some ways, Florida's endangered springs are a symptom of a larger problem. 在某些方面，佛羅里達的泉水乾涸，預示著更大的問題。(NPR)

【用】 該詞常用於環境、物種保護領域，如：endangered species 瀕臨滅絕的物種；endangered breed 瀕危品種。

## dispute [disˈpjuːt] n./v. 爭論

【例】Experts are predicting that the United States could become more active in settling disputes in the future. 專家預測，美國將來在解決爭端時可能會更加積極。(VOA)

【用】 常用片語：dispute about/ over 就……爭執；beyond dispute 毫無疑問；open to dispute 有問題的。

## accusation [ˌækjuːˈzeiʃən] n. 控告

【例】These accusations of improper behavior bring the taint of scandal to the group. 這些有關不當行為的控訴給這個群體／組織蒙上了醜聞的汙名。(BBC)

【用】 時事新聞中與 accusation 有關的片語：false accusation 誣告；be under an accusation 被控告；bring an accusation against 控告。

## apply [əˈplai] v. 申請；適用；運用

【例】Ever since British researchers produced Dolly the sheep in 1996, scientists have been trying to apply the same reproductive cloning method to human cells. 自從 1996 年英國研究人員製造出桃莉羊以來，科學家們一直試圖用同樣的方法來克隆人類細胞。(BBC)

【用】 apply 常與 for 連用表示「申請」，如：apply for a job 求職；apply for a visa 申請簽證。

## corporate [ˈkɔːpərət] a. 公司的；共同的；法人的

【例】To others, he is the financial industry insider who facilitated reckless corporate risk-taking that placed the national and global economy in grave peril in the first place. 對其他人來說，他作為金融業內人士，促使企業不顧後果地去冒險，這在最初讓國家和全球經濟陷入了險境。(VOA)

【用】 通常用在商業、社會領域，如：corporate culture 企業文化；corporate image 企業形象。

## marriage [ˈmærɪdʒ] n. 婚姻，結婚

【例】From now until the end of June, the Supreme Court is expected to rule on big issues: affirmative action and same sex marriage. 從現在到 6 月底，最高法院將裁決重大議題：平權行動和同性婚姻。(CNN)

【用】 結婚相關詞：proposal 求婚；wedding 婚禮；family 家庭；responsibility 責任；property 財產。

## reportedly [riˈpɔːtidli] ad. 據報導

【例】Meanwhile, cooler temperature and lighter wind reportedly are making firefighters effort a little bit easier. 同時，據報導，低溫和微風的條件使消防隊員的工作變得更簡單一些。(NPR)

【用】 該詞相當於句型：It's reported that...。

## elderly [ˈeldəli] a. 較老的，年長的

【例】It's thought that fewer than 500,000 people, mostly the elderly, speak it worldwide. 人們認為全世界只有不到 50 萬人會說這種語言，其中大部分是老人。(VOA)

【用】 the+ 形容詞，表示一類人，如：the elderly 老年人；the disabled 殘疾人。

## style [staɪl] n. 風格;式樣

【例】Sullivan says when she was writing and recording songs for her album she knew she had to develop her own style. 蘇利文表示在為自己的專輯寫歌和錄音時,她認識到必須發展出自己的風格。(VOA)

【用】 常見片語:life style 生活方式;in style 流行;out of style 過時的。

## interim [ˈɪntərɪm] a. 臨時的;暫時的 n. 過渡期間

【例】The opposition coalition announced a new interim government for Kyrgyzstan and said it would rule until elections are held in six months. 反對派聯盟宣布了吉爾吉斯新的臨時政府,並表示臨時政府將管理該國直到六個月後選舉。(VOA)

【用】 表「臨時」時,通常用於政治方面,如:interim provisions 暫行規定;也可表「中間的」,如:interim report 中期報告。

## district [ˈdɪstrɪkt] n. 地區

【例】Ten districts in the city have suffered power failures. 該市的 10 個區都停電了。(BBC)

【用】 指地方行政區域,要用 district,一般與生活相關;指大範圍的一個地區,可用 area。

## vital [ˈvaɪtəl] a. 極其重要的;生死攸關的

【例】This budget will allow Europe to keep engaging on vital global issues such as climate change, nuclear safety and development aid. 這個預算會讓歐洲持續關注重要的全球問題,比如氣候變化、核安全與發展援助計畫。(VOA)

【用】用於經濟、政治、文化、軍事等多個領域,表示其重要性,如:vital battle 生死攸關的戰役。還用於醫學領域,如:vital sign 生命跡象;vital energy 生命力。

## treat [triːt] v. 醫治；對待 n. 招待

【例】He said he and his co-defendants had only wanted to treat their guest to a couple of days holiday in Bavaria. 他說他和共同被告只想在巴伐利亞州款待幾天客人。(BBC)

【用】 在口語中，It's my treat. 表示「這頓飯我請客。」而在萬聖節時，固定用法 Trick or treat. 表示「不招待就搗亂」。

## deploy [diˈplɔi] v. 部署；展開

【例】In November the African Union approved plans for a West African military force to deploy to Mali. 11 月，非洲聯盟批准了將西非軍事力量部署到馬利的計畫。(VOA)

【用】 deploy 的賓語通常與軍事行動相關聯，如：deploy troops 部署部隊。

## slightly [ˈslaitli] ad. 輕微地

【例】When you're on the high salt intake you always have some extra salt in you and a slightly greater volume of blood. 當你攝入大量食鹽，體內總會有額外的鹽分和稍多的血液量。(VOA)

【用】 其反義詞為 seriously 嚴重地。都是對事物進行程度的比較。

## embargo [emˈbɑːgəu] n. 禁運

【例】Ecuador and Croatia were involved in regional confl icts at the time and were under an arms embargo. 當時厄瓜多和克羅埃西亞捲入了地區衝突，並被禁止運輸武器。(BBC)

【用】 常見用法：arms embargo 武器禁運；oil embargo 石油禁運。而 embargo on 表示「對……禁運」。

## retailer [ˈriːteilə] n. 零售商

【例】Benetton is the latest retailer to join the pact that calls for more rigorous safety inspections. 班尼頓是最新加入該條約的零售商，該條約要求開展更嚴格的安全檢查。(NPR)

【用】 與之相對的就是「批發商」，為 wholesaler。

## legacy [ˈlegəsi] n. 遺產；遺贈物

【例】That won't make it any easier to build on the legacy of the greatest manager the English game has ever seen. 在英國這項運動史上最偉大的經理人遺留下的江山上再創輝煌並非易事。(BBC)

【用】 片語 legacy system 表示「遺留系統」。

## secure [siˈkjuə] a. 安全的 v. 使安全

【例】But for the great bulk of the population, working longer is really the way to have a secure retirement. 但對於如此大量的人口而言，延長工作時間是保證安全退休的絕佳方法。(CNN)

【用】 其名詞形式為 security「安全」。secure state 表示「安全狀態」。

## mainly [ˈmeinli] ad. 大體上，主要地

【例】Some genuinely want to protect the environment; others may be mainly seeking a marketing edge. 一些人真正想要保護環境；另一些人可能只是在尋求行銷優勢。(NPR)

【用】 該詞由 main「主要的，重要的」衍生而來。

# Level 14

## confident [ˈkɔnfidənt] a. 自信的

【例】It makes me feel confident again about the future of Chinese operas. 這讓我對中華戲曲的未來再次充滿信心。(CRI)

【用】「對……有信心」用 be confident in sth./of sth.。

## predict [priˈdikt] v. 預言，預測

【例】A new American intelligence report this week predicted Asia's economic power rising in the coming years. 本週，美國的一條新情報報告預測，亞洲的經濟實力將在未來幾年內持續上升。(VOA)

【用】 predict 表「預測」，是基於一定理由之上的猜測；而 guess 是一般詞，主要用於主觀猜測。

## consistent [kənˈsistənt] a. 一致的

【例】This has been our consistent stand. 這是我們一貫的主張。(CNN)

【用】 搭配 be consistent with 表示「與……一致」。

## assembly [əˈsembli] n. 裝配；集會

【例】 Concluding its meeting in Budapest, the assembly called for decisive action against contemporary expressions of the extremism. 這場集會在布達佩斯落下帷幕，集會呼籲對當代極端主義果斷採取行動。(BBC)

【用】 用以指正式、大型集會，如：general assembly 聯合國大會；national assembly 國民大會。

## feature [ˈfiːtʃə] n. 特徵，特色

【例】It has experienced highs and lows in its history, but its abundant heritage and distinct features has allowed for its enduring artistic vitality. 它已經歷過歷史的大起

大落，但其豐富的傳統和獨特的特色使其具有經久不衰的藝術生命力。(CRI)

【用】 常見片語：distinguishing feature 特點；main feature 主要特徵；facial feature 面貌。

## retire [riˈtaiə] v. 退休

【例】It's dishear tening to see that we're losing people that we've known our whole lives, are moving to different parts of the country for work, to retire. 我們正在失去那些認識多年的人，看到他們搬到國內的其他地方工作、退休，這讓人感到沮喪。(VOA)

【用】 常用片語：retire from 從......退下來；retire into oneself 退隱。其名詞形式為 retirement 表示「退休」。

## branch [brɑːntʃ] n. 樹枝；分支；分部

【例】Insider trading is illegal, even for members of Congress and the executive branch. 內幕交易是非法的，即使是國會成員和行政部門人員也是如此。(NPR)

【用】 指「樹枝」，但引申為「分支」，如：overseas branch 海外分行；party branch 黨支部；branch company 分公司。

## hire [ˈhaiə] v./n. 租【用】，雇【用】

【例】The U.S. housing market is seen as recovering and U.S. companies are slowly starting to hire again. 人們認為美國房地產市場正在復甦，美國公司開始逐漸再次聘請員工。(BBC)

【用】 for hire 指「供出租（用的）」；hire out 出租；on hire 中 on 強調狀態，表示「租用」。

## gain [gein] v. 獲得；增加 n. 收益

【例】The performances gained much attention and concern over the future of Hui Opera. 演出為徽劇及其未來贏得了極大的關注。(CRI)

【用】　諺語有 No pains, no gains. 表示「沒有付出，就沒有收穫」。

## spill [spil] v. 溢出，灑落，濺出

【例】Beyond spilling drinks, severe clear-air turbulence can injure or kill passengers, and damage planes, too—it once ripped an engine off a DC-8. 除了會讓飲料灑出，嚴重的晴空湍流還會使乘客受傷或死亡，也會毀壞飛機——有一次，湍流曾使一架 DC-8 飛機的引擎脫落。(Scientific American)

【用】　常見片語：spill out 溢出；spill over 溢出；spill into 湧進。

## assistant [əˈsistənt] n. 助手 a. 助理的，輔助的

【例】Assistant Executive Director Paula Bramel says the trust is the only global organization dedicated to doing that. 助理行政總監保拉‧布拉默爾說，該信託基金是唯一致力於做這件事的全球性組織。(VOA)

【用】　通常用於管理領域，用以表示輔助性的。其動詞形式為 assist。

## aggressive [əˈgresiv] a. 侵犯的；挑釁的；有進取心的

【例】 For example, a rough and low-frequency call suggests the vocalizer is large and aggressive, while a clearer, higher frequency signals a small, nonthreatening animal. 例如，粗糙的低頻叫聲表示發聲者是體型很大且具有侵略性的動物，而更清晰、更高頻率的叫聲則標誌著一隻體型較小，沒有威脅的動物。(NPR)

【用】　該詞用於文化、歷史、軍事等方面，如：aggressive behavior 侵犯行為；aggressive attitude 侵犯態度。

## occur [əˈkəː] v. 發生，出現

【例】While it cuts the time it takes to first nod off and sends us into a deep sleep, it also robs us of one of our most satisfying types of sleep, where dreams occur. 雖然它減少了我們打盹的時間，讓我們進入深度睡眠狀態，但是它卻使我們少了一種最

令人滿意的睡眠──做夢的睡眠。(CNN)

【用】 常用句型：It never occurs to sb. that ... 我從來沒想過……。

## combine [kəmˈbain] v. 聯合，結合

【例】Researchers say these elements could have combined to provide an energy source for microorganism. 研究者稱，這些元素可以結合在一起為微生物提供能量。(BBC)

【用】「與……結合」，用 combine with 表示。

## abroad [əˈbrɔːd] ad. 到（在）國外

【例】These deeply unpopular austerity measures are part of the price this country is forced to pay for continuing financial support from abroad. 這些非常不得人心的財政緊縮措施是這個國家被迫為急需得到外國的財政支援所付出的部分代價。(BBC)

【用】 一般用 go abroad 表示「去國外」。

## administrator [ədˈministreitə] n. 管理人，行政人員

【例】But the administrator Patrick Juneau said he was just doing what the court had asked him to do. 但管理人員派翠克·朱諾稱，自己只是按照法庭的要求行事。(BBC)

【用】 常用於行政方面。注意：在法律領域，特指「遺產管理人」。

## survive [səˈvaiv] v. 倖存，繼續存在

【例】They survived a 5,000-mile journey across the Pacific. 他們在橫渡太平洋的 5000 英里的旅程中倖存了下來。(CNN)

【用】常用片語 survive on 表示「靠……活下來」，一般用於災難、天氣變化等領域。

## recognize [ˈrekəgnaiz] v. 認出，識別；承認

【例】This week, senators could decide whether the bill extends equal protections to homosexual immigrants whose relationships are not recognized under current federal law. 本週參議員可以決定該法案是否對同性戀移民也提供平等的保護，同性戀移民的合法地位在現行的聯邦法律中是尚未被承認的。(VOA)

【用】 其名詞形式為 recognition。在表「確認，承認」時，相當於 accept。

## wildlife [ˈwaildlaif] n. 野生動植物

【例】The decision was taken on the final day of a major international conference on regulating the trade in wildlife species. 該決定是在規範野生動物物種貿易的重要國際會議上的最後一天做出的。(BBC)

【用】 用於自然、環境等相關領域，如：wildlife conservation 野生動物保護；wildlife refuge 野生動物保護區。

## prosecute [ˈprɔsikjuːt] v. 對......提起公訴，告發

【例】They point out that only a tiny fraction of people caught trying to buy a gun illegally are ever prosecuted. 他們指出被抓獲的人中只有很小一部分曾因試圖非法購買槍支而被起訴。(NPR)

【用】「起訴某人」直接用 prosecute sb. 即可。其反義詞為 defend「辯護」。

## mostly [ˈməustli] ad. 主要地，大多

【例】USC (University Of Southern California) surveyed about 50 mostly female industry leaders and content creators who detailed the obstacles women face. 南加州大學對 50 位主要行業領導者和內容創作者進行了調查，這些調查對象大部分是女性，她們詳細地介紹了女性所面臨的困難。(VOA)

【用】 mostly 強調數量占多半，近乎全部；mainly 指主要部分，突出在一系列事物中的相對重要性；largely 著重範圍或分量大大超過別的成分。

## framework [ˈfreimwəːk] n. 框架，構架

【例】China has signed the framework for a freetrade agreement with Switzerland, a deal which could become Beijing's fi rst with a major Western economy. 中國已經與瑞士簽署了一項自由貿易框架協定，這次交易可能成為中國首次與西方主要經濟體達成的自由貿易協定。(BBC)

【用】 常用短語：basic framework 基本框架。

## damage [ˈdæmidʒ] n. 毀壞，損害

【例】Mackey said his hospital quickly canceled all lective surgery as his colleagues tried to repair he damage as well as they could. 麥基表示他的同事們將竭盡全力去治癒創傷，因為醫院迅速取消了所有的非急需施行手術。(NPR)

【用】 用於事故、疾病、災害等領域，如：serious damage 嚴重損害；brain damage 腦損傷。

## impose [imˈpəuz] v. 把......強加於

【例】The deal signed in Geneva commits the European Union to gradually lowering the tariffs it imposes on bananas imported mainly from Latin America. 在日內瓦簽署的協議要求歐盟逐步降低對香蕉的進口關稅，這些香蕉主要來自拉丁美洲。(BBC)

【用】 常用於不公正或被迫的場合，如：impose on 利用；強加於；impose upon 強加；impose pressure 施壓。

## profi le [ˈprəufail] n. 輪廓；側面；人物簡介

【例】 As CRI's Ding Lulu reports, it's hoped the new collaboration will help lead to the better safeguarding of users' and companies' online profi les. 據中國國際廣播電台丁露露報導，新的合作將有望更好地幫助維護用戶和公司的在線資料。(CRI)

【用】 用於企業, 如 :company profile 表示「公司概況」。

## negative ['negətiv] a. 消極的；負的，陰性的

【例】Based on the negative test results, all of the women in the family thought they were not at a heightened risk of breast or ovarian cancer. 基於檢測結果呈陰性，該家族中的所有女性都認為她們不具有患乳腺癌或卵巢癌的高風險。(NPR)

【用】其反義詞為 positive「積極的」。在醫學中，呈陰性，為 negative；呈陽性，則為 positive。

## reflect [ri'flekt] v. 反射；反映，深思

【例】This question reflects just how complicated and at times, how confusing the world can be. 這個問題反映了世界是多麼複雜，有時又多麼讓人困惑。(CNN)

【用】 片語 reflect on 表示「思考；反省」；而 reflect upon 表「回憶，回顧」。

## forecast ['fɔːkɑːst] v./n. 預報；預測

【例】The models forecast that by mid-century clear-air turbulence will be more violent, and transatlantic flights will hit it twice as often especially during the winter. 該模型預測到本世紀中葉，晴空湍流將更猛烈，跨大西洋航班遭遇這種情況的次數將為現在的兩倍，尤其是在冬季。(Scientific American)

【用】 常見片語有：weather forecast 天氣預報；market forecast 市場監測。

## advice [əd'vais] n. 勸告，忠告，建議

【例】In Germany, if you think your financial advisor has been giving you bad advice and messing up your investments, you can complain to the regulators. You can go to the police. 在德國，如果你認為你的財務顧問一直給你糟糕的建議，把你的投資弄得一團糟，你可以向監管機構投訴，也可以去報警。(BBC)

【用】「給某人一個建議」可以直接用動詞 advise sb. sth.，也可以用 give sb. an advice.

## controversy [ˈkɔntrəvəːsi] n. 爭議

【例】Doctor Fox stepped down after days of controversy over his ties to Mr. Werritty, who has no official role but attended Defense Ministry meetings. 福克斯博士在經過幾天的爭議後下台，這些爭議圍繞著他與威瑞特先生的關係，威瑞特先生沒有官職，卻參加了國防部的會議。(BBC)

【用】 controversy 側重指深刻的意見分歧；conflict 側重懷有敵意的爭論，有時靠武力解決；dispute 側重長時間的爭辯。

## extract [ikˈstrækt] v. 提取 n. 摘錄，提取物

【例】Indeed, study subjects who ate yogurt with just olive oil extract consumed fewer calories over a three-month period than those who ate plain yogurt. 事實上，在經過三個月後，只食用含有橄欖油提取物的優酪乳的研究對象比那些食用原味優酪乳的消耗的卡路里更少。(Scientific American)

【用】 quotation，citation 和 extract 均可表「摘錄」，但 quotation 常指篇幅較短的引語；citation 指學術、專業上的完全引用、摘抄；extract 指選錄或摘錄，一般較長。

## incentive [inˈsentiv] n. 刺激，動機

【例】The U.S. patent system, authorized in the Constitution, gives temporary economic incentives to inventors to advance science. 美國專利制度是經過憲法授權的，給予發明家暫時的經濟獎勵，以推動科學發展。(NPR)

【用】 常用搭配：tax incentives 稅收激勵；financial incentive 金融刺激。

## presence [ˈprezəns] n. 存在；出席，到場

【例】One thing that might be helping is the presence of J.B. Pritzker, a Chicago native who founded New World Ventures in 1996 to invest in technology startups. 傑伊‧羅伯特‧普里茲克的出現可能會推波助瀾，普里茲克是芝加哥本地人，他於 1996 年創辦了「新世界合資企業」，投資技術創業公司。(Washington Post)

【用】 在新聞發言稿中，常見句型為 Thank you for your presence.，表示「感謝各位的出席。」

## schedule [ˈskedʒuːəl] n. 排程表 v. 排定，預定

【例】A demonstration against privatization is scheduled outside the stadium during the opening event. 在舉辦開幕式的時候，體育館外將舉行反對私有化的示威遊行。

【用】 常見搭配：on schedule 按計劃；ahead of schedule 提前。在非正式場合，可以和 timetable 互換。

## unveil [ˌʌnˈveil] v. 公布；揭開

【例】President Obama has unveiled details of a bold new US initiative to study the human brain. 美國總統歐巴馬宣布了一項研究人腦計畫的細節，這項研究很大膽。(BBC)

【用】 veil 指「面紗」，加上首碼 un-，指「脫下，下來」。像這樣 un- 加名詞，變成動詞的詞還有：unmask，uncover 等。

## assist [əˈsist] v./n. 幫助，協助

【例】Meanwhile it's being reported local residents in Boston, including many participants of the Marathon, rushed to nearby hospitals to donate blood to assist with treatment of those injured. 同時，據報導在波士頓，當地居民與眾多馬拉松參賽者爭相前往附近醫院獻血，幫助治療傷者。

【用】 表示「幫助」的詞：ai 用於正式場合，站在提供幫助者的角度；assist 則是站在受助者的角度；help 用法廣泛，指一般性的幫助。

## tension [ˈtenʃən] n. 緊張；張力

【例】Some parties in the governing coalition want to set a clear time frame for elections to ease tensions. 執政聯盟中的一些政黨希望為選舉設定一個明確的時間框

架，以緩和緊張局勢。(VOA)

【用】 可指物理上的「張力」，如：surface tension 表面張力；也可指國家、組織之間或形勢、局勢的「緊張」，如：tension between countries 國家間的緊張局勢。

## cyber [ˈsaibə] a. 電腦的；網路的

【例】The Dutch government has announced plans to give police much greater powers to fight cyber crime. 荷蘭政府宣布將授予警方更多權力以打擊網路犯罪。(BBC)

【用】 與 Internet 相關，常用 cyber world 表示「網路世界」，而 cyber attack 表示「網路攻擊」。

## excess [ikˈses] n. 過量，過剩 a. 過量的

【例】We continue to issue fines in excess of $100,000 over and over again. 我們繼續一遍又一遍地開出超過 10 萬美元的罰單。(NPR)

【用】 常用片語：in excess 過度；in excess of 超過；excess profit 超額利潤。

## balance [ˈbæləns] n. 均衡，天平 v. 使平衡

【例】 To understand how all this balances out, ecologists monitor how forests take up CO2. 為了明白這一切是如何達到平衡，生態學家們監測了森林如何吸收二氧化碳。(Scientific American)

【用】 常見搭配：in balance 總而言之；in the balance 懸而未決；balance sheet 資產負債表。

## border [ˈbɔːdə] n. 邊界，邊境；邊緣

【例】Rocket alarms have terrified Israeli border communities near the Gaza Strip for years. 火箭襲擊警報多年來一直恐嚇著加沙地帶附近的以色列邊境社區。(VOA)

【用】 主要指國家領土範圍，如：border area 邊境地區；border trade 邊境貿易。

## request [riˈkwest] n./v. 請求，要求

【例】Last year,a group of experts examined studies of aspirin at the request of federal health officials in the United States. 去年，一組專家應美國聯邦衛生官員的要求進行了有關阿司匹林的研究。(VOA)

【用】 常見用法：request for 要求；at the request of 應......的邀請。

## artificial [ˌɑːtiˈfiʃəl] a. 人造的

【例】Most agree that creating artificial reefs is a good idea, but they are divided on how to do it. 大多數人都認同製造人造珊瑚是一個好主意，但他們對於如何製作人造珊瑚存在分歧。 (Scientific American)

【用】在電腦領域，artificial intelligence 表示「人工智慧」；在醫學領域，artificial insemination 表示「人工受精」；在建築領域，artificial lighting 表示「人工照明」。

## displace [disˈpleis] v. 取代，移走

【例】 Across the globe, local farmers are being displaced to make way for energy crop plantations. 在全球範圍內，當地農民流離失所，因為要給能源作物種植騰出空間。(Scientific American)

【用】 相當於 shift，replace by，均表示「取代」。

## affair [əˈfeə] n. 事情，事件

【例】And he explained why the international affairs budget should not be cut. 他還解釋了為什麼不應該削減國際事務預算。(VOA)

【用】 affair 通常指與工作、私下相關的「事件」，但注意 affair 還可表示「風流韻事」。

## essential [iˈsenʃəl] a. 本質的；非常重要的 n. 要素，實質

【例】We hope more efforts will be made to revive and develop China's local operas, an essential portion of Chinese intangible heritage. 我們希望投入更多的精力來恢復和發展中國地方戲曲，因其是中華非物質遺產的重要組成部分。(CRI)

【用】 一般用於社會、歷史、政治、經濟、文化等領域，如：essential condition 必要條件；essential component 主要部件。

## exist [ig'zist] v. 存在，生存

【例】The report adds that the best world possible would exist if the United States and China work together and lead international cooperation. 報告補充說，如果美國和中國願意攜手引領國際合作，世界就完美了。(VOA)

【用】 短語：exist in 存在於......；exist on 靠......生存。

## optimistic [ˌɔptiˈmistik] a. 樂觀（主義）的

【例】The officials said they were less optimistic about the political crisis in Madagascar. 官員說，他們認為馬達加斯加的政治危機形勢並不樂觀。(VOA)

【用】 其反義詞為 pessimistic 悲觀（主義）的。常用 be optimistic about sth. 表示對某事感到樂觀。

## direct [diˈrekt] a. 直接的 v. 指揮，指導；把......對準

【例】He directs one of the World Health Organization's 「collaborating centers」 on influenza. 他在世界衛生組織的一個防治流感的「合作中心」指揮。(NPR)

【用】 其反義詞為 indirect 表示「間接的」。

## worried [ˈwʌrid] a. 擔心的；煩惱的

【例】NASA was worried that the extra water could destroy the power supply needed for the spacecraft's return to Earth. 美國國家航空航天局擔心多餘的水會破壞太空梭的供電系統，導致太空梭無法飛回地球。(VOA)

【用】 常用句型：sb. feel worried about ... 某人對……感到擔憂。

## bury [ˈberi] v. 埋葬；掩埋

【例】Authorities in Bangladesh have begun burying the unidentified victims of the building collapse. 孟加拉當局已經開始埋葬在這次樓房倒塌事件中身分不明的受害者。(BBC)

【用】 bury one's head in the sand 形象地描繪了鴕鳥把頭埋在沙子裡的行為，通常這個片語引申為「逃避現實」的意思。

## defeat [diˈfiːt] v. 戰勝 n. 失敗

【例】Rejection—even repeated rejection—doesn't have to mean defeat. 被拒絕甚至是屢次被拒並不一定意味著失敗。(CNN)

【用】 常見片語：suffer defeat 遭受失敗；concede defeat 認輸。

## disrupt [disˈrʌpt] v. 擾亂；(使)中斷；使分裂

【例】By early Monday, around 40% of fl ights had been disrupted. 週一早些時候，大約 40% 的航班受到了干擾。(BBC)

【用】 disrupt market 擾亂市場。其名詞形式為 disruption，表示「分裂」。

## bureau [ˈbjuərəu] n. 局，辦事處

【例】The bureau of land management has announced recreation of restrictions on Federal land in Arizona. 土地管理局已經宣布在亞利桑那州的聯邦土地範圍內限制娛樂活動。(NPR)

【用】 熟悉的 FBI 就是 the Federal Bureau of Investigation，即「美國聯邦調查局」的縮寫。

## motivate [ˈməutiveit] v. 驅動;激勵

【例】I hope that in sharing my story I motivate others to find a way to make their dreams and passions a reality. 我希望透過分享我的故事,能夠激勵他人找到通往夢想和激情的道路,並將它們變成現實。(CNN)

【用】 該詞常用於被動語態,be motivated by ... 受......所驅使。其名詞形式為 motivation,表示「動機;激勵」。

# Level 15

## enormous [iˈnɔːməs] a. 巨大的

【例】She says the strategy has resulted in 「enormous success.」 她說，該策略取得了「巨大的成功」。(VOA)

【用】 形容「巨大」的單字很多，如：huge、immense。 huge 強調體積、容積的龐大； immense 更為正式，強調面積或分量的巨大； enormous 強調的是遠超一般標準。

## subject [ˈsʌbdʒikt] n. 主題 v. 使服從 a. 受......支配的

【例】 The budget airline insists that its staff were hired under British contracts and therefore were not subject to French rules. 該廉價航空公司堅持認為，其工作人員都是與英國簽訂合約的受聘人員，因此不受法國法規的管理。(BBC)

【用】 常見用法是：be subject to 表示「受到；服從」。

## stuff [stʌf] n. 東西；原料，材料 v. 塞滿

【例】 Even if Google is not necessarily the vehicle for achieving a lot of this stuff, they certainly are to be praised for getting us to be thinking about a lot of this. 即使谷歌不一定能使其實現計畫，但他們應該受到讚揚，因為他們讓我們思考了很多關於這方面的東西。(NPR)

【用】 通常用 and stuff 表示「等等，諸如此類」。作動詞時，stuff up 堵住。

## leak [liːk] v.（使）漏；洩漏 n. 洩漏

【例】Officials described the leak as serious but said there was no risk to the crew on board the International Space Station. 官方稱滲漏情況很嚴重，但對國際空間站的工作人員來說沒有危險。(BBC)

【用】 作名詞時，gas leak 氣體洩漏；oil leak 漏油。作動詞時，leak out 洩漏；leak off 漏泄。

## cover [ˈkʌvə] v. 覆蓋 n. 蓋子；封面

【例】Most of the aquatic plants are covered by algae. 大多數的水生植物都被藻類所覆蓋。(NPR)

【用】 cover up 指「掩蓋，蓋住」，cover with 指「用......覆蓋」。注意：在軍事領域，cover 表示「掩護」，如：Cover me. 掩護我。

## heat [hiːt] n. 熱 v. 加熱

【例】This extra heat can raise temperatures in cities by about one to three degrees Celsius compared to rural areas. 多餘的熱量可以讓城市溫度升高，比農村地區大約要高 1 至 3 攝氏度。(VOA)

【用】 heat 所指的「熱」，一般是物理概念，如：heat source 熱源；heat conduction 熱傳導；heat loss 熱損耗。

## extreme [ikˈstriːm] n. 極端 a. 極端的

【例】 That is why he loves extreme sports and is among the first in China to try them, such as diving, skiing and piloting. 這就是為什麼他喜歡極限運動，並成為中國第一批嘗試潛水、滑雪和駕駛飛機的人。(CRI)

【用】 在新聞中，與種族、政治相關事件會出現 extreme，表示「極端的；偏激的」，如：a supporter of the extreme left 極左分子的支持者。

## separate [ˈsepəreit] a. 分離的，分開的 v.（使）分離

【例】It's now been shown that the crystal is of Iceland spar, a form of calcite, which is known for its property of diffracting light into two separate rays. 現已表明該晶體是冰島晶石，是方解石的一種形態，以能讓光衍射成兩束獨立光線的特性而聞名。(BBC)

【用】常見片語： separate from 把......和......分開；separate into 把......分成；separate out 區分開。

## file [faɪl] n. 文件；檔案

【例】Under a new draft law, investigators will be able to hack into computers, install spyware, read emails and destroy files. 新的草案將允許調查人員侵入他人電腦，安裝間諜軟體，閱讀使用者電子郵件以及銷毀檔。(BBC)

【用】常用片語：on file 存檔。同義詞：document、paper。

## method [ˈmɛθəd] n. 方法

【例】The Twitter tracking method has its biases. 推特的追蹤方法有其傾向性。(Scientific American)

【用】method 指系統、科學的方法；而指一般的方法，用 way 即可。

## spot [spɒt] n. 地點；斑點 v. 發現

【例】But on Thursday, the crew spotted frozen flakes of ammonia suggesting a leak. 但是在星期四，機組人員發現了雪花狀的冷卻氨，這說明有地方洩漏。(NPR)

【用】口語中，用 hit the spot 表示「完全契合要求」，而 put someone on the spot 表示「為難某人」。

## mix [mɪks] v. 使混合 n. 混合；混合物

【例】Produced water is what comes up with oil and gas from deep earth deposits, but drillers also use tons of water mixed with sand and chemicals in the fracturing process. 採出水來自地球深部礦床，與石油和天然氣混合在一起，但鑽井工人在壓裂過程中也使用了幾噸混合了沙子和化工產品的水。(VOA)

【用】mix it up 是美國俚語，表示「激戰，大打出手；爭吵」。

## dawn [dɔ:n] n. 黎明

【例】The number of dead has slowly increased since the tsunami struck after dawn and there are fears it will keep on rising as emergency teams reach isolated areas. 海嘯之後，隨著黎明的到來，死亡人數在緩慢增加，人們擔心在緊急救援隊到達偏遠地區時，死亡人數還會上升。(BBC)

【用】 常用 at dawn 表示「黎明，天亮」，可引申理解為「開端；復甦」，如：a dawn for the economy 經濟的復甦。

## complex [ˈkɔmpleks] a. 複雜的 n. 綜合體

【例】Complex systems can and do arise from simple events, including random events. 複雜的系統確實源自簡單的事件，比如隨機事件。(Scientific American)

【用】 complex 表示「複雜」，側重內在關係，需透過仔細研究與瞭解才能掌握和運用；而 complicated 表示「複雜」，比 complex 語氣更強，著重極其複雜，很難分析。

## pattern [ˈpætən] n. 模式；圖案

【例】Scientists at Scripps and elsewhere are publishing a new study that looks at that globa breathing pattern in detail. 斯克里普斯研究所和其他地方的科學家正在發表一項新的研究成果，有關全球範圍內呼吸模式，觀察細緻入微。(NPR)

【用】 常見片語：growth patter 生長模式；design pattern 設計模式。

## fee [fiː] n. 費，酬金

【例】To her, the fee represented nothing less than a money grab. 對她來說，這筆費用支出相當於被搶劫。(CNN)

【用】 表示「費用，錢」的單字有很多，其中 fee 主要指上學、求醫以及找律師等付的費用；charge 常指提供服務時索取的費用；fare 側重指旅行中所付的交通費用。

## opinion [əˈpinjən] n. 意見，主張

【例】Opinion polls show the majority of Greeks are against an IMF-EU bailout, seeing it as foreign interference. 民意調查顯示，大多數希臘人反對國際貨幣基金組織和

歐盟的救助，他們將其視為國外力量的干預。(VOA)

【用】「依……的個人看法」，可以用 in one's opinion 來表示。

## enrich [in'ritʃ] v. 使豐富；使富有；濃縮

【例】Internet is invented to enrich our life rather than shackle us with a chain. 網路發明是為了豐富我們的生活，而非束縛我們的枷鎖。(CNN)

【用】 該詞由形容詞 rich 演變而來，表示「使富有」；相同構詞法的還有 enlarge，large 為形容詞「大的」，加上詞綴 en- ，變成動詞，表「擴大」。

## mental ['mentəl] a. 精神的；智力的

【例】Whenever there is a mass shooting by a lone gunman, the killer is usually portrayed by the media as a troubled loner with a history of mental illness. 每當有單人持槍引發大規模槍擊事件時，殺人者通常會被媒體描繪成一個有精神病史並處於困境的孤家寡人。(Scientific American)

【用】與 mental 相對的為 physical 「身體的」。常見片語有：mental health 心理健康；mental stress 精神緊張。 mental 也與「智力」相關，如：mental development 智力發展。

## award [ə'wɔːd] n. 獎 v. 授予

【例】The Nobel Prize medal awarded to the British scientist Francis Crick in 1962 for his discovery of DNA has sold for more than $2m at auction in New York. 英國科學家弗朗西斯‧克里克因發現了 DNA 在 1962 年被授予諾貝爾獎章，該獎章在紐約以 200 多萬美元被拍賣。(BBC)

【用】 award 一般在文藝、科學等領域出現，如：Academy Award 奧斯卡金像獎；Grammy Award 葛萊美獎。而作動詞時，用 award a prize 表示「授予獎項」。

## scheme [skiːm] n. 計畫；方案

【例】The emissions trading scheme was a centerpiece of the Rudd government environmental strategy. 排汙權交易策劃是陸克文政府環境策略的核心。(BBC)

【用】 新聞中常用的片語有：work out a scheme 制訂計畫；drawback scheme 退稅方案。

## resolve [ri'zɔlv] v./n. 解決；決心

【例】I'm 21 years old and I resolve to get a girlfriend this year. 我今年 21 歲，我下定決心在今年找個女朋友。(VOA)

【用】 新聞中常用 fail to resolve 來表示「解決未果」。常用片語還有：resolve the problem 表示「解決問題」；resolve differences 表示「消除分歧」。

## intense [in'tens] a. 強烈的；緊張的；專注的

【例】The fighting is far less intense than it was in the 1990s, but a political solution to Kashmir's problems remains elusive. 與 1990 年代相比，戰爭形勢遠沒有那麼緊張，但喀什米爾問題的政治解決方案走向仍然撲朔迷離。(BBC)

【用】 新聞中 intense 常形容強烈的感情，如：intense emotion 表示「激情」；intense anxiety 表示「非常焦慮」。

## permission [pə'miʃən] n. 許可

【例】With official permission, you can have a big picnic—or get married—in nearby East Potomac Park. 在得到官方許可之後，您就可以在附近的東波托馬克公園野餐或舉行婚禮。(VOA)

【用】 聽力中常出現的片語有：get permission 表示「得到許可」；without permission 表示「沒有得到允許」；written permission 表示「書面許可」。

## remark [ri'mɑːk] v./n. 評論

【例】He made the remarks as protests continued in a number of Egyptian cities. 當多個埃及城市接連抗議時，他發表了相關評論。(BBC)

【用】 常用片語有：remark on 表示「對……評論」；make a remark 表示「進行評論」。

## numerous [ˈnjuːmərəs] a. 許多的

【例】Alarms are found on numerous medical devices. 在多個醫療設備中都發現了報警器。 (NPR)

【用】 在表示「數量多」的時候，還可以用這些詞來表示：plentiful、many a、a numher of、plenty of 等。

## principal [ˈprinsəpəl] a. 主要的 n. 校長

【例】Those who can't afford any principal risk are in a different boat. 那些不能承受任何資本風險的人則處境不同。(New York Times)

【用】 學校相關詞：paper 論文； professor 教授； campus 校園； laboratory 實驗室。

## shortage [ˈʃɔːtidʒ] n. 缺少

【例】There are reports of at least two-hour flight delays due to staff shortages. 由於人手不足，報導稱航班將至少晚點兩個小時。(NPR)

【用】 在新聞播報中，各種「資源短缺」有：shortage of water resources 水資源短缺；food shortage 糧食短缺；power shortage 電力短缺；fund shortage 資金短缺。

## suffocate [ˈsʌfəkeit] v.（使）窒息而死

【例】Hayes became a grain bin safety activist after his 19-year-old son, Patrick, suffocated in a grain bin in Florida in 1993. 海耶斯 19 歲的兒子派翠克於 1993 年在佛羅里達州的一個糧倉內因窒息而死，此後他開始積極關注糧倉安全問題。(NPR)

【用】 常用片語 suffocate me 表示「令我窒息」。

## wrap [ræp] v. 包起 n. 圍巾

【例】We wrap up our first real effort in the electric car—Arina. 我們將首次實實在在的努力傾注在這輛名叫阿里娜的電動汽車上。(CNN)

【用】 聽力中出現的 wrap up 表示「使圓滿結束；勝利完成；最後達成」。

## elite [eiˈliːt] n. 精英 a. 卓越的

【例】The Volvo Ocean Race is held every three years and always attracts elite sailors from around the world. 沃爾沃環球帆船賽每三年舉辦一次，並總能吸引來自世界各地的精英水手。(CRI)

【用】 新聞中常用的固定搭配有：elite education 表示「精英教育」；elite athlete 表示「優秀運動員」。

## plead [pliːd] v. 懇求；為......辯護；提出......為理由（或藉口）

【例】Former Egyptian President Hosni Mubarak pleaded not guilty today in a Cairo court. 埃及前總統胡斯尼‧穆巴拉克今天在開羅法庭上為自己辯護，拒不認罪。(NPR)

【用】 法律相關詞：defender 辯護人；defendent 被告；plaintiff 原告；court 法院。

## collaboration [kəˌlæbəˈreiʃən] n. 合作；勾結

【例】This kind of collaboration between students and astronauts still exists aboard the International Space Station. 在國際空間站中依舊存在學生和太空人之間的合作。(VOA)

【用】 合作關係相關詞：coworker 共同工作的人；colleague 同事；fellow 同事的；mutual 相互的。

## character [ˈkærəktə] n. 性格；特性；角色

【例】One of his favorite characters is a man who lives in a shack on the beach and rents lounge chairs to weekend visitors. 那個住在海灘上的棚子裡，在週末把躺椅租給遊客的人是他最喜歡的角色之一。(NPR)

【用】 性格相關詞：honest 誠實的；courageous 勇敢的；virtue 美德；positive 積極的。

## expose [ɪkˈspəuz] v. （使）曝光；揭露

【例】Football's world governing body FIFA is to offer players and officials rewards and amnesties to persuade them to expose match-fixing. 世界足球管理機構——國際足球聯盟將獎勵並赦免球員和行政人員，目的是說服他們揭露球賽造假的情況。(BBC)

【用】 常用片語：expose to 表示「暴露；接觸」；expose problems 表示「揭露問題」。

## manufacturer [ˌmænjuˈfæktʃərə] n. 製造商；製造廠

【例】Sony and Philips, another electronics manufacturer, worked together to create a new storage device for digital sound—the compact disc. 索尼和另一家電子設備製造商飛利浦合作，創造了新的數位聲音儲存工具——雷射唱片。(VOA)

【用】 商家相關詞：distributor 經銷商；agent 代理商；advertiser 廣告商；retailer 零售商

## pain [pein] n. 疼痛 v. 使痛苦

【例】That man cannot look me in my eye and tell me we do not live this pain. 那個人不能看著我的眼睛告訴我，我們不用承受這種痛苦。(CNN)

【用】 醫療相關詞： analgesic 鎮痛劑；antibiotic 抗生素；aspirin 阿司匹林；capsule 膠囊；cure-all 萬靈藥。

## shrink [ʃriŋk] v. （使）收縮；退縮

【例】President Obama wants to shrink the deficit and promote economic growth. 歐巴馬總統希望縮減赤字並促進經濟增長。(VOA)

【用】 衣物上標有 shrink easily 是「容易縮水」的意思；片語 shrink from doing sth. 表示「畏縮不敢做某事」。

## compensation [ˌkɔmpenˈseiʃən] n. 補償（或賠償）的款物；補償

【例】The EU plans to provide those countries with some compensation. 歐盟計畫向那些國家提供一些補償。(BBC)

【用】 新聞中常常提到的 economic compensation 表示「經濟賠償」；經濟學上的 unemployment compensation 表示「失業補償金」；片語 claim for compensation 表示「索賠」。

## screen [skriːn] n. 螢幕 v. 掩蔽

【例】With a tap on an iPad, the local Fox station pops up on the screen. 在 iPad 上點一下，當地的福克斯台就會出現在螢幕上。(NPR)

【用】 常用片語有：screen resolution 表示「螢幕解析度」；on the screen 表示「在螢幕上」；projection screen 表示「投影螢幕」。

## swear [sweə] v. 詛咒；宣誓

【例】The candidate who won in the election swore in for being the president. 在競選中獲勝的候選人宣誓就任總統。(BBC)

【用】 swear by 表示「以......起誓」，後面常加名譽、神明等。相關片語還有 swear in，表示「使宣誓就職」。

## notably [ˈnəutəbli] ad. 明顯地

【例】The British diplomats had spent the night in the security of various EU embassies, notably the French mission. 英國外交官在各歐盟使館安全過夜，在法國使館尤為突出。(BBC)

【用】 notable 是形容詞形式，意思是「值得注意的，顯著的」。

## experiment [ikˈsperiment] n. 實驗 v. 進行試驗

【例】New experiment suggests that these activities may not be so great for the animals. 新的實驗表明，這些活動可能對動物的影響並不太好。(Scientific American)

【用】 表示「對……進行實驗」，要在 experiment 後面加介詞 on、upon 或 with。

## proof [pruːf] n. 證據；校樣

【例】Scientists have discovered proof that the first English settlers in America resorted to cannibalism to survive. 科學家發現的證據表明，首批來到美國定居的英國人曾靠食人為生。(BBC)

【用】 新聞中常提到的 onus of proof 表示「舉證責任」；proof of purchase 則表示「購買憑證」。

## recreation [ˌrɛkrɪˈeiʃən] n. 娛樂活動

【例】Today, parts of the river have been restored as a recreation area. 今天，該河流的一部分已被恢復成一個休閒區。(VOA)

【用】 休閒聚會相關詞：entertain 招待；masquerade 化妝舞會；binge 狂歡；primp 精心打扮。

## panic [ˈpænik] a. 恐慌的 n. 驚惶 v. ( 使 ) 驚惶失措

【例】Their research may also apply to other extreme situations, which could help us understand collective human movement in panics and riots. 他們的研究也可能適用於另一種極端情況，這將有助於我們瞭解人類在恐慌和騷亂中的集體性行動模式。(Scientific American)

【用】緊急情況相關詞：ambulance 救護車；stuck 被卡住的；contingency 偶然性；lifeguard 救生員。

## fill [fil] v. 裝滿

【例】In order to get tax exempt status, which is what it's called, those groups have to fill out an application and submit to other checks from the IRS. 為了獲得所謂的免稅地位，這些團體必須填寫一份申請表，並提交給美國國稅局接受其他核對總和調

查。(CNN)

【用】 在新聞中，常出現「填寫表格」的說法，可以用 fill in 或者 fill out 來表達。

## clog [klɔg] n. 障礙 v. 阻塞

【例】Nearly two weeks later he told her he was tired of being sent into massive storage bins clogged with corn. 兩個星期後，他告訴她已經厭倦了進入被穀物塞住的大穀倉。(NPR)

【用】 clog 作動詞時，後面加介詞 up 或者 with 表示「阻塞」。

## barrier [ˈbærɪə] n. 柵欄；障礙；屏障

【例】The report notes that consumer disgust, particularly in Western countries, remains a barrier to their wider consumption. 該報告指出，消費者的反感情緒仍然是擴大消費的一大障礙，尤其是在西方國家。(BBC)

【用】 新聞中常用的固定搭配有：trade barrier 表示「貿易壁壘」；natural barrier 表示「天然屏障」。

## consequence [ˈkɔnsikwəns] n. 結果；重要性

【例】One of the unexpected consequences of this is perhaps we do not value it as once we did. 其中一個意想不到的結果就是也許我們已經不像原來那樣珍惜它。(CNN）

【用】 新聞常用片語：as a consequence 表示「因而，結果」；in consequence of 表示「因為……的緣故，由於」；of consequence 表示「重要的」；而 of no consequence 則表示「不重要的」。

## deliver [diˈlivə] v. 傳送；接生

【例】As it did in 1993, the agency delivered a warning to the industry. 像 1993 年那樣，該機構向業界發布了一個警告。(NPR）

【用】 新聞中會用到的專有名詞：Deliver Fast 表示「快速交付；交貨快捷」；Deliver Time 表示「交付時間；交貨時間」。

## element [ˈelimənt] n. 元素

【例】Experts also warn that traditional Chinese opera must never abandon its roots and core elements. 專家還警告說中國傳統戲曲決不能忘了根，不能或背離其核心要素。(CRI)

【用】 跟 element（元素）相關的專有名詞有：essential element 必需元素；chemical element 化學元素；metallic element 金屬元素；optical element 光學元件

## commencement [kəˈmensmənt] n. 開始；畢業典禮

【例】 This is the last of the president's three commen-cement addresses this year, and his first at a military academy. 這是總統今年的三場畢業演講中的最後一場，也是他第一次在軍事學院進行演講。(VOA)

【用】 典禮的相關詞彙：guest 嘉賓；dining-table 餐桌；emcee 司儀；banquet 宴會。

## inaugural [iˈnɔːgjurəl] a. 就職的；開幕的

【例】 Some of his most famous words appear on the monument—the Gettysburg Address and his Second Inaugural Address. 他的一些最著名的演說中的話被刻在紀念碑上──蓋茲堡演說和他第二次就職演說。(VOA)

【用】 在新聞中常出現各種演講活動，例如：inaugural ball 表示「競選活動」；inaugural lecture 表示「就職演講」。

## apologize [əˈpɔlədʒaiz] v. 道歉

【例】 Acting commissioner wants to apologize on behalf of the Internal Revenue Service for the mistakes that we made and the poor service we provided. 代理官員希望代表美國國稅局，為我們犯下的錯誤以及劣質的服務而道歉。(NPR)

【用】 apologize to 表示「向……道歉」；apologize for 表示「為……而道歉」。

# Level 16

## fundamental [ˌfʌndəˈmentəl] a. 根本的；十分重要的 n. 基本原則

【例】Calling the financial crisis the outcome of a failure of responsibility from Wall Street to Washington, he said the time has come to seize the moment to make fundamental changes in the rules of the financial road. 他將金融危機稱為華爾街和華盛頓共同失職導致的結果，並表示現在是時候抓住機會，徹底改變金融規則。(VOA)

【用】 政治中的「基本」都是由 fundamental 表達的，如：fundamental principle 表示「基本原則」；fundamental change 表示「基本變化」；fundamental rights 表示「基本權利」。

## egregious [iˈgriːdʒiəs] a. ( 缺點等 ) 過分的；驚人的

【例】This is one of the most egregious cases we've seen in a long time. 這是我們在很長一段時間內看到的最驚人的案件。(NPR)

【用】 egregious 多用於貶義詞。相關的片語有：egregious conduct 表示「極端惡劣的行為」；egregious offender 表示「臭名昭著」；an egregious mistake 表示「大錯」。

## rid [rid v. 使擺脫；使去掉

【例】Now, the company is increasing its efforts to get rid of hate speech. 目前該公司正努力擺脫仇恨的言論。(CNN)

【用】 關於 rid 必須掌握以下重點片語：be rid of 被動形式，表示「免除；去掉；擺脫」；get rid of 表示「擺脫；解脫；除去」。

## unrest [ˌʌnˈrest] n. 不安，動盪

【例】The political unrest started over two years ago in Tunisia. 政治動盪在兩年多前始發於突尼斯。(VOA)

【用】 新聞中經常出現動亂、動盪等事件，如：industrial unrest 表示「行業動盪」；political unrest 表示「政治動盪局面」；civil unrest 表示「國內動亂；民間動亂」。

## contrary [ˈkɔntrəri] n. 相反 a./ad. 相反的（地）

【例】In fact, much evidence to the contrary has existed, open to their inspection. 事實上存在許多相反的證據，可以供他們檢查。(VOA)

【用】 on the contrary 表示「正相反」，常用作插入語。

## liberty [ˈlibəti] n. 自由

【例】The God who gave us life gave us liberty. 上帝在賜予我們生命的同時也賜予了我們自由。 (VOA)

【用】 Statue of Liberty 就是美國著名的「自由女神像」。

## repeatedly [riˈpiːtidli] ad. 重複地

【例】Something the president has repeatedly said he won't do. 總統曾多次表示他是不會做某事的。(BBC)

【用】 常用搭配有：repeatedly said 表示「多次表示」；explain repeatedly 表示「反覆說明」。

## silence [ˈsailəns] n. 沉默；寂靜 v. 使沉默

【例】 Finally the chief justice silenced Sotomayor, saying, 「Could I hear her answer, please!」 最後，審判長讓索托馬約爾安靜，並說：「請讓我聽聽她的回答！」 (NPR)

【用】 常用片語有：break the silence 表示「打破沉默，開口說話」；in silence 表示「靜靜地，無聲地」； keep silence 表示「保持沉默；保持安靜」。

## flat [flæt] n. 公寓套房 ad. 直截了當地

【例】The fire broke out in a flat in an old threestorey leather factory converted into apartments. 火災發生在一座老舊的公寓裡，這座公寓是由三層高的皮革工廠改建的。(BBC)

【用】 住宅房間相關詞： condo 商品房 ；residence 住宅 ；estate 房地產 ；villa 別墅。

## attach [əˈtætʃ] v. 連接；認為有（重要性、責任等）；使附屬

【例】But that doesn't mean that we attach any less importance to Pakistan and Afghanistan. 但這並不意味著我們對巴基斯坦和阿富汗不重視。(VOA)

【用】 常用片語： attach importance to 表示「重視」。

## thought [θɔːt] n. 想法；思考；關心

【例】It's not thought the new rules will have a massive impact. 未能想到的是新規則會產生巨大的影響。(BBC)

【用】 常用片語有： second thought 表示「重新考慮」； deep thought 表示「深思」。

## furlough [ˈfəːləu] n.（軍人、官吏的）休假 v. 給予休假；使停職

【例】Planned employee furloughs have also been called off. 雇員們計畫好的休假也被取消了。(NPR)

【用】 固定搭配有： furlough certificate 表示「准假證明」； furlough plan 表示「無薪假」； be on furlough 表示「正在休假」。

## disable [disˈeibl] v.（使）喪失能力；（使）傷殘

【例】A US jury has awarded damages of $240m to a group of disabled former workers for the years of physical and mental abuse at a turkey processing company which employed and housed them. 美國一陪審團對一群在火雞加工廠工作並住在那裡的前雇員們支付了 2.4 億美元的賠償，他們在工作期間遭受了多年的身心虐待而致殘。(BBC)

【用】 the disabled 表示「殘疾人」。

## reality [ri'æləti] n. 現實，實際

【例】Guo Chuan describes the stark reality the crew encountered during the nine-month race. 郭川描述了全體人員在為期 9 個月的比賽中所遭遇到的嚴峻現實。(CRI)

【用】 in reality 表示「事實上」。

## honor ['ɔnə] n. 榮譽 v. 給......以榮譽

【例】The obelisk—the tall, slender column of marble—honors the United States' first president. 這座高大修長的大理石柱即是方尖碑，它是為了向美國第一任總統致敬。(VOA)

【用】 關於 honor 常用的片語有： in honor 表示「為了紀念」； in honor of 表示「向......表示敬意；為......慶祝」。

## tend [tend] v. 易於；趨向；照管

【例】We all have our times, but I do tend to have an optimistic attitude. 我們確實經歷過磨難，但是我常常保持樂觀的態度。(VOA)

【用】 需要區分的介詞片語： tend to 表示「傾向於」； tend towards 表示「走向；趨向」； tend to do 表示「傾向於做某事」； tend on 表示「照料；招待」。

## preliminary [pri'liminəri] a. 初步的 n. [ 常 pl.] 初步做法

【例】A preliminary estimate from Oklahoma's Insurance Department puts the cost of the tornado at more than $2 billion. 根據奧克拉荷馬州保險部的初步估計，龍捲風造成的損失超過 20 億美元。(NPR)

【用】 新聞中常出現的片語： preliminary analysis 表示「初步分析」； preliminary stage 表示「初始階段」； preliminary round 表示「初賽」； preliminary scheme 表示「初步規劃」。

## cancel [ˈkænsəl] v. 取消

【例】Opposition protesters want the president to cancel an order expanding his powers. 反對派抗議者希望總統取消擴大他的權力的法令。(VOA)

【用】 相關片語有：cancel activity 表示「取消活動」；cancel out 表示「取消；抵銷」；cancel after verification 表示「核銷」。

## strengthen [ˈstreŋθən] v. （使）堅強；（使）堅固

【例】Tao says he hopes it can help the country develop and strengthen its economy. 陶說，他希望它能幫助這個國家發展及強化經濟。(VOA)

【用】 常說的「強化意識」就是 strengthen the awareness。

## outcome [ˈautkʌm] n. 結果

【例】You have to be in this together; we want the same outcome. 你必須參與其中，因為我們想要的結果相同。(CNN)

【用】 常用搭配有：test outcome 表示「測試結果」；evaluation outcome 表示「評鑑成果」。

## contend [kənˈtend] v. 與對手競爭；據理力爭；主張

【例】Lawyers for the Hopi tribe contended that the masks had been stolen. 霍皮部落的律師爭辯說，有人偷走了面具。(BBC)

【用】 商業競爭相關詞：competitive 好競爭的；competitor 競爭者；price 價格；monopoly 壟斷；millionaire 百萬富翁。

## overturn [ˌəuvəˈtəːn] v./n. （使）翻倒

【例】The lengthy amendment overturns earlier constitutional court rulings. 冗長的修正案推翻了先前的憲法法院裁決。(BBC)

【用】 同義詞有 destroy、throw down。

## recount [riˈkaunt] v. 描述 n.（投票等的）重計

【例】Capriles had demanded the National Electoral Council to recount Sunday's vote. 卡普里萊斯要求全國選舉委員會重新計算週日的選票。(CRI)

【用】 投票競選的相關詞： advocacy 擁護 ；cast 投票 ；electorate 全體選民 ；referendum 公民投票 ；suffrage 選舉權 ；voter 投票者。

## intelligent [inˈtelidʒənt] a. 聰明的；智慧的

【例】Typically, children with autism are very intelligent. 通常情況下，自閉症兒童是很聰明的。(CNN)

【用】 intelligent 有兩種含義，一是「智慧的」，如：intelligent control 表示「智慧控制」；intelligent system 表示「智慧系統」；二是「智力的」，如：intelligent behavior 表示「智力行為」。

## classic [ˈklæsik] a. 典型的；傳統式樣的 n. 文學名著

【例】From classic novels to modern films, we'll talk about the unique delights of people who can't really be trusted to tell their own stories. 從古典小說到現代電影，我們將談論在講述自己故事的時候所能感受到的喜悅，即使講述人並不完全相信。(NPR)

【用】 文學相關詞：poetry 詩歌 ；novel 小說 ；prose 散文 ；literature 文學。

## fairly [ˈfeəli] ad. 相當；公平地

【例】The body has just exercised this power in a fairly dramatic way. 該團體剛剛以一種相當激烈的方式行使了這種權利。(BBC)

【用】 常用片語有： fairly paid 表示「支付公平；公平薪酬」； fairly well 表示「相當不錯」。

## compete [kəmˈpiːt] v. 競爭

【例】Now several of the parties have decided not to compete in the parliamentary or state elections either. 現在幾個當事方已經決定不再參與議會或州的選舉競爭了。(BBC)

【用】 常用片語有： compete ability 表示「競爭力」； compete for 表示「為……而競爭」。

## oversight [ˈəuvəsait] n. 監督，照料；失察

【例】One argument is they have greater oversight than anyone's ever had before. 一種說法是他們的監督進行地比以往任何人都更嚴格。(VOA)

【用】 新聞中常出現的固定搭配： legislative oversight 表示「立法監督」； oversight role 表示「監督作用」； safety oversight 表示「安全監管」； detailed oversight 表示「細化監督」。

## submit [səbˈmit] v. 呈送；屈服；主張

【例】They were looking for evidence that the firms had submitted distorted data to price reporting agencies. 他們正在尋找這些公司向價格申報機構提交失真資料的證據。(BBC)

【用】 常用的提交資料的表達有： submit registration 表示「提交登記表」； submit applications 表示「提交申請」； submit article 表示「投稿」。

## select [siˈlekt] v. 選擇 a. 精選的；優等的

【例】She's a student at Savoy Elementary Schoo in Washington, D.C., one of the schools selected for the program. 她是華盛頓特區薩沃伊小學的學生，這所學校被選中參與此專案。(NPR)

【用】 詞義辨析： select 表示「精心挑選的」意思； choose 為用得最普遍的； elect 多用在選舉上。

## compile [kəmˈpaɪl] v. 彙集；編輯，編纂

【例】It's much harder work to compile. 編譯工作更難進行。(BBC)

【用】 圖書編輯相關詞：proofread 校對；adapt 改編；rewrite 重寫；abridge 縮短；omit 省去。

## outcry [ˈaʊtkraɪ] n. 強烈抗議；吶喊

【例】The new tax provoked a public outcry. 新的稅收專案引起了公眾的強烈抗議。(VOA)

【用】 抗議抱怨的相關詞： grievance 抱怨 ；remonstrance 抗議 ；demonstrate 示威 ； wrath 憤怒。

## crush [krʌʃ] v. 壓碎；鎮壓

【例】 Critics say the package of spending cuts, job losses, higher taxes and lower pensions is crushing the Greek economy. 評論家稱，削減開支、失業、稅收的增加和養老金的降低綜合起來破壞了希臘的經濟。(BBC)

【用】 常見片語： get/have a crush on 表示「迷戀」；crush in 表示「壓成；擠進」。在包裝上見到的 do not crush ，就表示「切勿壓擠」。

## stimulus [ˈstɪmjʊləs] n. 促進（因素）；刺激（物），激勵

【例】It was a strong suggestion that the FED is ready to try further stimulus. 這強烈暗示美聯儲準備嘗試開展更多的刺激行動。(BBC)

【用】該詞多與經濟有關，如：economic stimulus 表示「經濟刺激」；stimulus package 表示「刺激計畫」； fiscal stimulus 表示「財政刺激」。

## fame [feɪm] n. 聲譽

【例】She has experienced a stratospheric rise to fame. 她經歷了聲名鵲起。(CNN)

【用】 該詞的拓展詞是 famous ，表示「著名的」。

## depression [dɪˈprɛʃən] n. 憂愁；低氣壓；不景氣

【例】Extreme depression and disappointment were my first reactions to this unexpected accident. 極度的消沉和失望是我對這起意外事故的第一反應。(CRI)

【用】 Great Depression 表示「美國經濟大蕭條」；另外，economic depression 表示「經濟蕭條」，還可以說 economic recession。

## passion [ˈpæʃən] n. 激情；感情

【例】They appreciated his enthusiasm and his passion. 他們欣賞他的熱情和激情。(NPR)

【用】 法律中常說的「激情犯罪」就是 crime of passion。

## occupy [ˈɔkjupaɪ] v. 占用；(使)忙碌；(使)從事

【例】We do not seek to occupy other nations. 我們絕沒有占領其他國家的計畫。(BBC)

【用】 公司日常相關詞：jot 摘要記錄；undertake 承擔；memo 備忘錄；assign 分配。

## prone [prəun] a. 易於......的；平臥的

【例】Haiti is prone to disasters, but this huge quake is the worst to hit the Caribbean island state in two centuries. 海地很容易發生災害，但這次大地震是兩個世紀以來加勒比島嶼國家所經歷的最嚴重的災難。(VOA)

【用】 常用用法是 prone to 表示「有......傾向的」。

## accountability [ə,kauntəˈbɪlətɪ] n. 負有責任

【例】 Senate Minority Leader Mitch McConnel is demanding more accountability from the Obama administration. 參議院的少數黨領袖密契‧麥康諾要求歐巴馬政府承擔更多的責任。(NPR)

【用】 片語 fiscal accountability 表示「財政責任」。

## wealth [wεlθ] n. 財富；豐富

【例】One should not equate wealth with happiness. 人們不應把財富等同於幸福。
(CNN)

【用】「財富收入」相關詞：revenue 收入；saving 儲蓄金；abundant 豐富的；prosperity 繁榮。

## furious ['fjuəriəs] a. 狂怒的；強烈的

【例】Carla is still furious about the settlement. 卡里亞對結算的結果仍然感到憤怒。
(NPR)

【用】 furious 後面可靈活的加 with、over、about 等介詞，表示「對……感到憤怒」。

## offend [ə'fεnd] v. 冒犯；使厭惡；違犯

【例】The worst offending countries involved in the illegal ivory trade had been given a strict deadline to improve the situation or face sanctions. 從事非法象牙交易最猖獗的國家被給予了明確的最後期限，要求馬上改變現狀，否則將面臨制裁。(BBC)

【用】 常見用法是 offend against sth. 表示「違犯……」。

## precious ['prεʃəs] a. 珍貴的

【例】To me, it was a precious chance. 對我來說，這是一次很寶貴的機會。(CRI)

【用】 詞義辨析： precious 和 valuable 都有「貴重的」的意思。其區別是 precious 指任何無法用錢衡量的珍貴東西，尤其適用於失掉後無法補償的東西，還可用於人的感情方面；valuable 指任何值錢的或可以帶來巨額利潤的、非常有用的或受人珍視的東西。

## chamber ['tʃeimbə] n. 會議室；（槍）膛 v. 裝填

【例】Edward Rica is president of Alabama golf coast area, chamber of commerce.

愛德華 · 黎加是阿拉巴馬州高爾夫海岸地區的商會會長。(NPR)

【用】 chamber of commerce 表示「商會」。

## split [split] v.（使）分裂；裂開 n. 裂口

【例】They tried to split the organization. 他們曾經試圖分裂這個組織。(VOA)

【用】 詞義辨析： split, tear 這兩個詞都有「撕裂」的意思。其區別在於， tear 多指外力作用下的撕裂；split 既可指外力作用下的撕裂、分裂，也可指物體內部自動地分裂、裂開。

## permit [pə'mit] v. 允許 ['p4:mit] n. 許可證

【例】Now, he says, people must not permit Haiti's poorest citizens to return to the terrible conditions that existed even before the earthquake. 他表示，現在人們絕不允許讓海地的可憐的市民們再次處於糟糕的處境，即使在地震發生前景況已經不盡人意。(VOA)

【用】 常見用法有： work permit 表示「工作許可證」； residence permit 表示「居留證」； entry permit 表示「入境許可證」。

## hospitalize ['hɔspitəlaiz] v. 使入院；允許住院

【例】About 70 people were hospitalized although most have been released. 雖然大部分患者已經出院，但仍有大約 70 人在醫院中接受治療。(NPR)

【用】 生病住院的相關詞： frail（指人）體弱的 ；emergency 緊急 ；relapse 舊病復發 ； register 掛號。

## erupt [i'rʌpt] v.（指火山）爆發；突然發生

【例】The last time this volcano did erupt in the early 19th century, he says, it lasted two years. 他表示這座火山最後一次爆發是在 19 世紀早期，時間持續了兩年。(VOA)

【用】 其名詞形式是 eruption，eruption of volcanoes 指「火山爆發」。

## function [ˈfʌŋkʃən] v. 運行 n. 職責;函數

【例】Research is incredibly important in understanding the function of these genes. 要理解這些基因的功能,研究是至關重要的。(NPR)

【用】 常見用法: basic function 表示「基本功能」; social function 表示「社會功能;正式社交集會」。

## imminent [ˈiminənt] a. 即將發生的;急迫的

【例】There is little sign that this is at all imminent. 幾乎沒有跡象顯示情況已迫在眉睫。(BBC)

【用】 新聞中播報關於災難時會用到的片語: imminent danger 表示「迫在眉睫的危險」; imminent threat 表示「緊迫的威脅」。

## bumpy [ˈbʌmpi] a. (路等)崎嶇不平的;擾動的

【例】While economic growth continues at a healthy pace in developing nations, advanced economies are facing a bumpy road to recovery, says IMF Chief Economist Olivier Blanchard. 國際貨幣基金組織首席經濟學家奧利弗 · 布蘭查德表示,儘管發展中國家的經濟仍在穩健地發展,但是先進國家在恢復經濟的道路上遇到了困難。(VOA)

【用】 開車相關詞: uneven 不平坦的 ;tyre 輪胎 ;swerve 轉彎 ;break 剎車。

## motion [ˈməuʃən] n. 議案;動作;請求 v. 運動;打手勢

【例】His acting, singing and dancing changed the American motion picture musical. 他的表演、歌唱和舞蹈改變了美國的電影音樂劇。(VOA)

【用】 新聞中常見用法是 make a motion 表示「提議」。

## surround [səˈraund] v. 圍繞，環繞；包圍，圈住

【例】The common thread is to surround myself with those that share my love of music, my passion for music. 我們共同的想法是與志同道合的人在一起，分享對音樂的熱愛與激情。 (CNN)

【用】 左鄰右舍相關詞：dweller 居住者；neighbor 鄰居；neighborhood 附近；resident 居民。


## permanent [ˈpə:mənənt] a. 長久的；固定的

【例】It leads to many deaths or permanent disabilities. 這將導致多起死亡或永久性殘疾。(VOA)

【用】 permanent、eternal、everlasting、endless 等形容詞均有「持久的、永久的」之意。permanent 指總是處於相同的情況和地位，可長期持續下去，永久不變；eternal 語體較莊重，側重指永遠存在，無始無終；everlasting 語氣較莊重，側重持續不盡，或指開始後一直進行下去；endless 是日常用詞，指無盡無休。

# Level 17

## administrative [əd'ministrətiv] a. 管理的，行政的

【例】We have gone about this from the administrative standpoint and the federal district court has done exactly what we supposed to be doing. 我們是從管理者的角度來處理此事，而聯邦地區法院則嚴格照章辦事。(BBC)

【用】 政府政策相關詞：bureaucratic 官僚政治的 ；governance 統治 ；mandate 授權 ；legislator 立法者 ；enactment 規定。

## fantastic [fæn'tæstik] a. 奇異的 ；極好的 n. 古怪的人

【例】We have some fantastic short films, movies with costumes and beautiful dresses, thriller, romantic movies, animations. 我們有精彩的短片，以及內容含有華美服裝的電影，還有驚悚片、浪漫片和動畫片。(CRI)

【用】 常用片語：fantastic idea 表示「想入非非」；fantastic job 表示「幹得太好了 ；好樣的」。

## monitor ['mɔnitə] n. 監控器 ；班長 v. 監控

【例】Stephen Dukker says all you need to connect to a network is a keyboard and monitor. 斯蒂芬 ‧ 杜克爾表示，要連接到網路，你只需要一個鍵盤和一個顯示器。(VOA)

【用】 儀器相關詞：gauge 測量儀表 ；navigation 導航 ；microprocessor 微處理器 ；hardware 硬體。

## stabilize ['stebəlaiz] v. 使穩固 ；穩定

【例】The real estate developers will make adjustments according to the market demand, after a period of time, property prices will stabilize. 房地產開發商將根據市場需求進行調整，再過一段時間後，房價將會穩定下來。(CRI)

【用】 在新聞英語中，stablize prices 表示「穩定物價」；stablize the market 穩定市場

## dispensable [disˈpensəbl] a. 可有可無的；非必要的

【例】They are the 「outcasts」, ultimately dispensable who must build the conditions for a new life. 他們是「棄兒」，最終還是變得可有可無，必須自己去創造建立新的生活。(BBC)

【用】 在科技新聞中，專業片語 dispensable enzyme 是「非必需酶」的意思。

## import [ˈimpɔːt] n./v. 進口；輸入

【例】There are also plans to ease import restrictions and work continues on laws governing foreign investment. 此外，他們還計畫放寬進口限制並繼續制定有關外商投資的法律。(VOA)

【用】 片語：import from 表示「從……進口」。

## resort [riˈzɔːt] v. 求助；憑藉 n. 憑藉，手段；度假勝地

【例】He says American citizens living in the main resort areas of Mexico provide their own vote o confidence. 他說居住在墨西哥主要度假勝地的美國公民表達了他們的支持。(VOA)

【用】 常用片語 in the last resort 表示「作為最後一招，作為最後的解決辦法，不得己」。

## unacceptable [ˌʌnəkˈseptəbl] a. 無法接受的

【例】Currently, I haven't chosen any property. It's too expensive. I am still considering, the price is really unacceptable. 目前，我還沒有選擇購房，因為房價太貴了，我仍在考慮，房價實在令人難以接受。(CRI)

【用】 新聞中提及的相關片語：unacceptable product 表示「不合格品」；unacceptable terms 表示「不可接受條款」。

## abandon [əˈbændən] v. 離棄；完全放棄 n. 放縱

【例】He is an abandoned Indian children. 他是一個被遺棄的印度孩子。(NPR)

【用】　詞義辨析：abandon、desert、leave、give up、forsake 等動詞或片語均有「拋棄、放棄」之意。 abandon 強調永遠或完全放棄或拋棄人或事物等； desert 著重指違背法律責任和義務； leave 是普通用詞，指捨棄某事或某一職業； give up 是普通用語，側重指沒有希望或因外界壓力而放棄； forsake 側重斷絕感情上的依戀。

## lobby [ˈlɔbɪ] n. 大廳；遊說議員的團體 v. 向（議員等）進行遊說

【例】He's now a consultant for the gun control lobby. 他現在是一個槍支管制遊說團體的顧問。(NPR)

【用】　常見用法：departure lobby 表示「出境大廳；旅客登機報到處」；ticket lobby 表示「售票廳」；reception lobby 表示「接待大廳」。

## bilateral [ˌbaɪˈlætərəl] a. 雙邊的

【例】President Obama has arrived in Mexico for talks that are expected to switch the focus of bilateral ties to job creation. 總統歐巴馬抵達墨西哥參加會談，這次會談有望將關注焦點從雙邊關係轉向創造就業機會。(BBC)

【用】　雙邊關係相關詞：negotiation 商議；channel 管道；dialogue 對話；diplomatic 外交的。

## viable [ˈvaɪəbl] a. 切實可行的；能養活的

【例】Each year, Xu says he stays for several months in a foreign country such as Italy, France and Spain to observe local operas and try to find ways to make Hui Opera more viable and international. 每年，徐（導演）表示他都會在義大利、法國和西班牙等國停留一段時間觀察當地戲劇的情況，試圖找到將徽劇國際化的方法。(CRI)

【用】　表示「可能性」的詞語還有： possible 可能的 ；workable 切實可行的 ；practicable 可行的 ；feasible 可實行的。

## catastrophic [ˌkætəˈstrɔfik] a. 災難的;悲慘的

【例】Home mortgage giants were failing at a catastrophic pace. 住房抵押貸款巨頭正以災難性的速度倒閉。(VOA)

【用】 新聞中播報災難時常用片語: catastrophic failure 表示「災難性故障」; catastrophic collapse 表示「毀滅性破壞」。

## capable [ˈkeipəbl] a. 有能力的,能幹的

【例】Astronomers using NASA's powerful Kepler space telescope say they've identified two planets that appear capable of supporting life. 天文學家利用了美國航空局強大的開普勒太空望遠鏡,稱他們現已發現了兩顆似乎能夠支持生命存在的行星。(BBC)

【用】 能力相關詞: amiable 和藹的;creative 創造性的;dedicated;專注的;honest 誠實的。

## talent [ˈtælənt] n. 天資;人才

【例】The documentary shows how Hall developed a unique sound based on skilled studio engineering and the support of local talent. 這部紀錄片展示了會堂如何以強大的音響工程和當地的人才支援為基礎,做出了這種獨特的聲效。(VOA)

【用】 詞義辨析: talent、genius、gift 這幾個詞都可表示「天才,才能」。 genius 主要指在智力方面具有極其特殊和非凡的能力; gift 強調人天生具有的能力和品質; talent 主要指某一方面具有的「天資,才能」,需要後天的教育和努力。

## lifeless [ˈlaiflis] a. 無生命的;無生物的;無生氣的

【例】Sometime after that, he's filmed lied on the ground where he appears lifeless. 隨後,影片顯示他躺在地上,似乎已經死了。(BBC)

【用】 近義拓展: dead 表示「死的」; deceased 表示「已故的」。

## bless [[bles] v. 使有幸得到；為......祈神賜福（或保佑）

【例】May God bless him and may he rest in peace. 願上帝保佑他，願他安息。(VOA)

【用】 bless 這個詞經常用在口語中，比如：Bless me 可用來表示「驚訝、高興、沮喪、憤怒」的情緒，可譯為「哎呀！」在西方，當有人打噴嚏的時候，會有人對你說 Bless you！表示「上帝保佑你」。

## boom [buːm] n. 繁榮昌盛時期 v. 發出深沉有迴響的聲音

【例】 The International Energy Agency said global carbon emissions hadn't fallen because a boom in solar and wind power had been offset by increasing use of coal. 國際能源機構稱，儘管太陽能和風能有所發展，但仍然不足以抵消煤炭使用量的增長，因此全球碳排放量沒有降低。(BBC)

【用】 在美國口語中，可用 lower the boom（on）表示「一拳把......擊倒；嚴懲；對......採取嚴厲措施；完全禁止」的意思。

## rise [raiz] v./n. 升起；增加

【例】He says the rate at which his income rises is not in line with the rate at which property prices have soared. 他說房價飆升的速度與他收入上升的速度不吻合。(CRI)

【用】 注意其過去式和過去分詞分別是 rose、risen。

## parental [pəˈrentəl] a. 父母親的，父母的

【例】They certainly don't have access to paid parental leave or paid leave to take care of an ill family member. 他們當然不能利用帶薪產假或帶薪休假來照顧生病的家庭成員。(VOA)

【用】 parental leave 表示「產假」；parental testing 表示「親子鑑定」。

## conglomerate [kənˈglɔmərət] n. 企業集團；聚合物 v. 聚合

【例】Today, we're talking to a man who singlehandedly created a global conglomerate as well as an instantly recognizable brand. 今天，我們將與一位先生對話，他獨自一人創建了一個全球性的集團企業，和一個知名品牌。(CNN)

【用】 新聞中出現的固定搭配：transnational conglomerate 表示「跨國集團企業」；business conglomerate 表示「企業集團」；conglomerate merger 表示「多行業企業併合」。

## heal [hiːl] v. 使癒合 v. 癒合

【例】The city's FBI Chief Stephen Anthony said now they have been found, the process of healing could begin. 該市聯邦調查局局長史蒂夫 · 安東尼稱目前這些人已被找到，可以開始對他們進行治療。(BBC)

【用】 詞義辨析：heal、cure 這兩個詞的共同意思是「治癒」。其區別是，cure 多指內部疾病，而 heal 多指外傷；cure 有時強調突然或戲劇般的治癒，而 heal 常強調緩慢甚至長時期的治療過程。用於比喻時，cure 多指社會不良現象或個人惡習，而 heal 則指精神上的創傷或思想上的分歧。

## originate [əˈridʒəneit] v. 起源；創辦

【例】As the name indicates, Hui Opera originated from Huizhou and the surrounding areas of Anhui Province. 顧名思義，徽劇起源於徽州及安徽省周邊地區。(CRI)

【用】 originate 用作及物動詞時，接名詞或代詞作賓語，可用於被動結構；用作不及物動詞時，常跟介詞 in、from、with 等連用。

## dedicate [ˈdedikeit] v. 獻（身）；題獻詞於（著作等）上

【例】But, in a larger sense, we can not dedicate—we can not consecrate—we can not hallow—this ground. 但是從更廣泛的角度來說，我們無法為這片土地投入和奉獻，我們也無法將其神聖化。(VOA)

【用】 delicate 後面經常接介詞 to，表示「把（時間、精力等）用於；題獻給」等意思，比如：He dedicated himself to scientific research. 他將他自己獻身於科研之中。

## eventual [iˈventʃuəl] a. 最後的

【例】Stock markets have been gaining on heard of eventual deal as ministers begin a weekend of meeting in Brussels on how to solve the eurozone's debt crisis. 部長已經在布魯塞爾召開關於如何解決歐元危機的週末會議，受此消息的刺激，股票市場有所增長。(BBC)

【用】 表示「最後的」這個意思的詞語有： final 最後的； ultimate 最終的。

## rely [riˈlai] v. 依靠；信賴

【例】In some areas, the aquifer—which most Floridians rely on for drinking water—has dropped by 60 feet. 在一些地區，蓄水層已下降了 60 英尺，而這是大多數佛羅里達州人賴以生存的飲用水來源。(NPR)

【用】 rely 是不及物動詞，後面須接介詞 on 或 upon ，再接名詞、代詞、動名詞或動詞不定式作賓語補足語的複合結構。

## elementary [ˌeliˈmentəri] a. 基本的

【例】Standing outside the plaza tower elementary school, Obama pledged the federal government will help the community throughout the rebuilding process. 歐巴馬在廣場高塔小學門外承諾，聯邦政府將協助社區的重建工程。(NPR)

【用】 在學術中常用的固定搭配，如： elementary school 表示「小學」； elementary education 表示「初等教育」； elementary algebra 表示「初等代數」。

## invest [inˈvest] v. 投資；投入

【例】Turkey has decided to invest in nuclear energy. 土耳其已經決定投資核能。(BBC)

【用】 投資相關詞： consultant 顧問 ； financing 籌措資金 ；dividends 紅利 ；auction 拍賣。

## purchase [ˈpɚːtʃəs] n./v. 購買

【例】After hearing each clip, the subjects could bid between zero and two dollars to purchase the song. 在試聽每段音訊片段之後，試聽者可以花零到兩元購買歌曲。(Scientific American)

【用】 購物相關詞：coupon 優惠券；luxury 奢侈品；splurge 揮霍；stock 庫存。

## default [diˈfɔːlt] n. 違約；棄權 v. 不履行義務

【例】Share markets have taken fright, fearing that if Greece does default on its debt. 股票市場出現恐慌，因為擔心希臘在債務方面違約。(BBC)

【用】 實用片語：in default of 表示「在缺少……的情況下」；default on 表示「拖欠」，還有「未出席」的意思。

## checkup [ˈtʃekʌp] n. 全面檢查；審查；身體檢查

【例】Siblings of children diagnosed with autism may benefit for a checkup for related symptoms. 被診斷為自閉症的患兒兄妹們可以進行一些相關症狀的檢查。(VOA)

【用】 表示「體檢」的還有：physical examination；health check；medical examination。

## assault [əˈsɔːlt] v./n.（武力或口頭上的）攻擊

【例】A travel advisory by the Indian government earlier this week warned that Indian students in Australia face an increased risk of assault. 本週早些時候，印度政府發布的旅遊警告稱，在澳洲的印度學生被毆打的風險有所增加。(VOA)

【用】 案件相關詞：abduct 綁架；bullyrag 恐嚇；maltreat 虐待；mayhem 故意傷害罪。

## negotiate [niˈgəʊʃieit] v. 商議；順利通過

【例】It comes just three months after governments negotiated a deal to cut future

EU spending. 這件事情就發生在政府協商削減歐盟未來的支出三個月之後。(BBC)

【用】 negotiate、arrange，concert 都可表示為「經過討論或會談雙方一致成就某事」。其區別在於，negotiate 多指外交、交易或法律上等為某事進行談判；arrange 一般指私人之間進行的商定或商妥；concert 特指為取得協同一致所進行的協商。

## overwhelm [ˌəuvəˈhwelm] v. 氾濫；壓倒；使不知所措

【例】After being severely burnt by the crisis, the administration has been careful not to proruise too much, warning that the overhauled site won't work for everyone and could still be overwhelmed by traffic during busy times. 受到危機的重創之後，政府部門開始變得小心翼翼，不再給出過多承諾，並警告稱網站在維護之後不再是每個人都能登錄，且在流量繁忙時仍然可能發生頁面崩潰。(BBC)

【用】 其形容詞是 overwhelming，表示「壓倒性的」。

## eager [ˈiːgə] a. 熱切的

【例】 The law ends a 15-year fight that environmentalists and celebrities have waged against developers eager to build hotels, golf courses and luxury homes in the vicinity. 為反對殷切的開發商在附近建造旅館、高爾夫場和豪華房屋，環保主義者和名人與他們進行了為期十五年的鬥爭，而這條法律頒布後，結束了這場鬥爭。(BBC)

【用】 實用片語：eager beaver 表示「做事異常賣力的人；雄心勃勃的人」；eager for 表示「渴望，想得到」。

## cure [kjuə] v. 治癒 n. 療法；藥（劑）

【例】Autism is often diagnosed in childhood, it is a lifelong disorder, there is no cure for it. 自閉症往往在童年時期被診斷出，這是一種終身疾病，目前還沒有治癒方法。(CNN)

【用】 詞義辨析：動詞 cure、treat、remedy 都有「治療、醫治」之意。cure 主要指治癒疾病；treat 是普通用詞，指接受並診治病人；remedy 著重用藥物對病人進行治療。

## enhance [in'hɑːns] v. 提高

【例】He admitted giving horses in his care anabolic steroids to enhance their perfor-mance. 他承認，為了提高成績，他給自己馴養的馬服用過雄性激素。(BBC)

【用】表示「提高，加強」這層意思的詞語有：improve 提高；promote 促進；strengthen 加強。

## momentum [məu'mentəm] n. 動力；動量

【例】There's real momentum towards resolving the eurozone crisis, and that will be the bigges boost not just to the European economy but actually to the British econ-omy. 解決歐元區危機的勢頭良好，這不僅會大力推動歐洲經濟的發展，實際上也會大力推動英國經濟的發展。

【用】「保持經濟發展的良好勢頭」就是 maintain the good momentum of economic growth。

## integrity [in'tegrəti] n. 正直；完整

【例】The integrity tests would show whether an end is in sight to the environmental disaster that has been unfolding for the last 12 weeks. 完整性測試將揭示在過去的 12 週裡發生的環境災難是否已經快要結束。(CNN)

【用】 詞義辨析：integrity、honesty、justice 這些名詞均有「誠實、正直」之意。integrity 指品格純正，有高度是非感，正直誠實，受人敬佩；honesty 是普通用詞，側重為人忠厚、老實、正直、不欺騙、不說謊；justice 側重辦事或處事公正，公道不偏心。

## academic [ˌækə'demik] a. 學校的；學術的 n. 大學教師

【例】Last year, Friedman headed a committee of academics that took a serious look at the idea. 去年，弗里德曼帶領的一個學者委員會認真地研究了這個想法。(NPR)

【用】 聽力中談論學業常用這些片語：academic research 表示「學術研究」；academic year 表示「學年」；academic achievement 表示「學業成就」。

## sweep [swi:p] v. 打掃；席捲 n. 打掃

【例】The authorities have been swift to sweep up the street damage, tow away burnt-out cars, sandblast graffit. 當局迅速清理了街上的碎片，拖走了被燒毀的轎車並用噴砂機清除了塗鴉。(BBC)

【用】 其形容詞是 sweeping，表示「徹底的；廣泛的」。

## relative ['relətiv] a. 相對的；有關的 n. 親屬

【例】Human vocal tract shape has allowed us to do what our primate relatives can't. 人類聲道形狀使我們能夠做到我們的靈長類親戚所無法做的事情。(CNN)

【用】 在新聞英語中，跟 relative 相關的片語有： relative motion 相對運動； relative sensibility 相對敏感； close relative 近親。

## consecutive [kən'sekjutiv] a. 連續不斷的

【例】The win is the Canadians third consecutive women's ice hockey victory, with two of them coming over the United States. 此次獲勝是加拿大女子冰球的三連勝，她們曾兩度擊敗美國。(VOA)

【用】 consecutive interpretation 表示「交替傳譯」。

## rigorous ['rigərəs] a. 嚴密的；嚴格的；嚴峻的

【例】Sporns says the U.S. has an international certification process that is rigorous and will catch potential problems. 斯波恩表示，美國有著嚴格的國際認證程式，該程式不會放過任何潛在的問題。(VOA)

【用】 詞義辨析：rigid、strict、rigorous 均有「刻板的，嚴格的」之意。rigid 指沒有靈活性、機動性； strict 指在行為規則上要求嚴格； rigorous 側重指嚴格到毫不寬容的地步。

## unity [ˈjuːnəti] n. 團結；一致；聯合

【例】Speakers at the rally expressed sentiments of unity. 集會上的發言者們表達了團結的觀點。(CNN)

【用】 該詞經常出現在政治領域，常用表達有：unity is strength 團結就是力量；眾志成城；strengthen unity 加強團結。

## sentence [ˈsentəns] n. 句子；判決 v. 宣判

【例】A court in Argentina has sentenced the former military ruler Reynaldo Bignone to life in jail for crimes against humanity committed in the 80s. 因 80 年代犯下的反人道罪，前軍事統治者雷納爾多 · 比尼奧內被阿根廷法院判處終身監禁。(BBC)

【用】 依法判決相關詞： absolve 赦免；arbiter 裁決機構；intermediary 仲裁者；retribution 報應。

## portion [ˈpɔːʃən] n. 一部分 v. 分配

【例】It says a portion of profits from the project will be given as grants to social program. 據說該專案的一部分利潤將被作為社會專案的補助金。(VOA)

【用】 詞義辨析： portion、part、section 這三個詞都有「部分」的意思，其區別是： part 指任何整體中的一部分，是最常用的詞， portion 指各人分得的一部分， section 指對整體分割、區分或歸類後而形成的部分； portion 強調一份的量， section 常暗指各部分之間有明顯的界限； portion 多用於抽象事物， section 多用於具體事物， part 則既可用於抽象事物，也可用於具體事物。

## remote [riˈməut] a. 遠的；偏僻的；遠程的

【例】It's on a remote island halfway between Norway's mainland and the North Pole. 它位於挪威大陸與北極中間的一個孤島上。(VOA)

【用】 常用片語： remote education 表示「遠端教育」； remote control 表示「遙控」； remote monitoring 表示「遠程監控」。

## downturn [ˈdauntəːn] n. 低迷時期；下翻

【例】Amid a protracted downturn, the United States is now increasingly looking to revive its manufacturing industry as a way out of its economic woes. 在曠日持久的經濟衰退的背景下，美國現在越發地將重振製造業作為經濟困境的出路。(CRI)

【用】 近義拓展：slump 表示「大幅度下跌」；recession 表示「經濟衰退」；decline 表示「下降」。

## initially [iˈniʃəli] ad. 最初地

【例】Initially, the school had an art teacher but it didn't have money for supplies or an art club. 最初，學校有一個美術老師，但學校缺乏資金購買美術用品和成立藝術社團。(NPR)

【用】 表示「最初地」的單字還有：firstly 最初；originally 最初地；primarily 首先。

## encourage [inˈkʌridʒ] v. 鼓勵或支持某人；激勵

【例】After decades of estrangement, the United States sees engagement with Burma as a means to encourage further political and economic liberalization. 經過幾十年的隔閡，美國將與緬甸的合作視為一種手段，以鼓勵進一步的政治和經濟自由化。(VOA)

【用】 常見用法：用作及物動詞，encourage n./pron. 表示「鼓勵」；encourage doing sth. 表示「鼓勵做某事」；用作賓補動詞，encourage n./pron. to do 表示「鼓勵……做某事」。

## participate [pɑːˈtisipeit] v. 參與

【例】Most of his fellow sailors had participated in the Olympic Sailing Regatta, five were gold medalists, and three were silver medalists. 大部分跟隨他的船員都曾參加過奧帆賽，其中五人為金牌得主，三人為銀牌得主。(CRI)

【用】 participate、attend、join 和 take part in 都可作「參加」講。其區別是：join 指參加某團體或組織成為其中一員或參加活動，是非正式用語；attend 主要「出席」會議等；

participate 指參與活動並積極從事工作，是正式用語； take part in 指參加一項工作，在其中分擔一部分，也指參加活動並積極工作。

## persuade [pəˈsweid] v. 說服

【例】I am persuaded that such is the fact. 我相信事實如此。(VOA)

【用】 需要掌握的介詞片語： persuade sb. into doing sth. 表示「勸某人做某事」； persuade sb. of sth. 表示「使某人確信」。

## blossom [ˈblɔsəm] n. 開花 v.（植物）開花；發展

【例】The National Park Service suggests that cherry blossoms should be seen during three time periods. 國家公園管理局表示，櫻花應該在三個不同的時間段觀賞。(VOA)

【用】 常用片語： in blossom 表示「盛開；開花」。

## observe [əbˈzəːv] v. 注意到；觀察；評說

【例】In the sixteenth century, one astronomer suggested that navigators could observe the moon as it passed in front of different known stars to tell longitude. 在 16 世紀，一位天文學家表示航海家們能透過觀測月亮運行到已知星球的各前方位置，得知自己所在的緯度。(VOA)

【用】 observe、notice、perceive 這組詞都有「觀察」的意思，其區別是：perceive 指使用各種感覺器官去瞭解事物；notice 指觀察並注意到某個重要卻又很容易被忽略掉的細節；observe 指在方便有利的位置上注意觀察、研究某事物或現象，強調思想高度集中，態度嚴謹客觀。

## instruction [inˈstrʌkʃən] n. 命令；教學

【例】And he says it must start in the schools by giving all Indian children the same instruction on physical activity and diet. 他還表示這必須從學校開始做起，給予印度兒童在體育和飲食方面同樣的指導。(VOA)

【用】 instruction 在表示「教學」時常用單數形式，表示「指令，指示」時，常用複數形式。

# Level 18

## keen [kiːn] a. 熱心的；敏銳的；激烈的

【例】Julia Gillard's sworn in as the country's first female prime minister, but keen to mark the achievements of her predecessor. 國家的首位女總理朱麗亞 · 吉拉德宣誓就職，她熱切地稱讚了前任總統所取得的成就。(CNN)

【用】 常用表達： keen on 熱衷於，喜愛； keen competition 激烈競爭； keen interest 強烈興趣。

## precaution [priˈkɔːʃən] n. 預防措施

【例】The New York police department says there has been no specific threat against the city's subway system, but additional security has been put in place as a precaution. 紐約警察局表示，目前還沒有針對城市地鐵系統的具體威脅，但額外的安全保障作為預防措施已經發表。(VOA)

【用】 常用表達： take precautions against 對……採取措施預防； precaution against 提防，防範； safety precaution 安全預防措施。

## assess [əˈses] v. 評定

【例】For the first time, Mexico will have an independent body to oversee teaching and the curriculum and teachers and schools will now be assessed. 墨西哥將首次建立獨立的教育體系監管機構，現在課程、教師和學校都將接受評估。(BBC)

【用】 在新聞英語中，可用 assess a tax upon on land 來表示「徵收土地稅」。

## sentiment [ˈsentimənt] n. 思想感情；意見

【例】They showed consumer sentiment fell in April. 他們表示，四月消費者信心指數有所下跌。 (NPR)

【用】 其形容詞是 sentimental，表示「多愁善感的」。

## outbreak [ˈaʊtbreɪk] n.（戰爭等的）爆發；（疾病等的）突然發生

【例】The United Nations has warned Haiti to prepare itself for a potential spread of the cholera outbreak, which has killed more than 250 people. 聯合國警告海地需要預防霍亂爆發和大範圍傳播，因為它已經奪去了 250 人的生命。(BBC)

【用】 自然災害相關詞： avalanche 雪崩 ；blizzard 暴風雪 ；drought 乾旱 hurricane 颶風 ；landslide 山崩。

## quit [kwɪt] v. 放棄；離開，辭（職）

【例】After having threatened to quit on several previous occasions reportedly over the direction and handling of economic policy, Mr Abbas has now accepted his Prime Minister's resignation. 此前因為經濟政策的方向把控和處理等方面的問題，首相曾數次以辭職作為威脅，而這次阿巴斯先生已經接受了他的辭職。(BBC)

【用】 quit 經常用來表示「辭職」，我們還可用 resign 這個詞表示這層意思。

## needy [ˈniːdi] a. 貧窮的

【例】A new study says much of the money the federal government gives to needy college students through Pell grants is wasted. 一項新的研究表明，大部分聯邦政府透過佩爾助學金資助貧困大學生的資金都被浪費了。(NPR)

【用】 其反義詞是 affluent，表示「富有的」。

## tear [tɪə] n. 眼淚；破洞 [teə] v. 撕裂

【例】Police in Rome fired tear gas to disperse protesters, who'd smashed bank and shop windows. 羅馬警方發射催淚彈以驅散那些打砸銀行視窗和商店櫥窗的示威者。(BBC)

【用】 常用片語：tear down 表示「扯下；詆毀；拆卸；逐條駁斥」；tear off 表示「撕下；扯掉」；tear up 表示「撕毀；撕碎；拉掉」；tear out 表示「撕開，扯下」。

## mismanagement [ˌmisˈmænidʒmənt] n. 管理不善

【例】Protests against what's perceived a corporate greed and economic misman-agemen have been taking place around the world. 針對企業貪婪的行為和經濟管理不善事件的抗議活動已在世界範圍內進行。(BBC)

【用】 管理相關詞： superintendent 監管人 ；regulation 規章 ；managerial 經理的 ；super-intend 監督。

## ease [iːz] v. 緩和 n. 悠閒

【例】He wanted to see if putting patients into a sleep-like condition would help ease troubled minds. 他想看一下是否讓病人處於睡眠般的狀態就能減少煩擾的思緒。(VOA)

【用】 at ease 表示「安逸，自由自在；舒適」。

## wrongdoing [ˈrɔŋˈduːiŋ] n. 不道德行為

【例】Mr Blazer, an American, was due to step down from Fifa's executive board at the end of his term later this month, he's previously denied any wrongdoing. 布萊澤先生是一名美國人，他將於本月底任期結束時辭去國際足聯執行委員會的職位，此前他否認自己犯下了任何過錯。(BBC)

【用】 社會道德相關詞： harmony 融洽 ；ideology 思想體系 ；norm 規範 ；principle 原則。

## revolutionary [ˌrevəˈljuːʃənəri] a. 革命的 n. 革命者

【例】Some members of the interim authorities said he had been wounded and cap-tured by revolutionary fighters, but there's been no independent evidence of this. 臨時政府的一些成員稱他已經被革命戰士所擊傷並逮捕，但沒有獨立證據證明這一說法。(BBC)

【用】 政治新聞常用的固定搭配： revolutionary party 表示「革命黨」； revolutionary com-mittee 表示「革命委員會」； revolutionary guard 表示「革命衛隊」。

## amendment [əˈmendmənt] n. 改正；修正案

【例】He said the amendment should recognize the right to own slaves as property in states where slavery was permitted. 他表示在允許施行奴役制度的州，這一修正案承認了將奴隸作為私有財產的權利。 (VOA)

【用】 國際時事的相關詞： communique 官方公報 ；declaration 宣布 ；impeachment 彈劾 ；nationalism 民族主義。

## reward [riˈwɔːd] n. 報答；報酬 v. 報答

【例】When the music fulfills or even exceeds these expectations, the listener feels rewarded. 當音樂能夠達到，甚至超出這些預期時，聽者就會覺得得到了回報。(Scientific American)

【用】 其形容詞形式是 rewarding ，表示「有益的，值得的」。

## prior [ˈpraiə] a./ad. 在......之前

【例】 As most of you know, I didn't work in government prior to about a year ago now. 就像你們大多數人所知道的那樣，大約一年前我並不在政府工作。(CNN)

【用】 常見用法： prior to 在......之前。

## aboard [əˈbɔːd] ad./prep. 在船（車、飛機）上；上船（飛機、車）

【例】 The three astronauts aboard waved and smiled for after emerging from the capsule. 三名太空人從太空艙出來以後，在太空梭上招手並微笑。(VOA)

【用】 航空相關詞： aerial 航空的 ；ascend 攀登 ；upward 向上的 ；onboard 在飛機上。

## counter [ˈkauntə] n. 櫃檯 v. 抵制 ad. 相反地

【例】The seafood counter displays blue labels from the Marine Stewardship Council, an international, nonprofit organization. 這個海鮮櫃檯標著來自國際非盈利性組

織──海洋管理委員會的藍色標籤。(NPR)

【用】 常用表達： counter measure 對策；防範措施； counter attack 反攻，逆襲。

## guard [gɑːd] n. 警衛員 v. 守衛；防止

【例】Troops were reported to be guarding the key points there. 據報告，部隊正守衛著那兒的要塞。(CNN)

【用】 安全防範的相關詞： alert 警惕的；awareness 意識；precaution 預防措施 ；safety 安全 ；vigilance 警惕。

## wage [weidʒ] n. 工資，報酬 v. 開始；發動

【例】Obama says he wants Perez to play a big role in such issues as long-term unemployment, immigration and the minimum wage. 歐巴馬說他希望佩雷斯能在解決長期失業、移民及最低工資等問題上起到重要的作用。(NPR)

【用】 薪酬情況相關詞：payroll 工資單；payday 發薪日 ；remuneration 報酬 ；novice 生手。

## drag [dræg] v. 拖著腳步走；慢吞吞地進 n. 累贅

【例】The space agency is planning to capture a small asteroid, drag it to the moon and put it in orbit. 宇航局計畫捕獲一個小行星，並將其拖到月亮運行的軌道上。(NPR)

【用】 drag、draw、pull 意思相近，都表示「拖、拉」，其區別如下： drag 指慢慢地拖著笨重的東西，意味著所拖的東西阻力很大；draw 與 pull 相比，它通常指較平穩地，也往往是比較從容地拉；pull 是普通用語，指用力拉，與 push 相對。

## contemporary [kənˈtempərəri] a. 當代的；同時代的 n. 同代人

【例】 Concluding its meeting in Budapest, the assembly called for decisive action agains contemporary expressions of the extremism. 這場會議在布達佩斯結束，會議呼籲針對目前的極端主義表現要堅決採取行動。(BBC)

【用】常用表達： contemporary art 當代藝術； contemporary society 當代社會。

## harsh [hɑ:ʃ] a. 嚴厲的；粗糙的；刺耳的

【例】It is a strong feeling, but the harsh realitie s of costs and benefits are likely to be around for future generations. 這是一種強烈的感覺，但是成本和利益的殘酷現實都是未來幾代人要面臨的。(VOA)

【用】 常用表達： harsh reality 表示「嚴酷的現實」； harsh terms 表示「苛刻的條件」。

## faulty [ˈfɔːlti] a. 有錯誤的

【例】The first delay was weather-related, the second was due to a faulty valve. 第一次延誤與天氣有關而第二次延誤是由於一個閥門出現故障。(BBC)

【用】 常用表達： faulty item 表示「故障產品」； faulty goods 表示「次貨；劣等貨物」； faulty operation 表示「錯誤操作」。

## slender [ˈslendə] a. 修長的；苗條的；微薄的

【例】We have large floor plates for the offices, and then the building gets more slender to the top, and the lighter to the top. 辦公樓的樓板更大，而且越通往樓頂越窄，重量也越輕。(CNN)

【用】 形容人「苗條的」，還可以用 slim。

## suit [sjuːt] n. 一套衣服（或西服）；起訴 v. 合適

【例】 But he'll also expect Britain's NATO partners to follow suit by offering more forces themselves. 但他也會期待英國的北約夥伴照做並為自己提供更多的力量。

【用】 法律訴訟相關詞： accusation 控告 ；civil 民事的 ；damage 損壞 ；litigation 訴訟。

## rebuild [ˌriːˈbild] v. 重建；再形成

【例】So there has been rehabilitation and rebuilding of Mogadishu, and people were so happy and just were feeling some sort of relative calm. 所以，目前摩加迪休正在復興重建，人們很開心並開始感到相對平靜。(BBC)

【用】　知識拓展：首碼 re- 表示「重新；再」的意思。相關的詞有：reconstruct 表示「重建」；remake 表示「重做」；reconstitute 表示「重組」；reestablish 表示「重建」。

## denounce [diˈnauns] v. 譴責，公開指責

【例】Others say he should forcefully denounce the election. 其他人表示他強有力地譴責選舉。(VOA)

【用】　denounce 的近義詞辨析：eprove 的意思偏向公眾的譴責，多指訓斥；denounce 則偏向於公然抨擊。

## transition [trænˈziʃən] n. 過渡；轉變

【例】But we believe that now it is time to engage more and to help the transition move ahead. 但我們認為現在應該積極參與，幫助緬甸順利過渡。(BBC)

【用】　常用片語：transition period 過渡時期；smooth transition 平穩過渡；transition state 過渡狀態。

## simulation [ˌsimjuˈleiʃən] n. 模擬；模擬：模仿；假裝

【例】Researchers used climate simulations to fast forward to the year 2050. 研究人員透過氣候模擬預測了 2050 年的天氣。(Scientific American)

【用】　computer simulation 就是「電腦類比」。

## oust [aust] v. 驅逐；剝奪

【例】New leadership will often oust existing coalitions and surround themselves with a new team. 新的領導階層往往會驅逐現有的聯盟並任用一個新團隊。(CNN)

【用】 常和介詞連用，構成固定表達。如：oust from 表示「驅逐」；oust of 表示「剝奪」。

## downstream [ˈdaunˈstriːm]] a. 下游的 ad. 順流而下

【例】Heavy rains and flooding in states up river in the past week, are exerting enormous pressure downstream. 上週在一些州，大雨和洪水漫過了河床，傾斜而下。(VOA)

【用】 相關的固定搭配：downstream industry 表示「下游產業」；downstream processing 表示「下游處理」；downstream water 表示「下游水」；downstream transactions 表示「下游交易」。

## abduct [æbˈdʌkt] v. 綁架；誘拐

【例】Last summer the pensioner posse plus one accomplice abducted the financial advisor outside his house. 去年夏天，一隊領取養老金的人和一名同謀在財務顧問的房子外面將他綁架了。(BBC)

【用】 abduct 的過去分詞 abducted 可修飾名詞作定語，意思是「被誘拐的，被綁架的」。

## pandemic [pænˈdemik] a. 大範圍流行的

【例】The World Health Organization is warning countries to prepare for further spread of the H1N1 influenza pandemic in coming months. 世界衛生組織提醒各國要為預防未來數月 H1N1 流感的進一步蔓延做準備。(VOA)

【用】 診斷病情相關詞：infectious 傳染的；incurable 不能治癒的；remediable 可治療的；susceptible 易受感染的。

## waste [weist] n. 浪費；廢料 v. 浪費

【例】 The researchers say airlines may have to fl y more detours in the future to avoid it, a waste of time and fuel that ups emissions. 研究人員說，航空公司在未來

不得不設計更多的彎路航線來避開它，這不但浪費時間和燃料，還會增加排放量。
(Scientific American)

【用】 常用句型：It is / was a waste of time doing sth. 表示「做某事是浪費時間的」，如：It's a mere waste of time waiting any longer. 再等下去純粹是浪費時間。

## destination [ˌdestiˈneiʃn̩] n. 目的地

【例】Before Disney World, Silver Springs in Central Florida was for decades one of the state's most popular tourist destinations. 在迪士尼建立之前，位於佛羅里達州中部的銀泉幾十年來一直是這個國家最熱門的旅遊目的地之一。(NPR)

【用】 常用表達：tourist destination 旅遊勝地；destination country 目的國。

## chart [tʃɑːt] n. 航圖 v. 【用】圖表表示；製圖

【例】This chart basically shows what they might be. 這個圖表主要展示的是它們可能的樣子。(VOA)

【用】 片語 chart out 有兩個意思，一是「在海圖上標出」；二是「探查」。

## publication [ˌpʌbliˈkeiʃn̩] n. 出版；公布

【例】The publication was seen as an attempt to inflict damage on a political rival. 這一事件公布了人們認為這是在試圖加害政治對手。(BBC)

【用】 electronice publication 就是現在流行的「電子出版物」。

## downtown [ˈdaunˈtaun] ad. 往（在）市區 a. 市區的

【例】Cobo Center is home to the 2010 North American Auto Show in downtown Detroit. 科博會展中心位於底特律商業中心區，2010 年北美國際汽車展曾在這裡舉行。(VOA)

【用】 downtown 用作「在商業區」解時，一般與靜態動詞（如 live）連用；作「往商業區」

解時，往往與動態動詞（如 come、go、move 等）連用，表示運動的方向； downtown 無比較級和最高級。

## preserve [priˈzəːv] v. 保護；保存；醃制 n. 保護區

【例】She says, she wants to make choices that will help preserve the wild fish populations in the oceans. 她說，她希望自己做出的選擇能夠有助於保護海洋裡的野生魚群。(NPR)

【用】 在新聞英語中，有「維護」的意思，比如： preserve one's independence 維護某人的獨立；它還有「保藏、保存」的意思，比如： preserve food 保藏食物。

## entry [ˈentri] n. 進入；入口；條目

【例】A lot of the entry level jobs the young people used to count on, like those at clothing stores or restaurants for example are going to more experienced or more educated workers. 過去年輕人指望尋找的許多入門級職位，如在服裝店或餐館的工作，現在都招收更有經驗或接受過更好教育的員工。(CNN)

【用】 entry into 表示「進入」； entry form 表示「報名表格」； no entry 表示「不准入內；禁止通行」。

## circumstance [ˈsəːkəmstəns] n. 環境；[pl.] 境況

【例】 This explains that those complications and difficulties are following a pace thought by people who don't know the internal circumstances of the talks. 這就解釋了為何會出現人們所認為的複雜和困難的局勢，因為他們並不瞭解談判內情。(BBC)

【用】 新聞中出現的固定搭配： existing circumstance 表示「現況」； business circumstance 表示「經營情況」； adverse circumstance 表示「不利的處境」。

## whereby [weəˈbai] ad. 憑什麼；憑藉

【例】 I have asked the registrar to implement emergence procedures whereby the building remains closed but fit for purpose until such a time as we can open safely. 我曾讓登記員執行緊急程序，這樣這座樓房就能符合我們的要求一直關閉，直到我們能夠安全地將其打開為止。(BBC)

【用】 whereby 是關係副詞，也就是 by which，如：Whereby shall we find fault with him? 我們憑什麼指責他呢？ 可以改寫成 By which shall we find fault with him?

## vault [vɔːlt] n. 拱頂；撐竿跳；地下室 v. 用手支撐越過

【例】The Global Crop Diversity Trust said seeds and plant material are stored in what it calls a fail-safe location the Svalbard Global Seed Vault. 全球作物多樣性信託基金表示，種子和植物原料儲存在裝備有自動防故障裝置的斯瓦爾巴全球種子庫。(VOA)

【用】 bank vault 表示「銀行金庫」；vault cash 表示「備用現金」。

## profound [prəuˈfaund] a. 深切的；知識淵博的；深奧的

【例】As governments debate who is to shoulder greater responsibility for slowing climate change and paying for the damage, profound change, says Dr.Anond, should come from individuals. 各政府辯論應當由誰肩負起更大的責任，去減緩氣候變化並補償由此造成的損失，但阿諾德博士表示，每一個體都應該做出深刻的改變。(VOA)

【用】 詞義辨析： profound 和 deep 這兩個詞的共同意思是「深刻的」，都可以表示理論的深奧、學問的淵博及感情的深厚等。其區別在於： deep 可以用於具體事物，而 profound 則不能； deep 可表示顏色之深，而 profound 則不可以； profound 是正式用語，deep 為一般用語。

## inform [inˈfɔːm] v. 通知；告發

【例】People with anorexia see themselves as heavier than they actually are. But does this distorted self-image inform unconscious behavior? 患厭食症的人認為自己比實際體重要重，這種扭曲的自我形象認知是否說明這是一種無意識行為呢？

(Scientific American)

【用】 媒體傳播相關詞：disclose 揭露；informant 提供消息的人；introduce 介紹；report-er 記者；disseminate 散布。

## duration [djuəˈreiʃən] n. 持續的時間

【例】These longer duration missions and space dockings are essential practice for any kind of long-term, more permanent presence in space or a mission to, say, the moon. 如果想要在太空中存在的時間更久，或者有登月計畫，這些持續時間較長的任務和空間對接都是非常必要的訓練。(CNN)

【用】 在新聞英語中，與 duration 相關的片語有：test duration 試驗時間；exposure dura-tion 暴露時間；pulse duration 脈衝持續時間。

## platform [ˈplætfɔːm] n. 平台；月台；(政黨的) 綱領

【例】Actually, merchants, payment platforms, banks and consumers online are all victims of such behavior. 事實上，商家、支付平台、銀行和消費者在網路上都是這種行為的受害者。(CRI)

【用】 政治新聞常出現的片語：party platform 表示「黨綱」；in accordance with platform 表示「按照政綱」。

## enforce [inˈfɔːs] v. 實施；強迫

【例】European authorities are trying to enforce strict anti-smoking laws to save hun-dreds of thousands of lives each year. 歐洲當局正試圖強制執行嚴格的反吸菸法，這樣每年將拯救成千上萬人的生命。(CNN)

【用】 實施政策相關詞：implement 實施；permissible 容許的；rationalization 合理化；viable 切實可行的。

## flexibility [ˌflɛksəˈbiləti] n. 彈性；適應性

【例】White collar workers, high-paid workers, professional workers have more flexibility than they used to. 白領、高薪員工和專業人員的工作形式都比從前更靈活。(VOA)

【用】 近義拓展：adaptability 表示「適應性」；suppleness 表示「易彎曲」；elasticity 表示「彈力」；springiness 表示「富有彈性」；flexibleness 表示「柔軟性」。

## consumption [kənˈsʌmpʃən] n. 消耗（量）；揮霍

【例】 What are the potential pros and consumption of this? Christine Romans has some answers. 潛在的優勢和消耗是什麼？克里斯汀．羅曼斯已經有了答案。(CNN)

【用】 該詞經常用於經濟領域，常見用法有：popular consumption 表示「大眾消費」；consumption level 表示「消費水準」；high consumption 表示「高消費」。

## barrack [ˈbærək] v. 住入兵營 n. 兵營

【例】 Local security forces in Algeria say at least ten people were killed today in a car bomb attack on a barrack. 阿爾及利亞當地的安全部隊表示，在今天的汽車炸彈襲擊兵營事件中，至少 10 人被炸死。(VOA)

【用】 在軍事新聞中：barrack 的常用表達中：detention barrack 軍中拘留所。

## escape [iˈskeip] v./n. 逃脫；避免

【例】A day after around 50 wild animals escaped from a private zoo in Ohio, police say they have killed nearly all of them. 大約 50 頭野生動物從俄亥俄州的一所私人動物園逃跑，一天後，警方稱他們幾乎已經把動物都殺死了。(BBC)

【用】 監獄入罪相關詞：abscond 潛逃 ；exempt 免除 ；gaol 監獄 ；bail 保釋 。

## vary [ˈveəri] v. 變化

【例】Professor Jerry Seigel from the University of California, Los Angeles, conducted a study of the sleep times of a broad range of animals and found that they vary widely. 洛杉磯加州大學的傑裡 · 西格爾教授研究了不同動物的睡眠時間，發現它們之間有很大的差異。(BBC)

【用】 常用片語：vary between 表示「在兩種情況之間變化」；vary from 表示「不同於」；vary in 表示「在......方面變化」；vary with 表示「隨......而變化」。

## merely [ˈmiəli] ad. 僅僅

【例】It needs to be tackled from an educational and a social point of view rather than merely legislation. 這需要從教育和社會的角度來解決，而不僅僅是立法的角度。(BBC)

【用】 merely because... 表示「僅僅因為......」。

# Level 19

## partly [ˈpɑːtli] ad. 部分地；在一定程度上

【例】Her book became popular partly because she uses plain Chinese to explain difficult medical theories. 她的書很受歡迎，部分原因是因為她使用了淺顯易懂的中文語言來解釋艱深的醫學理論。(CRI)

【用】 partly cloudy 就是天氣預報中常說的「局部多雲」。

## dine [dain] v. 進餐

【例】One of the world's best restaurants based in Copenhagen has apologized after dozens of people who dined there last month suffering from vomiting and diarrhoea. 上月，數十人在哥本哈根的一家世界頂級餐館就餐後出現嘔吐和腹瀉，該餐館就此事道歉。(BBC)

【用】 必會片語：dine out 表示「在外吃飯」；dine at 表示「在……就餐」。

## supplier [səˈplaiə] n. 供應者；供應貨物等的人或商店

【例】Overnight, the demand far outstripped the supply and so the suppliers had to catch up. 一夜之間，需求遠遠超過了供應，因此，供應商必須迎頭趕上。(NPR)

【用】 近義拓展：provider 供應者；dealer 商人；contractor 立契約的人；seller 賣方。

## riot [ˈraiət] n. 暴亂；（色彩、聲音等的）極度豐富 v. 聚眾鬧事

【例】And historically, a boost in the cost of bread has led to riots across Egypt. 從歷史上看，麵包成本的上升已經導致了整個埃及的騷亂。(VOA)

【用】 a riot of color 表示「五彩繽紛」；a riot of sound 表示「人聲鼎沸」。

## stall [stɔːl] n. 貨攤 v. 停止；拖延

【例】Kids still prefer tasty snacks made by the stalls rather than a school lunch. 孩子們還是喜歡攤位上出售的美味小吃，而不是學校的午餐。(CRI)

【用】 food stall 就是「小吃攤」。

## namely [ˈneimli]] ad. 也就是

【例】There is no constitution code, namely no legal text by the name of constitution. 沒有憲法法典，也就是沒有以憲法為名稱的法律文本。(CNN)

【用】 namely 用於對剛提及的事物給予更多的資訊或說明，常用作插入語。

## freely [ˈfriːli] ad. 自由地；免費地；大方地

【例】The government is to develop plans to make publicly funded research results freely available to all. 政府將制訂計畫，將公共資助的研究成果免費提供給所有人。(BBC)

【用】 新聞中也經常出現其同根詞 freedom ，表示「自由」。

## crusty [ˈkrʌsti] a. 有殼的；易怒的

【例】Vacuuming the corn was a very slow process, especially because it was wet and crusty.　用吸塵器清理穀物是一個很緩慢的過程，主要是因為穀物潮濕且帶殼。(NPR)

【用】 crusty bread 表示「硬皮麵包」。

## dusty [ˈdʌsti] a. 滿是灰塵的

【例】 The film park lies only a couple of blocks away from a dusty, noisy and truck-loaded highway. 電影公園距離這條塵土飛揚、聲音嘈雜且有許多卡車經過的公路只有幾個街區遠。(CNN)

【用】 形容房間相關詞：neat 整潔的 ；messy 雜亂的 ；empty 空蕩蕩的 ；humble 簡陋的。

## accomplish [əˈkʌmpliʃ] v. 達到；完成；實現

【例】The 39-year-old northern Irishman accomplished the feat when he triumphed in the second of two rides in the Towcester north of London. 這位 39 歲的北愛爾蘭人在倫敦北部的托斯特一共進行過兩次騎行，在他的第二次騎行中，他完成了這一壯舉。(BBC)

【用】其形容詞 accomplished 表示「完成的；熟練的；有修養的」。

## convince [kənˈvins] v. 使某人確信

【例】We could not find any studies that convinced us that there was a causal link between teaching the arts and performance on test scores. 我們無法找到任何的研究使我們確信，教授藝術與考試成績之間存在因果關係。(NPR)

【用】 承諾擔保相關詞：allege 斷言；commitment 承諾；pledge 保證；trusty 可信賴的。

## compound [ˈkɔmpaund] n. 化合物；複合物；圍牆內的房群 a. 複合的 v. 混合；妥協

【例】According to military officials, the two rockets were supposed to target insurgents who they say were firing from a compound. 據軍事官員所說，反叛分子在一棟建築內開火，這兩枚火箭原來的射擊目標是他們。(NPR)

【用】 compound 一般用在化學方面，如：compound fertilizer 表示「複合肥料」；organic compound 表示「有機化合物」；chemical compound 表示「化合物」。

## outgo [autˈgəu] n. 支出；出口 vt. 支出；超出

【例】Through this program of action we address ourselves to putting our own national house in order and making income balance outgo. 根據這一行動方案，我們將致力於整修國家大廈並整頓財政，使收支達到平衡。(BBC)

【用】 支出消費相關詞：prepaid 預付的；tariff 關稅；kickback 回扣；disburse 支付。

## plain [pleɪn] a. 平的；簡單的；樸素的；清晰的 n. 平原 ad. 清楚地

【例】Your blunt, plain-spoken style has really stirred—are we going to hear more of that? 你直白而坦率的風格引起了爭論——我們還要聽到更多那樣的話嗎？ (CNN)

【用】 常用句型：It is/was plain to do sth. 表示「做某事很顯然」；It is/was plain that... 表示「……是很顯然的」。

## echo [ˈekəu] v./n. 回聲

【例】The sound of gun shots and explosions echoed through the centre of Srinagar after gunmen opened fire in Lal Chowk. 當槍手在拉爾集市開槍後，槍聲和爆炸聲迴盪在斯利那加市中心。(BBC)

【用】 軍事新聞中常出現的片語：radar echo 表示「雷達回波」；echo cancellation 表示「回波消除」；ultrasonic echo 表示「超聲回波」；echo sounder 表示「回聲測深器」。

## object [ˈɔbdʒɪkt] n. 物體；目的 [W4b'd9ekt] v. 反對

【例】The very idea of lassoing an object and towing it to Earth orbit sounds pretty preposterous when you first think of it. 剛開始的時候，用套索套住物體並將其牽引到地球軌道的想法聽起來很荒謬。 (NPR)

【用】質疑反對相關詞：denial 否認 ；lash 猛烈抨擊 ；rejection 拒絕 ；retort 反駁。

## uncertain [ˌʌnˈsəːtən] a. 不確定的；不可靠的

【例】Progress is not going to be even. There is going to be a period where it is going to feel very bad still and very uncertain. 進步的過程不會一馬平川。會有一段時期，你感覺情況將持續糟糕下去，且一切都很不確定。(VOA)

【用】 新聞中常出現的固定搭配：uncertain factors 表示「不確定因素」；market uncertain 表示「不穩定的市場」；uncertain systems 表示「不確定系統」。

## plagiarism [ˈpleidʒiərizəm] n. ( 文章、學說等的 ) 剽竊；剽竊物

【例】France's chief rabbi is leaving his post after admitting to plagiarism and lying about his academic background. 法國首席拉比承認剽竊和學歷背景造假，隨後辭去職務。(BBC)

【用】 跟 plagiarism 相關的詞語有：copyright 版權；issertation 論文；atent 專利。

## span [spæn] n. 跨距；一段時間 v. 持續

【例】It's one of those songs that really spans the gamut. 這是為數不多的跨越了全音階的歌曲之一。(VOA)

【用】 生活中常用片語：life span 表示「壽命；使用期限」；long span 表示「長跨度」；time span 表示「時間跨度」。

## dense [dens] a. 密集的

【例】The cortex is comprised of dense layers of nerve cells, and its thickness indicates the health of the brain. 皮層由神經細胞的緻密層組成，其厚度可以顯示大腦的健康狀況。(NPR)

【用】 dense 的常用用法：dense fog 表示「濃霧」；dense population 表示「稠密的人口」；dense concrete 表示「密實混凝土」。

## defend [[diˈfend] v. 保衛；為......辯護；為 ( 論文等 ) 答辯

【例】Mr. Brennan defended the policy during his confirmation hearing Thursday before the Senate Intelligence Committee. 在週四的聽證會上，布倫南先生在參議院情報委員會面前為這一政策辯護。(VOA)

【用】 被告辯護相關詞：clarify 澄清；defense 辯護；guilty 有罪的；impunity 免除懲罰。

## thick [θik] a. 厚的；密的 ad. 厚厚地

【例】An extra thick piece of bread is hollowed out to resemble a flat bread bowl. It is toasted to harden it and then filled with seafood chowder. 將一片超厚的麵包片挖空，做成一個扁平的麵包碗，然後再把它烤硬，用它盛滿海鮮雜燴。(CNN)

【用】 Blood is thicker than water. 表示「血濃於水」。

## tense [tens] a. 緊張的 v. 變得緊張；拉緊

【例】In a comment of a Russian TV channel she said that the situation in the country remains tense and difficult. 她在俄羅斯電影頻道發表評論說，該國局勢仍然緊張而難以應付。(BBC)

【用】 常用表達 tense up 表示「緊張」。

## efficient [i'fiʃənt] a. 效率高的；能勝任的；有能力的

【例】Cars are getting more efficient, and people are actually driving less. 汽車正變得性能越來越強，但實際上，人們已經不經常開車了。(NPR)

【用】 新聞中常出現的搭配：efficient production 表示「有效生產」；efficient market 表示「有效市場」；energy efficient 表示「高效節能」。

## tap [tæp] n. 龍頭 v. 輕叩

【例】When you hear an unfamiliar tune, how do you wind up either tapping your foot or plugging your ears? 當你聽到不熟悉的曲調而緊張起來時，你是用腳打拍子還是捂住耳朵？(Scientific American)

【用】 經濟新聞中，常用 tap into the market 表示「進入市場」。

## command [kə'mɑːnd] n./v. 命令；控制

【例】We have no change, that is to say she is still following those basic commands.

我們沒有做出改變，也就是說，她仍在遵循那些基本的命令。(CNN)

【用】 常見用法：command sb. to do sth. 表示「命令某人去做某事」。

## pretend [pri'tend] v. 假裝

【例】Research also shows that you won't get the same effect by just pretending to chew gum. 研究還表明，如果你假裝嚼口香糖就不會得到同樣的效果。(Scientific American)

【用】 pretend to 有多種意義，後面加動詞原形表達「假裝去做某事」。

## accidental [,æksi'dentəl] a. 意外的

【例】The hot line had an important purpose: to prevent accidental war between the two competitors during the period known as the Cold War. 裝熱線電話還有一個重要的目的：阻止兩個競爭者在冷戰期間發起意外的戰爭。(VOA)

【用】 新聞中的常用表達：accidental death 表示「意外死亡」；accidental damage 表示「意外損壞」；accidental explosion 表示「意外爆炸」。

## flame [fleim] n. 火焰；強烈的感情 v. 燃燒

【例】Families, young and old, brought flowers. Others lit candles. The pavement in front of the building is carpeted with flickering flames. 無論老幼，家人們紛紛買來了鮮花。其他人則點亮蠟燭。樓前的路面滿是燭光閃爍。(BBC)

【用】 常用搭配：burst into flame 表示「突然燃燒起來」；a flame of anger 表示「怒火」；go up in flames 表示「毀於一旦」。

## crack [kræk] v. (使)破裂；打開 n. 爆裂聲

【例】 For governments around the world, sustainable development is proving a tough nut to crack. 對於全世界各國政府來講，可持續發展仍然是重中之重。(BBC)

【用】 crack down 在新聞中經常出現，表示「鎮壓；取締」。

## frequent [ˈfriːkwənt] a. 時常發生的 v. 時常來訪

【例】We don't know whether it's because they have more frequent contact with poultry or if it's because of their physical condition. 我們不知道這是因為他們頻繁地接觸家禽而導致，還是因為他們自己的身體狀況。(CRI)

【用】 其副詞 frequently 表示「經常地」也很常用。

## license [ˈlaisns] n. 許可證；執照 v. 特許

【例】Professor Shahabi hopes to license this new technology to companies that already have navigation systems, such as Google and Apple. 薩哈比教授希望從已經擁有導航系統的公司得到這新技術的特許，例如谷歌和蘋果。(VOA)

【用】 證件相關詞：certificate 證書 ； visa 簽證 ； identity 身分 ； passport 護照。

## sufficient [səˈfiʃənt] a. 足夠的

【例】You should have sufficient funds to support yourself after you arrive in America. 你應該有足夠的資金能夠維持自己在到達美國以後的生活。(CNN)

【用】 常說的「綽綽有餘」就是 more than sufficient ；「自給自足的」就是 self sufficient 。

## visible [ˈvizəbl] a. 可見的

【例】From the walkway that overlooks the head spring, the water is still blue and crystal clear, with fish, turtles and alligators clearly visible. 從清泉上方的人行道俯瞰，水仍是碧藍清澈的，魚、烏龜和鱷魚都清晰可見。(NPR)

【用】 其反義詞是 invisible，表示「無形的；看不見的」。

## intrigue [inˈtriːg] v. 密謀;引起極大興趣 n. 陰謀

【例】The man never dirtied his hands with political intrigue. 這個人從不參與政治陰謀玷汙自己。(CNN)

【用】 常用片語: intrigue against 表示「密謀反對」; intrigue with 表示「與……密謀」。

## profitable [ˈprɔfitəbl] a. 有利可圖的;有益的

【例】The bottom line is if you ask them why they did it, it was because it was more profitable to do it that way. 底線是如果你問他們為什麼要這樣做,原因就是那樣做更加有利可圖。(NPR)

【用】 profit 表示「利益;有益於」。

## visual [ˈvizjuəl] a. 視覺的

【例】 Professor Rauschecker says large parts of the visual cortex became active during the sound and touch tests, but only in the blind people. 勞舍克爾教授表示,大部分視覺皮質在聽覺和觸覺測試中都變得很活躍,但這只針對盲人。(VOA)

【用】 感官相關詞: audition 聽覺 ; scent 嗅覺 ; tactus 觸覺 ; dull 遲鈍的。

## vast [vɑːst] a. 巨大的;大量的

【例】Petrobras has a very ambitious plan to spend over $200 billion on expanding production from Brazil's vast deep-sea oil and gas fields over the next four years. 巴西國家石油公司有一個雄心勃勃的計畫,他們要在接下來的四年花費超過 2000 億美元,用於擴大巴西巨大的深海油氣田的生產。(BBC)

【用】 常用片語: vast ocean 廣闊的海洋 ; vast majority 絕大多數 ; vast scale 大規模。

## minimize [ˈminimaiz] v. 將……減到最少;貶低

【例】I am determined to see that if the law is repealed, the changes are implemented in such a way as to minimize any negative impact on the morale. 我下定決心，如果這項法律被廢除，那一定要確保相關變動的實施盡量不給軍隊士氣帶來任何負面影響。(CNN)

【用】 其反義詞 maxmize 表示「將......最大化」。

## dissolve [diˈzɔlv] v. 使固體溶解；解散

【例】Former foreign minister Roza Otunbayeva says Prime Minister Daniyar Usenov has resigned, parliament has been dissolved. 前外交部長羅薩 ‧ 奧坦巴耶娃表示，達尼亞爾 ‧ 烏謝諾夫總理已經辭職，議會也已解散。(VOA)

【用】 常用介詞片語：dissolve in 表示「溶入」；dissolve fatigue 表示「消除疲勞」。

## deserve [diˈzəːv] v. 應得；值得

【例】Now, they are FA Cup winners and it is a story to breathe new life into the reputation of the old competition and on the day at Wembley, it was entirely deserved. 現在，他們成為了足總杯冠軍，而這一天在溫布利，這給這個歷史悠久的比賽注入了新鮮的氣息，這一切都名副其實。 (BBC)

【用】 You deserve it. 表示「這是你應得的」。

## comfortable [ˈkʌmfətəbl] a. 舒適的，舒服的

【例】Jorge Lorenzo recorded a comfortable win at Mugello to increase his lead at the top of the MotoGP standings. 豪爾赫 ‧ 洛倫佐在馬格羅輕鬆獲勝，穩固了他在摩托車錦標賽的領先地位。 (BBC)

【用】 comfortable seats 舒適的座位 ； comfortable feel 手感舒適。

## intervene [ˌintəˈviːn] v. 干涉；阻撓

【例】The United Nations call for the other member nations to intervene in the dis-

pute between the two countries. 聯合國呼籲其他成員國來調停這兩個國家的爭端。
(CNN)

【用】 詞義辨析：intervene 和 interfere 都可表示「干涉」。其區別是，intervene 指介入時間、空間或人際關係之中，強調夾在中間，常表示從中調解或從中阻撓；而 interfere 指介入某事或妨礙他人。

## partial [ˈpɑːʃəl] a. 部分的；偏愛的；不公平的

【例】This is only a partial explanation. 這僅僅是一個有偏見的解釋。(VOA)

【用】 常用片語：be partial to 表示「對......偏愛；對......特別喜歡」。

## recall [riˈkɔːl] v./n. 回憶；召回；取消

【例】 Their announcement followed the recall by the Swedish retailer IKEA of its meatballs after tests showed traces of horsemeat in one batch. 檢測顯示瑞典零售商宜家的一批肉丸中含有馬肉，隨後宜家召回全部牛肉丸並發表了聲明。(BBC)

【用】 常用表達：beyond recall 無法挽回；product recall 產品召回；recall to mind 回想起。

## succeed [səkˈsiːd] v. 成功；接著發生；繼承

【例】The talk can succeed if both sides are serious. 如果雙方都有認真的態度，這次會談就能成功。(VOA)

【用】 常用片語：succeed in/at 表示「在......方面成功」；succeed in doing 表示「成功地做了某事」。

## testify [ˈtestifai] v. 作證；表明

【例】Only when the passenger would like to testify can we get proof of their illegal behavior. 只有當乘客願意作證時，我們才能夠得到他們非法行為的證據。(CRI)

【用】 在新聞英語中：testify against 作對......不利的證明；hearsay tesitify 因果關係證明。

## ratify [ˈrætifai] v. 正式批准

【例】But before Delaware and the rest of the states could ratify it, the document had to be approved by a majority of the Constitutional Convention. 但是在特拉華州和其他州正式批准之前，這個檔必須先得到制憲會議大多數人的認可。(CNN)

【用】 在新聞英語中： ratify anaccord 簽署協定； ratify a convention 批准公約； ratify the arrest 批准逮捕。

## exposure [ikˈspəuʒə] n. 暴露；曝光；揭露

【例】So human cases identified since 2003 have been in people with prolonged exposure to infected poultry. 所以自 2003 年以來，人體感染病例都是長期接觸被受感染的家禽所致。(NPR)

【用】 常見用法：risk exposure 風險暴露；exposure to 暴露；economic exposure 經濟風險。

## assert [əˈsəːt] v. 斷言；堅持

【例】I've been advised by my counsel to assert my constitutional right not to testify. 我的律師建議我堅持憲法賦予我的權利，不去作證。(CNN)

【用】 在新聞中，assert 常用的表達有：assert one's rights 維護自己的權利；assert onself 表示堅持自己的權利。

## ideal [aiˈdiəl] a. 理想的；想像的 n. 理想

【例】This seems like a threat to the ideals that social conservatives hold dear. 這對社會保守派所堅守的理想似乎是一個威脅。(NPR)

【用】 詞義辨析：perfect，ideal 這兩個形容詞均含「完美的、極好的」意思。perfect 用於褒義，指某人或某物等達到理想中的完美無缺；用於貶義，則相反，指十足的壞；ideal 語氣較強，指完美到使人稱心如意的地步。

## accurate [ˈækjurət] a. 正確無誤的；精確的

【例】Experts say if it's used in the right way, this profile can help accurately identify people. 專家們表示，如果使用方式正確，這個檔案可以說明準確識別個人身分。(CNN)

【用】 新聞中會出現的用語：accurate measurement 表示「精確測量」；accurate positioning 表示「精確定位」；accurate record 表示「精確記錄」。

## inspire [inˈspaiə] v. 激發；鼓舞；給......以靈感

【例】The protests were inspired by weeks of continuing anti-Wall Street demonstrations in North America. 這些抗議是受到了在北美持續數週的反華爾街示威的啟發。(BBC)

【用】 常用 inspired by... 表示「受......啟發」。

## transit [ˈtrænsit] n. 運輸 v. 運輸；經過

【例】Bus rapid transit systems are not the answer for every city. 快速公車系統不一定對每個城市都適用。(VOA)

【用】 知識拓展：首碼 trans- 表示「轉變」、「變換」。例如：transplant 表示「移植」；translation 表示「翻譯」；transform 表示「使變形，改造」。

## consortium [kənˈsɔːtjəm] n. 財團；聯合；合夥

【例】The new aircraft was developed by a European consortium. 這種新的航空器是由一個歐洲財團研發的。(VOA)

【用】 consortium purchasing 表示「聯合採購」。

# Level 20

## wound [wuːnd] n. 創傷 v. 使受傷

【例】A multi-disciplinary team of doctors and nurses works quickly to save the life of a 60-year-old man suffering from multiple stab wounds. 一個多學科醫生和護士小組正緊急搶救一位 60 歲男子的生命，該男子有多處刀傷。(VOA)

【用】 傷痛相關詞：injury 傷害；disease 疾病；cancer 癌症；tingle 刺痛。

## oversize [ˈəuvəˈsaiz] a. 太大的 n. 特大型

【例】 Using only his feet, he twirls an oversize hat and ladles water into gourds hanging from his shoulders. 他僅僅用腳去轉動那個特大號的帽子，然後把水舀入他肩膀上掛著的葫蘆裡。(NPR)

【用】 其形容詞形式 oversized 表示「過大的，極大的」。

## speed [spiːd] n. 速度；迅速 v. 加速

【例】They provide power to the plane's four electric motors and allow flight in daylight and night conditions with the maximum speed of around 70km/h. 它們為飛機的四個電動機提供動力，使飛機在白天和晚上都能以大約每小時 70 公里的最高速度飛行。(BBC)

【用】 有關「度」相關詞：height 高度；slope 坡度；sensitivity 靈敏度；roundness 圓度。

## crucial [ˈkruːʃəl] a. 重要的；決定性的

【例】DesLauriers also says information from the public will be crucial in the ongoing investigation. 德斯里耶還表示來自公眾的資訊對調查的進行至關重要。(CRI)

【用】 常見用法：be crucial to 對……至關重要；crucial moment 關鍵時刻；crucial problem 決定性問題。

## heartbreak [ˈhɑːtbreik]] n. 心碎；傷心事

【例】Still, despite the heartbreak, many of the secretaries have been doing this for years, decades even. 不過，儘管這令人傷心，許多祕書這樣做甚至已有幾十年了。(NPR)

【用】 其過去式是 heartbroke，過去分詞是 heartbroken。

## minimum [ˈminiməm] a. 最小的 n. 最小量；最低限度

【例】They collect a minimum of 50 surveys each of spectators. 他們每人至少從觀眾那裡收集 50 份調查問卷。(VOA)

【用】 數學相關詞： maximum 最大值； limitation 極限； sum 求和； equation 方程式。

## principle [ˈprinsəpl] n. 原則；道德準則

【例】 Mr. Brown will say he's agreed in principle to send around 500 extra British troops to Helmand. 原則上布朗先生表示已經同意把大約 500 支額外的英國軍隊派到赫爾曼德省。(BBC)

【用】 固定搭配：working principle 表示「工作原理」； basic principle 表示「基本原理」； on the principle of 表示「根據……的原則」； guiding principle 表示「指導原則」。

## uncover [ʌnˈkʌvə] v. 揭露；揭開……的蓋子

【例】The justices said being able to crossexamine the analysts could help uncover any problems with the testing methods or results used as evidence. 法官表示，反覆詢問這些分析家才能有助於揭露有關測試方法和證據結果所存在的問題。(VOA)

【用】 cover 表示「遮蓋，掩蓋」，加首碼 un 則構成其反義詞 uncover，作「使露出，揭露」解，可指揭去物體的覆蓋物，使之露出原來的真實面目；也可指發現地下的礦產等；引申還可指揭露陰謀、揭開祕密等。

## belief [biˈliːf] n. 相信；信念

【例】It is my strong belief that willful violations occurred. 我堅信這是故意違規的行為。(NPR)

【用】 常用片語：belief in 表示「相信；對……的信仰」； religious belief 表示「宗教信仰」； firm belief 表示「堅定的信念」； in the belief 表示「相信」； beyond belief 表示「難以置信」。

## guide [gaid] n. 導遊；指南 v. 指導

【例】The new regulations give guide dogs and their owners access to public places and transport. 新規定允許導盲犬及其主人進入公共場所和使用公共交通工具。(CRI)

【用】 旅遊相關詞：monument 紀念碑； lodging 住宿； visa 簽證； luggage 行李。

## enterprise [ˈentəpraiz] n. 公司；事業；進取心

【例】In two thousand, the Rolex Watch Company of Switzerland honored him with the Rolex Award for Enterprise. 2000 年的時候，瑞士勞力士手錶公司為他頒發了「勞力士雄才偉略」獎。(VOA)

【用】 該詞經常用於經濟領域，如：foreign enterprise 表示「外企」； enterprise strategy 表示「企業策略」；joint venture enterprise 表示「合資企業」；private enterprise 表示「民營企業」。

## straight [streit] a. 直的 ad. 直接地；立即

【例】Why don't we talk about some other things rather than going straight to pathway to citizenship? 我們何不談論一些其他事情，而不是去直接向公民詢問。(CNN)

【用】 straight away 立刻 drive straight 長驅直入

## hint [hint] n. 暗示；線索 v. 暗示

【例】Such sensitivity to small carbon dioxide changes hint at a warm Arctic future.

這種對二氧化碳輕微變化的敏感性暗示未來北極將會變暖。(Scientific American)

【用】 常見用法：hint at 表示「暗示」；take a hint 表示「領會別人的暗示」。

## communication [kəˌmjuːniˈkeiʃən] v. 交通；通訊

【例】Over a period of time, China has always maintained close communication with all the relevant parties. 在一段時間內，中國一直保持著與相關各方的密切溝通。(CRI)

【用】新聞中經常用"交流"這個意思，如：communication with 表示"與……交流"；international communication 表示"國際交流"；intercultural communication 表示"跨文化交流"。

## reproduce [ˌriːprəˈdjuːs] v. 繁殖；複製

【例】Dolly the sheep was the first cloned mammal, but scientists have struggled to reproduce even the early steps in people. 桃莉羊是首隻複製的哺乳動物，但科學家在人類克隆上僅僅完成了初期步驟。(BBC)

【用】 asexually reproduce 就是生物學中常說的「無性繁殖」；reproduce sexually 即「有性繁殖」。

## blight [blait] n. 植物枯萎病；不良影響 v. 使......枯萎

【例】 The potatoes were destroyed by late blight, caused by the water mold Phytophthora infestans. 這些馬鈴薯因水黴晚疫病菌引起晚疫病，最後被全部毀掉了。(Scientific American)

【用】 植物狀態相關詞：lush 茂盛的；germinant 發芽的；withered 乾癟的；seedy 多籽的。

## emotion [iˈməuʃən] n. 情感；情緒

【例】They hope to identify how the wiring that controls impulsive and emotional behaviour changes as they get older. 他們希望能夠發現隨著年齡的增長，控制衝動和

情感行為的（大腦）神經線路會有什麼變化。(BBC)

【用】 常說的 EQ 就是 emotion quotient，表示「情商」；intense emotion 表示「激情」。

## translate ['trænsleit] v. 翻譯；轉化

【例】Further tests showed that increased brain volume translated into better memory. 進一步的研究表明，腦容量的增加意味著有了更好的記憶力。(NPR)

【用】 常用片語：translate into 表示「把......翻譯成......」。translator 就是「（筆譯）譯者」，interpreter 是「口譯者」。

## steady ['stedi] a. 穩定的；不變的 v.（使）平穩

【例】Guo ate a steady diet of dehydrated food during the voyage and drank water desalinated by a machine. 郭在航行中一直食用脫水食品，並且飲用經過機器脫鹽的水。(CRI)

【用】 詞彙搭配：steady growth 表示「穩定增長」；smooth and steady 表示「安穩的」。

## float [fləut] v. 浮動，飄浮

【例】 How I wished I had the power to enter that bright light and float with her through those beautiful forests. 我多希望我有能力進入這道明亮的光，和她一起漂過這美麗的森林。(VOA)

【用】 float 的基本意思是指在空氣中、水面上或其他平滑的表面上輕盈地漂浮或不費力地迅速滑動，引申可指匯率、價格浮動，也可指人漫無目的地游來蕩去。

## rough [rʌf] a. 粗糙的；粗略的；艱苦的 ad. 簡陋地 n. 艱苦

【例】Finally, then, we have a rough idea of the how the cost of oil breaks down. 最終，我們對於石油成本是如何失控的有了大概的想法。(BBC)

【用】 常見用法：rough road 起伏不平的路；rough draft 草稿；rough estimate 粗略的估計。

## evacuate [iˈvækjueit] v. 疏散；排空

【例】Governor Arnold Schwarzenegger is pleading with people in the path of the flames to evacuate as soon as they're told to do so. 州長阿諾德‧施瓦辛格懇求處於這條著火道路上的人們一旦得到通知就馬上疏散。(BBC)

【用】 evacuate 用作不及物動詞時，主語一般為「撤出」這一動作的發出者；用作及物動詞時，其賓語一般為撤出的地區，也可為被撤出的人（通常是老弱病殘者或戰時的平民）。evacuate 接介詞 from，可表示「從……撤出」；接 to 可表示「撤至……」。

## arise [əˈraiz] v. 發生；起源於；起身

【例】People were nice and polite and sweet, then the questions would never arise. 如果人們和善、有禮、親切，這樣的問題就永遠不會出現。(BBC)

【用】 arise 常與 from 搭配，表示因果關係，意思是「由……引起，起因於」。

## trace [treis] v. 追蹤；查出 n. 痕跡

【例】Official bilateral ties between the two countries can be traced back to as early as 1971. 兩國正式的雙邊關係最早可以追溯到 1971 年。(CRI)

【用】 常用 trace back 表示時間上的「追溯到……」。

## unannounced [ˌʌnəˈnaunst] a. 未事先宣布的；未通知的；突然的

【例】Competition officials turned up unannounced to the offices of energy companies in three European countries. 參與競爭的官員未經宣布，突然出現在歐洲三個國家的能源公司的辦公室裡。(BBC)

【用】 新聞中常用 unannounced visit 表示「突然訪問」。

## sober [ˈsəubə] a. 清醒的；不誇大的 v.（使）清醒

【例】Italy's next Prime Minister Enrico Letta expressed what he called sober satisfaction with his new team of ministers. 義大利下一任首相恩里科 · 萊塔表示，他對新的部長團隊的滿意程度絕無誇大的成分。(BBC)

【用】 常用 sober up 來表示「使......清醒」。

## mysterious [mɪˈstɪərɪəs] a. 神祕的

【例】In some areas, mysterious rings of grass with bare centers appear and thrive. 在一些地區出現了許多神祕的環形草圈，而草圈中間卻是光禿的地面。(Scientific American)

【用】 神祕相關詞：covert 隱藏的 ; dark 黑暗的 ; hidden 藏匿的 ; secret 祕密的。

## technical [ˈtɛknɪkəl] a. 技術的

【例】NASA engineers cleared the shuttle to fly on Sunday, after deciding there were no technical concerns to delay launch from Kennedy Space Center in Florida. 當美國國家航空暨太空總署的工程師們排清了導致延遲發射的技術問題之後，於周日在位於佛羅里達州的甘迺迪航太中心發射了太空梭。(VOA)

【用】 常見用法：technical support 技術支援；technical personnel 技術人員；technical co-operation 技術合作。

## standby [ˈstændbaɪ] n. 備用品；可信任的人 a./ad. 備用的（地）

【例】It will alarm you when a tornado was happening, or just get to know where the radio is, that's the old standby. 那個備用的舊設備會在龍捲風來臨時發出警報，或者只是幫你接收到無線電訊號。(CNN)

【用】 片語 stand by 則表示「支持；袖手旁觀；準備」。

## personnel [ˌpɜːsəˈnɛl] n. 全體人員；人事部門

【例】Job evaluation is a very sensitive part of the personnel system. 職位評定是人

事系統中非常敏感的部分。(VOA)

【用】 詞義辨析：personnel, personal 這兩個詞的詞形相近，但意思不同：personal 意為「個人的，私人的」，是形容詞；personnel 意思是「全體雇員，全體工作人員」，是名詞。

## occasion [əˈkeiʒən] n. 場合；機會 v. 引起

【例】How do you commentate on a state occasion? 你怎樣評論一個國事活動？(BBC)

【用】 新聞中常用 state occasion 表示「國事活動」。其他常用片語還有：special occasion 特別的場合；on the occasion of 值此……之際；on occasion 有時。

## prominent [ˈprɔminənt] a. 卓越的；突出的

【例】Republicans don't often make high-profile speeches at Howard University, one of the country's most prominent historically black schools. 共和黨人不常在霍華德大學做重要演講，霍華德大學是該國最著名的傳統黑人學校之一。(NPR)

【用】 常用表達：prominent feature 突出特徵；prominent character 主要特性。

## pursuit [pəˈsjuːt] n. 追求

【例】The government has begun a crash diet of automatic spending cuts in pursuit of better fiscal health. 政府已經開始實行自動削減開支的政策，使財政狀況有所好轉。(VOA)

【用】 in pursuit of 表示「追求」，如：in pursuit of happiness 追求幸福。

## incorporate [inˈkɔːpəreit] v. 包含；納入 a. 合併的

【例】I think it makes the music more natural to be able to incorporate the production just in your everyday life. 我認為如果能夠加入人們日常生活中的元素，這會讓音樂更加自然。(CNN)

【用】 實用片語：incorporate in 表示「使......成為......的一部分」，也可用 incorporate into 表示；incorporate with 表示「合併；混合」。

## shift [ʃift] v. 移動；改變 n. 轉換

【例】When these children become literate, become educated, that's going to cause a big shift. 當這些孩子能夠識字並變得有文化以後，他們身上將發生重大的變化。(CNN)

【用】 day shift 日班 ；shift key 換擋鍵。

## recruit [riˈkruːt] n. 應徵；新成員 v. 徵募

【例】She began recruiting volunteers age 80 and up from the Chicago area to test their memories. 她開始從芝加哥地區招募年齡為 80 歲及以上的志願者，以測試他們的記憶力。

【用】「招募」的相關詞：enroll 登記 ；beginner 初學者 ；conscript 徵兵 ；trainee 實習生。

## poll [pəul] n. 民意測驗；投票處 v. 對......進行民意測驗

【例】Viewer polls taken after this second debate, which focused on foreign policy, showed there was no runaway victor. 第二場辯論主要集中在外交政策上，辯論結束進行的觀眾投票結果表明還沒有明顯的獲勝者。(VOA)

【用】 政治新聞中經常會提到投票，其常用表達有：boycott the poll 表示「抵制投票」；conduct a poll 表示「進行民意調查」；declare the poll 表示「宣布投票結果」。

## disaster [diˈzɑːstə] n. 災難；徹底的失敗

【例】Like most big-city hospitals these days, Tufts Medical Center runs regular disaster drills. 這些天，塔夫茨醫學中心像多數大城市的醫院一樣也在定期舉辦災害演習。(NPR)

【用】 賑災救援相關詞：lifesaver 救生員 ；misfortune 不幸 ；perish 毀滅 ；refuge 庇護。

## innovate [ˈinəuveit] v. 革新

【例】A commentary on Shanghai Daily points out that innovation doesn't mean pile of documents. 《上海日報》的一篇評論指出，堆積文獻不等於創新。(CRI)

【用】 變革相關詞：modernize 使現代化 ； revolutionize 徹底變革 ； originate 發起 ； transform 改變 ； update 更新。

## strict [strikt] a. 嚴格的；絕對的

【例】Greece could be forced out of the euro if voters reject strict austerity measures demanded in return for rescue loans. 如果選民拒絕為換取救助貸款而實施嚴格的財政緊縮措施，希臘就有可能被迫退出歐元區。(BBC)

【用】 常用表達有： strict control 嚴格控制； strict with 對......要求嚴格； in the strict sense 嚴格說來。

## delicacy [ˈdelikəsi] n. 美味；佳餚；精緻；微妙

【例】 Shark fin soup is a delicacy in Asia, but its popularity is helping to decimate shark populations. 魚翅湯是亞洲的一道美味，但一旦普及會導致鯊魚種群可能會面臨滅絕。(VOA)

【用】 該詞常用於飲食方面，如： local delicacy 風味小吃； exquisite delicacy 精美佳餚。

## payout [ˈpeiaut] n. 支出；花費

【例】After two days of intense questioning from French judges, International Monetary Fund chief Christine Lagard has avoided criminal charges related to a controversial payout to a businessman while she was finance minister. 國際貨幣基金組織總裁克莉絲蒂娜‧拉加德在擔任法國財政部長時涉及一起備受爭議的案件，有關給予商人賠償，在經過法國法官連續兩天的緊張問詢之後，她被免於刑事起訴。(NPR)

【用】 該詞常用於經濟領域，常用表達如： payout ratio 股息支付率； minimum Payout 最小付款額。

## twister ['twistə] n. 不誠實的人；纏繞者；龍捲風

【例】Asked why the number of fatalities was so high, Nixon cited the 『total destruction』 left by the twister. 當被問及傷亡人數為何如此之高，尼克森列舉出了龍捲風所造成的「全部破壞」。(CNN)

【用】 tongue twister 英語繞口令 ； Mexican Twister 墨西哥雞肉捲。

## stab [stæb] v./n. 刺傷

【例】Someone stabbed a soldier in the neck over the weekend just outside Paris. 上週末有人在巴黎市外刺傷了一名士兵的頸部。(CNN)

【用】 stab knife 穿刺刀 ；stab wound 刺傷。

## contest [kən'test] v. 競爭；辯論 n. 競賽

【例】In the statement the Japanese bank said it would vigorously contest any suggestions of wrongdoing. 日本銀行在聲明中表示將極力反對任何有罪指控。(BBC)

【用】 常用表達有： speech contest 演講比賽； contest with 爭奪； close contest 勢均力敵的競爭（指競選等）； contest for 和……對抗。

## original [ə'ridʒənəl] a. 最初的；新穎的 n. 原件

【例】 The incidents of the presence of bute in the horsemeat were extremely low, less than 0.5%, and also the fraudulent link within the percentage was an original 4.6%. 馬肉中的保泰松含量非常低，只有不到 0.5%，而在存在欺詐現象，比率只有 4.6%。(BBC)

【用】 original edition 英文原版進口 ； original article 原創文章。

## ending ['endiŋ] n. 結局

【例】The government hopes this unsupervised, ash-based economy is ending. 政府

希望馬上結束這種毫無監管、現金交易的經濟模式。(VOA)

【用】 ending tag 結束標記 ； subtle ending 巧妙結束。

## oceanic [ˌəuʃiˈænik] a.（似）海洋的；生活於海洋的

【例】「We know that we cannot control them in the entire ocean,」 says James Morris, an ecologist with the National Oceanic and Atmospheric Administration. 「我們知道我們不能在整個海洋中控制他們，」 國家海洋和大氣管理局的生態學家傑姆斯 · 莫里斯說道。(NPR)

【用】 海洋相關詞：marine 海的 ；saltwater 鹽水的 ； deep-sea 深海的 ； sailing 航行。

## bond [bɔnd] n. 債券；聯結；契約 v. 結合

【例】Please therefore look upon each other as brothers and sisters whose national bond should not be broken. 因此，請讓我們彼此以兄弟姐妹相待，不要破壞團結。(BBC)

【用】 bond 常用於經濟領域，表示「債券」。如： corporate bond 企業債券 ； bond market 債券市場 ； bond fund 債券基金。

## equivalent [iˈkwivələnt] a. 相同的 n. 等價物

【例】 Many colleges and employers will accept what is known as a GED as the equivalent of a high school diploma. 許多大學和公司會將一般同等文憑與高中文憑視為效力相同。(VOA)

【用】 equivalent 指在數量、價值、時間等方面「相同的」，常用於「be equivalent to sth./ v-ing」結構中。

## oversee [ˌəuvəˈsiː] v. 監督；俯瞰

【例】The cabinet failed to agree on two important and hotly-contested issues: one was the establishment and membership of a commission to oversee general elections. 內閣在兩個重要的問題上未能達成一致，爭論不休，其中一個問題關於成立委員會、監督大選以及委員會的成員資格。(BBC)

【用】 監管相關詞： abide 容忍 ； administrate 管理 ； approval 贊成 ； supervisor 監督者。

## sacrifice [ˈsækrifais] n. 犧牲；祭品 v. 犧牲

【例】Now Memorial Day honors all the men and women who've sacrificed their lives in service their country. 如今，陣亡將士紀念日將紀念所有在服役時為國家獻出了寶貴生命的男女。(CNN)

【用】 常用片語： sacrifice for 表示「為……而犧牲」； at the sacrifice of 以犧牲……為代價。

## dependent [diˈpendənt] a. 依靠的；取決於……的

【例】Any limitation on this fundamental right of self defense makes us more dependent on our government for our own protection. 基本權自衛權受到限制，於是我們更加依賴政府，尋求保護。(VOA)

【用】 常見用法： dependent on 表示「取決於；依賴……」。其反義詞為 independent ，也很常用，表示「獨立的」。

## seasonally [ˈsiːzənəli] ad. 季節性地

【例】The Commerce Department says sales rose last month to a seasonally adjusted annual rate of 445,000. 商務部表示，經過上個月的季節性調整，銷售額增加到了 44.5 萬。(NPR)

【用】 常見用法： seasonally unemployment 表示「季節性失業」； seasonally variation 表示「季節變動」； fluctuate seasonally 表示「隨季節變動」。

## fluid [ˈfluːid] n. 流體 a. 流動的

【例】There's a new procedure instead of the traditional method of giving trauma patients large amounts of intravenous fluids such as saline. 這個新的治療程式取代了

給外傷病人進行大量靜脈輸液的傳統方法，比如輸生理鹽水。(VOA)

【用】 物質狀態相關詞： solidity 固態 ； gaseity 氣態 ； crystal 結晶體 ； molten 熔化的。

## myriad [ˈmiriəd] n. 無數 a. 無數的

【例】 Imagine a magic scroll, one that contains a myriad of stories and tells you a different one every night. 想像有一個魔法捲軸，裡面有無數個故事，而且每晚都會為你講述一個不同的故事。(CNN)

【用】 該詞用法與 lot 相似， a myriad of 與 myriads of ，表示「無數的」，後面加可數名詞複數或不可數名詞；另外， myriad 可以作定語，放在名詞前，修飾名詞。

# 新聞英語必備指南──關鍵字

作　　　者：金利 主編

發　行　人：黃振庭

出　版　者：崧博出版事業有限公司

發　行　者：崧燁文化事業有限公司

E-mail：sonbookservice@gmail.com

粉　絲　頁：https://www.facebook.com/sonbookss/

網　　　址：https://sonbook.net/

地　　　址：台北市中正區重慶南路一段六十一號八樓
815 室

Rm. 815, 8F., No.61, Sec. 1, Chongqing S. Rd.,
Zhongzheng Dist., Taipei City 100, Taiwan (R.O.C)

電　　　話：(02)2370-3310

傳　　　真：(02) 2388-1990

總　經　銷：紅螞蟻圖書有限公司

地　　　址：台北市內湖區舊宗路二段 121 巷 19 號

電　　　話：02-2795-3656

傳　　　真：02-2795-4100

印　　　刷：京峯彩色印刷有限公司（京峰數位）

## 國家圖書館出版品預行編目資料

新聞英語必備指南：關鍵字 / 金利主編 .
-- 第一版 . -- 臺北市：崧博出版：崧燁
文化發行 , 2020.10
　　面；　公分
POD 版
ISBN 978-957-735-993-3( 平裝 )
1. 新聞英文 2. 讀本
805.18　　109015619

官網

臉書

── 版權聲明 ──

原著書名《新聞英語高頻詞》。本書版權為清華大學
出版社所有授權崧博出版事業有限公司獨家發行電子
書及繁體書繁體字版。若有其他相關權利及授權需求
請與本公司聯繫。

定　　　價：420 元

發行日期：2020 年 10 月第一版

◎本書以 POD 印製